A SECOND LEASE OF LIFE

MADELEINE LÜTHI

Trafford
PUBLISHING™

*We at Trafford believe that it is the responsibility of us all, as both individuals
and corporations, to make choices that are environmentally and socially sound.
You, in turn, are supporting this responsible conduct each time you purchase a
Trafford book, or make use of our publishing services. To find out how you are
helping, please visit www.trafford.com/responsiblepublishing.html*

*Our mission is to efficiently provide the world's finest, most comprehensive
book publishing service, enabling every author to experience success.
To find out how to publish your book, your way, and have it available
worldwide, visit us online at www.trafford.com/10510*

 www.trafford.com

North America & international
toll-free: 1 888 232 4444 (USA & Canada)
phone: 250 383 6864 ♦ fax: 250 383 6804 ♦ email: info@trafford.com

The United Kingdom & Europe
phone: +44 (0)1865 487 395 ♦ local rate: 0845 230 9601
facsimile: +44 (0)1865 481 507 ♦ email: info.uk@trafford.com

10 9 8 7 6 5 4

ABOUT THE AUTHOR

Madeleine Lüthi was born and raised in Switzerland. She left her home country after completing her formal education then followed an innate curiosity and an eagerness to travel and see the world. Her novel *A Second Lease of Life* was inspired by friends and acquaintances made during her many years of backpacking around the globe.

She is now a citizen of Australia and lives a quiet life in a small mud brick house in the north of the State of Western Australia.

A SECOND
LEASE OF LIFE

PROLOGUE

Florence was now well into her second month traveling aimlessly in her truck around the vast brown land in the north of Western Australia, the land that's called the Pilbara, and she was well aware that this nomadic life was in danger of becoming permanent. She would usually stop under a big old gum tree, in a dry riverbed or simply in the wide open country where she would gather wood for a small fire and cook her evening meal. A solitary life it was, but her lonely days were usually rewarded by a magnificent sunset and this somehow made life alright again - at least temporarily.

But Florence had not always been homeless and driving around randomly with nothing but the clothes she stood up in. She had grown up in a decent home in a suburb of Brisbane. Her parents had been upstanding middle-class people who taught her right from wrong. She had been a lively child and reasonably good at her schoolwork. Her childhood was mostly untroubled and more often than not happy. There had been nothing wrong with her life then. She left school at seventeen, found jobs, had hobbies and interests, friends and fun.

Then, two months ago came the day when heaven and earth conspired against her and destroyed her home - her whole life.

It all happened on a day when she did her monthly shopping in town; it was a day that started as just an ordinary day but was to end in disaster of unimaginable proportions - a disaster which made her homeless and determined her present nomadic life.

Florence owned a nice old home out in the country. She had bought it a few years ago, quite spontaneously. It had appealed to her on first sight: wide verandas on all sides, big shady trees, flowerbeds and a vegetable patch. It was a little dilapidated but had potential nevertheless; and all of it was on four acres of land.

Around six o'clock on that fateful shopping day she was on her way back and as she approached her home, she could just see a small column of smoke rising right behind the last hill that separated her from her farm. It caused her no undue anxiety - not straight away - but as she turned the last corner where the three big gum trees formed an almost perfect archway across her track, she saw the origin of that little rising column of smoke. Her heart sank and an ominous feeling pervaded her whole being. Something was dramatically wrong. She felt a lump forming in her throat, she could not breathe. Then came the terrible realization that her house was not there anymore ... there was nothing now! What happened? Why was there just a black and charcoaled wasteland instead of her beautiful home with the red roof and the shaded verandas? The big old trees reduced to stark black skeletons ... why? What had happened to her home? Sitting behind the wheel in the driver's seat of her truck, she took in the devastation before her, and she turned to stone.

Everything was gone, reduced to a black and smoldering rubble; her house, the barn, the chicken shed, nothing was there now. All she saw was a crumbled heap of black and still smoking charcoal, pieces of blackened metal, disintegrated walls and some little flames still lapping at whatever they could find to keep alive a little longer.

A bushfire!

It had destroyed everything she had called home. What struck her hardest, however, was the realization that there was no more life, nothing anywhere, just complete silence all around. The fire had silenced the chickens and the geese, the cats and Buster, her dog; it had destroyed everything, everything. The life she had made for herself, her animal-family, the gardens, the fruit trees, all her beloved books, music tapes and discs, all destroyed and gone forever. And it had all happened in just one day. Slowly she became aware of the magnitude of the catastrophe she was facing and it was at that moment that she finally broke down. She gripped the wheel with both hands, lowered her head and disintegrated in hopeless, heart wrenching sobs. Poor Buster, she cried in her misery, you could not have gotten out of your pen, the fire must have consumed you alive.

She did not see her neighbors at first. They had all come to try and save her house but had arrived too late. When Florence was finally able to compose herself, she got out of her truck and, in as rational a voice as she could muster, thanked everybody for their concern and for their helpfulness. She gratefully accepted an offer of food and shelter on that first night, but decided the very next day to leave the place. There was nothing left of her life except her truck, the day's shopping and her guitar which had been on the passenger's seat that day for no apparent reason .

She left the following morning with no particular destination in mind; she did not look in her rear-view mirror or turn her head. She knew she would never see the place again.

If she had been a religious person, she might have wanted to blame God for this monumental injustice, but Florence had her own home-made philosophy and whatever higher authority was out there to make her vegetables grow, her chickens lay eggs and the sky turn red after sunset, she simply called it Nature. On that day however, no matter how high an opinion she had of Nature, Florence was sadly disappointed. Nature could have made a little effort to protect my home, she thought impotently. Nature could have issued instructions for the fire to go someplace else.

It was two months now since that fateful day, two months she had spent feeling sorry for herself and mourning the death of Buster and her entire animal family. So on that night, while sitting quietly by the fire until the last little flames had died, Florence made a decision: I must start to look ahead.

It's time to stop indulging in self pity, this is not like me, she instructed herself. The secret to living happily, she had long ago found out, was to be aware of all things around, to keep your eyes and ears open and your senses awake and alert.

"And that's just what I'm going to do starting tomorrow morning," she said out loud. "I can again make something of my life. I'm healthy in body and sane in mind. I have a fair amount of common sense, I'll be alright."

I

The footsteps on the bitumen were distinctly audible. Florence could tell that they were approaching her truck from the front. She had driven her vehicle into a parking lot that night; it was her first venture into the city after weeks of enforced camping in the bush. Florence had carefully avoided the big highways into the State Capital of Perth and made her way south to Fremantle. Now she was sitting comfortably on the loading tray facing away from the cabin, dangling her legs, cradling her guitar in her arms and picking out some tunes and singing along very gently. The approaching footsteps did nothing to diminish her enjoyment of the music she was playing ... not that night. Her mind and her heart were filled with optimism and confidence now that she had made her decision to stop blaming the elements for her loss. Her life was back on track again.

Florence had seen a flyer as she drove into the city earlier in the day, it advertised a folk concert and she knew instinctively that an evening of Blue Grass music would be just the thing. It will be the ultimate panacea for my soul and a booster for my optimism, she told herself. As she now sat on her truck replaying some of the tunes she had heard earlier on, she was in high spirits and paid no heed to possible danger inherent in the approaching of footsteps. She was filled with a joyful recklessness which allowed her to dismiss all thoughts of self preservation from her mind.

The footsteps clearly belonged to two or more people but they were still some distance away. Suddenly they came to a halt. One pair of feet now detached itself and seemingly approached her truck in a straight line across the almost empty parking area. Florence casually looked over her shoulder and saw a dark, fairly tall figure standing only a few feet away from her. He stood stock still, his hands in his pockets - a silhouette.

What does the man want? Why is he just standing there, looking at me and saying nothing? Maybe he's listening to my music, Florence reassured herself. The thought sprang simply from curiosity not from fear of the dark figure. She resumed her music-making without further ado and embarked on her own version of the last song she had just heard at the concert that night. She knew the tune well, she even knew most of the lyrics. Why then can't I get it right, she puzzled, maybe the wrong key? At that moment the dark figure spoke.

"Try A major, you'll find it works."

Florence heard, understood and followed the instructions. She chose the key of A major and went back to the beginning. It worked. She played a few bars until she ran out of lyrics, and only then did she feel the man's eyes on her back. He is looking at me, doesn't move ... strange guy. Should I say something? Thank him for giving me the correct key? Florence gently put the guitar down beside her on the truck, then turned to face the tall dark figure and in a casual tone of voice started to tell about the events of her evening.

"I've just been to a concert, folk music and that, you see, and the tune I had trouble with just then was one the band played, the last one, and .... well ... I liked it. Anyway, why were you so sure about the correct key?" And then it dawned on her: he is American. Florence knew just from the few words he said. All the musicians were American ...what if this guy should be one of those musicians? If it had been daylight she would surely have remembered his face but it was now too dark to see. That would be real embarrassing, she thought, I might just have made a monumental fool of myself? Too late to worry about that now.

Florence jumped down from her truck and placed herself squarely in front of the man and asked, "Are you...I mean, did you ...?" How to put this question subtly? Come on whoever you are ... help me out, she pleaded silently to herself. There was no immediate reaction from the man. If it had not been so dark she could have seen the smile on his face. But Florence did not see that.

"Was I one of the players in the Blue Grass band? Is that what you mean to ask me? Yes I am. I play the acoustic guitar."

Nice guy, she thought, answers his own question just as soon as he's asked it. "Yes I remember now, you sat on that stool right up front. You sang too, didn't you? It was a smashing concert. I enjoyed it, really did. It was so lively and, well, it was just what I needed to … to …" Why did I say that? He's not interested in my need for music to heighten my spirits. She decided to tell him anyway since she had already started.

"I needed the cheerful atmosphere your performance created to get my life back on track … somehow." Then, almost unconsciously, she took a step or two toward the dark figure, put her arms around him in an innocent and friendly hug and said simply, "It was a wonderful concert indeed." Her gesture was spontaneous, it was without affectation, it was simply her way of thanking this unknown musician for an enjoyable evening.

The man's arms automatically closed around her in a gesture as natural as hers had been. They held each other for a few seconds, then Florence dropped her arms and made a move to step back.

"Wish I hadn't made such a fool of myself a minute ago though," she mumbled partly into his jacket.

If her musician had heard her words, he did not let on. He had by then decided on a different course of action. He pulled her towards him once again and hugged her a little longer, a little tighter, pressing her gently against his body. Then, looking down at her, he waited until she lifted her head and looked at him.

"It's OK, we all make fools of ourselves sometimes. So don't worry," he said in a gentle and smooth voice.

That's OK then, she thought with some relief, and made no further effort to move out of his embrace. For some reason she did not even bother to analyze, Florence felt at ease enclosed by the unknown man's arms. Slowly now he lowered his head until he found her lips with his. Their kisses were slow at first, soft and smooth and unhurried. It was just perfect. Florence felt as though she was with an old friend after a long absence. They stayed in their embrace and kissed for what seemed an eternity. It was a wondrous situation, but then this whole evening had been a fairytale experience.

When the time came to take a breath, they disengaged and stood at arm's length facing each other, still unable to see each other's faces clearly.

"I'm Phillip," the man said soberly.

"I'm Florence."

That was all, no surnames, just Phillip and Florence.

Hey, that was real nice, Phillip thought after they had made their introductions. First a quick hug then the lingering embrace, a long kiss, no questions asked, no charming games, no need for long flirting or other seducing tactics, it all happened so naturally. And I'm sure that Florence enjoyed our closeness as much as I did. So much unexpected good fortune! Phillip considered himself no beginner in the art of seducing women. On this night, however, there had been no need for any of his seducing techniques to be put into practice, it had all just fallen into place. Aloud he said, "This is a pretty nice truck you got here. Is this where you live?"

"Yep, I have everything I need: a bed rolled up in the corner, just gets unrolled and pronto it's ready to be slept in. I've got cooking stuff and some food. I'm all right."

Phillip looked at Florence, hiding a smile, easy to do in the dark. He was intrigued by the simplicity of her way of life and by her uncomplicated and down-to-earth way of handling this situation. She had shown no signs of fear or apprehension when approached by a stranger in the dark. Knowing the type of life she lived Phillip had to assume that Florence did not get the opportunity to meet and kiss a harmless bloke like himself every other day. But now he needed to say something, and say it soon, or he might let this magic situation get away from him.

11

"I'm sure it is an interesting way of life, the one you have chosen. Umm … would you ... maybe ... care to spend one evening with me and the other musicians? We're staying at the hotel just across from here. We usually share a bottle of wine or something after a performance."

"Thanks for your invitation and yes, I would like that," she answered without hesitation. "I just tidy up my home," she said matter-of-factly. "Shall I leave it here?"

"Why not park it in the hotel parking lot. It is underground and it would be more secure there than if you just left it here in the open," Phillip explained. "Come on, let me be a passenger in your mobile house just for the short ride."

"OK, get in and give me directions," she said cheerfully.

During their short drive to the hotel, Phillip started to wonder why Florence had chosen to live on the back of a truck and how long she had lived this nomadic life. He was puzzled, but refrained from putting any of these questions into words right then. There was, after all, the prospect of good things to happen that night. Why spoil good luck by asking useless questions? Phillip was sure Florence knew that his invitation to share a glass of wine was tantamount to an invitation to sleep with him yet she didn't seem to worry about spending the night with a guy she had met only five minutes ago. Anyway, she has nothing to fear from me, he thought as an assurance to himself. I won't harm her, I would never attempt to make love to her if she did not consent. I am, after all, a decent guy. An odd feeling, however, stirred inside of him right then and he could not help asking himself: how can Florence be so sure of me, and why does she feel safe with me?

With the car stowed away in the hotel's guest parking, Phillip and Florence made their way up to the third floor where the musicians had their rooms.

"Do you want to take anything with you?" he had asked just before leaving her truck, "A change of clothes maybe?"

"I don't really own very much in the way of clothes, not even a warm jacket. I have lived up north and traveled through the desert where it's always warm. I more or less own what I am wearing. Should I take my toothbrush?" she inquired with a sheepish grin.

"Good idea," he said trying to keep a straight face.

Florence was, indeed, looking forward to a comfortable and enjoyable night in a luxury hotel. It was going to be warm and comfortable. The fact that comfort and warmth were also going to be ephemeral did not bother her right then. She was at the starting point of a new phase of her life and she was going to embark on this new phase by spending a night with a man she had only just met and would never see again. The irony of it almost made Florence laugh.

Phillip was in excellent mood that night as he and Florence made their way to his room. His good luck had been with him all the way. The thought of spending a night with Florence was exciting, she was fun and had a good sense of humor - Phillip liked her. The band was scheduled for only one performance in this city called Fremantle - never heard of it before. Tomorrow they would fly across the continent to another never-heard-of-place called Port Macquarie then to a music festival in another 'Port' ... Port Fairy or similar, and on and on for ten days. Life was good when they were on tour. When Phillip got to this point in his contemplations they had reached the third floor. They got out of the elevator and walked on the soft carpet along a silent corridor. It had doors at regular intervals on either side. Finally they reached Phillip's room.

"We all have our rooms on the same floor," Phillip said rather lamely. "Bob, the fiddle player, if you remember, is offering us all a glass of wine or champagne. He is our boss, so to speak." He opened the door to his room and showed Florence in. She entered slowly, looking to the left and to the right familiarizing herself with her new surroundings.

Phillip took off his jacket as soon as he had closed the door behind Florence and flung it casually over the back of the nearest chair, hoping to give the appearance of feeling at home in hotel rooms the world over, even though this was not an attitude or a confidence he truly subscribed to.

14

His performance that night however, was a complete waste of time since Florence took no notice of it. He watched her from the corner of his eye as she walked around the room, inspected the clothes recess and peered into the bathroom. She was barefoot, obviously enjoying the softness of the carpet. She slid her fingers gently over the buttons of the television remote control. He could see that she was fascinated by everything around her; she seemed to absorb her surroundings with the rapture of a child at a magic show, even though this was just a very ordinary hotel room, nothing like a luxury suite. Hotel rooms must be a complete novelty to her, Phillip mused. I wonder if she has ever actually paid for one and slept in it? He found that his mind was wandering to places he had no real intention for it to wander.

Finally Florence came to a standstill behind him and asked in an almost childlike tone of voice. "Please, may I have a hot bath? There is one in there, I've seen it and there are heaps of beautiful white, soft looking towels and lovely little cakes of soap. May I use all of that?" Her face started to glow with anticipation.

What's this? Is this all she wants? Is a hot bath all it takes to make her happy? I'll be damned if I ever understand women. Out loud however, he said, "Of course you may. You are welcome to whatever wonders the bathroom has to offer."

From inside the room, Phillip could soon hear the sound of water gushing into the bathtub and a few minutes later her voice came through the wall, crystal clear, as she sang. He did not recognize her song, it was certainly not one of the band's tunes this time. Phillip smiled to himself. He stood awkwardly in the middle of the room, hands in his pockets as he was wont to do when his mind was wandering. He was thinking about the girl in his bathroom. There was a kind of naïveté about her - or was it rather a complete lack of affectation? She seemed to approach every situation with an intensity to exclude everything else around her and Phillip knew that by doing so, Florence got a whole lot more out of life than most people.

The song was finished, there were no other sounds coming from the bathroom than the splashing of water and the dribbling sound of a washcloth being squeezed here and there as she was probably luxuriating in her bath experience.

He approached the door and called, "We are meant to be at Bob's in five minutes. Can you make it?"

Instant reaction. The plug was pulled out and he could hear the gurgling sound of water running out of the tub.

"I'll be out in two seconds," she declared. And true to her word, she emerged almost instantly from the steam-filled bathroom, wrapped in one of the hotel's bath towels.

"I'll be wearing the same stuff as before," she said a

16

little apologetically, "but I do have a clean T-shirt. Will that do?"

"It will have to, I suppose. You can borrow one of my sweaters if you like. It will be too cold for just a T-shirt."

She beamed at the prospect of a warm woolly sweater and Phillip was puzzled at how infectious her expression of delight was.

Florence knew she was going to meet the other members of the band and was looking forward to it. They would all talk about music, about today's performance and hopefully recount incidents which happened during other concerts. Florence knew that Blue Grass music originated in the State of Tennessee. She had read all about the city of Nashville being the musical center of the state. Maybe that's where they all came from. Florence briefly disappeared back into her paradise of a bathroom. A minute later she stood as if to attention in front of Phillip.

"Do I look alright? Good enough to meet your friends?" She asked seriously. Phillip was at pains to hide his smile. Nothing she wore was in keeping with anything. Her attempt at taming her hair proved a total failure and his sweater reached down to just above her knees; the sleeves were rolled up so as to let the tips of her fingers stick out. She was still barefoot, unable to resist the luxurious softness of the probably fully synthetic carpet and almost unconsciously he put his arms around her and pressed her against

17

his body. She nestled her head comfortably in his shoulder while he held her small figure inside folds upon folds of his own sweater. Neither of them found the need for words. It was all just perfectly wonderful.

Then a knock on the door and Mario's voice, "Are you coming over, Phillip?"

"We will be there in a minute," Phillip's voice had a mellow undertone. He and Florence disentwined themselves - slowly, reluctantly.

"That was nice, kid," Phillip said when he finally found his voice.

"...'but I ain't no kid,'" her answer came back with a cheerful laugh, "Don't you know the song? It goes something like 'people say she's a hell of a kid, but she ain't no kid and she's tearing or cutting or something me apart.' Shall I sing it?"

"No, to both questions. You don't need to sing it, we haven't got time for it right now, and no, I don't know the song. But it has just occurred to me that you have created a new name for yourself. I shall introduce you to my friends as Kid, how is that?" And later, he thought, I shall remember you as Kid, but he did not say.

"I like that, yes please do call me Kid." Her mind was racing: a new name ... perfect, just the thing I need to start on a new and more positive track in my life.

In Bob's room all the musicians had now gathered,

ready for their celebratory glass of champagne. Anita, Bob's wife, was there; she always liked to accompany the band when they went on tour. She was the only woman in the group that night. Mario had just come back after having called Phillip when the cork was about to be popped.

"What's up? Is he coming?" Bob looked up from the bottle he was in the process of uncorking.

"He said *we* will be over in a minute. Does anyone know who 'we' is? Where and when did he manage to pick somebody up this time?"

"I'm not sure, but I have a feeling it happened on the way back here just after the performance," Joshua said. "We will doubtlessly be introduced to our first Australian fan, guys." The irony of his statement was unmistakable.

Just then, Anita heard a soft knock and a second later Phillip and his 'pick-up' stood in the door. No-one got a clear picture of Phillip's latest girl right then since she shyly walked into the room behind Phillip. All the musicians took on a blasé attitude, some because they did not care who Phillip's latest conquest was, some because they were a little envious. Anita was quick to remind Phillip to make the required introductions.

"Oh yeah, of course, I meant to, I'm so sorry," he spluttered. "This is Kid. Kid, this is Bob, his wife Anita," he turned towards where she was sitting on the end of the bed, "Jim, our world class bass player, Joshua and Mario," and turning to all of them he now added, "Kid saw us all on stage a couple of hours ago."

Florence, now Kid, looked at them, one after the other. She was wide-eyed and there was an expression of expectancy and wonderment on her face.

What a sight this girl, with the unusual name Kid, Anita thought, barefoot, a sweater about ten sizes too big for her - probably Phillip's - covers the biggest part of a pair of well worn jeans, hair wild and curly and still wet from the bath, but the expression on her face shows alertness and interest.

Phillip's friends sat around the room wherever there was a place, on the bed or in armchairs. Kid, without the slightest hesitation, settled on the floor between the small table and the bed, and when Bob offered her a glass of champagne, she took it with both hands treating it delicately as if it were some sort of gift from the Gods.

"Thank you very much, very kind of you," she said politely, pronouncing the sentence in what everyone took to be perfect British English. Much later they would find out that it wasn't that at all. It was just one of Kid's many imitations of accents which she applied depending on the situation.

Everybody had stopped whatever conversation they had been engaged in and looked at Kid as though it was her turn to entertain them all. This was rather unfair since she was the newcomer to the group, but Phillip didn't seem to notice and failed to make any attempt at getting her out of an awkward situation. So Anita took things in her own hands, she turned to Kid and asked in a conversational tone of voice, "Did you enjoy our concert?"

"Oh, very much indeed," Kid beamed, "but... I had trouble getting in, you know." She had chosen a different accent for this pronouncement. "First it was the frayed jeans which were not good enough, then the ticket guy objected to my sandals ... I wore those rubber thongs that we all wear here. He said I did not conform to the dress code that the American musicians expected. Do you really?" she harmlessly addressed everyone around.

They were all laughing and shaking their heads 'no'.

"And all that time, I had the money for the entrance fee in my hand." Kid made a point in completing her story.

"How did you manage to make him change his mind?" It was Phillip who asked the question.

"Hmm," a mischievous smile came over her. "I was at my most stubborn. I placed myself squarely in front of the counter and pulled myself up to my full height and assumed a posture of authority, then I told the man that he was treating me unfairly and that the whole procedure was undemocratic in the extreme. That did it. He sold me the ticket and I walked in."

Nobody was quite sure whether Kid had told this story as a joke or not. Anita was intrigued but she had already decided that she liked Kid. She repeatedly glanced in Phillip's direction trying to define his feelings for his new girl, but all she could see was amusement, no more.

Kid then made a bold move to get the conversation onto another track. "I don't want to talk about myself, I am sure everyone of you lives a far more interesting life than I do," she said. How long had they played together. Were they all professionals. Did they tour the world over non-stop, had they been to this country before and much more she wanted to know.

After that, the conversation ran smoothly. The musicians told her a little about themselves. Kid listened with obvious interest. She paid attention to every detail no matter how casual or how trivial, and all the while she was enjoying every sip of her champagne to the fullest. Anita wondered if Kid had in fact ever tasted champagne before.

Slowly Kid started to feel more comfortable in her new surroundings. Anita watched her without staring and was surprised at how easy Kid was to please. She was alert, inquisitive, nothing escaped her and she was visibly enchanted by the atmosphere created by the group of musicians who she had heard in concert that night and, more than anything else, she was luxuriating in the warmth of her gigantic sweater. Maybe Kid lives in a cold, unheated house, and maybe she is financially unable to keep herself warm, Anita speculated.

Where and how she and Phillip had met remained as yet undisclosed. Anita had noticed that all through the conversation, Kid and Phillip had sat at opposite sides of the sitting area. Kid looked across to Phillip when he said or asked something. She smiled at him ... but then she smiled at everyone. Yet she didn't flirt with him or try to attract his attention unduly, even though he was the only person in the whole group to whom she had any sort of a link.

Phillip's sweater had to be one of the highlights of her evening. She stroked it and she cuddled up inside it, she clearly loved it. Anita's curiosity got the better of her then.

"Where do you live Kid? Tell us a little about your life, would you?"

"Well, I ..." she now shot a glance at Phillip as though for help, but none was forthcoming. "I had this pretty house, you see. It was a small farm, and I had a nice view too," she continued a little hesitantly. "It was a comfortable, though simple place, a long, long way away from her, way up north where it is always warm."

Maybe the reason for her lack of warm clothing, Phillip quickly calculated.

"From my veranda I could watch the sunset almost every evening. As I said, I ran a small farm-type-thing, you know, with a vegetable garden, herbs, fruit trees, chickens, all that. It was peaceful and gave me time and opportunity to contemplate and ... well, just be myself." At that moment a faraway look came into her eyes. She sat cross legged on the floor clutching her magical champagne glass in her hands and looking at the little bubbles which climbed up to the surface along the sides, and after a few minutes she continued almost dreamily, "It was all I had. A small family of a few cats and a dog. And about two months ago, I lost the whole lot ... in a bushfire."

Anita watched as Kid deposited her champagne glass carefully beside her, unfolded her legs and put her feet flat on the carpet. She hugged her knees to her chin and lowered her head. She was now no more than a heap of dark blue fluffy wool, bare feet sticking out at the bottom and a mop of curly blond hair falling down all around her head. At that moment, the sound of suppressed sobs came out of this pitiful bundle. Nobody made a move; nobody said a word. They all looked first at each other and then at Phillip. Wasn't it up to him to do something to help her, or to comfort her? Did he know all the details of what she had gone through? Did he know anything at all about this unusual but remarkable lady?

A few minutes later Kid made an effort to stop her tears and to continue her story. Anita now wished she had never asked about her life. But how could she have known? It had been no more than an ordinary conversational question.

"You see," she heard Kid's stifled voice next to her, "my dog, Buster, he was in his pen while I was away in town doing my shopping. And when the fire came through, he had no way of escape. The fire must just have ..." It became all too much for her, she almost physically disappeared in Phillip's sweater and she cried, and cried.

Phillip, for God's sake, Anita silently pleaded, can't you see the distress she is in?

Phillip *did,* and he made a move then. He walked over to where Kid sat on the floor, sat down beside her and put one arm around her shoulders the other around the front, thus completely encircling her. He said nothing, but bent his head so that his forehead touched the top of her head. After a while Phillip could be seen to whisper something in her ear. A question? It must have been since it almost immediately caused Kid to move her head up and down in agreement.

There was complete silence in the room for a couple of minutes, a silence that could have been due to annoyance or embarrassment at Kid's breakdown.

As the silence started to become uncomfortable, Kid said in a tearful voice, "I'm sorry for making such a scene."

With this she unwittingly saved a difficult situation of her own creation. She now made a conscious effort to stop crying and started to wipe her eyes and her nose ineffectually with the backs of her hands. At that moment Jim put the box of tissues on Kid's knees. He had obviously seen enough tears and heard enough sobs.

"Thanks," she said in a small voice looking up into Jim's face, "I'm OK now. I am so sorry for making such an idiot of myself. I thought I was finally able again to talk about the fire and the destruction of my home. It is just when I come to what happened to Buster ... I do apologize. I had such a wonderful evening, I feel I have spoiled it for you all now. Maybe I better leave ... back to my truck." She got to her feet and turned toward the door.

But Anita's mother instincts dictated that she get up and hold Kid back. She took her by the hand and made her sit down again. "Please Kid, sit down and have another glass of champagne. Don't worry about having spoiled our evening, OK?" Nobody objected to Anita's initiative.

Kid now sat demurely on the sofa between Anita and Phillip. She was composed again and proceeded to tell in a sober voice how it had all happened while she was away in the nearest town doing her monthly shopping. She told of how neighbors had been helpful and sympathetic, but that she had found it impossible to accept either help or sympathy for any length of time.

"I needed to be alone with my thoughts and with my grief over the loss of my little family. You see, I still had the vehicle, a four wheel-drive truck, and some money, so I bought a minimum of stuff, pots, pans, a cooker, a roll-up bed, that sort of thing, and went bush. Since then I have led the life of a nomad," she concluded.

"You and Phillip," Bob now asked, "how did you get to know each other? Will you tell us?"

Kid gave Phillip a look which made it clear that it was for him to tell that part of the story.

He did not argue. He looked around the room, a cheeky smile on his face then embarked on a outline of their meeting, embellishing his story with some of his own verbal niceties.

He is probably leaving out the more intimate bits, Anita thought. Everybody knew Phillip was a good actor and an excellent story teller and he soon had everybody in peals of laughter and that included Kid. Anita was grateful to Phillip for having brought back an element of cheerfulness to their evening. Still, an uncomfortable feeling somewhere deep within her remained. It would be nice if Kid could be more than just a number on a list of one-night stands for Phillip, it went rather absurdly through her head. I'd like to get to know her a little better. Anita knew that Phillip was a decent guy. She knew him to be gentle and inoffensive and he was certainly attractive. His own words now came to her mind, something she had heard him say just a short time ago, 'I enjoy women, even just for one night,' he had said and added seriously, 'I enjoy them, I don't use them.' But did Phillip ever have feelings of remorse or shame in the morning when he said good-bye to his one-night acquaintances? Kid did not seem to be the kind of girl who should be enjoyed for one night and consequently forgotten, Anita thought. One thing however, Anita was glad about: even though it is for just one night, it makes for a wonderful night for Kid. She seemingly lives and enjoys every minute of every day without speculating on results and propitious outcomes. Kid would not be one to ask for extras or try to hang on in the morning when the band left for the airport.

Little did Anita know that her thoughts exactly matched the ones Phillip had pursued while Kid was in the bath, a couple of hours earlier.

Kid's evening had started with a decision to embark on a more constructive path in her life. Meeting Phillip and being asked to his hotel to meet his musician friends she saw as a favorable omen - something like a first step on this newly designated path, a hot bath in Phillips bathroom, his soft woolly sweater, the champagne, the warmth of the room, sitting on a soft carpet and hearing all the interesting stories the musicians had to tell. With some embarrassment she recalled the scene she had made when she broke down in tears, but everybody had reassured her that she had not ruined their evening. So, that was OK.

As the party drew to a close, Bob reminded everyone to be ready at ten thirty the next morning. It was his job as leader of the group, Kid assumed, to make sure that all the administrative stuff was under control.

Do we have to talk shop now? Phillip thought with some impatience as everybody started to get ready to retire. By that time he was positively excited at the thought of pleasant things to come that night. He watched as Anita gave Kid a special little hug, wishing her all the best. He noticed that Anita liked Kid but she, like all the others, knew the band's policies of 'no strings attached'. Everything was OK.

As Phillip and Kid re-entered his room, he realized that Kid already treated it as her home, unconcerned by the fact that it was going to have this status for just one night in her life. But then, he reflected, she is a nomad, as she herself said, and nomads make a home every night in a different spot, in a different town, or in this vast country probably out in the open, on a beach, a river bank, who could tell. No need for a lot of imagination, therefore, to figure out that tonight's 'home' in Kid's eyes was luxury on a grand scale. It did not escape Phillip that her face was a little flushed, her cheeks had turned a nice pink and she radiated warmth and contentment. The champagne had probably played its part in enhancing her enjoyment of the evening.

On his way to the bathroom, Phillip wondered very briefly if Kid would come into the shower with him if he asked her. Maybe better not ask ... might shock her and possibly upset her ... no, it's not worth it. So he decided against this sudden scheme to improve an already perfect situation. He entered Kid's bathroom, closed the door, stripped and stepped into the shower. Kid's bathroom? I must be mad.

Before re-entering the room Phillip tied a towel chastely around his middle and as he now approached the bed all he could see was Kid's head sticking out of the covers, she was beaming with delight. He stopped at the first glimpse of her, shook his head in disbelief and broke into genuine laughter.

Kid did not understand his reaction. As far as she was concerned, there was nothing laughable about the way she sat in bed waiting for what was bound to become a night of lovemaking and enjoyment.

Phillip walked up to her side of the bed, bent over her and gave her a big, long kiss. Then he untied the towel from around his waist, dropped it at his feet and slowly, gently climbed into bed beside her. He proceeded to wrap her in his arms savoring the softness of her skin. She felt smooth and pliable to his touch. Her skin was warm and there was a healthy feel to it and she responded willingly to his touch. But she was so very small, so thin and insubstantial. Phillip started to wonder when she had had her last meal. Had she eaten nothing tonight because she spent her food money on the entrance fee to his concert? Was that why the two glasses of champagne went straight to her head? At that point he could not help but ask himself the obvious question: Should I have taken her for a healthy and wholesome meal rather than just the drink we all shared? After all, *we* all had our evening meal, didn't we?

Kid asked no questions and made no demands. She gave herself to Phillip naturally ... easily. Their lovemaking was unhurried and sweet. Kid could not put on a show, not even if she tried. She handled every situation in her own, natural fashion. Phillip was simply delighted. Kid was neither overwhelming and aggressive nor was she passive and boring. Everything was just so perfect, nothing short of sheer delight.

Later that night, Kid cuddled gently and contentedly against his chest. After saying goodnight to Phillip she went into a deep and peaceful sleep.

She woke up early, around sunrise; this had become a habit during her nomadic life. You went to bed with the sun, and you got up with the sun. It saved firewood or batteries in your torch, depending on where you spent the night. She wriggled around gently until she was sure she knew where she was. Phillip's arms were still around her, she felt warm and cozy and a little cheeky. She stroked Phillip's soft hair. It was smooth and flat, not rough and curly like hers, and it was long enough to touch the collar of his shirt. She looked at his sleeping face for a few minutes remembering his gentle greenish-hazel slightly hooded eyes, his soft, regular features, his sheepish smile. He was a handsome man, indeed.

Phillip now opened his eyes and remembering the previous evening and the night just gone, he gave her a big smile, then rolled over and kissed her without saying a word. They made love again under the covers in the rather chilly early morning hours.

Phillip could hardly believe his luck. Kid had come to him again in the morning, still no questions asked. He almost wish she *did* ask a few.

They stayed in each other's arms well under the covers for a while longer, then Kid started to move and sat up.

"You'll have to make sure you are ready and downstairs in the lobby at the right time. Is Bob in charge of the management side of the band?"

"Yeah, he is. He kinda got us all together and organized us into the band we are now. We are not professional musicians, as you know. We all work at our jobs to make ends meet." And as an afterthought, "I would love to be a full-time musician though ..." He left the sentence unfinished but by the tone of his voice Kid knew that there was truth and depth in what he had just said. Playing music obviously meant the world to him. And that was about the extent of her knowledge of this man's personality. The next thing she heard shook her out of her reveries.

"Thanks Kid," then a pause, "thanks for ... a very enjoyable time. It was great and ... well ... thanks for everything."

Kid was gobsmacked. Is this guy actually thanking me for having spent the night with him? Isn't it usually the other way round? What with men being God's gift to women and all that. Does he expect an answer, Kid wondered? What an extraordinary situation. She said nothing, just savored the last few moments of the warmth and comfort of the soft bed, the pleasant smell of soap and shampoo that emanated from Phillip, and then she decided that it was time to make a move.

Kid had not had a proper meal for close to twenty-four hours but that did not bother her. She would soon find a place where to park her truck and use her cooker to brew some porridge. Nobody has yet been known to starve to death after a twenty-four hour fast, she assured herself.

Phillip watched as Kid got out of bed shivering visibly in the cold morning air. Her slim body moved easily and unhurriedly across the room to where she had deposited her neatly folded clothes. Phillip closed his eyes in make-believe morning slumber, but he watched Kid get dressed and drag some sort of comb through her impossibly thick, rough hair. She picked up his dark blue sweater, the one she had borrowed the previous night, and pressed it lightly against her face. Phillip could not be quite sure of her next move since he had to look through closed eyes, as it were, but he guessed that she planted a kiss on it before putting it back down on the chair. Then she disappeared into 'her' bathroom.

Phillip knew he would have to make a move too. He

threw the covers back and started to tie last night's bath towel around himself just as Kid walked towards him, arms outstretched, her little plastic bag in one hand. Phillip was glad to see a smile on her face; her misery and helpless sobs the previous night had been difficult to cope with. He and Kid gave each other a last friendly hug, and it was only for one second, just before she turned away, that he saw a shade of sadness come over her face. It came and went.

"You can get some breakfast downstairs in the breakfast room, you know," he called after her just as she was about to open the door.

"But," she looked puzzled "I am not really an official guest, I mean a paying guest here. Do you think breakfast will still work?"

"Sure will. You just give them this room number. That should do it. You have to turn to the right as you get out of the elevator, past the reception desk. If the others are there, please tell them I'll be down as soon as I am ready. Can you do that?"

"Of course. Can I have anything I like ... I mean toast and jam and stuff, and coffee? It will all go on your bill," she asked over her shoulder just as she opened the door to step into the corridor.

With a little smile and a shaking of the head, Phillip said, "Sure, have anything you like, Kid."

"Thanks a lot." And with that she was gone, for good, he thought - maybe just a little unhappily.

Kid took the elevator to go down to the lobby, turned right as Phillip had told her and found that the corner area facing the T-junction on the opposite side of the entrance was set with small round tables, all covered white table cloths; on each of them were sugar pots, serviettes and a small flower arrangement. Neat, she thought, I'll get some juice, toast, marmalade and coffee; that will get me through the biggest part of the day. A few minutes after she had ordered, the other band members joined her. She debated for a second whether she should explain her presence. She did not want them all to think that she was presumptuous and greedy by assuming the status of a paying guest. But no one asked any questions of her.

"It's all right. Don't be shy," Bob encouraged her.

"Good," she said and tucked in. Kid sat facing the windows and turning her back to the reception desk and the elevator next to it. "Phillip will be here as soon as he is ready, he said to tell you." She didn't look at Bob.

Kid was sure about one thing, she wanted to be finished with her breakfast and gone before Phillip came down. They had said their good-byes, it was best this way. She absently watched the traffic move steadily in and out of the junction while enjoying her toast. Anita sat next to her on the right, Mario on her left, the others at the adjoining table talking shop. Kid had just taken her last swallow of coffee, she was now fishing under the table for her plastic bag getting ready to leave when she said in an even tone of voice still looking straight ahead, "Phillip is coming now."

Everybody peered out through the window, following Kid's eyes, trying to locate Phillip.

"Where?" Anita asked uselessly.

"No, not out there on the road, behind us, where the elevators are, of course," Kid said. Why, she puzzled, would Anita expect Phillip to come in from the street, silly.

The whole group now turned as one to face the reception desk and hence the elevator to see the automatic doors open and Phillip step out. Kid took advantage of that moment to disappear from the breakfast room.

Phillip approached his friends, said good morning all around, sat down and confidently ordered his breakfast. All six of them sat around the same table now discussing the continuation of their tour. A good thing the tables were round, you could sit any number of people around one of them. Phillip's food arrived, he started to attack his bacon and eggs with gusto.

All was still well then but about three minutes into his breakfast, things started to happen. Phillip jumped up from his chair as if stung by a hornet. He threw his napkin away. Alarm registered on his face. He scanned the breakfast area then the lobby, his eyes flashing wildly in every direction.

"Where is Kid? When did she leave? Where to?" He exclaimed rather pointlessly.

36

They all stared at him in disbelief. Nobody knew.

"I can't just let her go, or I'd never find her again in her nomadic life." He scooted his chair back roughly and started to run past the reception desk and out the door at full speed. Outside he made a sharp left turn and kept running. He was possessed by only one thought, 'I must catch her before she leaves the car park ... she must not drive off before I get to that exit.' But in order to achieve this aim he knew he had to run - and run fast.

At the very same moment, Kid was driving out of the underground car park. She too, made a left turn, then joined the flow of traffic. She knew instinctively that Phillip was running - running and trying to catch her. But where was he? She knew he needed to run - and run fast or she would not be able to see him in the rear view mirror before turning the next corner.

Suddenly, there he was. She saw him speeding out of the hotel's main entrance, his jacket flying in the wind. He turned in her direction. He must have sensed the exact moment when my truck would appear on the road, same way I sensed he was coming out of the elevator, Kid told herself. Telepathy? Kid didn't know much about this phenomenon but it sounded like a good enough explanation for the accurate information they both had on their respective movements.

Kid was amused rather than puzzled, even though surprise would have been a more appropriate reaction to this inexplicable situation.

She put her foot on the break and pulled over to the left hand side of the road. There she came to a halt with two of her truck's wheels on the pedestrian walkway. She never turned around in her seat, just watched the whole show in her rear view mirror. By the time she had turned the engine off and was out of her seatbelt, Phillip had come to a standstill beside the driver's side of her vehicle, breathless but visibly happy. The window was down and he reached inside the cabin with both arms, then grabbed her head, pulled it towards him and gave her a breathless kiss. No explanation was made, no questions were asked. Phillip just kept leaning against the door disregarding the existence of the world around him. He had succeeded in catching up with Kid before losing her forever. In a few minutes he would put his mind and his brain into gear and consider what possible surprises life could have in store for him but his rational thinking got him nowhere right then. As his breathing slowly calmed down, he still held Kid's head in his hands, a foot away from his face now. He looked into her eyes, stammered something unintelligible and suddenly there were tears burning behind his eyes. He tried to blink them back, but to no avail.

Kid to the rescue. She opened the door pushing Phillip back a couple of feet and left it standing open not caring that it was interfering with the flow of traffic. Drivers complained loudly and angrily. Kid took no notice. The real world around her had ceased to exist. She reached out, put her arms around Phillip and enclosed him in a tight hug. There was no need for words now.

After a while Kid said, "Phillip, I think we are obstructing traffic. Quick, lets get in the truck and drive ... somewhere. I don't know Fremantle any better than you do ... I'll just drive wherever the truck takes us."

Once inside the cabin, Phillip placed his right hand lightly on Kid's knee, he felt he needed some little physical contact just to make sure the whole situation was not a dream but reality. How could this happen? What was I thinking when I let her go? And just now tears. What the hell is the matter with me?

Then without further thought he said, "Kid, it feels like all this is happening on another planet – in another universe...."

The sentence was still hanging in the air when Kid piped up, "I know, a miracle, right? I like miracles. There are plenty all around, only not everybody sees them." She chuckled, "Too busy ... lots of people are too busy to appreciate the miracles in everyday life." She sensed rather than saw Phillip turn his head to look at her, and she also sensed that he was smiling.

They continued in silence after that exchange until they came to a half-empty parking lot close by the port facilities. They were surrounded by stacks of ugly containers of all colors and sizes. Kid turned the engine off, pulled the handbrake tight, then sat back in her seat and exhaled deeply as if she had just completed a major acrobatic exercise. They made no move to get out, just sat strapped in their seats and looked straight ahead.

Phillip was the first to try and put thoughts into words. He started slowly and chose his words carefully.

"Kid, we've got something special here, right? We need to hold on to that. We'll embark on a new life all our own. What form or shape this life will take, I have no idea. It can be in my country or I could join you in your nomadic life in this country, or we can both move to the North Pole ..."

Kid had been listening attentively to Phillip's words. She was sitting behind the steering wheel, holding it with both hands and looking closely at the dash board as if what she was about to say was written there for her to read.

"I give the North Pole a miss," she said, then she stretched her arms, laced her fingers together and turned them palms out. She leaned back in her seat placed her hands behind her head and relaxed. "It's like there is some bond between us ... don't know quite what to call it. A bond that makes each of us feel what the other does or thinks. It's like we were wired together. That's good fun, isn't it?"

She pressed her lips together while emitting a cheerful little giggle, then she was serious again, businesslike even.

"I think it's best to start our new life in your country...

yes, better than here. I've lost everything I owned in this country. You see, it's like this: I had made a big decision only yesterday, a promise to quit feeling sorry for myself. I knew it was time to start looking to the future. Then I happened upon your concert and I met you ... perfect timing."

Kid now dropped her hands into her lap, turned her head to face Phillip who had sat quietly through her whole speech. She lifted her left hand and tenderly laid it against Phillip's cheek without saying a word. Phillip turned his face slowly inside her palm and softly kissed the inside of her hand.

A little later Kid added nonchalantly, "We'll just take what life has to offer and deal with it one day at the time ... much better than to make plans and stuff."

Phillip could no longer suppress the laugh which had been building up inside him, "I'm sure that's the best way, Kid. Of course you are expert at dealing with life one minute at the time. You have already given me ample proof of that in just the short time we have known each other."

Kid was wide-eyed, "Have I?" was all she could say.

Their life together started right there in the cabin of Kid's truck, after one night spent together in a hotel room. Neither saw anything wrong with this approach. They knew nothing about each other, gave no thought to possible risk factors as part of the long-term nature of their decision, it was all based on instinct and intuition. Kid and Phillip knew there and then that they were going to love each other to the end of their lives.

On arriving back at the hotel that morning, Kid and Phillip were all business.

"OK, we have to make some important decisions and we have to make them now. The plane leaves at about one and you and I are both going to be on it." Phillip said.

"Yep. Will you buy my ticket? What happens to the truck? I have no clothes." Then she added, "You are wonderful, I'm so glad we found each other."

"Touché," was all Phillip said. They made their way back into the lobby hand in hand. Phillip's friends watched them in stunned silence. Phillip was all smiles. "I caught up with Kid, probably beat the world record as a sprinter in the process."

Blank looks from everybody greeted him. Turning to Kid he said, "We tour this country for ten days, then we all fly back to the States. You and I can make a detour, come back here and settle whatever needs settling. Then, since it's alright with you, we fly to glorious America and we will live happily ever after!"

Kid beamed and held on to Phillip's hand.

Less than a month later, Kid and Phillip arrived in America. To Kid that meant starting a brand new life in the 'Land of Opportunities' - the land of her future.

II

There were a few steps to be negotiated before arriving at the entrance to Phillip's apartment. Phillip inserted a key into the keyhole and pushed open a heavy wooden door, then stood back respectfully to let Kid enter first. She stepped into a hallway, slowly, carefully, looking around as if to ascertain that there were no ghosts looming anywhere.

"It's OK," Phillip said, "no monsters are waiting to devour you, at least not straight away."

Kid was nervous and she was glad of Phillip's joke to brighten up the situation a little. There should have been no reason for her nervousness since Phillip had already given her a detailed description of his home in the town of Knoxville which was indeed in the State of Tennessee, the cradle of Blue Grass music.

It was a spacious apartment; Kid thought of it more as a semi-detached house. It was built in red brick and joined by two identical houses on the right. Phillip's was the last one in the row and it had a sort of tower-like alcove on the left, which made for two rooms, one above the other, with windows on three sides thus letting in a maximum of light. There was a fair size kitchen with lots of cabinets all in white to give it an overall welcoming appearance; a dining room with a round table and chairs and a living room with a soft and comfortable looking lounge suite in light brown leather. Kid wandered from room to room absorbing everything without saying a word while letting an inexplicable feeling of home-coming flood through her whole being.

Phillip followed Kid. He was a little nervous and he felt somewhat insecure even though he found himself in his own surroundings. Why can't I just relax? It's almost as if *I* was suffering from culture shock, he thought. He gave explanations to unasked questions, made unnecessary apologies for untidiness and unwashed dishes which had been left in the kitchen sink since before the tour.

Finally he said, "Let's settle down and share a glass of wine. We could go out for a meal later - the fridge is kind of empty." He took Kid by the hand and led her to the lounge room. There he took two delicate, high stemmed glasses out of the cabinet, stood them on the low table in the centre of the room, uncorked a bottle and poured the dark red wine. They sat for some time following their own trains of thought, neither of them spoke, both were re-living the previous few weeks of fairytale life - a life filled with love and happiness. They had told each other almost nothing about family and background except that Kid, at thirty-seven was Phillip's senior by two years, that they were both single and unattached. "We have the rest of our lives to talk about mundane stuff like the past," Kid had said. They had lived like two teenagers in love for the first time.

Phillip finally broke the silence. "Kid, you are a country girl at heart, aren't you? Do you think you could live in this apartment? Wouldn't you feel like a caged bird after your nomadic life in Western Australia? I know you are adaptable and versatile, I don't mean to underestimate you but ... please, tell me the truth Kid."

"Right now I feel that I could live absolutely anywhere just so long as you were there with me," she said with a sheepish grin on her face. "I bet you didn't expect such a banal answer." Immediately after that however, she turned serious.

"I wasn't always a nomad, you know. I grew up in Queensland, in a suburb of the capital Brisbane. Remember I showed you on the map? My childhood was, I suppose, like anybody's childhood. I remember that when I was little most of my playmates were Italian. I often used Italian words at home with my parents but they didn't understand them. Both my parents' families had migrated from Eastern Europe some generations ago, and that made me just a regular Australian. Do you want to know all this?"

Phillip was giving Kid his undivided attention. "Yes, please Kid, tell me more."

"My parents have been dead for a long time. They died in short succession, first mum of cancer, then dad of a heart attack. I was barely twenty then. The way I remember, my parents were much older than everybody else's parents, but I might be wrong there. Anyway, as I had no more family – I never had any brothers or sisters - I decided to leave the east coast and make my way across the continent to the west. I did odd jobs here and there, in bars, working in shops, restaurants and on farms picking fruit. I always made a living somehow, just took what life had to offer and enjoyed it day by day. Why are you smiling?"

"It's just that … this life philosophy of yours … I've admired it from the very first day we met."

"Hmm … You realize of course that by living the way I did, I almost completely missed out on further education. I've never seen a university from the inside, I have no certificates or diplomas to my name … but that doesn't matter, does it? I can do all sort of jobs and I can cook and knit and grow vegetables and …"

"… and a million more things, I know darling. I've just made a decision, a big one, and I need to tell you straight away. OK, hold tight: I'm going to buy us a house … a house with a garden in one of the older suburbs … maybe where there are big old shady trees. What do you say?"

Kid looked at Phillip wide-eyed, "One with a back yard where I can grow tomatoes and lettuce and beans and if it's big enough potatoes and beetroots. In the front garden I'll have flowers in all colors ..."

"Time to take a breath Kid. I take it that you like my decision."

Kid simply nodded. "Sorry, I tend to get carried away sometimes. It sounds wonderful. When can we start house hunting?"

"Tomorrow morning OK with you?"

"Tell me Phillip," Kid said later on that first day. They were now comfortably settled in bed, both in a semi-sitting position, pillows stuck behind their backs, "your spontaneous decision to sell this apartment ... are you sure?"

"It was not all that spontaneous, not really. I had thought about it before we even got here, but today I suddenly knew. I want us to start our life together in a place all our own, in a place with no memories of the past, a place where we can start to live and enjoy our brand new relationship. This is really important to me, Kid. I want to be responsible for you and I want to care for you. I know you are going to tell me that you don't need looking after ... but I really mean to get this right."

"You almost sound vehement darling. Tell me all."

Phillip tried to shrug, not an easy thing to do when you are practically lying in bed. "I've owned this place for quite a few years, in fact it's the first and only apartment I ever had in this town. I told you that I grew up in Missouri, in St. Louis to be exact. That's quite a long way from here, I'll show you on the map. The reason I moved to Tennessee was none other than my interest in folk music and Blue Grass. I've played the guitar since I was very young and all I ever wanted was to be a professional musician, tour the country and play in every concert hall, make albums and CDs … all that. So I went to Nashville. I thought this would be the ideal place to start my career. But then … you know the rest."

He turned to face Kid and gave her a sad little smile. "There are thousands of people out there who make music, everyone wants to make a career but only very few make it to the top. After various wrong starts and a few near fits of depression I finally understood and changed tack."

"What did you do then?" In Kid's way of looking at life, failures to achieve an imaginary goal were no more than little hiccups; it was simply part of being alive. The important thing was to keep going.

"I put myself through college and became a journalist. I met Bob in Nashville, saw him play the fiddle with a band - we got talking. He was not a professional musician - still isn't, he teaches math at high school. Bob was about to move to Knoxville for a job and to marry Anita, and he told me he was determined to form a Blue Grass band. That was it. I followed, became part of his band and stayed."

Kid took a moment to digest all she had just heard then she asked, "Are your parents still in Missouri?"

"My parents are both dead. Mom died a long time ago, I was in my mid-twenties, I think. Poppa died last year, eight months ago exactly. I made it to the hospital in St. Louis ... was there when he died. I had never seen anybody die before."

"Were you and your Poppa close? Did you go visit form time to time?"

"Poppa and I got on well. We regularly talked on the phone - once a week, right up until the week before he died. I sometimes managed to visit when one of my reporting trips took me in that direction. Mind you, we used to have some fights - verbal fights I mean - when I was a soft-brained teenager but ... yeah, Poppa was a great person." There he paused for a moment then, "He wasn't sick or suffering, just old. He simply died of old age."

They sat in silence, holding hands. Kid felt that Phillip's mind was back at Poppa's death bed. She asked no more questions.

Phillip could still hear Poppa's last words. 'Please son, try to open your heart to your brother, promise me.' All he had done then was to concur with a nod but to Poppa it was a promise. Sadly Phillip had made no effort to keep that promise and if he felt a little guilty at the memory of that moment he was not prepared to let this guilt surface right then. He decided not to tell Kid. Poppa's words were meant for him only and Phillip had no intention of dealing with this issue - not right now and not in the near future.

It was a beautiful house, indeed, the one Phillip bought. What Kid liked best about it was that it had a veranda which went all along the front and around to one side making a lovely wide corner space, and another equally spacious porch at the back. There were no fences, neither between houses nor out front along the road and this, in Kid's mind, lent the whole suburb a friendly atmosphere - a kind of harmlessness, as suburbs go.

"It's like a forest where the houses are scattered among big old trees, rather than houses with man-made gardens around them," Kid exclaimed when she first saw the house.

And when they moved in, she was almost immediately in full swing decorating it. She crafted curtains, bedspreads, rugs, cushions; she dug flowerbeds and planted bulbs. Phillip marveled at her enthusiasm and her undisguised joie de vivre as he watched her float through her days and weeks.

One morning at breakfast Kid said unexpectedly, "Darling, since I know how much music-making means to you, I've been thinking … could we not make the big room on the left by the entrance into a music studio? I mean, set up all the musical paraphernalia permanently so that the band could practice there. It'll be fun for you to have all your friends right here and play, whether just for fun or to rehearse for performances, won't it? Do you think your friends would like my idea?"

What Kid didn't say was that a gut feeling told her that Jim, the bass player, did not like her and might consequently not welcome her idea of a music studio in her and Phillip's house. Better not mention that to Phillip, she thought, not right now ... not really important ... and Jim is after all his friend.

Phillip loved the thought of having a musical venue in his own home. "This sounds great, Kid, a wonderful idea. I'm sure your suggestion will be greeted with enthusiasm by everyone."

Kid had a great time living a life of leisure for the first weeks in her new country. She was determined to learn about its history, its culture and its people. Phillip was away during the day, either at the office or running around reporting and interviewing important people. He called her a couple of times a day for no other reason than just to hear the sound of her voice, and every evening Kid would deliver a report on the activities and findings of her day. Once she had familiarized herself with the layout of the town she started to include a few visits to the public library - her treasure trove of information. But she also had another source of information and it was her new friend Anita. The two women often met for a cup of coffee and a chat.

"That makes me feel terribly housewifely," Kid had told Anita on their first rendezvous, "but don't get me wrong, I do appreciate your friendship, it means a lot to me."

There were times however, when she would simply sit on the stone wall by the side of the river, dangle her legs and think about her life and immerse herself in meditations of her own making.

Every morning she gave Phillip a hug and kissed him good-bye before he left for work then greeted him in the same manner when he returned in the evening. Kid knew that she would perform this little ritual to the end of their lives. She was determined that her kisses would never become cooler or perfunctory ... never, because if they did it would mark the beginning of the end of their relationship - the end of their love. She could not imagine the morning after a quarrel when she would not embrace him at the front door or run into his arms on his return home because the quarrel had not been resolved and was still in their hearts. This would never happen. Her relationship with Phillip was sacred, everlasting. She knew she would love him to the end of her life.

Phillip loved to sit back every evening and listen to Kid's stories. He was delighted at how easily she adapted and how much enjoyment she got out of her daily activities. He was also aware that the day would soon come when

Anita would feel the need to inform Kid about his earlier and rather unsavory reputation as a bit of a womanizer. But I'm changing my ways. I *can* do it and I *will*, he resolved. Phillip was determined never to cheat on Kid, she was the most precious person in his life.

It was after one of her first exploring days that Kid told Phillip, "You don't worry about me, do you my love? I'm fine, I don't get bored and I don't feel lonely during the day when I'm on my own and not meeting with Anita. I mean, it's not like you had taken me to a village of mud huts with straw roofs on the edge of the Sahara Desert, or to a community where people live in tents made from animal hides in the steppes of Outer Mongolia. In this country at least I can understand people, I can speak their language and I can read the papers. My appearance is pretty much that of any other ordinary guy. People generally live in houses made of bricks, there are paved roads, cars, shops, markets, I can relate to all that. And then, there is …. " she started to giggle merrily.

"Please go on Kid," Phillip whispered in her ear, "before you lose momentum. I love it, and I bet you would have no trouble at all carving out a happy life for yourself in a mud hut in Outer Mongolia; it helps to be versatile."

"No no, the mud hut was on the edge of the Sahara."

"The Sahara, of course ... how silly of me."

After that the discussion disintegrated into helpless

laughter.

One evening as Phillip came home, about two months into their new life, he found her settled comfortably on the settee, a book in her lap. It looked like a big hardcover from the library. A history book, Phillip assumed, and he was almost sure it was about the Civil War and her favorite President, Abraham Lincoln. Kid got up briskly when he entered the room, and gave him her welcome home kiss, then sat down again with her book.

"What are you cooking, darling? It smells delicious."

"Casserole ... in the oven," she answered a little absently.

A minute later, Phillip's voice rang out from the kitchen. "Kid ... Kid."

Kid looked up from her book in alarm. A second later she heard Phillip's voice again, much louder that time and at least an octave higher, "Kid, come here, quick ... quick."

An emergency! Kid jumped up from her settee, flew past the breakfast counter and into the kitchen. "What happened? Are you hurt?"

Phillip stood dead centre in the kitchen, a big smile on his face. He opened his arms ready for an embrace and said, "Kid, will you marry me?"

"Come again? What's that got to do with the casserole in the oven?"

Phillip looked and sounded very serious when he repeated, "Will you? Please Kid?"

"You chose one hell of a moment for your proposal, Phillip. You're impossible ... and the answer is yes. Can we sit down and talk about this trivial little issue for a minute or two?"

Phillip took her in his arms and hugged her. Then Kid sat him down on a barstool at the counter, got a can of beer from the refrigerator and placed it in front of him. Phillip was seemingly floating in a different universe so Kid took charge of the situation.

"Why? Why all of a sudden? Isn't the life we are living just perfect? Why the need to make it official? I don't understand. Marriage ... it's just a piece of paper and signatures and stuff, isn't it?"

"That's not how I see it, darling. Call me old-fashioned but being married to you means everything to me - it's important to me. It kind of emphasizes my responsibility, my commitment. I really want to be married to you. I do understand your argument but ... can we agree to disagree and get married?"

In all Kid's adult life, she had never thought that anyone would marry her. Marriage was for other people; marriage was for people who enjoyed parties, for people who liked socializing, for girls who were pretty and desirable. When she was a teenager, her mother used to tell her that she looked ordinary, that she was ungainly and that she made no effort to look pretty. Her hair was dreadful, it was like a mop and she did not know how to behave like a lady. Mother probably meant well when she told her daughter that it was not grown-up to blurt out everything that came to mind. In short, mother had made it quite clear, that nobody would ever want to marry her. Kid, who of course went under the name of Florence then, started to believe her mother's predictions. She accepted the fact that she would remain single.

She was happy most of the time, she had fun, made friends and enjoyed life a day at the time while watching her school mates get married and have families. Now Phillip said it was important to him to be married to her. What next? All this went through her mind in flashes while she was sitting at the breakfast counter watching Phillip open his beer can.

"OK, let's get married tomorrow afternoon," she blurted in true Kid fashion, just exactly the way her mother had told her not to.

"I love you Kid. I'll love you to the end of my life and I promise I'll do everything to make you a good husband. I don't really know what that implies but everyday life will show me. I'll keep my ears, eyes and my mind open. That's what you do, isn't it? I'm so happy Kid …" tears were now very close to the surface.

Kid put her arms around him and whispered, "I'm happy, too. I know as little about married life as you do … so we are likely to make heaps of mistakes. But that's OK, life would be real boring without mistakes. We'll know how to handle them, nothing will ever interfere with our love, I'm sure of it."

Philip and Kid did get married and on that day Kid became Mrs McCabe. They organized a small party, invited their closest friends back to their home, nice and intimate. It was a memorable and unique day as befitted wedding days, but of course in Kid's life, every single day was memorable and unique.

Prior to the big day, the question of wedding rings had come up and it turned out that it would not be an easy issue to settle. 'I like a wedding band,' Phillip had said. 'One that I will wear on the fourth finger of my right hand, so that when I pluck the strings of my guitar it will sparkle, for everyone to see.' It was a statement, firm and unalterable.

Kid's idea had been rather more complex. 'A ring will be uncomfortable,' she had declared. 'You see Phillip, a ring is a bother when I work in the garden, it can easily catch on a twig or get lost when I pull weeds. No, I'd rather not have a wedding ring. What alternative do I have?'

Phillip had been quick with his answer, 'I shall get you a pretty little golden chain to put around your neck. Just be careful darling, when you work in the garden. Don't hang yourself on a tree by it.'

The night after their wedding party Kid lay awake for a long time. She was thinking about Phillip's father who had missed his son's wedding by only eight months. If he had lived, he would have been her father-in-law ... like a real father.

"I'm thinking about your Poppa," she said dreamily not knowing if her husband was still awake. "Do you think he would have been happy with me as a daughter-in-law?"

Phillip's voice came out from under the covers almost immediately, "I'm pretty sure he would have loved you, Kid. He would have loved your spontaneity and your cheerfulness ..." he left the sentence unfinished. Kid understood and did not pursue the subject further right then.

This last question made it clear to Phillip that Kid would have liked an extended family. Sadly she had missed out on a father-in-law but she did have a brother-in-law only she did not know that. Phillip wondered briefly if not volunteering information was tantamount to telling a lie. But he knew almost instantly that he could not talk about his brother David. He didn't want to talk about him and he didn't want to think about him either. Quite involuntarily his thoughts now went back to his mother who had died of a broken heart many years ago. Poppa didn't agree with me on that, Phillip remembered, but I just know. It was her sorrow and her anguish and grief, all to do with David, that killed her. Her death was David's fault. She died because of what he did to her, he was horrible. Suddenly Phillip's mind was awash with little wisps of memories. Why, he wondered, do I fill my mind with difficult stuff on the happiest day in my life? He turned to face Kid now, took her in his arms and held her tight against his body in an effort to push every vestige of unrevealed family history into the furthest corner of his unconscious mind – for the time being.

One evening shortly after their wedding day Kid attempted to cook her first Indian Curry. It was the evening of her first and successful job searching day. She and Phillip had discussed the issue of Kid going out to work. Phillip, predictably, was unimpressed. 'I can and will provide for both of us,' he had argued, but he knew full well that he could not make Kid into a lady of leisure. She was far too dynamic for that sort of life. That had been an easy disagreement to settle and it had been their first one.

Kid had the book open on the table beside her and was carefully following the recipe, step by step. It was a beautiful cookbook with color photos of every dish. Phillip had given it to her only a week ago. It was important, it said in the introduction, to measure all the spices very accurately; too much of one or too little of another could easily ruin the whole dish. What a challenge.

"What are you cooking, darling? It smells delightful," she heard Phillip's voice from the hallway.

"Curry ... Madras Beef Curry. Hold on, I need to concentrate on the spices ..."

A minute later, Phillip walked into the kitchen, a broad

smile on his face.

"From the new cookbook?" he asked and put his arms around her waist from behind and read over her shoulder. "Needs to simmer for one hour, it says here."

"I know, gives me plenty of time to tell you about my new job. Yes you heard right, my new job."

"I better sit down before I fall," he said chuckling happily. "I think we might need a glass of wine to go with your news."

"It was like this," she said once the curry was simmering and they sat side by side on the sofa. "I saw a note pasted on the door of this restaurant-type shop. 'Job vacancy' it said, so I went for it. The place is called Alfredo's, do you know it? Italian place ... beautiful ... real Mediterranean looking, you know with pictures of Adriatic beaches with lines of colorful sunshades, Tuscan landscapes, Florence, Sienna, Capri, the lot."

"Darling, the job. What is it?"

"I was getting to that. There is more than one vacancy. In fact Alfredo and his wife Giovanna need an extra pair of hands everywhere, kitchen, shop, restaurant, and they have functions too. Don't quite know what they are though, do you?"

"Invited guests only - not open to the public, a company celebration maybe ... something like that."

"Uh-huh. Alfredo wants me to work on all the jobs,

you know, switching from one to the other just like that. They are very nice people. We did the whole conversation in Italian, but I had to mix in some English words ... for the ones I didn't know. Remember I told you I played with Italian children when I was little? I still remember quite a lot. Many of Alfredo's patrons are Italian too, so he likes me to work in the restaurant and ..."

"Try and take a breath from time to time. I go and check the curry." Phillip said and ran to the kitchen.

"I start my job tomorrow, mid-morning," Kid called after him, "so I can work through the lunchtime rush. I'm so excited."

"I'm glad you are, Kid. I like to see you happy."

Kid's curry was a success but the rice that went with it wasn't. It was sticky and mushy, but that didn't matter. Phillip ate anything Kid served.

After another bottle of wine and a not very interesting movie on TV, Kid and Phillip made their way upstairs - time for bed. "There is something I'd like to talk to you about, Kid."

"Is it bad?"

"No ... no, not really. You might not even find it very interesting. But it is something I need to tell you ... can't keep it to myself."

They were both sitting in bed, the little bedside light still on. Phillip started awkwardly. "You know Kid, when we first got together … none of my friends believed in … well, in the workability of our relationship. No one trusted me to be faithful to one person for any length of time. It's because I had a bit of a reputation … you see, as a womanizer."

Kid giggled merrily. "I can't see that that is a crime. It only means that you picked up pretty girls easily because you are so irresistibly attractive to women, right?"

"Oh, shut up Kid, I wanted to have a serious conversation with you." Phillip did all he could trying to sound irritated at her ridiculous assertion.

"I'm sorry, darling but I just had to say that. I am serious now."

"Apology accepted," Phillip said and lightly kissed Kid's cheek. "All this ... this reputation ... it's in the past now. I have changed. All I want is to be with you, make you a good husband. That's what I needed to say to you."

Kid leaned her head against his shoulder then turned to look into his eyes. "I realize now that this was difficult for you to say and I am sorry I made a joke. But I still don't understand why you felt the need to tell me, darling?"

"Umm … I just didn't want you to hear it from Anita. I know you two are good friends, she might want to inform you, maybe warn you. I wanted you to hear this from me. That's all."

"OK," Kid said matter-of-factly, "now I know." And as

an afterthought she added, "You are probably right, Anita will want to warn me, meaning of course to be kind and helpful. It often happens, you know, that people want to help when help is not even asked for. It's a silly practice, sometimes even a little dangerous. I mean, it can be interpreted as meddling and interfering, can't it. It's what they always do in soap operas, mainly in the bad ones."

Phillip chuckled. "True. Still I do feel better now that it's out."

Phillip had decided to write his weekly column at home that day. He had also bought a bunch of flowers for his wife and stuck them in a bottle so they would look fresh when Kid came back. He knew the flowers she liked best: the more rough looking type, with long stalks, lots of leaves and a variety of colors. Phillip never forgot the day, at the very beginning of their life together, when he brought home twelve dark red roses, hoping this would please her. Phillip had to smile at the mere thought of what happened then. Oh, she liked them alright, and when she put them into a vase she had said, 'I wonder why roses are supposed to convey love between humans more than other flowers. I am pretty sure every other flower thinks of roses as being arrogant and haughty. Sure, roses are pretty and they do have a nice scent. That probably gives them a high status in flower society, but we don't often consider flower psychology, do we?' Who, other than Kid, had ever heard of flower psychology?

Kid's noisy arrival shook him out of his reverie. She had just completed one of her working days at Alfredo's.

"Have you earned our daily bread at home today, darling?" she asked after having given him a warm kiss. Then she went to the kitchen and Phillip could hear her thinking aloud about the events of her day and about what to cook for dinner.

Suddenly and without warning she addressed him with, "Why was President Lincoln at first unpopular? I mean, he won the Civil War for the Union, didn't he? And then...."

By that time, Phillip had learned to match the speed of Kid's mind leaps. "Hold it," he said from behind his newspaper, "one thing at the time. I am not so sure about unpopular. He was elected in an orderly fashion, after all, however with only a marginal majority I believe. Also, Lincoln was born in the State of Kentucky which was one of the Southern States, right?" Phillip sometimes wished he could remember more details of his country's historical facts. Kid was so inquisitive, she was on her way to be better informed than he was. "But Lincoln was a Senator of Illinois when he was elected President. You probably know better than I."

"Shouldn't think so," she said. "But in his Inaugural Speech he never said he was an abolitionist ... is this the right word to use?"

Phillip chuckled and finally lowered his paper. "I suppose you mean to ask wasn't he anti-slavery. He was non-committal on the subject of slavery at the beginning of his Administration in 1861. But I believe he always endeavored to abolish this dastardly practice, only he hoped it would not have to be done at the cost of a Civil War. His main concern was to keep the Union together."

By this time Kid had decided on Quiche Lorraine for dinner. "Hmm ... makes sense. He was tall, about seven feet, wasn't he? And do you think it is true that he said, and I quote, 'it's neither heaven nor hell, it's simply purgatory'. And would you know what he was talking about? Marriage," she said answering her own question. "Not very flattering for his wife ..."

Phillip let that sink in for a while, then "Kid?" he asked.

"Yes my love." The reply came in a voice, lacking every trace of emotion. She was all business.

"My darling wife," he tried again. "Correct me if I'm wrong, but I assume that you have spent the entire afternoon at the public library, while I sat here earning our daily bread."

This statement generated instant reaction. She now switched her priorities from President Lincoln to affection for her husband. She came out of the kitchen into the lounge room and settled comfortably in Phillip's lap, giving him her full attention.

"Darling, yes I did go to the library on my way back

65

from Alfredo's. I need to learn more about my new home-land's origin and history, and I just happened to pick up this very interesting book on the life of ..."

"... Abraham Lincoln, right? Sounds like he may not have been very happily married, and yes he was tall and very thin, but maybe not quite that tall. The important thing however, is that he won the Civil War for us in 1865 - or for the Union." Phillip always gave Kid's questions serious consideration and answered as explicitly as he knew how.

"And then he was assassinated, wasn't he, just as he started his second term. Very sad," Kid said with feeling. She was still sitting on Phillip's lap, her arms loosely around his shoulders, she then got up and continued with dinner. Phillip resumed his paper-reading.

The next thing he heard, "Thanks for the beautiful flowers, darling. Good of you to put them in water, I know they are grateful for that, no matter the horrible bottle you stuffed them into."

Phillip had nothing to add .

On this particular day as Kid worked at Alfredo's restaurant in her capacity as a waitress she was introduced to Father Pasquale. She had served him at table not knowing that he was a priest since his clothing gave nothing away. But she had heard him speak Italian to Alfredo and Giovanna so she spoke to him in the same language.

When the busiest time came to an end and the bulk of

the restaurant's work shifted to the kitchen and to cleaning and tidying up, Alfredo called her and asked her to come into the family room. This was where she was formally introduced to Father Pasquale.

Father was a little taller then she, he was lean and had large dark eyes, pronounced eyebrows and high cheekbones, his hair was black and curly. He was a handsome man and he had a friendly sparkle in his eyes. Kid liked him immediately.

"I am pleased to meet you, Kid," he said when Kid walked into the family room. They shook hands and made a few minutes worth of small-talk, interrupting the business discussion in which Father had been engaged with Alfredo.

"Didn't mean to interrupt. Please continue." Kid said, but her curiosity soon won over her politeness. "I always wanted to know what sort of work a priest did besides doing mass and confession," she blurted. But as soon as her words were out she had a feeling that it had been the wrong thing to say. I might just have given away the fact that I'm not a Catholic and that I know nothing at all about the workings of his Church, she thought with some embarrassment.

Father smiled, turned to Kid and started to answer her question concerning the work of a priest. "There is a lot to do, you know," he said, "Sometimes I wonder if my attempt at improving the world is maybe more than I can handle."

"Like what exactly, Father? What do you do to make

the world a better place?"

"Well for instance, I'm running a crèche for all the little children and babies. You see, there are many single mothers, and they all have to work during the day, and often they are not financially in a position to afford childcare facilities. We also look after some elderly people who live on their own, some are permanently wheelchair bound. We take them to the park in good weather, or to the shops. And there is of course all the administrative work. I do, indeed, say mass and hear confession, Kid, and often I take the catechism class – these are the usual obligations of a priest."

Father's list of tasks to be fulfilled lengthened and Kid soon understood the extent of his worries.

"It is almost impossible to find enough helpers," Father shook his head sadly. "You know, it's all volunteer work - unpaid, you understand…." The sentence trailed off. He made no attempt to finish it.

"I can give you a hand here and there, Father," Kid piped up. "I mean, just helping. I don't have any official qualifications, you know, like nursing or caring for the elderly or for babies, but I could still be useful, somehow, just help whoever is in charge, maybe." Then she turned to face Alfredo, "I could fit in some hours between my working shifts here, couldn't I Alfredo?"

Alfredo nodded.

Father was silent for a few moments as if deep in

thought, then he lifted his head and looked directly at Kid.

"You are very kind, Kid. This is a truly generous offer, thank you. Yes, I can already think of a dozen jobs where we could use an extra pair of hands."

After that the conversation went on almost exclusively in Italian. Father rattled off a list of activities that were in need of an extra helper: Setting up the church hall for the occasional function or lecture, trestle tables for tea and coffee and refreshments, tidying up after, work in the gardens around the church and lots more. Kid could tell by the change in Father's voice that he was getting excited at the prospect of a new volunteer.

"I have also just recently started to run a number of soup kitchens, you know, food and shelter for the poor and the homeless. There are now two places where these people can go for a meal and have a shower any time during the day and where it's warm and comfortable." He stopped to take a breath and in a somewhat resigned voice he continued, "There are unfortunately, many poor and destitute people in the streets of our city. I also hope to be able to offer accommodation – at least temporary – to homeless mothers with children. So you see Kid, lots to do."

While listening to Father's words, Kid could not help but cast her mind back to her Italian childhood friends in the Brisbane suburb. They were all Catholics and they went to mass every Sunday. Kid would have liked to join them sometimes but her parents didn't want to hear of it. They made her believe that all the Catholic priests did was to inculcate the fear of God into their parishioners. Now she had proof that her well intended parents were wrong. Father Pasquale does not do that, he helps people, he is a good man. I just hope its alright to work for him without being of the Catholic faith, it went through her mind.

"Father," she started uncertainly, "I have to tell you that I am not a Catholic. Is it still OK to work for your Church?"

Father lowered his head for a second in an effort to suppress a little smile. "It is quite alright, Kid. God isn't a stickler for such trifling things as these. Your work will be appreciated."

Kid had always gravitated towards the people who were left behind by society, the homeless and the destitute. She would hand out whatever happened to be in her bag, a sandwich, a piece of chocolate or an apple but after listening to Father, she now saw an opportunity to help the needy - and to help them big time - at shelters organized by the Church, truly a valid outlet for her unquenchable altruism. From now on I am really going to be instrumental in making the world a better place, she told herself with some satisfaction.

The day Kid met Father Pasquale threatened to end

in disaster almost as soon as Kid got home and showered Phillip with her elation over her latest engagements. No matter how hard Phillip tried to share Kid's enthusiasm at having found a way to improve the plight of the downtrodden and the homeless, an inbuilt insecurity got the better of him. Now that Kid worked almost every day at Alfredo's restaurant, at the shop or in the kitchen, and from today she had about another eight hundred jobs with the Catholic Church - would there still be time for him - for the two of them? He knew he should not try to stop his wife from organizing her daily occupations the way she liked but his lack of tolerance and his fear instantly showed on his face.

"I'm sorry darling," she said without preamble, "I was selfish. In my excitement I went a step too far. I should have discussed all this with you before making a commitment."

"*I* am the one who is selfish, Kid," there was a melancholy tone in his voice. "I want you to be happy, I really do. I'll work on this hang-up of mine and on my insecurity. I know I have a lot to learn."

From that day on, Kid juggled her working hours at Alfredo's and at Father's carefully. She and Phillip continued to spend Saturdays or Sundays in the park having a picnic, throwing a Frisbee or feeding ducks. The band played their regular evening gigs on the weekend. Phillip's and Kid's married life was in top shape.

III

Phillip sat behind the wheel of his comfortable Nissan sedan heading west on the highway to Nashville. He was on a three-day reporting trip that would take him all the way to Memphis or at least as far as the airport. This was his first assignment away from home in his married life. He had embraced Kid and kissed her intimately before he left and the feeling of her body pressing against his and the softness of her lips still lingered in his mind as he now increased the distance which separated them. But slowly he felt the effect of the purring sound of the engine and the monotony of the highway starting to conjure up unwanted memories. It was stirring some hidden feelings of guilt at misleading Kid by not revealing the truth of his brother. And what about the promise I made Poppa? I am not keeping it – I never really meant to. This thought started to hurt Phillip; it made him sad. His wife had a right to be privy to all this information,

Phillip was well aware of that. On a few occasions he had come precariously close to blurting out the whole invidious truth of his brother but every time his courage had deserted him at the last moment.

Now, alone in his car with all the windows up and with hours of driving ahead of him, Phillip found himself talking aloud. "I can't keep Kid in the dark. The longer I prevaricate, the more this whole thing turns into a skeleton-in-the-closet-story, and the closer I get to becoming a liar. Maybe I could just turn north once I'm in Memphis, drive to St. Louis and pay my brother a visit. I should just tell him that I'm married and that I don't ever want him to meet my wife. But what if Kid asks to be introduced? What do I do then?" But there was not enough time to include a side trip to St. Louis. I wouldn't be able to speak to David anyway, he still scares the shit out of me. Phillip conveniently found a host of excuses to justify the cancellation of his long overdue visit to his brother.

Phillip remembered the day, a long time ago when he was in his mid-teens - the day that had determined the antagonism he was still carrying in his heart and in his mind. And maybe in my soul too, if I have one of those, he added unhappily to his thought. David had appeared in his family home unexpectedly, when in fact he was supposed to be in the hospital. I was too young then, Phillip reflected now, and I didn't really understand why my big brother was in hospital or what was wrong with him. All mom had told me was that the doctors were treating him and making him right again.

Yet suddenly David tore into our home, said something unintelligible that sounded like, 'not going back' and 'they're trying to kill me', his speech was a little slurred. He seemed totally out of focus. Phillip remembered clearly that mom tried to reason with David but he just didn't get it, instead he turned into a savage brute. There was a sort of feral strength in him, something untamable, as he started to destroy everything in sight. Chairs flew against walls, the table with everything on it was turned upside down, there was broken glass, shattered lampshades, total chaos. When Phillip got to this point in his replay of that fateful day, his hands were shaking, his breathing became uneven, he felt cold sweat run down his back. He had to stop the car, get out and stamp his feet to clear his head.

Even though Poppa had told him later that David was a different man now and no longer violent Phillip could not think about this day without reacting like the teenager he was then. I went and hid under my bed that day, coward that I was, instead of helping mom to calm David down. Phillip could still picture the situation in his mind; it was as clear as if it had happened only last week. And all the while I was sure that David was going to kill us both. But then he didn't hurt anybody - not himself either - he just demolished the lounge room, then disappeared. Apparently David never went back to the clinic after that.

I was only very young then, Phillip recalled, but I knew that what happened that day changed mom. Dave had hurt her, broken something inside her. That's why I don't want to have anything to do with him, ever again. Phillip found himself hopelessly entangled in these memories of a long time ago. He knew he had to tell Kid the truth. This whole thing would drive him mad if he kept it locked inside for much longer. I've promised to make Kid a model husband, and being truthful is certainly one of the most important ingredients needed for the fulfillment of that promise. He wondered briefly whether Kid had not already noticed that there was something on his mind. What with the odd kind of telepathy that existed between them ... it just might be possible.

That 'odd kind of telepathy', as Phillip thought of it, had indeed given Kid a somewhat shadowy idea that there was something on her husband's mind, something that troubled him and on occasion made him a little tense. But she knew not to nag; nagging was ugly and bad for their relationship. So she relied on her husband's goodwill and sincerity; she knew he would talk to her when he was ready.

Phillip would be back this evening in time for dinner, he had told her over the phone. Kid had spent most of the afternoon tidying up, dusting and vacuuming around the house. She wanted to make her husband feel welcome and she knew that it was the small things that counted. She had missed Phillip over the last three days. They had spoken on the phone several times a day even though they had nothing concrete to say to each other. Their conversations had been no more than repeated declarations of love and affection. But then that's what you do when you're newly married, Kid convinced herself even though she didn't have a clear idea of what people did or had to do when they were newly married.

On the evening of Phillip's return, he and Kid sat comfortably in their lounge over coffee after they had had their dinner.

"Phillip," Kid said seemingly out of the blue, "I just saw a shadow cross your face. Anything? Do you want to talk about it?" This was the overture to the newly-married's very first in-depth conversation. But we won't argue, Kid reminded herself, not at all, we'll just be talking seriously the way two people do when they find themselves on the threshold of a new and shared life.

"Yes Kid," Phillip said, took a deep breath then assumed his serious-talk-posture. He sat on the edge of the soft seat, knees apart, elbows resting on thighs, hands clasped prayer fashion in the middle. He looked down at his feet when he started.

"I have a brother. I don't know him well ... I saw him

last at Poppa's funeral." Kid opened her eyes wide. About two dozen questions formed instantly in her mind but she managed to curb her curiosity and uttered none of them. Phillip continued. "My brother is a misfit ... been in and out of jail most of his adult life ... he is a semi-moron and he is dangerous. He is in prison as we speak."

"Let's go visit him in prison, Phillip," Kid said, interest and optimism written all over her face.

"Kid, I've just painted the picture of a murderous monster and all you have to say is 'let's go see him'."

"He is still your brother and now my almost-brother, he can't be all bad. Anyway, why didn't you tell me earlier? I had a feeling that you were mulling something over in your mind for some time."

"Well, I'm telling you now," he snapped, but realized his mistake as soon as the words were out.

Kid looked at him with a mixture of hurt, disappointment and confusion. I was entitled to ask that question, wasn't I? She thought. If I had brothers or sisters, I would have told Phillip straight up. Phillip's voice shook her out of her thoughts.

He sounded deflated, guilty and a little sad when he said, "I'm sorry for snapping at you Kid. I didn't mean to … I shouldn't have. I know I ought to have told you about my brother. It's just all very difficult." He went and knelt down in front of her, took both her hands in his and lowered his head. "Please Kid, forgive me and yes, it is true that I've been agonizing and struggling with this issue. I wanted to talk to you about it all, and I felt more and more guilty the longer I kept it inside me. I'm honestly sorry ..."

Forgiveness was instant. "Forgiven," she pronounced solemnly.

"Thanks Kid." He sat down beside her now as he continued, "His name is David. He is older than I by just over ten years. We got separated when I was very young and most of what I can tell you is what Poppa told me later. He always tried to keep in touch with Dave ... I didn't. Right now he is in jail because he killed somebody."

"On a murder charge? Is he on death row?" Kid had read a lot about the death penalty and she was adamant that this medieval practice should be abolished sooner rather than later. Now her own going-to-be brother seemed to be one of the victims.

"No no, he is serving a sentence of about five years for manslaughter, you know accidental killing. He was apparently provoked and got into a fight ... that's how it happened. He is in jail in St. Louis."

Kid was somewhat relieved after Phillip's explanation. "Why don't you like him, Phillip? What did he do to you?"

"He came to our home, I was only about thirteen or so, and he behaved like a maniac and destroyed everything. He was completely out of control and he scared me to death. He was meant to be in hospital but had broken out, and from then on he kept getting into conflict with the law … break-ins and that, in and out of jail. Sorry, my account is somewhat disjointed."

"Yes, it is rather. I go and make some fresh coffee, gives you time to reorganize your thoughts of the past."

But Phillip was now set to give his own interpretation of how David disrupted his and his parents' lives. His opinion had been locked in position when he was only in his teens and he had never been able to make any adjustments to it since. He followed Kid to the kitchen, talking uninterruptedly while she busied herself with brewing coffee.

"David was drafted and sent to Vietnam when he was around twenty. I was only a child and didn't understand anything about that conflict then. He was away for possibly three or four years. My parents were in constant fear of receiving a message telling them that Dave had been killed. One day I was told that he was back in the States, in Texas somewhere, and shortly after he was brought back to St. Louis, to some military hospital."

Kid had made a fresh pot of coffee, she carried it back to the lounge room, set it on the low table and poured two cups. She did not interrupt her husband, asked no questions even though she was dying to know why David had been taken to hospital. Was he injured? Lost arms or legs? Did he have scars from bullet wounds all over his body? Was he disfigured by burns?

Phillip read her thoughts. "David came back in one piece, so to speak, physically intact. Mom told me he was traumatized which I didn't understand ... still have trouble conceiving the exact meaning of it. I can only tell you what I saw on that one afternoon when mom took me to see my brother. He was lying on a hospital bed on his back, he was covered by a white sheet, eyes open, didn't move a muscle. He didn't seem to see or recognize us, didn't say 'hi' or anything, his skin was sort of grayish ... I thought he was dead. Now this next bit is second hand. Doctors told mom and Poppa that David would remain like a vegetable for the rest of his life. Something had happened in the war, nobody knew exactly what, but it had somehow killed his mind, his brain. But my brother fooled everyone, doctors and psychiatrists alike, and came out of his coma - his temporary death. You have to know Kid, that David is about six foot eleven and physically as strong as an ox. He is also a karate expert."

Phillip now told of David's karate training, first harmlessly as a school kid at a martial arts school in St. Louis. Later, when he was drafted, the military shamelessly exploited this talent of his and used it to their own advantage. He told how Dave was offered the best karate training, first in Florida then in Okinawa where apparently, karate originated.

Phillip could still hear Poppa's angry words, 'They made him into a killing machine so they could use him out there in the jungle of Vietnam'.

"So," Phillip continued his story, "he was in this clinic where they treated him with drugs and therapy to get his mind back on track again, but my savage brother refused to take his medication. He fought like a wild animal, nobody could make him do anything he did not want to do, he was just too strong for anyone to grapple with. That's when he started to get into trouble with the law. He broke into shops, gas stations, warehouses and such. He did it all alone and unarmed, stole nothing in the places he broke into, never hurt anyone. He was just wild and … mad."

Kid had been listening in stunned silence. When finally she found her voice, she said, "But Phillip, none of this explains why you dislike him so much."

"It was after the episode at our home. He disappeared and we had no news from him for many months. That really hurt mom ... she loved David like he was her own son. Sorry I forgot to say, she was *my* mother, David's step mother. His biological mother died when he was no more than about five or six. Mom was never the same after David changed into this untamable monster. He just left then and didn't care any more about her. That's what eventually killed mom, I'm sure of it. She wanted to help him and he refused. He ignored her kindness and her love. He could have come back, mom and Poppa would have taken him in again even after … but he never came back. I know mom cried a lot because of him, because she didn't know where he was, what sort of life he lived, whether he was OK."

"Did she ever see him again?"

"Yes, a few times. Poppa always tried to keep in touch. My parents went to see him in a couple of places. I didn't go because I had to go to school. I used to stay with my aunt Mavis and my cousins." Phillip took a break then added almost tonelessly, "David never wanted to come back home."

Talking about his family was taking its toll on his nerves, his breathing was labored and his hands shook visibly. Poppa's words were again ringing in his ears 'David refused to come home because he was embarrassed and ashamed of what he had become', but Phillip could not get himself to tell Kid.

"When did you speak to him last, Phillip?"

"Umm ... I saw him at mom's funeral. I was very upset, didn't really want him to be there since I hold him responsible for her death. He was at Poppa's funeral too, but he was shackled and flanked by two cops. I didn't go near him."

"Does he still suffer from trauma symptoms now?"

"I can't answer that, Kid … just don't know."

There was silence between them. Kid had draped her arm around Phillip's shoulders in a gesture to assure him that she appreciated his effort to enlighten her on the difficulties of his past. She had kept all her senses alert and absorbed her husbands words one by one. But there has to be much more to this story, she knew instinctively. She had easily discovered gaps, inconsistencies and question marks and her inbuilt stubbornness dictated that one day she had to get to the bottom of this issue of brother David. But not right now. It was late, Phillip had had a busy day and had done a lot of driving, yet he had not interrupted his narrative with excuses like 'I'm tired' or 'let's go to bed'. Kid knew how to appreciate this.

A brother, a savage brute, a karate expert, a war veteran, a criminal, a semi-moron - my new brother - my family, Kid mused now as she lay pleasantly spent and relaxed in Phillip's arms. These were her most divine moments and she was not going to ruffle them now with questions and doubts about the truthfulness of Phillip's account. Tomorrow, she thought, I'll go to the library and find out about trauma and symptoms, about stuff that happened in that conflict in Vietnam and about the length of sentences for manslaughter. Once I'm better informed, Phillip and I will talk again. And with this rational conclusion planted firmly in her mind, she fell into a deep and untroubled sleep.

Kid was working at Alfredo's restaurant. It was the middle of the rush-hour and she was in full swing serving customers, calling orders to the kitchen, clearing tables and re-setting them for the next set of patrons. Kid liked her job, she was efficient, she put her heart and her soul into her work as was her habit with all jobs she had held in her life. She and Phillip had had their breakfast of cereal, fruit, toast, jam and coffee sitting side by side at the counter. She had given him her good-bye kiss and hugged him tight at the door before he left. The previous night's revelations were not mentioned, neither were Kid's intentions to gather information relevant to her brother.

It was about two thirty when she finished work. She and Giovanna sat together in the family room for a few minutes and relaxed over a cup of coffee then Kid drove to the public library. She knew her way around quite well by now and today she headed straight for the medical section. She found a few volumes on 'Post Traumatic Stress Disorder'. She took them to an empty table and started to read.

A few minutes into her reading she shook her head with frustration. She found that the text was laced with medical expressions unfamiliar to her, she leafed quickly through to another chapter then another, then she closed the book and opened the next one. "That's better," she whispered to herself, "reads more like a story - something written for ordinary human beings." She took out her notebook and started to copy: 'symptoms: involuntary re-experiencing of traumatic distress in the form of nightmares and flashbacks.

Insomnia, periodic depression, emotional detachment from other people. Health effects including abnormalities in hormone function and possibly pain-perception both over- or under-emphasized. Often patients seek physical medical care when in fact they are more in need of mental healthcare.' Now she re-read what she had written and started to wonder which one of these symptoms could be responsible for David's antisocial behavior. She needed to ask Phillip about that.

Her next task was to deal with legal matters. She made her way to a different section, chose a whole stack of books and went back to her table. It only took her a few minutes however, before she found that she was hopelessly struggling with legal jargon. This is impossible, I'll never find anything I can understand, Kid realized. She was close to tears by then.

"OK if I sit down here?" said a voice right next to her.

She looked up, saw a young man in a colorful tracksuit top. He had a crew cut, wore jeans and loafers and carried a pile of books under his arm, ready to start studying. She noticed that the man sported a number of small silver ear rings.

"Yes, of course," she said trying to hide her tears, then she shoved her books to one side, "Sorry, I'm taking up the whole table."

"You don't look very happy. Is it the books you are studying?"

"Yes, they're law books and I can't understand a damn thing …"

"Maybe I can help. I'm studying law … only in my first year though, but please, try me."

Kid looked up and a glowing smile replaced her tearful expression in a second. "Great, thanks. I need to know about manslaughter charges. A person I know is serving a sentence," she lied but quickly corrected herself, "I mean a person I'm going to know. How many years would he be in prison for that? High security or just sort of medium? And then …"

"I'll answer one question at the time, OK? The sentence would be four or five years, depends on the circumstances and on the judge. He would probably not be in a high security prison. What else?"

"Are there visiting days and times? I mean where you can be in the same room and talk directly to the prisoner, not the sort of phone communication through a glass partition that they show in movies."

A little smile appeared on the face of the law student but Kid did not see it. She was all business.

"There would be visiting days. You'd have to call first and the prisoner has a right to either accept or refuse a visit."

"I see. Do you have time for one more? You're here to study, aren't you?"

"I am but it's OK, I have time."

"You see, what I know is that this man was provoked into a fight and … that's how it happened. I mean, since he didn't *start* the fight he shouldn't have been convicted in the first place, right?"

"Umm ... provocation, you see, is not a defense, that's not how it works."

Kid thought about that for a while knowing that injustice was staring her in the face, then she asked meekly, "Are prisoners treated well? Do they get enough to eat? Can they watch TV and read books? In the movies they always fight and kill each other in prison, don't they?"

The student could no longer hide his smile, "Maybe you watch too many movies and you take them too literally. Movies are for entertainment … not always true. Maybe in China or North Korea or … I don't know … other dictatorships, and in the death camps during World War II prisoners were treated abominably ... but here … ?"

"Thanks, your answers really help me a lot. The person I'm talking about is kind of my brother, that's why I'm concerned. By the way, my name is Kid."

"I'm Jeffrey, I'm glad to have been helpful."

Kid shook hands with Jeffrey, thinking it was the appropriate thing to do, then gathered her things and made her way home. One part of her was exhilarated at her findings, another part of her felt just a little guilty because Kid knew for a fact that she was not going to divulge the information she now had to her husband, at least not right away. Phillip did not like his brother, not one bit, that much she had understood the previous night. Has he told me all the reasons for his antagonism, or could there be more to it? He holds his brother responsible for his mother's death, Kid thought, at least in an indirect sort of way. But that's an opinion he formed at the tender age of about thirteen. He might never have considered making a re-assessment of this theory over the last twenty years or so. There were two possibilities, she reasoned as rationally as she could. Either there was something more to his story - something that he did not want her to know, or else her darling husband was suffering from a monumental hang-up - a hang-up he had never questioned or tried to put into perspective. His Poppa had probably kept him posted on his brother's whereabouts and developments on a regular basis but Phillip was unwilling or unable to believe his father's words, ergo he would not repeat them to her.

Kid was now turning into her driveway and carefully maneuvered her little Toyota into the garage, turned the engine off but kept sitting behind the wheel. She suddenly realized that both she and her husband were now keeping little secrets. We are only a few months into our marriage, she thought unhappily, and already we are not completely truthful with each other. It's not right, is it? Kid did not mean any harm by keeping her findings to herself for the time being. She did it because Phillip would say that she was jumping the gun, that she was already making plans to visit David even though she hardly knew anything about him. And Phillip would of course be right, an inner voice told her. What bothered her more than anything else however, was the fact that her husband had only mentioned David's negative characteristics. He had made no allowances for possible remnants of trauma symptoms which might be responsible for his bad behavior and that was not fair either. Just then Kid looked into her rear-view mirror and saw Phillip's car turn into the driveway and stop behind her. Right, forget about all my speculations, she ordered herself, cope with what comes a minute at the time. In this way I can handle anything.

They embraced and kissed then walked into the house hand in hand.

"We'll have a little music session tonight," Phillip informed her enthusiastically. "I had a call from Bob, we're doing an extra gig on Friday. OK with you darling?"

Everything to do with music was always OK with Kid. She loved music-making as much as Phillip did. Husband and wife often spent time together in their music studio, both played guitar and sang. Kid also knew how to harmonize on the keyboard and occasionally improvised on the tin whistles. These were some of their most exhilarating moments - moments when Kid felt that she was truly wired to Phillip's heart and to his soul. Kid liked to call the band's rehearsals 'home concerts' - concerts at which she alone was the audience. There was just one issue that marred the perfection of these music-sessions and that was Jim's evident dislike of her. Everybody felt it but nobody knew the exact reason behind it.

After the band's sessions Kid would proudly play host to Phillip's friends serving drinks and coffee; if given enough notice she baked cookies or cakes.

"Sounds wonderful Phillip," she said and once inside, "Darling, on Friday evening I'll be helping Father at the church, I've already promised. So I won't be able to come with you and the band and hear your concert."

A rather unreadable expression appeared on Phillip's face for a second but before it had time to turn into disappointment, she added quickly, "I'm helping Father to prepare the Church hall for Saturday … a lecture of some kind. They are expecting a guest speaker … must be somebody high up in their hierarchy." There she interrupted and gave a cheeky little smile, "probably with an awful lot of ecclesiastical elbow. Father wants everything to be perfect, flowers in the right places, trestle tables with coffee and tea-things ready and all that … I do tend to talk too much sometimes, don't I?"

Phillip loved Kid's interpretation of the hierarchy of

the Church. He had by then given up on a build-up of disappointment.

During the course of her prattle about that Friday's job, Kid had made a decision. She wanted to make use of her time with Father and tell him about her scruples at withholding information from her husband. She needed to know if not telling was the same as lying.

Father and Kid had been working side by side in the Church hall arranging tables and chairs, washing cups and saucers, and all the while Father had had a distinct feeling that there was something on Kid's mind. The expression on her face alternated between troubled and anguished. All during her work she was nervous, she tripped over the edge of the mat, knocked over a chair and dropped a porcelain cup while drying it.

When we finish here, Father thought, I'll ask her, make it easier for her to come out with whatever it is that's bothering her. But before he got to the end of his thought, Kid could contain her worries no longer.

She didn't look at Father when she blurted in typical Kid fashion, "Tell me Father, when you know something and you don't tell because you are not asked, is it like telling a lie? Is it like cheating? Is it bad? I mean if you knew that telling would cause unhappiness or anger, then you wouldn't, would you. Better to shut up then, right?" She was at the end of her tether and finally turned to look at

Father. She saw a weak smile playing in his eyes and he nodded.

"Whether it is a sin or whether it is cheating, only the person who is in possession of the information can determine," he said. "Let's put it this way: if you have knowledge of something and you don't divulge it, then you hold your own counsel first and make sure that not telling is helping rather than hurting. Would you like to tell me what exactly you have in mind, Kid? Let's go and sit down in my study, we're finished here for today."

Kid took a deep breath, then she said, "It's like this Father." Now she truthfully related her husband's revelation of his brother David, Phillip's dislike of him, her suspicions that Phillip had not told her all, her own doubts about David being the cause of his mother's death and finally her own initiative of finding out about issues related to this man who was now her brother, too. "You see, Father, from the moment Phillip mentioned a brother, I was determined to get to meet him, no matter whether he is a scoundrel, a prisoner or, as Phillip said, a semi-moron. I didn't quite understand this last bit anyway. I'm entitled to be introduced to him, aren't I? I can't understand why Phillip still holds a grudge after all the intervening years. I never had a brother of my own, but the way I see it, if you have a brother you love him, period. You do not argue with Providence, right?"

Father was the master at keeping a straight face in most

situations. He knew this issue was important to Kid even though her choice of words often bordered on to the comic. "I would say that, yes you are entitled to get to know your brother-in-law, but so far you have no real evidence to prove that your husband is keeping secrets from you. Don't underestimate the effort it cost him to talk about his family. Maybe he feels that you might put yourself in danger by meeting David. Your husband is concerned about your wellbeing, he feels responsible for you Kid. You have to consider every aspect of this before coming to conclusions ... before suspecting your husband of cheating and accusing him of not telling you the full truth."

"You're on Phillip's side, aren't you Father."

"I am not on anybody's side Kid. But I am afraid I have to give Phillip credit for telling you as much as he did. Maybe he had carried the burden of this knowledge in his heart for some time and maybe he too, felt that not enlightening you made him into a liar. This is a big issue in his life and in your marriage, Kid."

"So what do I do? I really want my marriage to work, Father. I love Phillip ... from the bottom of my heart I love him ... and I like to see him happy. But if he should stop me from getting to know his brother, then I would have to go against him and we would argue and fight and the whole marriage would be up shit creek."

"Kid, I think your overheated imagination might be

taking you a step too far," was the best Father could do after Kid's last exclamation of fear and distress.

Kid lifted her hands palms turned upwards in a deprecating gesture, "Sorry, Father."

Father continued in a serious tone of voice. "You understand Kid that talking about your research at the library will not jeopardize you marriage, on the contrary, your relationship with Phillip could benefit from it. Honest and well-intended dialogue could open up new channels through which you could explore deeper into your relationship. Occasional disagreements and little arguments will be short-lived and have no derogatory consequences since your strong bond of love will always be the foundation of your marriage. It would take much more than a superficial hiccup, as it were, to damage or even destroy the love which is holding you two together as a unit, right?"

Kid looked up at Father, nodded her head and gave him an uncharacteristically rueful smile. She needed a few more moments to digest the meaning of Father's speech.

"That makes a lot of sense. I'm feeling more confident now ... yes that's what it is. I just know that our relationship will weather this fickle issue of divulging or not divulging information. Thank you Father for your kind words."

Phillip entered by the backdoor and found his wife sitting on a straight backed chair at the dining table engaged in serious knitting. She was in the process of crafting the first sweater for her husband. She had chosen soft, fluffy, royal blue wool with some Alpaca mixed in. Kid had meticulously measured her husband back and front, width, length, shoulders, sleeves, then she had drawn a pattern on a large checked piece of paper marking all the measurements and alongside each the number of knitting stitches required. Now she was in full swing knitting, her steel needles clicking along rhythmically.

"I'm back darling," Phillip called as he closed the door behind him. Husband and wife met in mid-laundry for their welcome-home kiss.

"When you've taken off your coat, please will you stand straight and turn your back to me … need to measure the real thing now."

Phillip dutifully did as Kid asked, he turned, stuck his arms out akimbo and did not move a muscle.

"Good, it'll fit. Do you want a polo neck or a round one so the collar of the shirt can stick out?"

"Polo neck please, right up to my ears. The wool feels nice and soft."

That afternoon, Kid had brought back a pizza from Alfredo's for dinner. She had already prepared a big mixed salad to go with. It was three days after her talk with Father. The subject of David had not been mentioned again, but the enforced silence had irked both of them repeatedly. Neither wanted to be the first to open a new can of worms by uttering the name of their mutual brother.

Finally it fell to Kid, the more courageous of the two, to break the ice. "Phillip, please tell me more about your brother." She came straight to the point. "You know he is not going away just by us shutting up about him."

Phillip closed his eyes for a moment, then looked at Kid and shook his head just minimally, "I've already told you all I know. The way I see it this chapter is closed."

"But it can't be. I mean to meet him, introduce myself to him ... we are all family now."

"You don't know what you're getting yourself into, Kid. You could get hurt, the guy is dangerous, he is unpredictable and ... he is mad."

"But his mad destruction sprees all happened ... what, fifteen years ago or even more. He could have changed, calmed down. People sometimes reform while they're in prison, you know, become better people."

"I can't imagine a rogue like him being reformed and turn into a God-fearing do-gooder inside the Missouri State penitentiary. You're such an incurable optimist, Kid."

"You are being sarcastic and I can't handle sarcasm, you know that Phillip. I firmly believe that we should both go and pay him a visit. Did your Poppa visit him in jail? You said he always tried to keep in touch."

"I don't want anything to do with him. I don't want to see him or talk to him. I'd much rather forget that I have a brother altogether."

"Are these your final words?"

Phillip agreed with a nod of his head but could not get himself to say 'yes'.

"OK, I need to tell you that I have made some inquiries about stuff at the library and I have also talked to Father about this new brother of mine."

"You told Father? Everything I said? I was hoping you would keep this to yourself. I mean, it's nobody's business, really."

Kid had never heard Phillip speak so condemningly, so harshly. She felt a lump form in her throat and breathing became difficult. Phillip affected not to notice . "But … but Father is a special person ... a holy man you know. He is on a direct communication line with his God. I know that for sure. He and his God talk to each other ... prayers and that, and Father knows how to keep a secret, like what he does with people's confession-secrets."

To her surprise, she now saw Phillip's stern expression mutate to a weak little smile. He got up, walked around the table and came to a halt behind Kid's chair. He put his hands on her shoulders, bent his head and briefly kissed her unruly hair.

"Tell me about your inquiries, Kid."

Kid took a deep breath trying to blink back her tears while Phillip sat down on the edge of the table facing her. "I looked up 'Post Traumatic Stress-something-or-other'

97

because you said David was a semi-moron." From there her account became more and more incoherent but it was now too late to stop her, "... and Father said that talking about what's deep inside of us would bring us closer together and that it was not altogether irrational of me to want to meet David since he was going to be my brother and then I tried to find out about David's sentence of manslaughter and law stuff and life in prison and if he was treated well and given enough to eat and … and …" there she finally came up for air. "Phillip, why do you dislike him so much? Is there something I need to know maybe, something that's difficult to say? I never want to argue with you … I love you Phillip."

She said it all in one go giving Phillip very little or no chance to answer any of her questions, so he opted for just the one statement, "I love you too Kid, always."

They got up and cleared the table. Kid washed the dishes and Phillip dried them, put them away, wiped the table clean then shifted the two wine glasses and the half-full bottle to the lounge room. The silence which had taken hold of both of them and which now engulfed the whole house was not however, one fuelled by tension, rather it contained elements of a new-found goodwill - a sign that their love had prevailed.

"I'll read you my findings about trauma symptoms first," Kid started, once they sat down again sipping their wine. She took out her notebook and read what she had copied at the library without however, referring to brother David. Then she told about her legal endeavors and the help she got from the kind law student. "When will David be released, Phillip? Did Poppa tell you? And please, what else did Poppa tell you?"

"Poppa frequently talked to me about David, over the phone and when I visited," Phillip said seriously. He always meant to co-operate with Kid, it had been his steadfast intention to be truthful and honest, it was all part of being a good husband. He continued, "Poppa maintained that David was neither a lunatic nor a criminal. Poppa held our government entirely responsible for David's irrational behavior. He used to say 'the government first made David into a professional killer and even decorated him for his valiant service, and later in his home country, the same authorities put him behind bars for doing that which they had trained him to do'. Pretty radical, eh? David was his first-born son, and I believe that the death of David's mom almost killed him. My aunt Mavis, Poppa's sister, told me that Poppa had been suicidal for some time, that he had undergone counseling and treatment, and that David, as a very little fellow, had stayed with her and her family while Poppa spent some time in a psychiatric clinic of some sort. I think he met my mom in one of those clinics, she was a nurse."

"And David's mom? Do you know anything about her?"

"I saw a couple of photos of her. She was very pretty,

long thick blond hair all the way down to the middle of her back and she had beautiful blue eyes and a radiant smile. I believe she was tall and athletically built - excellent tennis player, apparently."

"Does David remember her at all?"

"Don't think so."

"Phillip?" Kid asked, her voice a little more tentative now, as if she wasn't quite sure if what she was going to ask could upset the fragile truce she and Phillip had established. "Did your Poppa believe that David was indirectly responsible for your mom's death? Did you ever discuss this matter?"

"We did talk about it, yes, and Poppa did not agree with me. Makes no difference, though."

Better not pursue this any further, Kid reasoned. This seemed to be as far as Phillip was prepared to go. But Kid's inherent stubbornness was by no means defeated. After what she now knew, she was more than ever determined to meet this guy David, and it was at that moment that, for the first time, she heard this little voice that was telling her it was going to be *her* job to unite the two brothers. It proved to be a very persistent little voice; it called to her again and again. Sometimes she tried to ignore it, other times she dismissed it as a disturbing element, one which meant to disrupt her marriage. But deep in her heart she knew that it was her duty to help Phillip overcome his dislike of his brother. Her fertile imagination however, didn't stop there. She soon told herself that it had been Poppa's wish that his two sons should open their hearts to each other and become real brothers. This straightforward thought confirmed her earlier conviction that she was now meant to bring the brothers together again since Poppa had not been able to do so in his life time.

Kid said none of this that night as they sat sipping their wine, instead she took Phillip by the hand, "Let's go upstairs, darling," she said, nothing more.

But Phillip's mind dwelled on the subject of his brother long after they were both comfortably in bed. "Kid, will you tell me more about your conversation with the priest?"

"Yes ... well, I made a bit of a blunder right at the start. I asked if not telling was the same as lying and then I said that I was afraid that if we argued ... then our marriage would be up shit creek."

"You said that to the priest?"

"Well yes, it just slipped out. I didn't think, but Father didn't admonish me, he just said that I was exaggerating a bit."

"Kid, you are incredible. But somehow, you know, I admire your way of blurting out exactly what's in the forefront of your mind. This spontaneity makes you so honest, so real, it doesn't even matter that it might shock people on occasion. I often wish I could learn not to bottle stuff up inside of me until it hurts."

"You have done well tonight, Phillip, talking about this issue which has been bothering you for so long. The best thing might be to mix my straight forwardness and your reluctance, shake it vigorously, then distribute the outcome fifty-fifty."

Phillip laughed softly and reached across for Kid's hand.

"Father said that it was beneficial for a relationship to go into difficult and even unpleasant discussions. He said that little upsets didn't matter because our love would sort things out again."

"Uh-huh … that's true, isn't it? But Kid, could we not tell our friends about David just yet? Let's make sure we know where we stand and how we feel about it all first."

Kid had been bursting to tell the story in all detail to Anita and to Giovanna but now that Phillip had asked her to keep it to herself, she agreed that a little compromise on her part was in order. "I promise," she whispered in Phillip's ear.

It had been a busy day for Kid. She had worked through the rush hour at Alfredo's, then she gave two hours to Father, cleaning and tidying his mansion. Father had asked her for this special favor even though it was not part of her voluntary work at the parish. Now she was driving home with a dozen shopping bags on the passenger seat beside her. Phillip and his musical friends, were at home doing some serious rehearsing for a special performance on the weekend. She could hear the music through the partly open window of the music studio as she turned into the driveway. She sat quietly behind the wheel and listened for a while before getting out and making her way into the house. The tune was being interrupted, somebody said something Kid could not understand, a few chords were sounded tentatively, the banjo player seemed to disagree, Bob counted … two, three then everybody came in good and strong, it was all part of the game – all part of the fun. Kid started to unpack her shopping bags leaving things for the dinner she had planned on the bench, then made her way noiselessly down the hallway to the music room, stopped at the door and listened.

When the song came to an end she clapped loudly, once again an audience of one, and exclaimed, "A virtuoso performance, fit to be put on record."

A little later, they all settled down in the lounge room for drinks. Phillip could almost feel the effort Kid was making not to talk about her new brother but she had promised and Kid always kept her promises. The musicians were still talking shop, when Kid's voice shook Phillip out of his thoughts.

"Do you know Alfredo's restaurant, Mario? That's where I work." And then without warning, she switched to Italian. She said something containing the name Visconti, and to everybody's surprise Mario answered spontaneously in the same language.

"What's this?" Jim sounded annoyed, "would you mind talking in a language civilized Americans can understand?"

Wrong thing to do, Kid thought, I always knew Jim couldn't stand me. She had just given him the perfect playing-field to air some of his pent-up antagonism. "Sorry Jim," she said, "but we Romans consider ourselves a very civilized society ... have done so for a long time," she improvised.

Nobody was quite sure if Kid was sarcastic or just plain Kid. Mario to the rescue.

"I hardly knew I was able to speak the language of my ancestors. Not Roman though, Kid, Venetian. It was a harmless exchange, Jim. Kid informed me that she was introduced to my parents at Alfredo's."

"Do you know the place, Mario? Go there often?" Phillip asked.

"My parents do, they are personal friends of Alfredo and Giovanna. It's nice there, the sort of place where homesick Italians go to recharge their nostalgic batteries from time to time. Have you been to any of his ... well, intimate evenings yet, Kid?"

"Not yet, but I can't wait."

Phillip was glad that an amicable ambiance had been

re-established thanks to Mario's nonchalance. If there was one thing Phillip was unable to handle, it was squabbling amongst his friends ... and on his home turf. What's the matter with Jim? What's niggling him every time Kid is around, he wondered? Phillip could easily imagine Jim's reaction if Kid should announce one day, probably in vintage Kid fashion, 'I have a brother, you know, he is in jail and he is a very nice guy' or something of that ilk.

IV

It was Saturday, a warm and sunny day in late spring. Trees and shrubs had woken up from their long winter sleep and grown their first tender new leaves. Colorful flowers appeared along the roads, in gardens and flower boxes; the new season was in full swing. But prisoner McCabe saw none of the beauties of nature, felt none of the soothing warmth of the sun. For him it was just another day, the same as yesterday, no different from tomorrow. He was sitting in the recreation room watching television, a ball game, then some advertising, then another game, it didn't really matter. It was one way to pass a few hours of the day and it left him with less time to think or worry about his future - about his life. It was visiting day in the Missouri State penitentiary, one of those days when prisoners could actually meet their friends and families face-to-face, not across a glass partition and speaking into a phone. But this bonus meant nothing to David McCabe, he had no family and no friends. Nobody came to see him now since Poppa's death. How long ago was that, he wondered? Time was hard to keep track of when every day was no more than a monotonous repetition of the previous one. Will my brother ever come to visit me, forgive me and make friends with me again? Poppa assured me that he would. But then Poppa died and Phillip never came. Why did Poppa die so suddenly? All these and many more sad thoughts coursed through David's mind - questions with no answers - questions he was ill equipped to deal with.

David had always wanted to be friends with his little brother. Through all the bad years he had never stopped loving him. But Phillip had turned his back on him, Phillip was unforgiving, and Poppa had been wrong. Phillip never even acknowledged my presence at Poppa's funeral, David reflected sadly. He was ashamed of me, ashamed of being related to a guy in handcuffs, a guy who had to be guarded by two armed police officers so he wouldn't escape - or kill anybody. As if I ever would.

In all the time David spent in jail he had never planned or attempted an escape, he just knew he wouldn't be capable of outsmarting the authorities. All David knew was how to fight, and it was fighting which had gotten him where he was now. As David proceeded with his introspection, his spirits sank lower and lower, he was on a direct road to one of his depressions. He knew the feeling and the hurt it caused in his chest. The tears would start to flow, his breathing would become difficult and in the end he would feel utterly alone and totally useless. Still he was determined not to take any medication ... never again.

David never forgot the time he spent in the hospital right after his return from the war – the time when he had been helpless and unable to defend himself. But as he recuperated from his temporary death – because that's how he thought of that period in his life - and re-gained more and more of his former strength, he also remembered the wise words of his Japanese karate master – so many years ago. 'You can control your emotions and fend off depressions through meditation and controlled breathing', his Sensei had said. Now was the time to follow his master's instructions. When David got to this point in re-playing his past, he started to clench and unclench his fists, then he placed his hands firmly on the tabletop in front of him, pushed himself into a standing position and started to control his breathing. It took him a few minutes to concentrate and find his centre of gravity. Now he stood tall and straight, solidly balanced on both feet, in the perfect karate stance. There were a few men in the room; they turned to watch David but said nothing. They had seen it all before: McCabe, the karate fighter who had scared the living daylight out of everybody at one time or another, was simply doing his 'thing'. You didn't need to understand, nobody could, but everyone knew that David was in possession of an odd kind of otherworldly power of concentration. Everyone who had seen him fight simply accepted this fact and stayed out of his way when times got rough.

But times hadn't gotten rough now for some time. It was directly after his Poppa's death that David had miraculously changed his ways. Poppa was well aware that there had been times when his son had terrorized this whole place. Any fight, any argument, used to draw David like a magnet, and those situations would invariably take him right back to the jungles of Vietnam and like a robot he would fight anyone in sight ... and that included armed security guards.

Towards the end of his life, Poppa had urged David to give up fighting and to stop the violence and the aggression and David had promised to calm down. He had willed himself to turn his back whenever there was a fight and to walk away. As a reward for good behavior, David had been allocated a time and place where he could execute his karate routine - that which he called 'kata'. To anyone who cared to watch him, David seemed to be moving in a different world as he performed what looked like an acrobatic performance from outer space. Before and after he would be on his knees, sitting back on his heels in quiet meditation.

On this Saturday when most prisoners enjoyed an afternoon in the company of their loved ones, David quietly left the recreation area and made his way back to his cell. The expression on his face gave none of his inner turmoil away. He needed the solitude of his special karate space to find his inner peace.

V

Phillip and Kid were seemingly floating through life, their marriage worked like clockwork to the surprise of all Phillip's friends who had witnessed that relationship's rather wayward start one night in Australia. Phillip bought flowers for his wife two or three times a week and took her out to shows and concerts. Kid contributed to the smooth functioning of her marriage by trying out new recipes, by improvising and creating ever more delicious and beautifully presented meals. They had picnics in the park on weekends, exhilarating performances with the band on stage. Life was simply perfect ... or was it? How could anyone guess at the undercurrents of tension that ran through this perfect marriage since there were no visible cracks in the veneer, no angry words between them, no known disagreements? Their skills of bottling up and hiding issues of importance had reached state of the art by then. The issue of brother David had not been settled satisfactorily; their discussions, although honest and truthful, had been basically insufficient to satisfy Kid's curiosity and her need to meet her new brother.

Phillip debated in his conscience whether to give in to Kid's unspoken demand or to continue his obstinate silence and hope it would eventually all just go away. There were times when playing perfect marriage was almost unbearable for both of them. Kid didn't want to nag. Phillip hoped she never would as he would not have been able to handle it. The situation became more and more abstruse. And then came the day when Kid broke down.

If it had happened at home while Phillip was at work or late at night in bed when Phillip was asleep, it wouldn't have been such a big drama, but Kid chose the most devastating moment for her breakdown.

She was sitting behind the wheel of her Toyota driving home from Alfredo's restaurant. Suddenly her eyes filled with tears, her vision blurred, her head buzzed, her hands and her whole body started to shake uncontrollably. She held on to the steering wheel in a feeble attempt to keep the swerving car on its wheels, but it was all to no avail. Two wheels left the road and were soon on the pedestrian walkway. Through a mist of tears she saw the stone wall approaching fast, but there was nothing she could do to make it go away. She slammed into it, heard the deafening noise of the impact, then she closed her eyes and tried to die.

From a distance she could hear the screeching tires of the police car, the blaring siren of the ambulance, lots of voices of people she didn't know. Kid did not open her eyes or lift her head; she could taste blood but made no effort to find out where it came from.

Somebody helped her out of the driver's seat, guided her to the nearby ambulance where a nurse kept wiping her face and tilting her head backward. Kid felt no pain. Her real suffering was deep inside her heart and the only thoughts she could muster were with her darling husband Phillip.

Phillip had spent the biggest part of the afternoon at the airport interviewing two politicians. Now he walked briskly back into the office, his paperwork tucked under his arm ready to finish the job. Suddenly he saw faces filled with apprehension and uncertainty all around. But before he could inquire into the reason for this doom and gloom atmosphere one of his mates took him by the arm.

"Phillip, there has been an accident … Kid. The hospital called just a short time ago … she will be OK, just get there as fast as you can."

Phillip turned deathly pale and started to feel dizzy; he held on to the desktop trying to put questions into words, but never quite made it that far.

"Come on, I drive you there. Forget about asking questions."

Ten minutes later Phillip stood at the reception desk of the main hospital, "I need to see my wife ... accident ... McCabe, Kid McCabe ...please ..." he stammered.

The nurse understood his disjointed sentence, led him along a corridor then opened the door to Kid's room. "Don't stay long and when you come out, the doctor would like a word with you, OK?"

Phillip nodded and went in. Kid lay on a bed, under a white sheet, he saw a small bandage across her nose. Her eyes were open but looked red and tearful, her face was bruised and her right wrist was bandaged.

"Are you in great pain, Kid?" was all Phillip could say.

The minute Kid saw her husband's face and heard his words, a renewed fit of crying took hold of her. She shook her head, "No pain," she said, "all my fault ... ruined the Toyota ... I feel such an idiot ... sorry Phillip."

Phillip stroked her hair out of her face, gently kissed her forehead, then he too, was in tears. "I love you Kid ... I'm the one who is the idiot ... forgive me ..."

Just then, the nurse quietly entered the room. She stopped in the doorway and watched husband and wife in their awkward embrace. She did not have the heart to interrupt, instead she stood quietly enjoying the unguarded display of two people sharing real, genuine love. Many a time in her job nurse had to witness a fabricated show of affection between a person and the injured partner; a façade enacted to hide feelings of guilt, maybe a confirmation to themselves of how flat and insipid their relationship had become over time. Now she walked up behind Phillip and tapped him lightly on the shoulder, "Patient needs to rest now."

Once they were out of Kid's earshot she reassured him that his wife was going to be OK and showed him to the doctor's office.

"Please sit down here Mr McCabe," the doctor said matter-of-factly and closed the door to his office. Phillip did as he was told, he said nothing. "Your wife will be fine, that's the main thing," he said even before he took his seat behind the desk. "She hit her face - her nose to be precise - against the steering wheel. This caused a profuse nose bleed, but nothing more. The nose is not broken and the bleeding has been stemmed soon after the accident but the bruise will be visible for a while. Her right hand got jammed somehow, her wrist is sprained but the x-ray shows no broken bones ... so no great drama on that front. No other car was involved in the accident, no pedestrians were hurt. Your wife caused the accident for no apparent reason. She was found sobbing in the driver's seat of her car directly after the accident, in fact she was quite hysterical. Can you tell me anything? Any idea?"

Phillip took a deep breath, looked straight at the doctor

115

and said, "I think I know doctor, what happened. Kid and I have ... how shall I say ... unresolved business. It's an issue of great importance to my wife ... and I have stubbornly refused to talk about it. It weighed as heavily on my mind as it did on Kid's ... I was just about ready to loose my nerve and have my own accident."

This provoked a little smile on the doctor's face, then it disappeared again, "Are you going to resolve this 'issue'? You know, Mr McCabe, that you can get counseling. Have you given that a thought?"

"I hadn't, no, but I am aware that counseling can help. I'll certainly discuss it with my wife. Maybe we'll try opening up and talking honestly first. You see doctor, I'm the real culprit in this matter ... I'm the one who stubbornly refused to deal with the issue ... my wife is much more open and extrovert than I am ... she just didn't want to nag or upset me, I suppose."

"So, you're saying that it was her anxiety that led her to loose control over her vehicle and sent her into spasms of weeping?"

"I'm sure of it, yes. I should have seen it coming, but ... I was too selfish ... too obstinate. But now I've had my wake-up call ..." Phillip let his sentence dwindle down to nothing.

The doctor understood, nodded and said as a parting piece of advice, "If you need help, you can inquire here at the hospital."

"Thanks ... thanks for your concern, doctor."

The following morning Phillip fetched Kid from the hospital. She sat demurely in the passenger seat as he focused all his concentration on driving. They walked into their home, slowly, carefully, the way one enters the empty house of somebody one barely knows. They both hedged feelings of uncertainty, of shame mixed with confusion and sadness. Phillip knew he had to tackle the topic of his brother, no excuse to prevaricate now.

"I see my mistake, Kid. I knew you wanted to talk about David but I somehow couldn't. I mean to discuss this issue now ... honestly and truthfully."

Kid nodded.

"You want to meet him, don't you? Tell me what you have in mind."

"I think," she started haltingly, "I believe that it is our duty to let him know that we think of him as family. He doesn't know that you are married ... that he has a sister-in-law. My understanding is that you have not contacted him since Poppa died, right?"

"I have never contacted him, Kid, even while Poppa was alive. It was always Poppa who did. He told me rather more than I let on. Poppa assured me that David was no longer the savage he used to be and that he had recovered quite well from his traumatic experiences of the war. But

117

Poppa also said that David never talked about what really happened to him out there in the war. David apparently talks a little slower than your average guy but he is not moronic. He understands and he can think. Poppa also believed that my brother was not responsible for mom's death. He maintained that mother and son had talked things through on one of their encounters and that mom had forgiven him. I find all this hard to believe even now, but then ... no father would want to paint a picture of his son as irredeemably bad, right?"

Kid might not have heard this last sentence, since she now referred to another period of Phillip and David's life. "When you were very young, Phillip, before David was drafted, do you have memories of that time?"

"Umm ... the earliest I remember is when I was about four or five. Dave was then already an adolescent, you understand. My memories of that time are rather childish of course, like ... I seem to see David hanging out the washing for mom, he also liked to do housework, washing floors and windows and that. Not much in the way of useful memories I'm afraid."

Phillip stopped there but Kid could feel that he had a whole lot more to say. Their discussion had begun as soon as they entered the house and they still found themselves standing in the hallway. We might as well sit down, she thought wistfully, since this is turning into truth-telling-

118

time on a big scale. "Let's have a cup of coffee, shall we, and sit down," she suggested.

"Sure, you sit, I make the coffee, Kid. So where was I ... ah yes, Dave was very tall even then ... at least I thought he was since I was still almost a baby. He was into sports at school ... and with a vengeance, and he learned karate. Don't know when he started that, but I seem to remember seeing him in his white outfit with a belt that changed color at regular intervals." The coffee was ready, he poured two mugs and put one in front of Kid on the dining table but he didn't give her a chance to say or ask anything. "We didn't fight like brothers are wont to do, I mean we couldn't ... too big an age gap between us. He was kind of ... gentle, took me by the hand when we crossed the road and that. He wasn't good at school though, but I don't remember that, mom and Poppa told me later. He looks like his mother, blue eyes and blond hair ... always had it long and got into trouble at school because of it."

By then Kid was wondering if Phillip was aware that he was now portraying his brother as a nice, harmless, good-natured lad. So David's demolition sprees later in life, she figured, had to be the result of damage done to him during the war. Something must have happened to change his whole personality.

"May I interrupt? Did Poppa think that David had lost some of his memory because of the trauma? And that thing

119

about 'malfunctioning hormones' that I read about, does this mean that his ... you know ... sex life went belly-up, maybe?"

"Poppa didn't say, but ... it's possible. I have read about guys who came back from the war and found that they were sterile as a result of having been in contact with some chemical weapons." Phillip reached across the table and took hold of Kid's hand, the one which was not bandaged. "Kid, I'm OK now. I'm glad I was finally able to talk. Let's start organizing a visit to St. Louis prison, OK with you?"

Kid beamed, "Thanks darling. I'm sorry about the accident ... sorry I lost control."

Phillip simply shook his head, but he smiled now.

VI

Alfredo was checking his watch for the third time in as many minutes. Unusual for Kid to be late for work, he thought, without letting us know. Just then the phone rang. "Pronto," he said, assuming it was Kid.

"Alfredo, I had an accident, damaged my wrist … I should have called earlier, I'm real sorry …"

"What sort of accident? Are you alright?" Alfredo was alarmed and genuinely concerned.

Kid now embarked on a detailed account of what had happened but omitted the real reason for her loss of control for the time being. "I'm alright, it's just a bandaged wrist and a bruised face. Umm ... there is something I need to talk to you and Giovanna about. May I come in this afternoon?"

The important issue Kid had in mind was none other than her request for some time off from work - time needed to go and meet her brother in St. Louis. Phillip had already made inquiries concerning visiting times and days at the prison. He was organizing time off from his own job and now Kid had to do the same on her side. Her employers took the news of a long-lost brother who was in prison with astonishing calm and understanding and agreed to give her as much time as she needed. Her next step was to inform Father Pasquale. Kid didn't think to make an appointment, she simply turned up on Father's doorstep.

It happened to be one of those days when Father was expected to be in at least three places simultaneously. Half of his voluntary staff was sick with the flu, the heating had broken down in the annex where he had the baby crèche, the storm had brought down a tree and landed it on the roof of the church hall and the phone was ringing uninterrupt-edly. Father had found a minute to grab a sandwich and was still holding the crust in his hand when he heard the knock on the door. Alright, one more problem is not going to kill me, he thought and went to open up.

"Sorry Father to interrupt your lunch," Kid said, "Don't look at my bruised face, just an accident. But all is well. We are going to St. Louis, you see. It has all worked out nicely and you have helped heaps. So now I'm going to meet him. I'm so excited. I won't be able to work for you for a few days. Can you let me go? This is really important. I already know what I'm going to say and ask ... dozens of questions ..."

At this point Father had to put his foot on the break. "It's also important to take a breath from time to time, Kid. Makes life much easier."

"Sorry. I tend to get carried away a bit when stuff happens."

Father threw his head back and laughed. "Listening to you is a little like doing a cryptic crossword, but I think I got it. Take as long as you need for your important meeting with your brother-in-law," he said, "or should I say your brother? I know that's how you think of him, right? Kid. I'm glad things worked out 'so nicely' for you and Phillip even though it was at the cost of an accident."

"Thanks Father."

Father put his arms around her in a friendly hug. "Take care now, and have a safe journey."

"Alright," Phillip announced, "we've got the information, all we need now is for my brother to OK our visit. What will we do if he refuses? He can, you know."

"Pessimist," Kid said, "after all you told me, I firmly believe that your brother will just love to see you … and maybe me, too."

David heard his name called over the speaker system; he was sitting on the edge of his bunk minding his own business. Now what is it? I've done nothing wrong, have I? That's what prison life did to you. The smallest little issue, only marginally out of the regular routine, and the first thing you feel is suspicion, the second is guilt. Have I done something wrong and if so what? He made his way dutifully down to the ground level, expecting the worst. The duty officer motioned him to enter the office. David stood straight and relaxed making the six foot tall armed officer look small and insignificant.

"We just had a call from your brother." David raised an eye brow but did not reply.

"You do have a brother, right?"

"Yessir."

"He wishes to come and visit ... with his wife, your sister-in-law."

David looked straight at the officer, incomprehension written on his face, "Sister-in-law, sir?"

"That's what he said. Do you accept his request for a visit?"

"Yessir." David's affirmative answer was immediate.

"He lives in Tennessee and needs to get organized. He will call back to make detailed arrangements ... day and time, OK? He just wanted to know if you'd agree to see him.

"Sure, thank you sir." David turned around and walked out of the office.

The officer watched the tall man walk down the hall. His movements were smooth and well coordinated. At that moment the officer's mind involuntarily went back to the time when David McCabe terrorized the entire prison sin-gle-handedly with his deadly fighting skills. It was not just his physical strength and his size, it was the speed and the precision with which he executed his movements that set him apart from all the other fighters. The officer and all his colleagues had noticed however, that since the death of his father some months ago David had slowed down. He keeps out of trouble ... doesn't take part in fights any lon-ger, the officer mused and he was inwardly glad of it. David McCabe isn't a bad guy. There isn't that mean streak in his eyes that I saw and even feared sometimes in my job. David just doesn't have the makings of a criminal somehow. The officer had to smile at the thought of how quick David had been to accept the visit from his brother. There had never been a mention of a brother ... and now there was a sister-in-law as well. Interesting.

A day and time was set for the visit. Phillip and Kid both got a week off from their respective jobs, a week they would use to acquaint - or re-acquaint in Phillip's case - themselves with their mutual brother. They had decided to go by air, it would be more relaxing and give them more time to spend in Phillip's home town. Kid was in high spir-its, her mind and her thoughts unencumbered by issues of the past. She was ready to deal with a new phase of her life, one which was going to incorporate a brand new brother.

Phillip's mood tended more towards ambivalence, after

all he, unlike Kid, did have memories of his brother. What will my very first impression of my brother be? Phillip asked himself. How will I feel when I see him in prison garb, probably sporting a crew cut? Phillip knew he had to look up at his brother. David was huge and lean and muscular. Or had years of prison life reduced him to a cadaverous looking guy with sunken cheeks and hollow eyes? That's what Phillip had seen on the day his mom had taken him to the clinic, shortly after David's return from Vietnam. But conjuring up old images was not a productive approach ... better to keep an open mind the way Kid proposed to do. That thought made him feel a little more confident, at least for a while, but his mind just could not come to a full stop. Questions and doubts kept surfacing. What will I say to him? How well can he talk now? According to Poppa, his brother had improved, but then ... Poppa was hopelessly prejudiced. He needed to convince himself that his firstborn son was a good man, that he was harmless and upstanding, that there was nothing wrong with his head and his mind, that he was a decent guy: an ordinary, harmless, good guy who just happened to be spending years behind bars. What a paradox!

But all these reflections still did not answer Phillip's initial question, namely 'how will I feel once I actually stand in front of my long-lost brother? What will this encounter do to me, to my mind and to my feelings?' Phillip kept up his mental debate for the duration of their flight to St. Louis. Kid sensed what was going on in Phillip's mind, and as was her habit she stuck to her cheerfulness as if trying to transfer some of it to her husband. And it worked ... to some degree.

David was told when to be ready for his visitors. He was looking forward to it but he was also a little uncomfortable. Dates and times were difficult issues for him to keep track of, days of the week could easily get mixed up. But he knew that for this unique event it was crucial that he get things right, so he had to rely on the competence and wisdom of his cell mate Chuck. They had shared a cell for some time now and had formed a close friendship.

"I won't let you miss this once-in-a-life-time visit, Dave," Chuck joked, "just put your whole life in my hands for once." There had been more than one occasion when Chuck had to put *his* whole life in *David's* hands.

The warden had reminded David to wash his hair, make sure he had a clean shirt and a decent pair of jeans to wear, and to clean his fingernails. David never paid much attention to his appearance but expecting visitors changed all this. Now he scrubbed up and made sure to look presentable.

As the time of his brother's visit drew closer, David became aware of tension, something seemed to lodge itself in his throat or thereabouts. He tried to relax through controlled breathing but the sensation did not go away. What David was experiencing was simply excitement. But since this was not an emotion he was familiar with, he did not know how to deal with it.. There had never been any reason for excitement in the monotony of prison life.

Kid and Phillip held each other by the hand as they approached the monstrous, gray, intimidating prison building. This helped them to overcome at least some of the trepidation they both felt. They were greeted by the sight of uniformed guards and armed security officers; heavy steel gates were clanging, the ominous sound of keys jangling, chains rattling ... then the first security check. They had to extend their arms and legs and let themselves be patted down.

Kid felt as though she herself was now one of the inmates. She closed her eyes and pretended it was not happening. She had to leave her little backpack at the desk in exchange for a large green tag. Now she came out of her cubicle and joined Phillip in a semi-dark and cold hallway. She held her head high and gave her husband a smile displaying a confidence she did not really feel. They joined a group of visitors who all fiddled nervously with their green tags, nobody looked directly at anybody else, there were no audible conversations, no smiles, only sadness all around. Now they were all herded down a dark, spooky passage like sheep about to be slaughtered. At the end of the tunnel-like corridor a door opened to reveal a fair sized well lit area with tables and chairs in neat rows. A coffee machine in the corner gave the place an almost innocuous appearance. Kid held on to her green tag as though it was the most precious object in the world.

They stood motionless for a minute and observed the distressing scene which unfolded before their eyes: families temporarily reunited, people of every walk of life, black, white, Mexican and Asian, moms and dads hugging sons, wives embracing husbands, children running around, rowdy and loud, people sitting at tables opposite each other, engaging in urgent, maybe intimate conversation. Kid started to scan the room for a brother she had never seen.

"There he is now," with a movement of his head Phillip indicated a tall man. His blond hair was short, badly cut and still wet from the shower. He wore a blue T-shirt and a pair of tight, well fitting jeans. Rather too sexy for the occasion, Kid thought rather irrelevantly. The two brothers walked slowly towards each other, Phillip a little uncertainly, his brother with lithe and elastic movements. It's like he walks from his shoulders down, Kid mused, Americans tend to use their legs. As the brothers came to a halt and started to talk to each other, Kid felt as if she was eavesdropping.

"Hi Dave," Phillip's voice was flat and dispassionate, "you look fit." He almost said 'prison life obviously becomes you' but decided to swallow that part.

David nodded. "Hi," he said in a deep voice. Nothing else.

"Dave, this is my wife, Kid."

Kid bent her head right back the way you do when looking up at a five-storey building and locked eyes with David for a second, "Hi David, I'm your new sister."

"… in-law, Kid," Phillip supplied.

"Well, yes. Same thing … almost." Then she turned partly to her husband and whispered from the corner of her mouth, "Tell him to sit down … can't see him … too high up." It was meant for Phillip's ears only but David had heard and understood.

"I'm sorry," he said unnecessarily, then moved to the nearest table. All the tables were bolted to the floor, the chairs weren't. The trio sat. No conversation was forthcoming.

What's happening to Phillip's eloquence, Kid wondered, she had never known him to be stuck for words. The two brothers seemed to silently scrutinize each other. What was going on? Kid decided to save the situation.

"Phillip and I … we have been married for five months now," she announced importantly. "We live in Tennessee, Knoxville, to be exact. Have you been there?"

David looked at her, seemingly speechless.

Kid continued undeterred, "Phillip bought us a beautiful house, you know with a garden front and back. I'm planting fruit trees and vegetables for next year. There are already flowers out front. Maybe you don't want to know all this ... it's my first trip here ... to Phillip's and your home town. Phillip is going to show me the big arch. I saw a picture of it." Now she turned to face Phillip. "Am I talking too much, darling?" But without waiting for an answer she turned back to David and said in a mellow almost motherly tone of voice, "Are they treating you OK here, David? Do you get a big healthy breakfast every morning? Because that's important."

Phillip shook his head almost imperceptibly and rolled his eyes. David saw but made nothing of it. He found Kid's narrative interesting, easy to follow. He liked her quaint accent but had no idea of its origin.

"Yeah, we are fed well ... breakfast and all ... never go hungry."

"You two haven't seen each other in a long while, right? Maybe you want to talk and be sort of brotherly ... without me being present."

"No no, Kid, you stay." Phillip's reaction was instant. He reached out and took her hand in his.

"Last time I saw you ... was at Poppa's funeral," David said slowly, "but you were ashamed of me because I was shackled then."

So he can put together a complete sentence, Kid thought with some satisfaction, not the moron Phillip portrayed him as. David's voice shook her out of her contemplations.

131

"Poppa came to see me … a few times. Why did he die so suddenly?"

"Poppa died because he was old, simple as that, and I don't know about ashamed, I just didn't want to talk to you. You know why."

"But it's not true … about mom. It's not true what you think. Mom and I talked … later. She understood … I apologized and all."

"*You* apologized? Doesn't sound like you." But Phillip did remember Poppa telling him just that, only he was not going to admit to it, not just then.

Are they going to start fighting? Kid was alarmed. She could not let that happen. She had a feeling that it was Phillip who was being stubborn. He just couldn't let go of his dislike of David. Kid had long started to suspect that the picture Phillip had painted was that of an unresolved conflict in his own mind. It's like an obsession, one that has been with him for a very long time, Kid thought, and he has no memories with which to correct it.

But no fight ensued, instead David continued doggedly trying to get his point across, "I know I frightened you that day … long ago … with my bad behavior, but I wasn't going to hurt you. I was … I don't know … not myself … didn't know what I was doing half the time. But I'm not like that any more. Didn't Poppa tell you …?"

"Yeah, he did. He told me you were now a calm, harmless, inoffensive model of a son," Phillip spat, a dangerous note of sarcasm in his voice. "If all that is true ... why are you inside, I'd like to know."

Kid had never been one to understand or use sarcasm and she wondered now if David understood the undercurrent in his brother's voice. She had her answer almost immediately when David said, "It is true. I've been on good behavior ... for a long time now. I don't fight any more. Why do you still hate me so much, Phillip?" David had not understood Phillip's sarcasm.

"Oh come on Dave, I don't hate you, 'hate' is a big word ..." He found no appropriate way to finish this half-baked sentence.

"Poppa always said you would find a way to open your heart to me again."

Now Phillip was completely taken aback. David is using the exact same words as Poppa used on his death bed. Is he aware of that, or is it just coincidence? From far away he heard Kid's voice. "Phillip, what is it?"

"Nothing darling," then addressing David again, "Is that what Poppa said to you? Is it really, David?"

"Yep."

"I'm not sure about 'opening my heart' but I mean to change my attitude some, that's why I'm here now. Kid wanted to meet you ... so I did some thinking. Can you remember what mom said ... on the day you mentioned?"

"She said … she said she understood that I had acted … out of frustration … that I was not to be blamed … that some of the trauma-stuff was responsible … She said she loved me."

"Why didn't you come home?"

"Because … I knew I was not quite right … in my head. I never took the medication in the clinic, remember? I needed to make my own way … live my own life. Later I would come home again but not then. Mom died … of a heart attack Poppa told me … not because of me." David's explanation was understandable even though it came out slowly and a little incoherently.

Phillip watched David's facial expression and he could see his need to think before making a statement. There had to be remnants of his trauma at work, maybe that was why he kept getting into conflict with the law … and that was probably also why he was here now. Phillip started to wonder then if he had been too hard on his brother, if his judgment had been clouded by his youthfulness, by the immature mind of an adolescent. Maybe I *am* suffering from a hang-up, as Kid told me. Phillip decided right then that he was going to forgive his brother, but being rather unfamiliar with the practice of forgiving, the best he could do was to reach across the table and tentatively place his hand on David's wrist for a second. Dave would understand the gesture … no need for words.

"How long before you get out of here, David?" he now asked trying to cover over unwanted emotions.

"Not sure. Time got changed … some time ago."

Weird way of answering a straight-forward question, Kid thought. "Which way did it get changed? Longer or shorter?"

"Longer. Too much fighting ... but no more now," and turning to Kid, "I guess Phillip told you about me … about what happened and that. Were you scared … scared of me?"

"Oh no, not at all. I'm not one to get scared easily you know."

This off-handed remark provoked the first little smile on David's face. "What happened to your hand, Kid?"

Kid had hoped he would not see the bandage around her wrist. She had put on a sweater with sleeves slightly too long so they would cover it. It obviously hadn't worked. "I …umm … it was like this: I was driving my little sedan and suddenly there was this stone wall ... it just came at me and ...bang ... I smashed into it … hit my face against the wheel … lots of blood. All my fault … I was a real idiot. Ruined the car, so I'll get a bicycle now … safer on the road …"

"Excuse me, Mrs McCabe," Phillip said in mock anger, "what's this about a bicycle? I never said anything like that and I have no intention of getting you one of those. Safer you think? No way!"

By now, David was laughing out loud. Kid affected not to notice. "Does that mean I get a new car?" She asked cheekily, then to David, "Do you know much about cars?"

"Yeah ... a bit ... learned some in the military. They taught us some useful stuff too."

Now this could mean a lot of things, Phillip thought. They obviously taught a heap of useless stuff, like firing guns, throwing grenades and other destructive activities. He now started to wonder how many more useful skills David had learned in the military, whether he had a trade, qualifications for some job or other. How had David made a living all these years ... and with his handicap? Phillip was lost in a string of questions, all of which had been triggered by just one short remark made by his brother.

"How much longer can we stay?" Phillip asked.

"I don't know these things ... you'll hear a sort of bell when you have to leave. Umm ... will you come again, both of you? I'd like to talk some more ... I'm not too good at conversation though. They're doing classes here ... all sorts. Took me a long time to start ... I am ... I have lots to learn before I get out ... my head, my mind got stuffed-up."

Suddenly, David felt the need to communicate, to own up to his mistakes, to ask questions, to get to know his brother and his new sister-in-law. It didn't matter now that his speech was disjointed, that his sentences were incomplete. He was gripped by the fear of running out of time.

136

He wanted to stretch this magic situation to the limit. There was his initial sensation in his chest again and this time it was laced with an unfamiliar urgency.

"You lead interesting lives, right? I want to know ... know about your lives, jobs, hobbies, everything. My life ... it's been a mess ... a complete waste. I'm ashamed. The teachers ... they are good, nice guys, try to help us. The authorities might tell you ... about my release ..." David was by now talking as if in a race against time. His speech became more incoherent by the minute. Finally, in hopeless frustration, he buried his head in his hands, then pressed his fists into his eyes as if forcing tears back inside his head.

Kid got up, walked around the table to David's side then gently put one hand on his shoulder. "We'll come back, David. We have taken a week off. There will be time for a lot more talk between us, OK?"

David lifted his head. "Thanks," he said looking straight ahead and seemingly focusing on a point in his mind.

The sound of a buzzer rather than a bell could be heard a short time later.

End of visit.

Kid considered giving David a hug good-bye but then thought better of it. She shook his hand and turned away.

Emotions were the one thing Phillip had not considered in connection with this first visit to his brother. He had approached the event rather half-heartedly and unconvinced of its usefulness, but David's desperate attempt to cram as much into this encounter as possible, his urgency, his helplessness and the fear that this might be his last chance to talk to his little brother, had provoked unwanted but undeniable emotions. I have shunned my brother for all these years yet now I see him in a different light ... after just one short encounter in the visitation area in the prison, Phillip realized with some surprise.

The tears had come and gone, now the two men composed themselves as best they could.

"Thanks Phillip for coming."

"We'll let you know about the day and time of our next visit, OK? I'm glad we came. Take care now." With that, Phillip turned, took Kid by the hand and together they made their way to the visitors' exit.

VII

Phillip had booked a room in a hotel - not one of the very expensive ones - in his home town, rather than to stay with his aunt Mavis. He did it for two reasons: one, because he knew how much Kid loved hotel rooms and two, because his aunt was not an easy person to get on with. He feared that she might not take to Kid. It was all a bit of a worry.

The hotel room, as far as Kid was concerned, was luxury on a grand scale, a big TV set with remote control, a small refrigerator, shower and bath tub, as much hot water as she liked. The bed was covered by a colorful quilted bedspread, under the window she saw a heater or cooler depending on the season.

"This is like when you are on a honeymoon, isn't it Phillip? But then, every day of my life with you is a honeymoon." Kid was glowing with happiness.

They had come back to their hotel after seeing David,

now they changed, showered and got ready for dinner. Phillip had suggested a number of restaurants, Greek, Italian, Chinese; he knew St. Louis like the palm of his hand. The French restaurant won, the McCabes decided to splurge.

Kid and Phillip were seated at opposite sides of a round table, it was covered by a stiff, white tablecloth which almost reached to the floor. Their meal had started with a fish dish accompanied by a glass of white wine, now they were well into their second course of filet mignon accompanied by a bottle of red wine. Neither Kid nor Phillip had mentioned their encounter with David, not because they were hiding feelings, impressions or emotions but simply because they were both enjoying their delayed honeymoon, so to speak.

"I've been thinking, Kid," Phillip said, "I would like to pay a visit to my aunt Mavis and her family while we're here. I feel it would be the decent thing to do. Do you mind?"

"Not at all, darling. I'm acquiring more family by the day. Sounds good. Could you tell me a little about her while we're indulging in our culinary extravagance. Actually, I might have to skip dessert." They had almost finished their third course of cheese - one piece of Roquefort one of Camembert.

"Same here," Phillip said, "shall we have coffee in a little while?" Kid nodded. "Here comes some family history then, just tell me when you had enough and I'll put my foot on the break. Aunt Mavis is my father's sister. There was another sister, Lynn, who I never knew. She died young, I believe of a tumor. Poppa was older than his sisters by about thirteen or fourteen years. OK, let me start some way back. The McCabes were Scottish, my great-grandparents – maybe even great-great-grandparents - migrated to the States. They lived in Cincinnati and owned a hotel and public house as they were known … quite a big business it was. You know, there were still horse-drawn carriages and the owner of the hostelries also had to provide food and shelter for the horses, there were stable boys and all that. The business was passed down to my grandfather – or great-grandfather - as was the custom, but when it came to my Poppa's generation things changed. He and his sisters had other careers in mind. Poppa started as a builder, later he studied architecture and interior decoration. He had his own business and did well. But as I told you, life dealt him a few hard blows: the loss of his first wife, David being drafted and sent to Vietnam, then his second wife's death - my mom - but he kept his business going right through it all. Mavis was a school teacher and her sister … I'm not sure, I think she went into nursing. Are you terribly bored, Kid?"

"No no, just keep going. I'll interrupt you soon enough when I'm either bored or overly interested."

141

"Right, I get it. Now, the McCabes were … what can I say … thoroughly decent and upstanding people. They believed in hard work and honestly earned money, they were law-abiding, had no debts, never accepted hand-outs. All this is still deeply ingrained in my aunt Mavis. I'm sure you can see where this is heading …"

"Yes I know. Your brother does not fit into your aunt's law-abiding concept so she wants nothing to do with him. I might equally not fit into her idea of 'upstandingness' … good word? … no trade, no career, no hard earned money. Is that what you are thinking, Phillip?"

Phillip nodded but his face showed amusement rather than unease. "That ... and also Mavis is a bit of a snob, or can be. Money and social standing are of great importance to her." Here he shook his head laughingly. "She always had this idea that I should marry money. She tried to matchmake once, would you believe it. It was the daughter of a rich banker she had in mind for me."

Kid's turn to laugh. "And you did not oblige? How naughty of you." Coffee and liqueur had arrived, Phillip was holding Kid's hand across the table, they were in fits of laughter.

"But she always liked me, never David, you were right there. He wasn't intellectual enough for her liking. Is it still OK with you to go see her? We needn't stay long if she should make it awkward for you. She was good with Poppa though, looked after him right to the end …"

"Give her a call tomorrow, darling. Will you take me on a sight-seeing tour around the city? Can't wait to see that 'Gateway to the West'. We can go inside it and right up to the top, it said so in the brochure." What Kid was referring to is a monumental archway constructed of a light colored metal which sparkles like silver in the sun. It stands tall and elegant in a park along the river's edge. "I'm getting a little tired now, maybe too much of that magic French liqueur," she added sleepily.

It wasn't until the following morning over a 'healthy breakfast' that David was mentioned, and surprisingly it was Phillip who said without preamble, "Can you imagine how hard it's going to be for David once he is released … you know, to re-integrate into a life he is probably quite unfamiliar with by now? Did you notice how he had trouble putting thoughts into words? I believed him though … about mom … I don't think he would tell a lie …"

"Phillip, I don't think he *could* tell a lie. Once you start lying you have to remember the first lie you told, then tell the second one and make sure it follows, otherwise you get caught. I doubt David would be capable. His mental gaps and his slow thinking mechanisms ... it's a little like a blessing in disguise. One thing though, I'd like to know more about his life, I mean the periods he did not spend in jail. He mentioned something about classes that he attends in jail, didn't he? What sort of classes … what do you think?"

143

Kid can be almost as incoherent as David, it went through Phillip's head. In answer to her question however, he said, "On a hunch I would say literacy classes, Kid. We might find out when we see him next time. There is also this business about karate. According to Poppa, his karate skills are all he was left with, so to speak, when he emerged from his trauma, and I believed Poppa when he told me that David was a master in the art of karate. Poppa saw an article about him in some paper, and a photo. David had won a competition of some kind ... 'star material' was the word Poppa read out to me over the phone that day." Phillip took a deep breath before he continued, "This whole thing ... I mean the martial arts stuff ... it kind of frightens me."

"Hmm ... are you thinking of a combination of deadly fighting skills and trauma symptoms? Maybe he also gets flashbacks like it said in the book ..." Kid did not need to finish her sentence. The possible danger it suggested was crystal clear to Phillip.

"What happened to you while you and David talked yesterday? I felt it - you know that silly telepathy - I felt some sort of vibrations. Remember I asked what was the matter?"

Phillip nodded, the question came as no surprise to him. "David said," he started haltingly, "I would or should find a way to open my heart to him, right? These were the exact words Poppa said to me on his deathbed. They were his last words. Coincidence?"

"And are you?"

"I feel I'm opening something … not sure if it is my heart, though."

Kid was happy with this answer, she did not take the issue further.

"I've had a wonderful day Phillip, and I'm exhausted, but I'd still like to go to that bar-type-thing it said on the flyer, and listen to some music."

Kid was sure getting the hang of being on a honeymoon. On that day, she got to see her Gateway to the West, and once there she insisted on going right up to the top, nothing else would do. She didn't mind having to wait in line for over an hour outside the arch, then another thirty minutes inside before stepping into the small elevator which took them to the top. Phillip had seen and known the monument all his life but had never even considered doing the tourist thing and going inside, yet now that he had he was as exhilarated as Kid.

"Look at those microscopic ants down in the streets," he said looking out through the small windows at the top of the arch. "That's us … in everyday life, isn't it?"

"Yeah, seeing people as tiny ants reminds me so much of how I felt in Australia ... while camping out in the middle of nowhere. I felt just like one of those little ants myself then. It makes you think that you are not so terribly important ... not really." At that moment Phillip wished more than ever that he could have experienced some of Kid's solitary post-fire camping life.

In the afternoon, Phillip had gone to the Court House to inquire about David's sentence and the date of his release. Kid had opted not to join him on this mission, she wanted to go back to the museum she and Phillip had been to earlier on. Together they had walked through the rooms but had not spent as much time as Kid would have liked. There was an exhibit of old photos and maps and artifacts of the two explorers William Clark and Meriwether Lewis who had made their way to the west coast at the beginning of the nineteenth century. She copied out names of people and places, the route the explorers followed, and finally she got to the then President, Thomas Jefferson, who had ordered the exploration and sent the two men on their way. Kid had found her second most favorite President and her second most favorite period in American history.

Afterwards, on her way to the prearranged meeting point with Phillip she had come across the flyer announcing a gig. She was sure Phillip would know the place and the band. After all, this is where he grew up and lived most of his life, she thought, forgetting that he had left more than a decade ago and that the music scene might have undergone some changes in the meantime.

Phillip and his aunt had agreed on dinner the next evening, another visit to the prison was convened for the following day - a busy honeymoon schedule, indeed.

Aunt Mavis was all smiles as she opened the front door to let her nephew and his wife in. She gave Phillip a hug and extended her hand to Kid to be shaken in the appropriate fashion for two people who had become family by default, as it were. Kid was in high spirits, she was alert and ready to be acquainted with more of her husband's family.

"May I call you aunt, too?" she asked as soon as Phillip had introduced her.

Aunt Mavis affected not to hear her question, instead she turned to Phillip, "It's been such a long time. You haven't been back here since the funeral, have you?" After that she talked about her late brother, about selling his house, about her health or rather her ill health, about her family and all the while she simply ignored Kid's presence. They all sat in the lounge room. John, the husband, was serving pre-dinner drinks of Martini, white and red.

Kid held her head high, she listened attentively to everything that was said. She didn't worry about being excluded from the conversation. She filed all this under: family-stuff. But Phillip didn't like what he witnessed. He knew that Mavis was ignoring Kid deliberately, and this irritated and annoyed him. He kept up the façade for a while longer but his patience was slowly fraying at the edges.

"This is Kid's first time in St. Louis," he now said, deliberately including Kid in the conversation. "We actually went right up inside the arch, like proper tourists. It was a first for me, too."

"It was beautiful," Kid piped up, "but at the same time it gave me an odd feeling, you know, looking down at people living their daily lives not knowing that they were being watched. Do you know what I mean, aunt Mavis? I almost felt as though I was eavesdropping on the world."

The look on aunt Mavis' face as she turned to Kid seemed to say 'never heard such balderdash'. Everybody in the room read it ... everyone except Kid. She was too full of enthusiasm after two exciting days in Phillip's home town. All her senses were tuned in to the beauties of life and the love for her husband. She carried on undeterred.

"Did Phillip tell you that we paid David a visit? That was kind of the initial issue, the one that determined our trip here." The moment her words were out, the atmosphere in the room seemed to change, the suave and rather smug family talk was replaced by a silent bitterness. A shroud of anger, incomprehension and perplexity hung over everyone's head.

It was aunt who spoke first. She was shaking ever so slightly but mustered a fairly non-committal tone of voice. "Did you really, Phillip? I was under the impression that you had erased David from your life a long time ago."

"I thought I had, but ... Kid asked to meet him, and Kid is entitled to meet her brother if she so wishes. Yes, we were at the prison ... we spoke to David. Look, we don't have to talk about this if you find it disturbing."

"I'm sorry, aunt Mavis, I didn't mean to upset you, just wanted to tell you about all we've done and that. Phillip told me about David and what happened to him ... I never had a brother, you see, now I do."

Aunt Mavis quickly and effortlessly changed the subject. She had no intention of hearing any more about this man who was a criminal and not fit to be considered a part of her family. "So, where do *you* come from, Kid. Your accent ... can't quite locate it somehow."

I've really put my foot in it. Why did I have to mention David, she admonished herself, when I knew full well she doesn't like him? I know that aunt's silly small talk about my accent is merely a veneer - just a way to hide her annoyance. But I cannot play her game. So she answered aunt's question truthfully.

"I'm from Australia but I hoped my accent had changed some since I've lived with Phillip. I'm trying to sound more American."

"And where did you meet?" she continued her interrogation.

"We met in Western Australia, a place called Fremantle. Phillip was on tour with the band, and we met in the car park. I lived on my truck then, you see, and had been traveling around for some time, right out in the desert and through the open country. Western Australia is beautiful, very big and empty. I was playing Phillip's song but in the

149

wrong key. Phillip said I should try A major, so that's how we met." Kid knew she was talking too much, that's what she usually did when she was nervous. She shot a glance at Phillip, saw him smile. Safe to continue then, she thought.

But aunt had different ideas. "I see, let's go in and have dinner, shall we?"

Maybe I saved the situation with my detailed account, Kid thought and congratulated herself silently. Aunt was generally in charge of the dinner conversation and of the topics to be discussed, so Kid got a dose of family history whether she liked it or not. Her daughter, Phillip's cousin, was now married and had a baby and lived in ... Kid had never heard of the place ... her son had his own business and a dozen employees and was making good money. She obviously did have a thing about money. Phillip's career got some attention too. Was he not thinking of going into business? Surely with his university degree ... and why was he still spending so much of his time on an unprofitable hobby like music-making? There she goes again, Kid thought, but it's none of my business. It was during dessert that aunt Mavis came back to the subject of Kid's origin.

"So I take it that you are a country girl, Kid."

Kid couldn't be sure if this was a question, so she said as cheerfully as she knew how, "I am rather, yes. I chose to live in the country once I grew up. But I started life in a suburb of Brisbane, that's on the east coast of Australia, you know, where it is always sunny and warm. I started to work my way west after my parents died."

"What work did you do?"

"Oh, I did any odd job that I could get, farm work, bars, restaurants, hotels, anything ... I didn't mind."

"I see, and now that you are married ... how do you spend your time and how do you like city life? I suppose you find that it holds a lot of temptations ... going out, shopping etc."

Again a nondescript half-question. Kid got more and more puzzled. She didn't even understand the meaning of aunt's last remark so she tried, "Well ... I ... I like my new life, we have a beautiful house with a garden ... I do quite a bit of gardening, you know ... but I work too, in an Italian restaurant, and I help the local priest ... as a volunteer ... and ... why did you say 'shopping' was a temptation?"

As Kid struggled on painfully doing her best to oblige with honest answers, she could feel Phillip's impatience build up, but now there was more ... she sensed frustration, maybe anger. Unusual for Phillip, but what was even more unusual, now he spoke up.

"Aunt Mavis, why are you interrogating Kid like this? You've been treating her with condescension and disrespect ever since I introduced her. I'm not having any more of this."

"Come, come Phillip. I'm only asking a few harmless

questions," Mavis said in a cowardly way trying to counter Phillip's outburst.

"No, these were not just harmless questions and you know it. Kid has tried to answer you honestly and truthfully. She does not, as a habit, use sarcasm or insinuations. You have been unpleasant to her all evening ..." Phillip was by now shaking with outrage and indignation.

Kid was speechless, she had never seen this side of her husband. In fact, she hadn't believed him capable of making such strong accusations. Like from far away she now heard aunt's voice which carried a distinctly hypocritical undertone.

"What is it with you, Phillip? I've always known you to be so well-mannered and soft spoken ..."

"I have no intention of being well-mannered or whatever, I'm not putting up with any more of your abominable treatment of my wife. You can either apologize now or we're leaving."

Silence in the room. Well said my darling, Kid thought with some satisfaction but made sure not to show any signs of her cheekiness. Phillip, true to his word, got up from his seat, walked around the table to Kid's side, took her by the hand and walked her to the door.

"You can't just leave like that," John said lamely, "Mavis didn't mean ..." but he didn't get any further. Mavis stormed out of the dining room.

Phillip looked at his uncle and said, "Yes, I can and I will, and Mavis did mean exactly what you and I both understood. The only one who did not understand is Kid. Thanks for dinner." And with these parting words, Phillip and Kid left aunt Mavis' house.

"I drive us back Phillip ... safer this way."

Phillip handed Kid the keys of the hire car without a word of objection. She drove carefully, they did not speak until they were back in the hotel room. Phillip was visibly shaken, his breathing was uneven, he was close to tears.

"I've never done anything like this before, Kid. Mavis was right when she said I'd always been well-mannered, but today I just couldn't put on this hypocritical show of smooth talk and all-is-well crap. Something got me, it was all too important to just put up with and ... and I don't regret what I've said and done, no way. You couldn't have understood her deviousness Kid, you don't function that way, but I knew. She was incensed because you don't have a university education, because you work at what she considers menial jobs. She insinuated that since you were a country girl and lived in the city now, you were probably spending money on a lot of nonsense - and spending *my* money to boot. She was simply horrible, condescending and a damn snob."

"Right, now I get it. You did warn me, though. What's going to happen now? Do you think she will apologize?"

"I don't think so … she does not know how to apologize … and I don't care."

"Darling, I've never heard you be so forceful, you really told her what you thought of her, eh? Please, calm down now, let's go downstairs to the bar and imbibe a night cap, shall we? And then … lots of nice things to come …" Kid said cryptically, put her arms around Phillip and gave him a long and intimate kiss.

Much later that night and long after their lovemaking, Kid lay awake and pondered the extraordinary events of her evening. Phillip had spoken up on her behalf, and he had done so in very strong language, and by so doing he had now created a unbridgeable rift between himself and his aunt and her family. She remembered him saying that his usual well-mannered behavior was hypocritical and would have been cowardly tonight. My darling husband must have taken his life in both hands when he gave Mavis a piece of his mind, she thought fondly, it must have been no mean feat and needed a lot of courage. Kid remembered Father's words now. 'As you learn more about each other', he said, 'through in-depth talk, you will strengthen the bond of love between you'. Is that what we have done tonight? Is that what you meant, Father?

VIII

"Not hungry today, Dave? What's the matter?"

David sat in front of his lunch, deep in thought, he did not immediately respond to his mate's concern. He and Tony had served close to five years together in this prison, they were both Vietnam veterans which made them something like brothers. Tony was of slight build, his dark curly hair and brown eyes he had inherited from his Sicilian ancestors, but unlike his father and grandfather who had been laborers on construction sites, Tony had ambitions. Rather than to construct buildings and bridges, he wanted to design them.

He had decided at an early age that he was going to go to university and study to be an engineer, but then he was drafted. Suddenly, the decisions for his future were made by others, university had to take second priority. His life was turned upside down from one day to the next. He never mustered the same enthusiasm again after his return. He let himself drift into the world of drugs and crime and finally found himself in the penitentiary in St. Louis.

He and David didn't have much in common and under ordinary circumstances would probably never have become friends. But there were no ordinary circumstances any more once you had spent two years in the jungles of Vietnam. In prison, David had rescued Tony on a number of occasions when he was viciously attacked by prison gangs. David was the fighter and rescuer of vets, that was his job. Intellect did not play much of a part in his life.

"I've had a visit from my brother ... first time ... he and his wife are coming again to see me this afternoon. I'm ... all in a turmoil inside ..."

"You'll be alright, relax ... you are the one who knows how to relax every muscle in your body, right? I've seen you do it."

David nodded. "This is different though. I want to make friends with my little brother ... we hadn't spoken for ... many years ...don't want to stuff up ..."

"Just take it easy ... ask one question at the time, answer one at the time. You can do it."

"Thanks Tony."

Kid and Phillip's second experience of the security procedure on entering the prison building was less intimidating; they both knew what to expect and had hardened their senses and emotions accordingly. It had been David's unequivocal wish to see them once more before they went back home … and a promise was a promise.

David was already there when Phillip and Kid entered by the visitors' entry. "Thanks for coming again." He had obviously rehearsed this introduction. He remembered that Kid had found his size intimidating the first time so now he made sure they all sat down, then he began to organize his thoughts and his questions. One at the time, he could hear Tony's words, but Phillip beat him to it.

"I've been to the Court House to inquire about your release. Ten more months to go, on good behavior. Can you do it?"

David nodded. "Yes, I'm trying real hard. You earn some privileges with good behavior you know … I got time and a place to do my karate practice. I'm also allowed to teach it to small groups … on certain days."

"Sounds good. May I ask what got you in here?" Kid's curiosity was running away with her.

"Umm ... you can ask, but my memories are kind of blurred … happened out west ... California. Never meant to get into trouble again by then … but those guys knew I was a member of the local karate club … they must have done. They provoked me … stupid ... like, 'you and your fancy fighting', stuff like that … 'try some proper street fighters'. Middle of the afternoon, those idiots … I remember saying I didn't want to fight. Umm … I can still see the first punch coming toward me … then … nothing ... don't know … maybe I thought I was back in the war … just went on autopilot … can't remember. Next thing I knew, I was in the lock-up. One of the guys died in hospital twenty-four hours later. That's it."

Kid was close to tears, Phillip was stunned, David feared that he had been too incoherent to be understood.

"How many guys, David?" Kid asked. She was determined to get to the bottom of this monumental injustice which had been done to her brother.

"I think four … real big guys ... all of them black."

Who is he to talk about 'big guys' Kid wondered. "You're talking about big guys, when you are six foot eleven yourself. Doesn't make sense."

"What's that? I'm not six eleven. I don't know anybody who is."

"Yes you are. Phillip told me, I'm sure of it."

Now David proceeded to get up from his chair almost majestically. He stood in what Kid considered to be his perfect karate stance and pronounced, "I'm exactly six foot five, OK?" Then he sat down again.

Phillip had sat silently right through the entire exchange. He was aware of course, that he had exaggerated his brother's size out of proportion.

"Are you both happy now?" he asked looking from Kid

to David, then back at Kid, a smug grin on his face. That's when it hit him. "I wish I had a mirror so I could hold it in front of you two," he said. "I only just saw it. There is an incredible resemblance between you. You guys could go as brother and sister any time. I mean, it's not just the blue eyes and the color of your hair, it's your features, chin, cheekbones, the shape of your faces … I don't believe it."

Kid beamed. "I like it … yes, that's fun, a real brother."

David was speechless. He didn't know what to make of this, and in one of his typical mind leaps he asked, "Would you like some coffee? There is a coffee maker in the corner."

"I go and get it, David," Kid volunteered.

As soon as she was out of earshot, Phillip addressed his brother in a serious tone of voice. "You realize Dave, that once you get out of here you need to get your act together and start leading the life of an ordinary guy. You have to get a job, find a place to live, look decent, pay tax and all that - and the main thing, you stay out of jail. Do you think you are up to this?"

"I hope so ... I'll try. It hasn't been easy … my head and my mind got fucked out there in the jungle, you know that. Maybe I can get some help … same as some of the vets get."

"Come on Dave, you were getting a lot of help when you came back but you blew it all by running away and be-

159

having like a lunatic. Poppa told me that the authorities just gave up on you after a while."

"My wild behavior was an outlet … you know … for my frustration, can't you see…"

Just then Kid came back, proudly carrying three Styrofoam cups at the same time. She placed them carefully on the table, one in front of David, one for Phillip and her own she kept in her hand. "Please, don't interrupt your conversation," she said, hoping she had not missed anything important. But David was not ready to give an explanation of his last statement, not in front of his sister-in-law. It already feels like she is my sister, it crossed his mind.

"May I ask questions David? I've got heaps of them." Rather than give him a chance to answer she jumped in with both feet and asked, "The martial arts part of your life … that's important to you, isn't it? Do you do your whatever-you-call-it-kata-type-thing every day? But I understood that you guys are not allowed to use your skills in everyday life, I mean in earnest, or to make money using them, is that right? But apparently Poppa said that …"

"You are asking a dozen questions all in one go. Umm … could you do one at the time?"

"Sorry. Tell us about your martial arts involvement, please."

"It's the most important thing to me … kind of all I was left with after I came out of hospital. During the war … I was ordered to use my karate skills … against the enemy … even though I didn't like to. I did a lot of damage … then once I was back home ... fighting got me into trouble ... with the police, with the law."

"That does sound unfair," Phillip said pensively, "but there could be jobs in your life as a civilian using those skills. I'm thinking … a bouncer for instance, or body-guard, right?"

David laughed, but it was a humorless laugh. "Yes, I've tried that ... both of them ... but it was no good. The bouncer job … they sacked me because I was too danger-ous. Bodyguard? I liked that, but they wanted a guy who … who blended in with the crowd, you know … invisible, just there to protect the important person. I didn't fit, did I ... sticking out a head above everyone ..."

Even though there was a certain sadness inherent in David's stories, Kid and Phillip couldn't hide a stifled little laugh.

David took no notice. He exhaled deeply, then contin-ued, "I've never really been able to keep a job … any job … for very long. Don't know … I often feel I don't belong, somehow … can't do anything right." He stopped for the briefest moment, then added, "I'm no good at relationships either." David did not look at his visitors, instead he fo-cused on some images of the past which now appeared in some recess of his mind. "I was told that I was married to the dojo – to karate."

"By a lady? And ...?"

David gave a deprecating shrug of his shoulders, "Yeah ... and she was probably right."

There was silence for a few minutes.

"Sometimes I can't even keep up with people's conversations ... like when Kid asked more than one question ... makes me feel like such an idiot. A good thing about being inside ... I can just go and be alone ... when I feel empty and useless. Please tell me about your lives ... about stuff you do. I haven't spoken to anyone from the outside world, not since Poppa ..."

That was Kid's cue. "Well, I told you that we had this beautiful house and garden. Also, I'm working at an Italian restaurant, a few days a week. Real nice people, it's a shop and pizza parlor and all, and I also work with the priest at the parish sometimes and Phillip ... he plays with the band. Do you know about the band? They are good, Blue Grass and folk and all. That's how we met ... in Australia. I used to be Australian, aunt Mavis said she couldn't place my accent. She was not nice ... didn't like me, and Phillip told her in no uncertain terms that she was horrible. She doesn't like you either, right?"

Now she turned to look at Phillip, gave a little shrug of her shoulders as if to say 'sorry, I know I talk too much but David asked, so there'.

"We have to go back home in two days … jobs you know … we went right up to the top of the arch yesterday in a cute little elevator, and I went back to the museum, you know where the water spouts are. What else did we do, Phillip?"

"I think you gave quite a comprehensive account, Kid." And in David's direction, "Did you follow all that?"

"Yeah, I liked it."

Just then the buzzer announcing the end of visiting time could be heard and a shadow seemed to cross David's face. His clear blue eyes lost their newly acquired shine for a second. He said nothing. But Phillip and Kid had noticed it simultaneously and neither liked the thought of him going back to his cell alone, wherever that was and whatever it looked like. They both knew David was going to be sad.

"David," Kid said a little uncertainly, "maybe we could stay in touch … by phone. Do you have the use of telephones here? And would you like that?"

"That would be good. Don't know the number or the rules. Nobody ever called me."

If he says one more sad word, Kid thought, I'm going to cry. Instead she got up and shook David's hand good-bye without showing her tears. After only two short talks with her new brother she already knew that she could like him, didn't matter that he was a criminal or a traumatized war veteran or a dangerous professional fighter.

IX

Kid drove her new white Ford sedan carefully up the driveway and parked it in the garage. She was very proud of her new car; it had four doors, comfortable seats covered by light brown sheep skins, a reasonable sized boot for all her shopping bags and it sported two delicate dark blue lines along the sides. Phillip had bought it for her directly after their return from St. Louis. He had never uttered a word of admonishment for wrecking the Toyota. The reasons for the accident were still all too vividly present in his mind. He had never stopped blaming himself for Kid's breakdown.

Kid had done her shopping after working at Alfredo's, Phillip was already home and there was also Mario's car parked on the curb. He and Phillip were best friends and Mario often came for a drink and a chat. He was a good guy, Kid liked him. He was always full of fun and laughs and he was also a lawyer. Kid liked to read and watch courtroom drama. Lawyers occupied a high ranking in her mind and she had a lot of respect for their cleverness to bring justice where justice belonged. Mario lived with his parents in what he called a high income neighborhood. He had told Kid once with a sheepish grin, "My Mama spoils me rotten, you know, the traditional and accepted behavior of an Italian mother toward her only son." Yes, Kid liked Mario.

She opened the boot, gathered her shopping bags then made her way in through the back door. She could hear Phillip and Mario's voices over the volume of the television in the lounge room.

"I'm back," she called in her usual way. No reaction. She took two steps into the laundry and even before she entered the house proper she could feel a tinge of unpleasantness in the air. Something was wrong, she could feel it, her senses did not often deceive her. Her usually so efficient telepathy had not clocked in and given her a warning note - a somewhat disturbing thought. OK, if there is a problem it's Phillip's not mine. I'm not going to do the housewifely thing and say 'what have I done wrong'. She made her way past the dining room into the kitchen, placed all her bags on the floor then walked up to her husband and put her arms around him following the pattern of her self-created ritual. Phillip felt cool to her touch, there was an unresponsiveness she was unfamiliar with.

"Hi Mario," she said, not showing either misgiving

or alarm. "I go and get started on dinner. Are you staying, Mario?" But before Mario could answer, she said, "There is something ominous looming in this house Phillip. Will you enlighten me?"

Phillip followed her and stopped on the dining room side of the breakfast counter. "Kid, I don't like your off-handedness. This is not like you."

"No ... I suppose it isn't. Are you two into a drink? Wait, I get a small glass of wine for myself then we sit down and talk." When she had poured her wine she pronounced, "Now."

Phillip's expression showed a mixture of puzzlement and annoyance. He shot a glance at his friend searching for a little help but got nothing from him.

"Maybe I should leave you to it," Mario said. "... none of my business."

"No need ... please stay." Then Phillip addressed Kid directly, "Kid I'm disappointed, you made me a promise and you broke it. Remember, you were not going to advertise the fact that you had found a brother – or rather a brother-in-law. It seems that you went and did just that. Why?"

All things fell into place for Kid then. She had met Anita for one of their regular coffee chats a few days after returning from their delayed honeymoon to St. Louis and had, during the course of her account, told Anita that she had met Phillip's brother David, that he was in jail but that she did not think of him as a criminal. She remembered her exact words, 'he seemed like a decent sort of guy'. Anita had obviously told her husband and he had related the news to the other band members.

"I told Anita over coffee one day. But I was under the impression that the promise had become obsolete since we had now made contact with your brother. I mean, we both realized that he is kind of OK, even though he is in jail ... and anyway he'll be out soon so she is likely to see him ... So I thought that cancelled the secrecy surrounding the whole issue."

"A promise doesn't just become obsolete because of intervening events, you know that, and we have not discussed it and have not agreed on letting the cat out of the bag, right?"

"No, that's true but ... you changed your opinion about him, the one you had formed so long ago, didn't you? So now it's just like having a brother ... like everyone else can have a brother. I can't see why it's such an issue and why you are so touchy about it."

"There is no justification for breaking a promise, no matter what. I trusted you. I didn't want to hear from Bob that I had a criminal for a brother."

"I, for one, don't think he is a criminal. We know that he has problems, mental, psychological or whatever ... difficult stuff to deal with. It's just that he made a mistake somewhere along the way ... that's what landed him in prison, that's all. I don't understand why you're in such a tizzy. Is it just the principle - the principle of not sticking to a promise - that upsets you so much?"

Phillip was shaking his head in complete incomprehension. "I've never known you to be so ... so argumentative, so aggressive, Kid."

At this point, Mario ventured rather levelly, "I'm sorry Phillip, but in my opinion, Kid does have a point. What harm is there in admitting to having a brother ... whether he is in jail or in the Pentagon is neither here nor there. There are a lot of people in jail who have made no more than a mistake, guys who lost it once and later regretted it, guys who committed crimes out of love and consequent jealousy, guys who'd require medical help rather than incarceration. It's true, you know, the simple fact that someone is in prison doesn't mean he is a thoroughly bad guy."

Phillip had listened to Mario's dissertation without interrupting him. Now he said, "This is the lawyer in you speaking, is it?"

"To a degree, yes, but I also happen to believe that legal injustices *are* committed at times. Sometimes they are later conveniently overlooked and swept under the carpet, in an effort to conceal the fact that some people are suffering undeservedly."

Kid was pleased with the approval she had gotten from

Mario. She wondered however, if Phillip had been embarrassed in front of all his friends by Bob's statement.

"Phillip, does everyone in the band know and did they all embarrass you with questions? I'm sorry I blurted it out to Anita ... I should have kept my mouth shut."

Phillip nodded. There was the smallest trace of a conciliatory smile in his eyes. "Bob knows and Mario ... and no, we didn't talk about it in detail. I'm sorry I overreacted a bit just now. It's my hang-up again Kid. I have to start getting used to the idea of being one of two brothers."

Kid knew she was forgiven. She silently thanked Mario for his mediation and said, "I will start preparing dinner now." Only then did she put her arms around her husband and whisper in his ear, "Sorry darling, and don't be angry with me. I love you."

Peace was re-established, Phillip helped Kid in the kitchen, Mario set the table, conversation during their meal touched on every topic under the sun, including the new McCabe brother. Mario proved to be a treasure trove of information on the subject of prisons, trials, sentencing, good behavior, release conditions - all issues related to David and his future. Kid had complete faith in the truth and the value of Mario's opinions and of his knowledge; she saw him as the professional, the legal expert. The fact that he was still only at the beginning of his legal studies conveniently escaped her.

"David will probably need some help and assistance after his release," Mario said seriously at one point. "People who have spent a number of years in prison invariably find themselves in a changed world once they are released. It's not always easy to re-adjust to everyday life. You know, just ordinary stuff like how to function in public places, dress properly, handle traffic, shop in big shopping malls, behave correctly in bars and restaurants, that sort of thing."

This was pretty much what Phillip had previously hinted at. "But what about when it comes to dealing with bureaucracy - issues like job hunting, filling out applications and that?" he asked.

"Umm .. are you suggesting that he might have literacy problems?"

"I am .. only suggesting though, but there is a possibility. He seems to be attending classes in prison. Could that be it?"

"Possible, yes. He might be able to read - I mean he would know the letters - the problem would most probably lie with writing. The moment he settles down somewhere, he'll have to fill out forms, open a bank account, sign contracts, buy a car, insurance, a house. But he can get help with all this after leaving prison."

Phillip knew right then that he and Kid were following the same line of thought concerning David's new life as a free citizen. Would he be able to handle money and make qualified decisions? Did he have memory gaps maybe? Was he still suffering from the aftermath of his traumatic war experiences? Phillip was almost sure that Kid, in her unstoppable philanthropic fantasies, would want to bring David right here under their roof so she could offer him the necessary guidance and assistance. I can just see her mothering him, he added rather unkindly in his mind. From a distance, he now heard Kid's voice.

"Thanks Mario for all your expert information. I guess it's all part of being a lawyer ... I mean having to deal with people in David's situation."

Mario shook his head as he said, "I'm still a long way from being a lawyer, Kid. You know that."

"You're just being modest," she said. "Let's have coffee in the lounge."

It was a few weeks after that evening with Mario that Kid suggested to her husband, "Darling, I think we should contact our brother. We did, after all, promise him. You haven't changed your mind about this, have you?" Kid had chosen a Friday evening as the ideal moment to raise the issue of David again. It was a warm evening in late summer, they were enjoying a pre-dinner drink on their back veranda where they could catch the last rays of the sun through the big old oak trees in the neighbor's garden and further down along the avenue.

"No. I've been thinking about it, I meant to discuss it

with you. I'm not so sure that I know what I'm going to say to him, though. It's like ... I don't really know the guy who is my brother. Those two encounters ... they were kind of significant. I keep re-playing them in my mind but I don't quite know where to go from here."

"But you have shed some of that fixed animosity, haven't you? You spoke to him in an almost brotherly manner.".

Phillip gave her a little smile as he said, "Almost brotherly ... yes, you can call it that, I suppose."

"Well," Kid started rather pompously, "it's like this: David is likely to become a permanent feature in our lives, we both know that, right? I mean he is our mutual brother and we are the only family he now has. The help Mario mentioned ... I wonder if David even knows he is entitled to any. I bet he was never a beneficiary of those assistance programs for veterans. If his literacy skills should really be ... umm ... around his ankles, as it were, it's quite likely that he never even made any inquires about assistance. And the authorities, rather than to take the initiative and extend a helping hand would just as gladly abandon him - one person less to bother with. That kind of thing."

Phillip looked unhappy since he knew full well that Kid had a valid point there. "Not a very flattering chapter in our recent history, is it Kid? I have a feeling that you have long ago decided to ask David to come and stay with us so we can give him the assistance he needs. You are really just presenting me with a fait accompli, right?"

"I have thought about it, that's true and I know I am steamrolling you a little but I wouldn't make a definite decision of such magnitude without discussing it with you first. You know, if he were to settle here in Knoxville, he would be close enough for regular contact then. He needn't actually live under our roof."

Phillip smiled and took her hand in his as they sat side by side, "I'll suggest it to him over the phone, OK?" After a minute he continued as if in a monologue, "I feel somehow more mellow towards David after having seen him and spoken to him. His savage destruction sprees seem a long way away now. I'm glad I finally opened up. All these past years it was like a compulsion to keep only the bad memories of him in my mind. I don't really know what made me do it. Poppa always wanted me to make friends with David again. He often hinted at it but it never really penetrated my stubborn brain. I've carried this fixed mind-set around with me for such a long time. I'm sorry I caused you so much hurt by being prejudiced and obstinate and opinionated and ... simply a pain in the neck."

Now he leaned over and kissed Kid's cheek. The sun had set by then but they could still see the red glow between the trees. They sat for a few more minutes watching the red turn to orange and finally fade away.

X

Kid and Phillip were not the only ones to worry about their brother's future after his release. In the penitentiary of St. Louis, David too, did some serious thinking on that subject around that time.

He was working as part of a small labor gang on the other side of the newly added wing of the prison. They were cementing the floor in the new ablution block and whitewashing the walls. It was just as well that Kid did not know about this or she would surely have been incensed and would instantly have compared the process with the nineteenth century practice by which convicts were made to construct their own dungeons. She had not forgotten the history lessons of her school days in far off Australia. David of course, knew none of this.

He and his mates were not shackled hand and feet the way the convicts in Kid's history book used to be, their prison was after all not maximum security. They were wearing their prison working clothes, all had shed their shirts and the sun was relentlessly burning their naked torsos on this hot day in late summer. David did not mind hard work, he was fit and strong. Working also took care of a few hours a day - hours in which he was unable to replay his conversations with his brother and think about the problems he was going to face in the future as a free citizen.

During the time since those two magic days when his brother and sister-in-law had come to visit, David's life – his whole existence – had undergone substantial changes. An unfamiliar feeling of expectancy and excitement had now almost permanently taken hold of him. There were moments when his exhilaration mirrored a smile on his face, and there were others when the approaching difficulties in his future life frightened him and made him feel almost physically sick. These were the days when he skipped lunch or dinner, not breakfast though. Phillip's wife had said that breakfast was the most important meal in the day, so he stuck with this. He liked Kid. He liked her openness and her friendly smile. But she does talk a lot, he remembered, like a radio, never stops ... only when she runs out of breath. Kid spoke with a curious accent, too. She had told him that she came from Australia but David couldn't quite remember where to place that country. A memory gap as a result of what happened in the war? Possible.

But there were a number of things David *could* remember and in all detail - stuff that happened years ago, when he and Phillip were children. Poppa had often talked to him about the family when he came to visit and he had assured David that his memory was not stuffed - not completely. Must concentrate on my reading and writing classes though, he told himself. Where has it all gone? I'm almost sure I knew earlier in my life. I seem to have lost the most basic everyday living skills ... everything except karate.

All this was involuntarily coursing through David's mind as he was making his way back to his own compound that afternoon after work. He and his cell mate had come to an agreement: Chuck would help David with literacy, figures, sums, telling time, days of the week, months and dates and David would instruct Chuck in karate, breathing techniques, relaxation and meditation. Now David had showered and changed and was back in his cell – it was time to put his brain into studying gear.

Chuck was a clever guy. He had been in business on the outside, all types of business. He sold swimming pools, talked people into buying insurance or real estate, but his repeated successes and the prospect of making more and more money had made him greedy and had ultimately landed him in jail. Embezzlement was the word he used to describe his crime, a word that made no sense to David. All he knew was that Chuck had a good heart; he was honest and he was a good friend.

"Having one of your good days, Dave?" Chuck greeted David. "Your moods have been going up and down like a yo-yo lately."

"Yeah, I'm feeling happy today … don't know … maybe I'll be hearing from my brother soon. His wife said they would keep in touch … by phone."

"Right, what that means is: learn all you can so you'll be ready to face the outside world when you are released."

After these words of advice, the two men sat down at their small table. Chuck started to write down five and six digit numbers for David to read out. Then he reduced them to three digit numbers and asked David to add, then some to subtract. He gave him columns of prices in dollars and cents to add up, dates to read out, weekdays to be recounted in their correct order. David was slow, he made mistakes but he plodded on doggedly.

"Am I doing alright?" he asked, "getting somewhere?"

"Yeah, fine," Chuck said half-heartedly. He knew only too well that his teachings were no more than a feeble beginning and that David still had a very long way to go before being able to function like an ordinary guy - a free citizen. "Time to put your literacy cap on Dave. What time does your class start?"

"At … umm … five-thirty. From five-thirty till six-thirty, right?"

Chuck smiled and sent him on his way.

Phillip's phone call came that same evening.

David was in the recreation area when his name was called over the speaker. Tony and Chuck sat on opposite sides of the table next to his, they were in the middle of a game of chess. David did not understand the game, he had watched his two best mates, had listened to their instructions on how to play it but in the end it was too complicated, too confounding and he gave up. He sat at a right angle to the television set and looked straight ahead..

"David, that's you they're calling. Down to the office where the phones are, go go go." Tony called over his shoulder.

"Uh-huh," David said. He had not heard his name. He made his way towards the bank of telephones down by the entrance, he was floating through the air, his feet never touched the ground, or so he thought.

"McCabe, phone number three," he heard from far away.

Must pull myself together, he told himself seconds before he lifted the receiver. I've tried to prove to Phillip that I'm not the moron he remembered me to be ... I'll have to keep this up. "Hello, David speaking," he said into the receiver then waited.

"Hi David, this is Kid. Is everything OK? You don't sound very happy ... is this a bad time to call? Sorry, we couldn't give you any warning ... we were told to call after seven, any day ... are you there David?"

"Yes Kid." He could just hear his brother's voice in the background, something like 'slow down Kid'.

"Sorry, I talk too much, don't I?" she said assuming David had heard Phillip's words. But she was not about to slow down now that she had made contact with her new brother. She told about everything that came to her mind. She gave a description of her new car complete with details of appearance and interior mechanisms. She talked about her work at the restaurant and concluded with, "Alfredo had a function, you know, and I served all his special guests." She rattled on about her gardening efforts. The fruit trees she had planted were now shooting nicely, some of the vegetables were ready to be picked, lettuce, spinach, a few cucumbers. Then she switched to Phillip's gigs with the band and the music studio in their own front room, and on and on. Finally she ran out of breath and stopped.

David had not said one word, never interrupted her. "I'd like to see your garden, Kid. I used to do some gardening when I was little ... helped my mom. We used to have vegetables ... and a plum tree in the back yard." He knew Kid was smiling ... or he thought he knew, so he continued in his very own disjointed fashion. "I remember the conversations we had here, the three of us. I keep re-playing them in my mind ... trying not to forget anything. Can you speak Italian ... you said it was an Italian restaurant, right? I have a mate who's parents are Italian ... no, Sicilian I think."

Kid stood stock still at the breakfast counter, she had been holding the receiver to her ear all this time and never uttered a word. Phillip started to wonder if David was still on the line. He had never been privy to a more outlandish phone conversation.

"I'll give you Phillip now and ... oh, next time we talk I'd like you to tell me about martial arts, would you do that? What color belt do you have?"

"I have a Black Belt, Kid. I'll tell you about karate if you like."

"Hi brother," Phillip's smooth voice came on the line. "I'm sure glad you and Kid have such a lot of topics to discuss," he said it without a trace of sarcasm. "There are a couple of issues I'd like to put to you, though ... just for you to think about, no need for instant decisions OK? It's about what you will do and where you'll go when you get out. Do you have any concrete plans yet?"

"No. Give me time to think."

"Sure. Another thing. I had a massive falling-out with our aunt Mavis last time I saw her. She doesn't like Kid ... she was horrible. I know she does not like you either - never has as far as I can remember." He heard David chuckle at the other end of the line. "...which makes Kid and I your only family. So here is my proposition: Would you consider starting your new life, as it were, somewhere close to where we live to make it easy for contact ... or do you have a home somewhere, a place where you spent time, have friends and that? But as I said, no need to rush into a decision. Kid would like you to be close to us. You and I … we are also *her* only family."

"I need to think this over some, but thanks … for … well, for suggesting it. I'm making a real effort now … to, you know, to learn all the stuff again … all the things that have somehow been wiped out in my brain and my mind. You know what I mean?"

"I think I know." Phillip paused then added, "but there is no need to be ashamed, if that's what worries you," and fearing that he might get overly sentimental he rushed on, "I can't talk too long. Kid and I are going out tonight, there is a band here in town, guys I have heard in Nashville some time ago. We'll call you again. In a couple of weeks ... OK? It's got to be after seven, as Kid told you."

"It's been great talking to you and to your wife. Gives me plenty to think about … life is kind of different now since … since I have something to look forward to. Take care now Phillip and thanks … and to Kid."

"Yeah, you too." And that was the end of the first ever phone conversation between Phillip and his long-lost brother.

XI

Phillip's suggestion took a long time to come to fruition. In the meantime, summer had given way to autumn, the leaves of all the trees in town had turned to brilliant reds and yellows and after that last show they all fell down on the ground. Kid told Phillip in utter amazement, "Why can't they go like our Australian trees? They drop some of their leaves all year round but they always make sure there are still some left on the tree. Here they shed the whole lot in one fell swoop, then they stand naked for six months. Makes no sense."

Winter had now set in, Kid's first in her new country. Winter also brought some novelties into the lives of Mr and Mrs McCabe. Kid wore a coat with a hood, boots lined with fur, gloves and a woolly scarf around her neck. They no longer had their picnics in the park; instead she and Phillip spent long evenings enjoying the comfort of their centrally heated house. David's release was now a mere three months away and still no definite plans for his future had been made. Phillip had repeated his suggestion during three consecutive phone calls to his brother, then he had upgraded it to 'you could come and stay with us for starters. We have a spare room … no problem', but David had not been able to decide. He neither declined nor accepted his brother's offer. The closest he came to giving an answer was 'if I stayed in your house I would interfere with your life … can't do that'.

"Kid," Phillip said out of the blue while they were having their breakfast, "I firmly believe that David *will* need all the help we can give him, he just doesn't want to own up to it. Maybe he has to be told to come here. I suppose he would know how to obey orders, that's what he had to do in the army first, then in jail. Suggestions don't seem to work with him."

"Possibly, I hadn't thought of it that way," Kid said a little absently since all her thoughts were on the evening's dinner. She and Phillip had invited Anita, Bob and Mario and Kid was going to cook one of her curries - a different one again. She did not believe in cooking the same dish twice when there were hundreds of them in her cooking book. "Tonight it's going to be Ceylonese Chicken Curry. I've already got all the ingredients, and as small side dishes I'll serve yoghurt, cucumber and pickles … it says here: 'to cool the palate and to add sweetness'. Sound good?"

"Sure … delicious."

"But there is always the rice. I can't ever get it right somehow."

"OK, I'll be in charge of the rice tonight, and if it turns out mushy and sticky I'll take the blame."

Kid giggled merrily, then she turned serious and said, "Do you think they will want to talk about David? I expected it the last time we were at Anita's but … not a word."

"Nobody mentioned him, at least not in my presence, since that first time. I must have really over-reacted that day. But I've done a lot of thinking since then. Now that we have decided that we are going to have him stay here, it's inevitable that he will meet all my friends. They can then form their own opinions of him. I just hope Jim will be OK, he can be a bit of a pain in the neck, you know."

"I've noticed. Any idea why?"

"Difficult marriage … it's been on the rocks for a long time ... he has two small children. He seems to project his anger and his frustration on the people around him, not an unusual thing to do but unpleasant, nevertheless ... he is a world class bass player though Has Anita opened up the subject of our brother again?"

"Yes, more than once, she'd like to know all the details … his past and everything. She sees it as a good topic for gossip ... I don't agree with that so I usually say nothing."

Phillip smiled. "I was a real idiot for making such a fuss over your spilling the beans that day. More coffee Kid?" he said and went to get the pot from the hot plate. "Hey, I'm just having a brainwave."

"Good, tell me quick before it makes you spill all the coffee."

"Right. I'm thinking ... on the day David is released ... what about we drive to St. Louis and pick him up outside the prison, then take it nice and slow on the way back, make a few stops - a little vacation for the three of us. What do you say?"

Kid beamed, she was amazed and exhilarated all at the same time. "Yep, and while we're in St. Louis we can go see that place we didn't make last time, remember, the house where Scott Joplin used to live. In the pamphlet it said he was the 'King of Ragtime' right? And then we'll stop in Memphis and we go to Beale Street where all the musical venues are and we can hear oodles of concerts there ... and while in Nashville we might go to that recreation park that I've read about where there are musical performances al fresco and ..."

By then Phillip was shaking with laughter, "Yes of course, and much much more Kid. I take it that you approve of my brainwave, yes?"

Two decisions had been made by default that morning. One that David was going to be told, no longer asked,

185

where to start his new life, and two that Kid and Phillip would make the trip to St. Louis by car to pick him up and turn the journey into some sort of a vacation.

XII

The prison building had lost almost all of its ominous and intimidating aspects on the day Kid and Phillip approached it for the third time, but its apparent harmlessness was really only a matter of the mind. In Kid's case it was merely an overdose of optimism, based on the certainty that this was the last time they would ever have to see it.

It was the day of David's release. Kid and Phillip stood at the edge of the car park on the opposite side of the road, their eyes fixed on the heavy metal double doors. They waited and waited.

The drive from home had taken two days and it had included a couple of the sightseeing spots on Kid's list. On arriving in St. Louis they had decided to splurge and had booked a room at an expensive hotel and enjoyed another four-course meal at their French restaurant. Memphis was scheduled for the return trip which would include brother

David.

While waiting, Phillip reflected on the last few phone conversations with his brother. David's reaction when presented with our ready made plans for his immediate future, Phillip thought with some amusement, was almost exactly the one I had predicted: David knew how to obey orders. Phillip had tried not to make it sound like a military order but at the same time he had not been prepared to take 'no' for an answer. David was bound to become a permanent feature in his and Kid's lives, and offering to accommodate him in their home was the right thing to do. The practical side of their decision they would have to play by ear - they knew as yet so little about their brother.

Now the heavy doors slid back to frame the tall and erect figure of David. He took on a stance which could easily be seen as readiness to attack ... attack what ... freedom ... his new lease of life? It was mid-morning on a cold day in early March, a pale sun peeped through the clouds as if trying to make this very first day of David's life as a free citizen an inviting and a promising one. Phillip and Kid approached the open prison gate hand in hand and when they came to a halt and stood face to face with David, Kid let go of Phillip's hand and in a spontaneous gesture she put her arms around her brother's waist - this was about as high as she could reach. David dropped the bag he had been holding in his hand and shyly, awkwardly wrapped his arms around

Kid's small body. Hugging somebody, Phillip thought as he watched, must be a completely unfamiliar greeting procedure to him, maybe even a little frightening. David held Kid for no more than two seconds then loosened his arms, turned to his brother and gave him a big, warm smile.

David was a free citizen.

Here came Kid's rehearsed lines, the hug had not been planned. "Welcome David. Welcome to ... our world ... and to us." Then she turned to Phillip as if to ask, 'did I do alright?'

"Good to see you Dave, you look great. Let's get away from here, nobody wants to look at this monstrosity of a building any longer than necessary." While they made their way to the car, Phillip asked, "Is there anything you like to do? Anywhere you'd like to go?"

David stopped in his tracks seemingly to concentrate, then answered with his own question. "Do you know where Poppa and mom are buried?"

"Yeah I know and so do you. You were there, remember?"

David shook his head. "Would you mind taking me there?"

"Fine. Do you ... want to get some flowers ... before ...?"

"No ... just like to see."

They all piled into Phillip's car, David automatically

took the back seat. An odd atmosphere prevailed in the vehicle, nobody spoke during the short drive to the cemetery.

"You two go, Phillip," Kid said once outside the gates, "I wait on the bench under that big tree over there."

The two brothers walked slowly along the small walkway past a row of tombstones. Phillip knew the exact location of his parents' graves. "May I leave you to it, Dave? I go back to where Kid is waiting."

"Yes," was all David had to say. He seemed to have entered a different world.

"Phillip, do you think that David is just a tad weird, or is this merely the upshot of my fertile imagination?"

Phillip chuckled. "Rather weird, yes. His wanting to go to the cemetery is certainly the last thing I expected, but then ... we were not to expect anything at all, were we Kid? Can you see him over there? What is he doing?"

"I can explain, darling. He is in his meditation position – so I assume he is meditating. He told me on the phone once that he meditates before and after his karate-what-d'you-call-it, the bit he does every day. It's all part of his variety of martial arts ... concentration, breathing techniques, relaxation ... all that. He might sit there for hours ... and we might freeze here in the meantime."

"Sounds promising." Phillip smiled and put his arm around Kid in an effort to keep her warm. "Still, it's his first day and we've decided not to push him, right? So we just let him feel his way back into our world again, even if this means waiting in the freezing cold."

"Phillip," Kid's question came without warning, "I've often wondered when I help Father in the shelters ... do you think David has been homeless like the people I feed there? You know, living in the streets, exposed to the cold at night, dirty and smelly and horrible?"

"Sounds awful ... even more so when it's your own brother. I don't know Kid. Maybe one day he will tell us."

"Father tells me that our *society* is responsible for people being homeless and destitute and addicted to drugs and all. He also says that black people are more vulnerable than white people because ... because ... I don't really know why Phillip. I thought everybody had the same rights in this country."

"It's a very complex issue darling. Sure, officially we all have the same rights no matter whether we are black, white or any other color but ... it's the circumstances in which people grow up that can determine their lives ... dysfunctional families, parents on drugs, conflicts with the law, all that. Still, it's unjust and shameful."

Like on cue Kid took over then, and in inimitable Kid fashion she stated the obvious. "But we are the richest and most powerful country in the whole world, aren't we Phillip? So there is lots of money and other resources ... you know, clever people and institutions and that. Poor and homeless people shouldn't even happen in the first place."

"I am in complete agreement with you. Unfortunately, that's not how it works, I'm sorry darling."

While Phillip and Kid were in the process of solving the problem of homelessness in the United States, David got up from his kneeling position, he bowed his head briefly toward the graves the way he did when entering or leaving the dojo mats, then turned and walked back out of the cemetery and joined his brother and sister. He had indeed been meditating by the side of his parents' graves. At the conclusion of his meditation he had thanked them for their love and kindness, he had apologized for his misconduct and had promised never to go back to prison.

Phillip recognized a serious, somehow impenetrable expression on his brother's face -an expression that seemed neither to invite nor even to tolerate interference or questioning. Kid understood the message he gave her by squeezing her hand and they drove in silence until they were on the highway out of the city and heading south.

"There are three graves, Phillip," David's words came slow and indistinct. "One is my first mom's then mom and Poppa, did you know?"

'My first mom' Phillip reflected, not 'my real mom' ... an unusual way to put it. "Yes I knew. Can you remember your real mom?"

"No, only that she sat on the edge of my bed at night

before I went to sleep ... and that she folded my hands together somehow ... then she said something like God was looking after me and that she and God and Poppa all loved me. That's what she said ... that's all I know."

"Do you still know how to pray, David?" Kid asked .

"No ... gave it away. Out in the jungle ... when I saw people die ... innocent women and children ... I understood that no God was looking after anybody ..."

Phillip closed his eyes briefly, took a deep breath to stop himself from pursuing the issue further. An intense and heavy silence ensued and it hung over their heads for a long time. Finally Phillip pulled up in a parking lot outside a gas station which was joined to a diner. "Anyone for some coffee? Maybe a bite to eat?"

"Good idea," Kid said and started to get out of her seatbelt. Phillip got out on the driver's side, then opened David's door from the outside. David sat immobile both hands palm down beside his thighs. Phillip noticed that he held on to the seat cover so hard, his knuckles were almost white. Something was happening to David. His eyes had narrowed and turned a steely blue, his features hardened, his jaw was firmly set. He was staring past Phillip at a tourist coach from which emerged a group of young tourists, all similarly dressed in padded jackets, caps, jeans and knee-high leather boots. They were Japanese.

Phillip turned around and watched the group as they

193

stepped out of the coach in single file but he could not make the connection between the tourists and his brother's strange behavior. When the last tourist had left the bus, David showed signs of waking up. He clenched and unclenched his fists, gave his head a vigorous shake then undid his seatbelt and got out without a word of explanation. The whole incident had lasted for no more than a few seconds, Kid had been fumbling with her backpack on the passenger's side of the car and had seen nothing.

The three of them were sitting at a corner table with their hamburgers and chips when Kid suddenly remembered that she had forgotten to get a drink. Phillip was quick to take advantage of her absence from the table and asked, "What happened Dave ... just then?"

"Umm ... all those people who came out of the bus ... Chinese weren't they? I saw them all turn into enemies ... you know in Vietnam ... all wore identical caps. My head is just so fucked Phillip. By tomorrow I probably won't remember any of it."

"They were harmless Japanese tourists, they tend to dress almost alike, the identical caps were probably some fashion thing." Then he scanned the room, "Where is Kid?"

"Over at the drink machine ... talking to some guy."

"How do you know? You weren't even looking that way."

David shrugged, "You learn to see all around you ... part of karate training ... useful in the jungle when you are surrounded by the enemy."

That's how far he got when Kid returned with a medium size cup of coke and a cheeky smile on her face.

"Tell you what happened," she announced before she even sat down. "OK, I was at the machine getting my drink, right? Then I hear a voice close to my ear, a foreign accent - Middle East I'd say ... very civilized, very polite. 'Where do I get my cup?' he asks and 'How do I work the machine?' So I told him to go and buy the cup first, then I went ahead and demonstrated how to get the ice from the middle tap, 'then you select your drink,' I said 'you push upward with your cup very gently and wait until it's full'. Nothing wrong with that, is there?"

"Nothing wrong at all," Phillip said with barely disguised glee. "Continue."

"Well, when my cup was full, I pulled it back and said a little off-handedly 'and there you are ... piece of cake'. The man opened his eyes wide and said 'no thank you'."

David had been following her story carefully, watching her lips and her every gesture and when she came to her last word he broke into genuine laughter. Phillip joined in, wondering however, if she had not made it all up on the spur of the moment.

Kid saw through him, "It's true ... happened just like I

said.'"

Little did Kid know that her silly little story, even though true, had inadvertently helped to restore a carefree atmosphere between them. But their return trip proved to have more surprises in store for them.

Kid was adamant that they get to Memphis before sundown. She had studied the map and knew that the highway would take them to West Memphis, that part of the city which was in the state of Arkansas, and from there they would cross the mighty Mississippi river into Memphis, in the state of Tennessee. She had seen pictures in her library book of the gigantic bridge which spans the biggest river in the country.

"We need to make sure we cross it in daylight," she had said the moment they started to plan their trip. Now they were under obligation to keep time. What Kid and Phillip didn't know was that David had no intention of staying overnight in Memphis. Memphis held memories ... bad stuff had happened to him here, a long time ago when he was still wild and aggressive. In his mind he could still see the street corner where he had stood watching a police officer mistreat a poor, weak, homeless man. In his overzealousness, David had intervened on behalf of the homeless guy, and as always happened, the minute he started to fight he found himself back in the jungles of Vietnam, and then no one, not even an armed cop, was ever a match for him. But assaulting a police officer was a big mistake and he was made to pay a heavy penalty for his rescue operation. This all came back to David in flashes and pictures as they neared the city of Memphis. David knew he had to tell his brother to drive right through the city without stopping. I'll close my eyes and pretend I'm somewhere else. Phillip would understand and do as he was asked and if his wife had other ideas Phillip was not to give in to her.

"Can we stop somewhere here," he heard Kid's enthusiastic voice, "before we cross the bridge, so I can get a real good look at the river?" David guessed that Kid had initiated the plan of staying over in Memphis. She probably wants to go to as many clubs and musical performances as possible, hopefully all through the night, he thought. I just have to stop her.

As they stood in a little park-like area that gave them a good view of the river, David said without preamble, "Phillip, I don't want to stay in Memphis ... I can't ... let's just drive right through without stopping."

Phillip lowered his head. "Hang on," he said. Kid stood a few steps away from him, he went up to her and put his arm around her shoulders then started to confer with her in a confidential manner. "Kid, David won't stay the night in Memphis. He just told me. I don't know why, not yet. But I'm not game to oppose him right now ... he still scares me. I'm sorry Kid. What do we do?"

"But I'm going to hear all the bands play and ... you promised. I'm amazed at how easily you give in to David's caprices, Phillip."

"I don't understand it myself. Could we come to a compromise Kid? I promise that we'll do another trip to Memphis, just you and I, and spend all night listening to music but tonight, let's just drive through and spend the night somewhere ... where David feels safe. Can you accept that?"

Kid nodded. "OK. It seems that we are taking turns in doubting our initial impressions of our brother. I thought of him as a nice and ordinary guy, no moron at all ... then he struck me as distinctly weird this morning, right?"

"And I was convinced that he was no longer savage and dangerous, now I admit to being scared of him." Phillip continued Kid's parable. "Maybe together we could write a psycho thriller, eh?"

"Right, you do the writing, I do the research. Still, I mean to get to the bottom of his tantrum-like rejection of Memphis. Brother David doesn't scare me, I'm just annoyed."

Phillip pulled her to him, kissed her unruly hair and said, "You'll probably succeed in making him tell us about his Memphis hang-up."

Kid giggled and nodded. Now she turned to David, looked up into his face and said, "It's OK brother. We'll drive right through but we have to stay overnight some-where ... between here and Nashville. Good enough?"

"Fine," was all he said.

What a damn stick in the mud, Kid thought. Hasn't he ever learned to say thank you?

If Kid was disappointed at missing out on the music scene of Memphis, she did not show but her mind was firm-ly set on the course of action she was going to take this very evening at whatever hotel they were going to spend the night. Phillip, true to his word, stayed on the highway after crossing the bridge and drove through the city of Memphis forsaking Beale Street with all it's musical magic. About half an hour after leaving the last suburb he pulled up out-side an hotel chosen at random.

"How is this Kid? Look alright to you? David?"

David nodded.

Kid squeezed Phillip's knee. He understood her mes-sage, got out of the car and made his way to the reception desk. Kid and David were left inside to wait, and that's when Kid saw her moment to settle a score with her brother. She turned sideways in her seat so she could see David, then ad-dressed him, "David, you do realize that the change of plan we made to accommodate your refusal to stay overnight in Memphis has made me sad? And I'm disappointed too. Does that mean anything to you? No? Did you even think of how I might feel?"

"I didn't ... I realize I should have. Kid, I just couldn't stay but I will tell you why. You have been good to me ... you and Phillip ... I didn't mean to cause you ... pain."

Just then, Phillip stuck his head through the window. "Let's go park the car, I secured two rooms for the night. There is a restaurant on the first floor, we're going to have our first family dinner." His cheerfulness was so infectious, both Kid and David broke into happy laughter.

Phillip had booked the room next to his and Kid's for David. He accompanied his brother inside. "Will this be OK David? Kid and I are next door," he said a little uncertainly.

"Sure fine. Must cost you a lot of money?"

"It does, but don't worry about it, after all it's not every second day that you acquire a new/old brother. We'll come and get you when we are ready for dinner ... in about half an hour. I'm starving."

"I'm real sorry to have upset Kid. I promised to tell her ... why I couldn't ... stay." David put one hand on his brother's shoulder. "I feel such an idiot."

"Never mind that now. I've promised her another trip to Memphis." Phillip was surprised by his own conciliatory attitude.

Kid had to wait until the end of their dinner to get David's promised explanation. "I got into trouble in Memphis once," he said as they were about to finish their meal. "I was arrested there. Didn't hurt anyone ... just helped a homeless guy out of trouble ... but overpowering a cop is a real big offence ... uniformed guys are ..."

"... a different species," Kid finished his sentence a little cheekily.

David nodded in agreement. "I didn't want to be seen and maybe recognized by ... anybody. No more fighting in the streets. Sorry Kid."

Kid had been listening attentively to David's disjointed account of his unfortunate experience in Memphis. So he helps the underprivileged, she thought, that's alright. Maybe his heart is in the right place after all.

"I'm helping the homeless people too, you know. I work in Father Pasquale's shelters, serve meals and that. What did you do to the cop? Wasn't he armed? He could have shot you. Karate fighters only use their hands, don't they? Bet the cop felt a real fool when you defeated him. What happened to his gun?"

"Umm ... lots of questions. Better to ask one at the time Kid. I'll try. The cop *was* armed ... they all are ... but I know how not to get shot. I just knocked the gun out of his hand, and once ... once he was flat on his back I pinned him down. And ... umm ... we karate guys use more than just our hands, we use feet, hips, shoulders, every part of our body."

"Right. But if you touch the gun ... that's bad, isn't it? That's what they say in crime movies. Did the homeless guy escape?"

"I think so ... but *I* didn't ... and I never touched the gun."

Phillip listened to the conversation between Kid and David but was unable to take part. He was amazed at the matter-of-fact way in which his wife and his brother had discussed David's crime and his modus operandi. As if this was no more than an everyday occurrence, he thought. They are on the same wave length – they speak the same language. Kid never stopped surprising her husband.

It was David's voice which pulled Phillip out of his reverie. "They tried to shoot me in prison ... the authorities did. I was doing a lot of fighting then ... long time ago."

Kid shook her head in disbelief. "The authorities? In prison? I thought you were going to say the enemy ... during the war."

"They tried it too ... many times."

Time to change the subject, Phillip decided. "Another glass of wine, Kid? David, a beer?" It worked. Kid and David did not proceed with their war topic.

Later that night in Kid's and Phillip's room there were a few more issues concerning David to be discussed. "I've been thinking all evening Kid, what if tomorrow morning we find David's room empty ... not a trace of him ... never see him again. I mean, it's possible, he might just take off."

"I think you are just a tad paranoid, my darling. Why on earth should he ... without a word? But then of course, he can be unpredictable as we have found out today. I'm almost as bad as you."

Once they were cuddled up together in bed, Kid said, "Your brother is very good looking. Did you notice how the lady in the dining room shot him admiring glances? She kept coming back to our table and afterwards she whispered to the others behind the counter."

Phillip had not noticed. "Do *you* think he is good looking?" He asked cryptically.

"Well, yes ... nice blue eyes and he is fit and sexy looking." And after a second, "Don't worry, just an observation. David evidently does not know about these things."

"What things?"

"You know, flirting, seducing and that. I think he is a proper stick in the mud in that respect."

After this confounded and rather pointless conversation, they were both in fits of laughter.

David woke up well before sunrise - his internal clock was still tuned to prison schedule. He opened his eyes, took in his surroundings in a matter of seconds, then relaxed safely back into the softness and the warmth of the big double bed and reflected on his new life. He was looking forward to a good day. They were going to drive all the way to his brother's home, he would be seeing the garden Kid has described and her fruit trees in the back yard. Forgotten were the previous day's mishaps, just as he had suggested to Phillip they would be. It never occurred to David to run away. Why when everything worked like clockwork.

He got out of bed, pulled the curtains back. The sun was still a long way from rising but the horizon already showed a faint glow suggesting that the new day was on its way. David assumed his meditating position and faced east. He sat very still, his breathing slowed down and became even and rhythmical. He sat motionless for he did not know how long. This had been a part of his morning routine in prison, the other part - the physical part - he had to forego on this day. If he proceeded, he knew he would create havoc in the hotel room. Must check the time, he reminded himself and consulted the digital alarm clock on the bedside table. That's easy, you just read the figures - if need be aloud - then you know. He took a nice hot shower got dressed in the same jeans he wore the previous day; but he had one fresh shirt. Other than that and a pair of sneakers his bag contained only his karate gear and some papers. Then he walked confidently out into the corridor and down to the breakfast level. Phillip and Kid were not there so he sat down and asked for a cup of coffee and while waiting he watched the sun which was now in the process of rising.

It was about ten minutes later when Phillip went and knocked on his brother's door. He found it unlocked, he entered and found the room empty. David's bag lay conspicuously on the bed. "Kid, he is gone," he said back in his room.

"Nonsense, he is probably having breakfast. I go and check ... mother instinct you know." She gave Phillip a reassuring kiss and made her way downstairs.

David sat alone at one of the little square tables, a cup of coffee in front of him; he seemed to be deep in thought. He heard his name called from the direction of the elevator, turned around and smiled at Kid.

"Phillip said you were gone ... he meant you had run away," she said cheerfully as she sat down next to him. "Did you sleep well? And did you do your karate-thing – the one you told me you did first thing every morning? Did you order breakfast or just coffee?"

"No, yes ... I mean no." David shook his head helplessly then said, "Kid why do you ask so many questions in one breath? How does one answer ... I need some help here."

Kid felt ashamed for being so insensitive and thoughtless. "You inadvertently did the right thing, David. When someone shoots a dozen questions at you in one go, you tell them to slow down ... ask one at the time. Did you sleep well?"

"I did ... my first night in a nice big bed rather than in my bunk in the cell."

"The karate-thing?"

205

"No Kid, I need a little more space for that. One day I'll show you." The breakfast question had now become superfluous since, right then, they were joined by Phillip who naturally took charge.

The trio were on their way east, heading for Kid and Phillip's hometown of Knoxville. Kid sat behind the wheel, David in the front passenger seat. Phillip sat in the back watching his brother and trying to second-guess his impressions of a world and a life he had been shut away from for over five years.

David saw and absorbed everything around him, buildings, the countryside, traffic coming and going. All of it he observed seemingly without turning his head one way or the other. Fragments of last night's dinner conversation echoed in Phillip's mind, 'I know how not to get shot', that's what Dave said. What did he mean? How about ... let's say ... a sniper fifty or a hundred yards away. Can he see him too, just like he sees stuff which he is not even looking at? Does he have some sort of exceptional peripheral vision ... is this really part of karate? Phillip was rudely pulled out of his reflections when he heard a loud 'bang' directly behind him. He felt the vehicle starting to swerve from side to side.

Kid was driving in the right-hand lane on the highway approaching Nashville.

Everything happened very fast from then on.

David was out of his seatbelt in a flash, he leaned across

206

and held on to the steering wheel. "Break slowly, Kid," he cautioned. "Hold tight ... everyone. Now stand on the break hard ... good." The car came to a halt. "Keep steering Kid,... turn to your right. Phillip, we're going to push ... out of the line of traffic." David was in complete command. He and Phillip pushed the car to the side, traffic passed harmlessly on their left.

Now Kid got out on her side and walked around to see what had happened. "Oh, I shredded a tire," she exclaimed, but there was no shock or fear in her voice. "I know how to change the wheel," she said, then she turned to David and said approvingly, "that was good how you kept the vehicle on its wheels. I thought we were going to roll. You had more strength in your arms than I even though you had to lean across. That was lucky, eh?" And with these final words Kid opened the boot and went to work getting the tools out. David had trouble hiding a smile. Phillip stood two steps away, he was in complete shock ... he was speechless. Kid's last words thrown in casually and off-handedly still reverberated in his ears. Out loud he said, "Lucky you still had a little bit more strength in your arms than Kid, eh David ... the understatement of the century."

By then, Kid had already started to loosen the nuts, not an easy task for someone of her size and caliber; Kid was no more than five foot three.

Finally, Phillip sprang to live again, "Let me, darling,"

he said.

By that time David had taken the spare wheel out of the boot and placed it directly next to the rear wheel. "Maybe we won't need the jack. Just get all the nuts almost off ... yeah like this," he said. "I'll grab the bum end of the car and lift ... just high enough for you guys to take the old wheel off and slip the new one on."

"Good," Kid was enthusiastic, "I count one, two and on three you lift, OK?" She was too preoccupied to notice the brothers shooting glances at each other trying to keep straight faces. She counted and David, with the strength of an ox, lifted the bum end of Phillip's vehicle. Kid took the old wheel off, Phillip put the new one on then David slowly let the car down again. The whole operation had taken no more than a minute. Kid was jumping up and down with excitement.

Phillip shook his head, turned to David and said, "You are mad brother, but thanks."

"I keep driving darling, you are too nervous. I'll stop for coffee ... soon as I can," Kid was genuinely concerned about her husband's wellbeing.

This was the only unexpected incident on their trip home. They arrived at their house in Franklin Drive just before sundown.

XIII

The three McCabes settled in nicely. Kid called their set-up a 'ménage à trois', a description Phillip vehemently and determinedly rejected.

"Well, there are three of us living under the same roof," Kid argued her point.

"But your fancy expression implies details I'm not prepared to even consider."

Kid giggled merrily. "Tell me what those implications are, darling. You're the clever one here."

"It means that the three people all share sexual activities ... everyone with everyone. Do you still think your ménage à trois-thing is appropriate?"

"Oh dear no - not at all." Kid said putting on a stiff upper lip.

This was David's fourth day at his brother's house. Two of those days had been weekend-days, settling-in days, enjoyment days, but now a new week had started and David was ready to go out and find work. Then he was going to buy a car, find accommodation and become independent. It had taken David a little while to shed his inhibitions and to accept Kid and Phillip's genuine hospitality. David found himself in a new and different world; hospitality had never been an issue in his previous life. One unforeseen and unpleasant incident had however, taken place on Saturday evening. David had been deeply disturbed then, and the mere thought of it still hurt him now.

On Saturday afternoon, Phillip and his musical friends had had a rehearsal session in the music studio. They were preparing for a gig on Sunday night at a venue which had only recently opened. It had become routine that at the conclusion of their rehearsals the musicians would shift to the lounge room for a shared drink. This Saturday was no different. Nobody however, had expected Jim's unaccountable animosity and belligerence to be provoked so dramatically by Kid's introduction of David.

While the musicians were rehearsing, Kid and David were out in the garden. Kid never interrupted or disturbed their musical sessions. She and David checked the fruit trees she had planted the previous year, but this was still only the end of March, too early to see signs of shoots, too cold for her bulbs to show growth.

"Let's go inside," Kid suggested, "I'll get some nibbles

ready to serve with their drinks when they are ready. We can go and hear their performance tomorrow night. Would you like that?"

"Sounds great. May I ... help you in the kitchen Kid?"

And this was where the musicians got their first glimpse of David.

Kid had shown him how to make a nice display of cheese, tomatoes, olives, cucumber and other little goodies that she had chopped up, now she carried the plate and a bowl with biscuits into the lounge room. David turned to face the sink, bent down and washed his hands, then he followed Kid.

"This is my brother David," she announced to the room at large. Then she turned to David for the continuation of her introductions. Kid was determined to get this bit right. "David, this is Bob, the leader of the band, this is Joshua, Jim and Mario."

David said a collective 'hi'. Kid noticed that he took each man's measure carefully. He is making sure, she thought, that later he'll be able to pair names and faces correctly.

"What do you mean, *your* brother? Come on Kid, cut out the nonsense," Jim spat almost instantly.

"Yeah well ... OK you win, he is Phillip's brother, but that still makes him almost my brother, just look at us ..." She placed herself right next to David, on tiptoe; but even by doing so, her head never even reached as high as David's shoulder. It only took seconds before everyone roared with laughter ... everyone except Jim. He was in no mood for jokes. He didn't like Kid and now he didn't like David. He had never bothered to inquire into the reasons for his dislike. He was quite content with keeping his antagonism in place.

"So where do you live, David? You've never come to see you brother, at least not since I've known him. Or are you moving here, is that it? What do you do?"

David was standing in the back of the room. Now he considered what to do about so many questions, all fired at him by a guy who had already decided that he didn't like him. "You've got a lot of questions. Which one would you like me to answer?" he finally asked.

Kid was hard pressed not to show a smile on her face. Well done David, she thought with some satisfaction.

Jim shook his head in disgust, "Oh forget it," he said.

Mario took over. "Kid, the resemblance between you and David is awesome. You could easily pass as brother and sister ... slight difference in height maybe," he added with a smile in Phillip's direction.

Kid giggled happily.

But Jim was not through with questioning David. "Where do you live, David? If it's not asking too much."

"Umm ... I mean to stay here ... make a new start. I'll get a job ... set myself up."

"You just can't answer a question, can you. So, what do you do ... I mean for a living?"

It would be an easy thing to shut this guy up, David thought. What the hell is the matter with him? If he keeps this up ... but no, I'm not going to do anything to him, not in my brother's home ... not anywhere for that matter. Finally he settled for, "I've done different things ... for a living ... in the past. But it's better if I you don't know, so stop questioning me, OK?"

David stood tall, alert and centered. It was his usual stance, but to all the people in the room it looked very much like he was preparing for a fight.

David's last sentence really got Jim's heckles up. If he wants a fight, he thought confidently, he can have one. Jim jumped up from his seat, took a few steps and came to a halt dangerously close to David, his fists clenched, his chest stuck out - the position of the street-fighter. Jim was only a couple of inches shorter than David, he was slim and fit, he thought himself a match for anybody including David.

David did not move, his arms hung loosely by his side, his long fingers stretched, his shoulders down, chin slightly tucked in bringing his spine into a straight line right to the top of his head; his features were hard, his eyes fixed on something nobody saw.

Why was it that all Jim's friends who knew him to be a bit of a fighter, suddenly feared for his safety? Why was everyone scared of Phillip's brother, the good looking guy who could be Kid's brother, the guy with the soft voice - the guy they knew nothing about?

Phillip stood stock still, he turned pale. He too, was terrified but he was the only one who knew why.

Kid however, did not share the discomfort of the terror-loaded silence which predominated. David had promised never to fight again, she felt secure in the knowledge of his sincerity. She was watching with interest the show of two people face to face, like two roosters about to kill each other. Kid knew no fear ... none at all.

Nothing happened. One, then two minutes passed, David watched his tall, dark and handsome opponent very carefully, he didn't miss even the slightest twitch of a muscle. David knew exactly how he was going to handle this situation. He would duck out of the line of the man's punches when they came and then he would run ... run as fast as he could and as far as necessary. Jim would be completely stunned to see someone back out of a fight, David thought with some amusement, he would be too perplexed to run after me. No fight will ensue in my brother's house ... never again.

Kid was the first to sense that an unease, an insecurity was taking hold of Jim. And she was right.

Jim felt that something was in the air, a sphere of power seemed to surround this giant of a guy. What's going on here, he asked himself in alarm, as he was transfixed by David's dangerously piercing eyes. First he is too dumb to answer a simple question and now he holds a room full of people in check. Is he going to tear the whole house down? It was at that moment that his anger and his frustrations were replaced by fear. He shot a quick glance around the room and saw a copy of his own panic mirrored in everyone's face - everyone's except Kid's, of course. Kid has absolutely no concept of fear, he thought, but then she wouldn't, she is just plain mad.

Time I stopped this nonsense, Kid told herself. If Jim only knew how little chance he would have in a fight against David - David the professional karate fighter. Without further ado, she walked up to the two men, placed herself right between them facing Jim and pronounced, "Alright, that will do, go sit down," then turning to David she said, confidence written all over her face, "I know you would not fight, but do sit down now David ... this is a peaceful place."

"Sure Kid, and no ... I wasn't going to fight Jim." Then he looked at his brother and said in a very low voice, "Never again Phillip ... I've promised you."

A collective sigh of relief could be heard around the room. Everybody was expecting an explanation and an apology from Jim but none was forthcoming so they all pretended nothing had happened.

Jim sat back in his seat and looking at Kid's expression

of innocence made him want to scream. Kid had always irritated him, from the moment she appeared on the scene. He never wanted her to be Phillip's partner. Did Kid really think she had what it took to make Phillip change his ways? As long as anyone had known Phillip, he had always been a philanderer and he had never made much of a secret of it. And then, overnight, Phillip was to become monogamous, faithful and all that ... Kid must be mad to believe it. But deep inside, Jim knew he was wrong. Phillip and Kid's love was there for everyone to see ... at least for all those who enjoyed experiencing other people's happiness. His own marriage had been on the rocks for a long time and was now threatening to break down completely. Why should others have it so good? Kid comes from nowhere, she is neither beautiful nor sexy. Why does she make such an excellent partner for Phillip? It's just not fair, that's what. He envied her, and he envied Phillip. It hurt him to see them happy and carefree. Jim knew that it was his own attitude that blocked all avenues that could lead to a friendship between him and Kid, still he did nothing to remedy the situation.

After having re-established peace, Kid put her arms around her husband. She needed to feel his body against hers - the softness of his lips on hers. "Darling, I did the right thing, didn't I?"

"Yes Kid, but I know it should have been me ... I just didn't get my act together in time. Thanks Kid."

Later that evening while the three McCabes sat in their lounge room, harmlessly watching television, David suddenly said, "You know Phillip, I could have wiped out that guy Jim in about two seconds flat. I could see his street-fighter tactics written all over him ... they're so slow ... God it was tempting ..."

Kid and Phillip looked at each other in utter amazement. So he did consider doing one of his stints, it went through Phillip's head, the consequences don't bear thinking about. "What stopped you?"

"Umm ... this is a different world now ... no place for fighting ... I made a promise." And after a minute's consideration, "I'd like to find out about martial arts schools ... if I can enroll and become a member of a club ... it will give me access to a dojo ..."

It was now Monday morning, Phillip was ready for work, Kid was scheduled at Alfredo's for the afternoon shift in the shop. David had only just emerged from his room; he wore his only pair of jeans, no shirt and he was barefoot.

"Do you own any clothes at all, Dave? No good offering you the use of any of mine ... nothing would fit," Phillip said laughingly.

"I own two shirts, one pair of jeans, sneakers, that's it."

"Might be a good idea to buy some clothes before applying for jobs ... make a good impression and that."

"Nope, need a job first to get money for clothes."

Phillip smiled, "Bit of a catch twenty-two, eh?"

David did not understand the reference to the movie he had watched on television in prison, so he said nothing. That's when Phillip made his spontaneous decision.

"Kid and I will lend you some money," he said, then turned to Kid and took her hand in his for reassurance. "You buy some decent clothes and shoes, get a proper haircut and when you start earning money you pay us back ... interest free. You also need wheels ... can't get anything done without. You have your license don't you?"

"Maybe expired."

"OK then, that's the first thing." Phillip was filled with an unusual amount of organizational energy. "Get ready and I'll take you to the licensing office ... I'll be leaving in about three seconds."

David smiled, sprinted upstairs and came back down complete with shirt, shoes and probably socks.

Fixing David's driver's license proved to be no big deal. Phillip had considered for a minute what to do if his brother should have to fill out a form that he was unable to read. But his worries, fortunately, had been unfounded.

"My reading and writing skills aren't great ... but sufficient," David said, having read Phillip's thoughts. "Remember I told you I took classes in jail?"

"Good, I just pop into my office, then I take you back home ... Kid will take over. You'll be in good hands," he said with that sheepish grin David remembered from way back when Phillip was only a young teenager.

"David, look at this," Kid said as soon as David was back. "I've found this here martial arts school in Market Street, it says Karate underneath; and there is also the university martial arts department, and this ... but it says Judo club ... maybe no good, but let's get some clothes for you first."

It was only once they were in the men's clothing department of the shop that David said with a note of resignation in his voice, "Kid, I had better tell you first up ... I'm no good with colors. Will you choose them and please make them easy for me?"

"Are you color-blind? Oh well, no problem." How can I make colors easy for him, she puzzled. Best to just buy jeans or black slacks, anything goes with that. Wonder what would happen, she thought a little mischievously, if I bought him a pink shirt, some bright green pants, an orange jacket and purple shoes. Instead they went home with white and light blue button down shirts, a beige woolly sweater, a pair of black slacks, black leather shoes and a light brown leather jacket with a zipper. It didn't need much for David to look respectable, he had been a good looking man even in his prison outfit.

But now it was time for Kid to go to work, "I'll be finished at ... five thirty," she said uncertainly.

"I'll be fine Kid," he said and for no apparent reasons and for the very first time, he put his arms around her and drew her to him. Kid felt squashed inside David's big strong arms. She knew she would not be able to free herself if she so decided - David made her feel like a little garden gnome. But she soon realized that the hug must have been as unexpected to David as it had been to her.

He stepped back, looked confused and said, "Don't know what got into me. See you after work." It had been the first hug that *he* initiated. David could feel the touch of Kid's body against his for a long time after no matter how brief the hug had been.

David's decision on how to spend this day, or at least the hours of Kid's absence, was made the minute Kid told him about the martial arts school. Job searching had suddenly taken second priority. Kid had left the street map on the table, she had drawn a circle around the place of her house, he would figure out Market Street and how to get there. I take a bus or even walk all the way there. I'll take my karate gear with me, just in case they have a class that I can join. The prospect of being inside a dojo was so exhilarating, there was no holding him back now.

He approached the building in Market Street that Kid had indicated. There was a small sign pointing to the side entrance saying 'Martial Arts School' and it had the name G.J. Blythe underneath. David tried the door handle and found the door unlocked. He ducked his head and entered, then walked along a corridor which led to the basement. There were signs at every corner and every time he read one he silently thanked his teacher in the penitentiary who had spent so much time and patience helping him with his reading. It was, David guessed, about the middle of the afternoon. He noticed a number of rather rowdy youngsters running along the corridor laughing and jumping about, swinging their bags and throwing them through the air. David guessed they were karate students on their way to the dojo. "Is this the way to the karate school?" he asked one of the boys.

"Yeah, at the end there, to the left. You could have come in from the other side of the building. Are you joining our school?"

"I've come to see ... if I can become a member."

"You can talk to Robert, our instructor. He'll be here in a moment. Just follow us."

"Thanks," David said and smiled. He smiled because he was talking to karate students, because he was going to witness a karate class and because this was a world he understood - this was his world.

Robert was preoccupied with some paperwork when he heard a deep voice beside his little makeshift desk.

"Hi, I'm David. I'd like ... to become a member of this school."

"I'll be with you in a second," Robert said and finished ticking off the names of the students. Now he put his pen down. "Right. You want to enroll," he said, then turned his head and found himself looking at a giant of a man who stood perfectly straight as if concentrating in readiness to start a karate class. The man's face wore an expression of intent.

"Yes, that's what I meant."

What is it about this guy? Robert thought. He seems to fill the whole dojo with his presence. "You want to be a student? Join a class?" he asked a little uncertainly, then, "Have you done any karate before? Oh, by the way, I'm Robert."

David looked down at Robert who was in his karate gear, complete with Black Belt, ready to take his class. It was at moments like these that David wished he was some six inches shorter so he wouldn't have to look down on people - people he would prefer to look up to.

"Yes, I have."

It needed no more than David's three words to fill Robert with an unmistakable feeling of excitement. It's a bit like when you go fishing, he thought with some irony, you feel a little tug at your line and you know instinctively that you've got something big. Robert knew he was in the presence of a Sensei – a master.

"What grade?" was the only thing he managed to ask.

"Umm ... I have my Black Belt." David was well aware that this was an unusual answer but he had to tell the truth then brace himself for the consequences.

So that was it: a Black Belt who wants to enroll as a student and join a class - rather incongruous. Then he heard David's voice again.

"You are about to take this class, aren't you? Please ... I can wait. OK if I watch?"

Robert found himself involuntarily staring at David for what seemed a long time. "Do you have your gear with you? Like to join this class?" Then without waiting for David's answer he called to one of the students, "Ralph, would you show David to the changing room please?"

A few minutes later David bowed himself onto the dojo mats. The students were lined up from the highest grade to the lowest starting from the left as they were facing their instructor. David joined the line at the end, on the right. He then followed the teacher's instructions alongside all the others, and if he noticed some curious looks from some of his fellow students, he did not let on. David was perfectly happy to feel the mats under his bare feet and to inhale the atmosphere of the dojo; students could stare as much as they liked. At the conclusion of the class, the students were all made to lower themselves into a kneeling position, sitting on their heels and facing their master for a few minutes of absolute silence.

After he had bowed himself out, David thanked Robert for letting him take part in his class. It had been his first experience in a dojo for over five and a half years, but no one needed to know that.

"We have to discuss a few issues here, David," Robert said once they were both in their street clothes.

"Sure." David was floating on a cloud of happiness. His new life had truly begun now.

"What's the story? You're a Black Belt, you want to become a member and a student at our little school. Nobody knew we had another Black Belt in town."

"I'm new in town," David started slowly, carefully. He knew he could get this right, he was, after all, on his home turf, so to speak. "I got my Black Belt when I was about eighteen ... before I was drafted. The military offered me top training in Florida then in Okinawa ... then they sent me to Vietnam."

Robert listened and watched attentively, he already had a clear idea of the hidden implications in David's first statement. Karate as a weapon in man-to-man fighting in the jungles of Vietnam; he got the picture.

"That's about it. I never lost or forgot any of my karate skills but ... I was not so lucky with my everyday living skills. Do you need to know any more ... details, or can you accept what I said so far?"

Robert simply nodded. He took some time to formulate

a reply. "I can accept your story, David, but I'm not in charge of this school. I'm just one of the instructors. I got my Black Belt six months ago. OK, let me tell you about this institution: it was founded by Mr George J. Blythe about thirty years ago and he's been running it sort of single-handedly from the very start. Mr Blythe himself was only ever marginally involved in martial arts but it had always been his wish and his dream to get young people involved in the art of karate. He is now in his seventies and he is still the boss, he has the last word - he hires and fires, if you know what I mean. Oh, he is a nice old bloke. I, for one, get on well with him. Now your case, I'm sure you understand, is a little out of the ordinary, right?"

David shrugged but said nothing.

"I'll tell you now what *I* would do if I was the boss ... then I go and tell the old man and try to persuade him to agree. We'll enroll you alright, but not as a student, we'll employ you as an instructor. This is only a small set-up as you can see. We will probably never again get the chance of acquiring a master of your caliber."

"Why do you say that? You hardly know me ... I haven't proved myself yet."

"I've watched you ... I just know. I sensed everything I need to know. OK now, do you have a job? A place to live? How much time can you spare? How many classes can you take in a row? Do you teach beginners, children, anyone?"

David started to laugh. He hadn't meant to, but Robert was even worse than Kid in the way he rattled off questions. "Could you take it a little slower? One question at the time?"

Robert stopped to think for a second. David did say something about having lost his everyday living skills, he remembered, could this be part of it? "OK, job?"

"Not yet."

"Place to stay?"

"I'm staying with my brother and sister-in-law at the moment."

"So you have plenty of time." A flat statement. "How do you feel about teaching?"

"I'd love to, beginners, kids, advanced students, big or small classes ... I take anybody."

"Good ... now money. If we can give you sufficient classes to make a decent income, would you be prepared to take it as a full-time job?"

David gave that some thought. "I never meant to make money from martial arts - not after Vietnam - but this sounds tempting. Yeah, I'd accept."

"I'll talk to the boss, let you know tomorrow or the day after. Don't worry, I already know he will just love my suggestion. So there ... guaranteed full-time employment. By the way, I can tell you right now that once you start teaching here, the university martial arts department will soon know and they'll want to kidnap you in a hurry. You'll have to find out how many classes you can fit into twenty-four hours, eh?"

When it came to exchange phone numbers, David had to admit that he did not know his brother's by heart. He was no good at memorizing figures ... one of those things.

One more of those things, Robert thought. He gave him his own number instead. The main thing was that he had secured a top instructor for Mr Blythe's school.

XIV

That night as the little McCabe family sat around the dinner table David announced, "I got a job ... probably full-time."

Kid's fork clattered down on her dinner plate, "Tell us all," she exclaimed glowing with excitement. Phillip simply raised an eyebrow and waited.

David explained, at his own pace, what had taken place that afternoon and finished with, "Robert said not to worry, and that his boss would agree with his suggestion. I have to contact him ... this is his number." And with that he fished Robert's calling card from his pocket and handed it to Kid and Phillip.

"Robert Connor," Kid read, "Architect and then heaps of letters that I don't understand, must be his titles. Is he a nice guy, David?"

"Yeah, real nice ... I can soon start to pay your money back."

"Did you ... umm ... did you tell Robert about your past and that? You know ... your recent past?" Phillip asked carefully.

"No, nobody needs to know."

If Phillip and Kid were unconvinced, they made no show of it. The subject was dropped and dinner continued.

The revelation of David miraculously securing a job was followed later on by an in-depth discussion between Kid and Phillip. The statement of 'nobody needs to know' just didn't sit well with Phillip. Did this ignorant but well-intended brother of his realize that his criminal record could not be discarded quite so easily, he wondered? To Kid he said, "People will want to know about his past, where he came from, what he did and all. His criminal record will be dogging him for the rest of his life, you realize that Kid, don't you."

"But if he never offends again, never goes back to jail ... well, his bad past doesn't really matter then, does it?. I mean, we don't build our lives on the mistakes we've made, do we?"

Phillip turned sideways in bed and put his arms around his wife. "I should have known you'd see it from the positive side only, darling. Sure, you and I and most other people have also made mistakes, only ours have not landed us in court rooms and prison cells. I know it's not fair but the fact remains that David has to live with a written record of his mistakes. If he wants a loan from a bank, insurance for a car or a house, a job in some big company maybe, or even a visa to go to some foreign country, his record will be checked and pronto ... he's in the shit."

"So he'll have to tell this man Robert that he was in jail, how many times, why and how long for, the whole damn caboodle. And Robert will tell his boss and David's job is down the gurgler."

"Maybe not Kid. You see, what karate is concerned, David is obviously in a class of his own. If the school wants him badly enough and if on top of it, he proves to be a decent guy, then his record won't stop them."

"Darling, there is something else I've had on my mind concerning our brother. Remember those trauma symptoms I found in the book? Do you think David is suffering from some or all of them?"

"I'm no psychologist Kid, all I know is that he is a slow talker, right? His thinking and talking mechanisms must have been damaged somewhere along the line, but then - you have noticed this too - he has become a very good listener ... by default. He needs to really concentrate on what is being said so as to be able to give the correct answers."

"Can't cope with more than one question at the time though."

"Yeah, but there is nothing really wrong with that. He seems to have recovered from his trauma ... he's shown no signs of violence right? He has been an easy and trouble free house-guest."

"Do you know, yesterday when he saw the flowers on the dining table, he looked at them in some sort of amazement, and when I told him that you had bought them for me - like to say that you loved me - he was completely thrown ... couldn't understand. 'Phillip gave you flowers?' he said 'to tell you that he loved you?' David must have forgotten all the niceties of ordinary people's lives."

Phillip shook his head in the dark for all this gesture was worth, "I'm sure he can learn again Kid. I'm glad there have not been any unmanageable situations."

"... and there won't be any darling, David is OK."

But they were wrong.

Phillip heard it first. He could not quite make out what it was: heavy breathing like somebody running long distance, then a bang against the wall. Phillip was wide awake within a fraction of a second. He pushed himself out from under the covers, sat bolt upright and listened.

Then came the voice, David's voice, in absolute terror, 'no, no' and 'run, for God's sake, run'.

Phillip woke his wife who was curled up beside him. There was no time to be gentle, "Kid, wake up quick, listen, David is in trouble." Phillip held Kid by the shoulders and spoke very close to her face.

Kid was in a sitting position in a flash, "I can hear him.

What do we do?"

They put their bathrobes on, "I go, Kid. I just have to shake him out of it, wake him up and he'll go back to sleep." Phillip sounded very competent. Kid wondered why.

Phillip went across to the other room, opened the door and walked right in. In the pale ray of light which came through the half open door from the hallway, he could see his brother thrashing about in his bed. He was screaming and lashing out in all directions. David had thrown all his covers off the bed, his naked body was glistening with sweat, tears were streaming down his face – Phillip saw an expression of absolute terror and it frightened him.

Phillip took hold of David's shoulders and shook him, "Wake up, Dave. Come on, wake up," he said urgently. Just as David calmed down somewhat, Phillip felt Kid's hands deftly slipping a damp wash cloth and a towel onto the bed. Then she disappeared back out of the room as quietly as she had entered.

Phillip sat down on the side of Dave's bed and started to wipe his brother's face, neck and chest. David was breathing heavily as though he had just run a marathon - or maybe gone through a fight of life and death. It was obvious that he did not know where he was, and that whatever he had been fighting was still threatening him.

"OK now Dave, calm down. Everything is alright," Phillip was not quite sure about the sort of things one had to say to get someone out of a nightmare. What is a nightmare in the first place? Just a dream, only rather unpleasant? Phillip realized just how ill-equipped he was to deal with the job he was confronted with. Not so competent after all. I need to make him feel safe ... get him to see where he is and who I am, Phillip thought feeling quite helpless and perfectly useless. He was also close to tears. He wished Kid were near to help him be strong; Kid was by far the tougher of the two.

David finally calmed down, opened his eyes and recognized his brother. He assured him that he was awake and back with the living. Phillip sat on the bedside, both hands still on David's shoulders. A minute later he wiped his brother's face again, brushed the sticky hair out of his eyes, then he toweled his neck and chest before pulling the covers back up.

David lay quite still now, his eyes closed. He was exhausted. Phillip held his wrist and felt David's pulse. It was racing. They remained in silence for a while.

"Thanks Phillip ... thanks for being here. Sorry I woke you up, it's ... I'm OK now."

"David ... what happens when you have that nightmare?" Phillip had not meant to ask this question, it just slipped out.

David rolled his head from side to side on the pillow. "You don't want to know. It's horrible…"

"But is it the same thing every time, or ... or what?"

"Phillip," David said as he pushed himself up into a semi-sitting position, "I have never told anybody ... I don't know if I can. It's the last thing I experienced in Vietnam ... or at least it's the last thing I know. After that ... I think they shipped me home. I was of no more use to them then ..."

"'Them' being the US military?"

David kind of nodded. "There was a mistake, I think ... the bombs were dropped in the wrong place ... I think they were ... maybe I'm wrong."

David was talking to himself now, trying to get some order into the chaos in his head. The horror he saw was the same, every time all through the years. It never changed never diminished. Fear and panic were perpetuated in these gruesome images he saw and lived through again and again. "Maybe it did not matter to them where the bombs fell ... there was fire everywhere ... napalm, the whole village in flames ... everybody ... oh shit ..." tears ran down David's cheeks, he sniffed, wiped his face with the towel then carried on with his garbled account. "All my mates ... we were not even told ... the bombs just rained down on us ... killed every one of us ... at least I think they did ... never saw anybody again ..." At this point, David was sobbing bitterly, covering his face with his hands, his whole body shaking.

Phillip wished he had not asked the question which was now causing such misery. What did Dave mean by 'every one of us'? Why then was *he* here and no burns or scars on him? Before he knew it, Phillip found that he had asked yet another question. "Where were *you* then? … not with your mates?"

David was going to tell all he knew, whether Phillip asked questions or not. In fact it didn't even matter to him now what Phillip wanted to hear. He shook his head, opened his eyes and started to talk staring at the ceiling. "In a ditch … in the mud ... don't know how I got there … buried in the shit up to my neck. I couldn't see anything … pitch dark. Maybe my eyesight was gone, my voice, my mind ... nothing worked. Nobody around ... I ran, I screamed … I think I did. I told everybody to run … maybe I did nothing at all. Everything was on fire, just flames … and later embers ... then silence. Then I wake up."

Phillip now tenderly bent over his brother, put his arms awkwardly around his neck and shoulders and rested his head on David's chest. A little later he felt the touch of David's arms tentatively around his waist. Both brothers were now crying.

XV

It was mid-morning on a Friday, the time Kid reserved for cleaning and tidying up her house. She had already done the washing and had just finished scrubbing the kitchen floor and the bathroom tiles. She liked everything to be shipshape when her husband came home. Phillip was and had been since the day they met, the most important person in her life. She loved him unconditionally and would do so to the end of her life.

Spring was now in full swing, the front garden was filled with colorful flowers which Kid tended carefully and spoke to frequently. It was her firm belief that all plants - trees, flowers and vegetables alike - absorbed spoken words and responded to them in the same way cats and dogs respond to tender loving care given them by their master.

David was no longer living with them now, he had found accommodation for himself in very much the same fashion he had secured a job. He and Robert had become friends almost from the start of David's employment. Robert had finally decided to buy the house he had had his eyes on for some time and had spontaneously asked David to be his house mate. It was a beautiful old house built in the colonial style with spacious rooms and wide verandas on two levels, and the kitchen, Kid had decided at first sight, was big enough to play football in. The house had not been lived in for some time and looked quite dilapidated. It needed a new roof and new foundations, Robert suspected white ants in the woodwork, the plumbing and electrical wiring needed to be replaced, walls taken out, staircases to be renewed. Robert and David had come to an agreement right at the start: Robert would make all the plans for the renovations, David was to be the builder-in-charge and consequently live rent-free.

The morning David surprised her with his news was still vivid in Kid's mind as she whizzed around her house with the vacuum cleaner that morning. Genuine happiness had emanated from David, he had scooped her up in his arms and lifted her high up in the air - his way of showing his affection. "I'll miss you, Kid," he had blurted, "but I won't be very far away ... we can always keep in touch."

It had been quite a struggle for Kid to get out of her brother's embrace, and once she stood on her own feet again she could finally back out of his attempted kiss; kisses were

237

strictly reserved for Phillip, no matter how fond she was of her brother.

"I meant no harm Kid," David said innocently, "just wanted to kiss you because I'm so happy ... because you have been so good to me ... just like Phillip kisses you when he is happy."

"David," she had admonished, "kisses are for husband and wife only, not for brother and sister. You have to remember that." She had felt like a school teacher indoctrinating her children with the rules of socially acceptable behavior. She had despised herself but had seen no alternative. David just did not know the stuff everyone else knew, so he had to be told. When she got to this point in her replay of that day, the phone rang.

"Kid," she heard an unfamiliar voice, "I'm Timothy, I work with Phillip. He asked me to call you ... it's to do with his brother ... and you shouldn't panic, he said."

"Right, I'm sitting down, please continue ... and by the way, he is my brother, too," she said.

"I see," he said but didn't see at all. "David jumped into the river to save a small child who had fallen in while chasing a ball or something. Phillip has been dispatched to report on the incident which is why I'm calling you. David and the child will be taken to St. Mary's hospital. Phillip would like you to go there, make sure David is alright ... take some dry clothes for him. Could you do that?"

"Yup, no problem," she said confidently. "Is the child OK?"

"Apparently, yes. Thanks Kid ... have to go."

Kid dropped everything she was doing, grabbed her backpack and her car keys and drove straight to Robert's office. "Sorry to barge in on you Robert," she blurted breathlessly, "David jumped into the river, I need to get him some dry clothes, please can I have the house key. I promise to bring it back." It all came out in one single breath.

Robert placed the keys into her hand. "Is he OK?"

"I ... I think so. Thanks," and she was out the door in a flash.

Kid approached the reception desk at St. Mary's hospital. "I need to see David - David McCabe. He was brought in by ambulance ... a few minutes ago," she improvised. "He is my brother."

Somebody took over. "I know who you mean. Follow me." The nurse led Kid along a corridor that smelled of window cleaner, Kid decided. Nurse opened a door to the left and motioned Kid to go in. The scene which presented itself to Kid then hit her like a punch in the stomach. David lay on a hospital bed, his eyes were closed, the lower part of his body was covered by a white sheet, a pair of thin plastic tubes were connected to his nose. Kid saw a screen which displayed a multitude of skinny lines following each other in quick succession along peaks and troughs - she understood none of it.

She now turned to the nurse; all the color had drained from her face. She stood stock still, she was speechless. "He looks ... dead. Is he, nurse?" she finally asked in a trembling voice.

"What are you saying? He isn't dead ... at all. David," she called out, "your sister is here with some dry clothes."

David opened his eyes and turned his head, "Thanks Kid," he said in his usual voice.

Kid almost melted on the spot with relief then took the few steps to his bed. Someone had toweled his hair and brushed it out of his face.

"That was clever of you to save the little child." She said with studied off-handedness. She was not going to let on that she had been devastated at the thought of his demise a minute ago.

"Swimming is one of the things I *can* do Kid."

"Uh-huh," she consented, "I brought some dry clothes for you. I wait outside." Then she felt bad about being so un-sisterly, she bent down and lightly stroked his forehead. "Glad you are alive David," she said, then she turned and followed the nurse back to the front desk and the waiting area.

As she settled down with a book to wait, she noticed a well dressed gentlemen - gray suit and tie - at the front desk. He was gesticulating animatedly trying to get a point across. Kid started to do some conscious eavesdropping.

"I've just seen my daughter, she is fine," she heard and then something she could not make out. The following words however, she understood perfectly, "The man who saved her ... is he OK?" Now Kid was in the picture. She jumped up from her seat, crossed the hall and came to a halt next to the gentleman who seemed to be close to a nervous breakdown. "Sir," she said, "the man who saved your daughter will be fine ... I've just seen him. His name is David McCabe, he is my brother. ... I'm Kid McCabe."

The man looked at Kid and exhaled with relief. "I'm so glad to hear it, thanks. My name is Joseph Goldberg. I am the father of the child whose life your brother saved," and turning back to the desk, he asked, "Please, may I see Mr McCabe?"

"He'll be here shortly sir. Would you like to wait?"

Kid and Mr Goldberg sat down side by side in the waiting room. Kid was fidgety and nervous but too proud to show her lack of control openly. Instead she did what she always did at moments of nervousness, she talked and talked.

"My brother, you know, he is a real good swimmer, he is unafraid ... he is very strong at six foot eleven ... almost ... and my husband is reporting on the incident .. he writes for the Telegraph, you see. I know that David jumped right down into the river from the terrace of that restaurant ... do you know the one I mean? Maybe it will all be on television today. Sorry sir, I tend to talk too much when I'm nervous." At this point she had to take a breath.

Mr Goldberg's expression, luckily, showed no signs of annoyance or impatience and that gave Kid green light to carry on. "How old is your little girl, and what's her name? She must have been playing or something in the park right there on the riverbank."

Mr Goldberg smiled now, "My daughter's name is Sarah and she is four and a half years old. She goes to pre-school and ... yes I believe the teacher sometimes takes them to the park, but I don't know how the accident happened. We will doubtlessly read your husband's article in the paper tomorrow."

Kid beamed, she was so proud of her husband's cleverness. At that moment, the glass sliding doors opened and David walked through, a doctor by his side. They exchanged a few words, shook hands, then the doctor disappeared back into the corridor. "That's him," Kid said unnecessarily then she and Mr Goldberg got up from their seats. "You look pale David, do you want to sit down for a while?" She took hold of his upper arm and tried to steer this giant of a man to the seat she had just vacated.

"Don't worry Kid, I'm not about to collapse."

Kid ignored that. "David, this is Mr Goldberg. He came to see you."

He sure is a big man alright, Mr Goldberg mused, but

not six eleven, no way. With some amusement he noticed the strong physical resemblance between David and Kid. How amazing, he thought, since the two are obviously not sister and brother ... maybe in-laws. It hadn't taken Mr Goldberg much to figure that out.

"I'm the father of the little girl whose life you saved. I've come to thank you, Mr McCabe ... I'm so grateful for what you have done for me and my family ... I hardly know how to express my gratitude."

"Is your little girl alright, sir?" was all David said.

"Yes she is, and thanks again. Umm ... before you go, there is something I would like to say: If ever there is anything I can help you with Mr McCabe ... please don't hesitate to call me ... call me anytime ... I mean it. Here is my card."

David was not quite sure what to make of this. He would need to read the calling card he now held in his hand and that would take some studying. "Yes sir," he said awkwardly, "and thanks."

On the drive back to Robert's office Kid addressed David, a note of genuine concern in her voice. "Are you fit enough to teach this afternoon, David? I think you might need some rest, you look all gaunt and pale."

David shook his head and laughed, "Come on Kid, stop worrying about me. Can't remember the last time anyone worried about my health."

Kid felt tears stinging behind her eyes but bravely blinked them back. "Things are different now, alright? So stop comparing with ... with your bad times, will you? Phillip is writing about your rescue mission in his paper. Why don't you come for dinner tonight."

"Thanks Kid, I'd like that. I finish at ... eight. I'm learning, eh?"

XVI

"Kid I'm starving. When is this brother of ours coming?"

"Darling, he works until eight, then he needs to shower and make himself presentable. He'll be here shortly. Most days he doesn't finish until ten at night, you know."

In other words, Phillip assumed, we're lucky to be able to have dinner at eight thirty rather than towards midnight.

Kid was in the kitchen, occupying herself with dinner. She had already announced to Phillip that there was going to be a surprise but kept details to herself.

. "David's rescue today, that was a noble act, wasn't it?" Kid called across to the lounge room and over the volume of the television.

"Very ... it was also brave ... *and* it was successful. They just got him into the ambulance as I arrived on the scene, so we didn't get to talk. I was told that he collapsed after he dragged the girl out of the water. He apparently gave her expert mouth-to-mouth resuscitation - one more thing they taught him in the military, I guess."

"This act of bravery ... this will surely cancel out his bad record, right? So he need no longer worry on that score," Kid said with finality.

My wife, the inveterate optimist, Phillip thought, but refrained from telling her how wrong she was. The next thing he heard was, "He likes doing house work - David, I mean - or he *would* like it if he could remember. Maybe he knew at some stage in his life ... before everything went belly-up. He kept watching me perform my housewifely duties while he was here. He sure makes a big effort to learn." There she took a breath, "Why don't you answer my questions?"

"What questions? You haven't asked any yet," Phillip said his voice deadpan. He turned the TV off, expecting that this opening could well develop into an interesting conversation.

"Uh-huh," Kid said. "Did you know," she now changed tack, "that the name of a three-stringed harp in Afghanistan is rhubarb?"

Phillip was prepared for almost anything but that. He did not reply.

"Just thought I mention it," he heard Kid's comment casually thrown in, and a minute later, "You see, if he keeps that up then mine will become unnecessary."

"Which one of yours?" Phillip asked, by now having trouble keeping a straight face.

"What's this? You make no sense Phillip, none at all."

"Sorry."

Silence for a minute. My turn, Phillip decided, to keep the nonsensical conversation afloat. "Did you know that there was a farmer somewhere in the mid-west who started to breed chickens with four legs so the consumer could have four drumsticks per bird?"

"Remarkable," Kid said uncertainly.

"It's true. So why don't we start breeding four-legged chickens in our back yard and you could go every night, just before their bedtime, and play them a lullaby on the rhubarb."

After this punch line, Kid and Phillip were in peals of laughter and that was how David found them on his arrival for dinner. He watched them for a minute then joined in to their laughter not having any idea of the nature of their joke.

"Come in and sit down David," Phillip said once he was able to speak again. "We'll tell you later about our home-spun joke. You're wearing your Sunday best ... getting good at your color scheme, eh?"

"Nope, I'll never be good at colors. Your wife chose these clothes for me ... if the colors are good, congratulate her not me. Hi Kid," he now called in the direction of the kitchen.

"Hi David, you can't come into the kitchen because

I'm doing a surprise."

David shot a glance at Phillip but when he got no help from there he said uncertainly, "It smells real nice."

"Yes, but that's not it. Can't you tell the difference between a chicken dish and a surprise?"

"Sorry."

"Come in and lets sit down in the lounge since we're not allowed in the kitchen. By the way ... congratulations on your incredible rescue of the little girl this morning."

"Oh, cut it out, Phillip. Hey, look I've got this card from the father of the girl. It says 'finance-something-or-other'. Is he a banker you think? He said that if I ever needed help I should go and ask him. He must have meant money, right?"

"Looks like it. Well, you never know ... maybe one day you get into a tight spot ... it's nice to know that someone means to help, eh?"

"Dinner is ready," they heard from the kitchen. The table was already nicely set for three people. A bottle of wine as yet unopened stood by the side of Phillip's place. They all sat down to eat. David asked for a glass of water. "You don't drink any alcohol at all?"

"No, not really, never have. Slows me down ... interferes with my concentration ..."

Phillip couldn't stop himself from pursuing this a little further. "Say ... if you had one can of beer before teaching a class, the students would find your movements too slow or not accurate, that sort of thing?"

"No, the students wouldn't notice anything at all ... but *I* would know."

"In other words, you would still be 'out-karateing' everybody else even with some alcohol in your bloodstream ... or in your head or wherever?"

"Sure." An unalterable fact. David did not see that his statement could be misconstrued and consequently interpreted as sheer arrogance on his part.

But both Kid and Phillip saw it. He could get himself into no end of trouble with stuff like that, it crossed Phillip's mind, but all he said was, "I know that you did not mean to show off David, but you have to be careful with pronouncements like this."

David gave this some thought. "It's true though," he insisted. He had not understood Phillip's warning. Instead he now launched into a story concerning one of his karate achievements of a long time ago.

"You know, at one time - I was in California then - some guys from the karate club I was a member of, got me to take part in a tournament - a sort of competition. They told me there was a lot of money in that. I never wanted to make capital out of martial arts but I needed money right then. The bastards ... didn't tell me ... you didn't make money by participating, only if you won the whole damn thing ...

249

then you made money, and there were Black Belts from all around the country. I had only just gotten out of prison then and ... anyway I don't know much about money or about tournaments for that matter."

Kid and Phillip got the picture of the situation without having to confer. Some guys were having fun with David, they realized his shortcomings and were wanting to make him the laughingstock among club members and karate fighters countrywide.

"What happened David?" Kid asked a straight forward question but refrained from mentioning that she knew about the newspaper article Poppa had seen and read out to Phillip.

"Well, I went ... first to San Francisco ... was refused because I wasn't registered with some organization. The guys had known all along ... just wanted a laugh. But by then I was determined: I was going, and I was going to win." David gave a deprecating shrug of the shoulders but he smiled. "Once registered I went all around the country, to Boston - coldest place in the world - then New York, Philadelphia, Baltimore and other cities ... last one was Washington - beautiful place, I still remember. There were karate fighters from all over the world ... Europe, Japan ... everywhere."

"Tell us about the tournaments."

David chuckled as he thought back to that time. "I won

them all ... everywhere ... enjoyed every minute of it ... made loads of money. ..."

"You must be joking. What did you do with all that money?"

"Yeah well ... I lost it all ... doesn't matter now. I was stupid ... they all knew I was an idiot ... used me and took my money."

"How? Where?" Kid exclaimed, she was outraged by the injustice inflicted on her brother.

"Las Vegas ... have you been there Kid? Full of gambling places ... some guys make lots of money there, I lost all mine. I didn't know how to do it ... guys borrowed my money, telling me they would double it for me ... then I never saw them again."

An uncomfortable silence hung over the three McCabes. "Come on, doesn't matter now ... it's all in the past," David said and smiled. "Lots of people, when they win money ... they get attacked and robbed ... I never got attacked ... just cheated and laughed at."

David had just admitted that it was due to his own inadequacies that he was robbed, cheated and made fun of. He was fully aware of his predicament yet he kept his optimism; he never gave up wanting to become an ordinary guy. How amazing, Phillip reflected. The essence of David's story however, is that my brother is the unchallenged master in one field, and is on the next to bottom rung of the social ladder in most others. Phillip knew it sometimes happened that people who distinguished themselves in one field, very often missed out on an over-all well balanced character. He now remembered a mate of his at university who fitted into just that category. The guy had an almost computer-like memory for languages, quite exceptional, yet in everyday life the guy was an absolute nutcase. But with David it's different, isn't it? David would probably have been an ordinary guy had it not been for some man-made fuck-up he was made to take part in against his own better judgment. And like by some miracle, he now found himself with his prodigious talent in martial arts still intact, yet with only a limited range of everyday skills - a sad situation. At that point Phillip was rudely pulled out of his reverie.

"Ready for my surprise everybody?" he heard Kid's voice like from far away. "I don't need any help ... I've got it all under control."

Kid's big surprise was in fact no more than an apple crumble for dessert but she had added some extra spices, some cinnamon and star anise and she was mighty proud of her achievement. At the very beginning of their marriage Kid had announced that she never made desserts, ergo this one went under 'surprise'.

"Tell us about your job as an instructor, David. Do you find it difficult to take new classes ... people you don't know ... different grades and that?" Phillip was genuinely interested in that subject, it was not just a maneuver to re-establish a pleasant atmosphere after the previous sad story.

"I like teaching karate ... it's the only thing I know how to do, don't forget. I really love children's classes ... I get on well with kids ... always have."

"You tell us that you love children ... didn't you ever want to have children of your own, David?" Kid asked innocently, but she soon realized that it had been entirely the wrong thing to ask.

David jumped up from his seat as if pulled by elastic bands. He turned to face Kid, his eyes flashing. "Of course I did but ... my whole life got fucked-up ... for God's sake ... and you know it," he spat at her viciously.

Kid was having none of this. She was on her feet facing David, defiance written all over her face. "Don't you talk to me like this ... or I'll throw you out of our house ... and I mean by force, hear me?"

Phillip had been watching this unreal scene unfold before his eyes, first with amazement, then with mounting annoyance culminating in absolute horror. Was David once again going to destroy a lounge room like he did years ago? Was it going to be *his* lounge room - *his* whole house - this time? And what was Kid talking about? How was his skinny little wife planning on tackling this giant - this world class fighter - and single-handedly remove him from the house? Phillip's mind boggled. And now, for the second time in his marriage - the second time since his visit to aunt Mavis - Phillip gathered more courage than he knew he possessed. He got up, ready to put an end to this quarrel, when to his surprise, he saw David take two steps back and look straight at Kid. Phillip was sure he saw traces of fear in his brother's eyes. What's happening here, he asked himself, and he could hardly believe his ears when he heard David's words.

"No Kid ... please, please don't ... don't attack me ... I couldn't handle that ... can't fight you ..."

What can I say now, Phillip thought, will I ever understand anything about this guy who is my brother? Then he remembered the conversation he and Kid had had some time ago – the conversation about David's possible sexual handicap. So Kid should have known not to ask that question, Phillip thought a little helplessly. Admittedly, it was a rather inconclusive discussion but still ... Kid obviously never believed that David could be either sterile or possibly impotent. Phillip however, was now wondering about the latter. He felt an urge to find out once and for good but couldn't really see how to go about it.

When he reached this point in his introspection, Kid had seemingly decided that she had overreacted. He heard her say rather pompously, "It's OK David ... don't be afraid ... friends again."

Phillip was completely baffled, he had no words to

express the incongruity of the situation, so he went and wrapped Kid in his arms instead and gave her a long, warm kiss. He was unaware of the fact that David watched this intimacy with interest. He too, wanted to kiss Kid, but so far he had failed.

The dinner finished in perfect harmony, the incident was not mentioned again. David didn't stay very late, he always started his days before dawn in the dojo.

Much later that night when Kid and Phillip were comfortably cuddled up in their bed, Phillip said with studied casualness, "How could I have gotten so scared when I have my wife by my side to deal with trivial little hiccups like a murderous brother who is about to destroy our home and possibly kill us both?"

Kid giggled merrily and said. "But David was afraid alright, you saw it."

XVII

It wasn't long after David's heroic rescue mission and the subsequent near drama over dinner at the McCabe's home, that Kid found herself in hospital once again. But this time it was not a car accident which put her there.

Kid and Father had been working in tandem at the homeless shelters all through the cold winter months. It was now the end of May, and although the days were longer and warmer, the homeless people still needed to be fed and looked after. Father and his Church had recently opened a place for homeless women with children and Kid, along with two other volunteers, was now partly in charge there.

Phillip was away on a two-day reporting trip which meant that Kid could stay later at the shelter. It was already dark by the time she left. She slipped her backpack over her shoulders and walked two blocks, then turned left into the parking lot where she had left her car. She saw the three men coming her way, she even thought she vaguely recognized them from one of the shelters. She paid no heed and continued confidently on her way. But she was not to reach her car that night. As she drew level with the three men, they stopped and asked her for money, only a small amount, enough for a cup of coffee. Kid slipped off her backpack, opened the zipper and took out her purse. Right then two hands snatched the purse while two more hands pulled at her backpack. Kid struggled and desperately tried to hold on, then she felt a jerk at her upper arm and a vicious blow to her back. She fell to the ground but was still conscious when the first kick landed in her ribcage, then came the second kick and her head hit the pavement with such force that she passed out almost immediately. She didn't know that the men took her purse and ran away, and nobody noticed a fourth man who had materialized seemingly from nowhere, seen the backpack lying abandoned in the street, picked it up and ran in the opposite direction. By then, there were only a few books, a newspaper and a handkerchief inside, but the backpack itself, the man calculated, could fetch some money if he was clever.

Somebody must have called the police and the ambulance, because when Kid opened her eyes, she found herself surrounded by men and women clad in white. She felt two plastic tubes stuck to her nose. Everybody talked nicely to her and seemed to be concerned about her wellbeing.

"What's your name?" Kid heard a voice from far away.

"Kid ... Kid McCabe."

"Can you tell us what happened?" It was a kindly police lady who spoke to her.

Kid thought for a minute then, "Three men ... they wanted some money ... I think they took my purse ... I fell and hit my head. It's nothing ... I'll be fine."

"Can you describe the men?"

Kid could have described them but she didn't want to. She knew they were poor and homeless, she didn't want them arrested and prosecuted, so she lied, "No ... it was too dark to see."

"How can we contact your family, Kid?" the nurse asked in a gentle voice.

Not knowing where to contact Phillip right then she gave David's phone number and simply said, "My brother." Then she asked for Father to be contacted. "Please, I would like to see him," she said and recited that phone number too.

The police officers were asked to leave the room, Kid felt sore and ashamed and unhappy and very disappointed. Is that what I get for helping the homeless, she thought miserably? Why did they hurt me when I was trying to give them the money they asked for? Since she had no answers ready, she closed her eyes and conjured up her favorite picture of Phillip and waited.

She heard the small click as the door opened, then Father entered the room quietly and came to a halt beside her bed. He looked down at her battered face. "The doctor told me what happened, Kid. How are you feeling?"

"It's not so bad Father, I'll be out of here in a tick." She reached out and touched Father's hand, "Father, please sit down here on the bed, I need to tell you something - and this is for your ears only."

Father braced himself for something hilarious, he knew how unpredictable Kid could be. He sat down as he was asked and bent his head close to hers so she could whisper whatever secret she had in store for him.

"Father, I've lied to the police. I said it was too dark to see the attackers but I think I know who they were ... homeless guys ... seen them at the shelter ... but I don't want them to be arrested. Is this a big sin, or just an averagely big one, you know, a well-meant one? Do you reckon God will consider forgiving me? Please Father, you can talk to him ... tell him that I'm sorry for lying but get him to understand that it was a necessary lie."

'An averagely big sin', Father repeated in his mind, now she asks me to make a phone call to God on her behalf ... what next? But since her question was sincere and his answer important to her, he said, "I'm quite sure God will forgive you, Kid. He'll understand." He gave her hand a little squeeze and got to his feet.

"Thank you Father," Kid said sounding relieved. The world seemed to be in order once again.

Right then, the door opened and David flew into the room, and with three big strides he stood by her bedside. "Kid, what's this?" he said, his face registering a mixture of concern and puzzlement.

"Does my face look that awful?"

"Yeah, you look horrible."

"Thanks ... you are a real booster."

"Your eye is all bloody ... the whole side of your face is kind of bashed." Then he remembered something and changed tack. "Are you in pain Kid?" he said choosing a different key and a milder tone of voice.

"Yes, a lot of pain," she said feeling a little piqued after his previous remark.

"Poor Kid," he said and started to stroke her face very gently with his huge hand. "Why did you let these guys snatch your purse? And why the hell didn't you defend yourself?"

"Why? Because I don't know how ... I'm only little and I'm no karate fighter ... that's why. Will you teach me? I don't ever want to be so helpless again."

"Yeah, I'll teach you Kid. If only I had been there when they bashed you, Kid ..."

"...you don't need to go on. I know, you would have wiped them out in about three seconds flat and that would have been your one-way ticket back to jail." Now she turned to Father who had been listening to their conversation with some amusement. "Father, this is my brother David." Then back to David, "This is Father Pasquale."

David opened his eyes wide. "You are Kid's priest?" Since it was not a real question, David did not wait for an answer. "We had a priest come to see us ... you know when I was inside ... but I never went to his meetings ... just couldn't."

"Why couldn't you, David?"

"Well, you see, sir, I knew that God wouldn't bother forgiving someone who has sinned as much as I have ... too big a job."

"You would be surprised at how well God can handle hundreds of forgiving-jobs all at the same time. He is the master of multi-tasking ... and please call me Father."

"Right. A mate of mine ... he told me about the forgiving procedure the priest organized for them ..."

"It's called confession, David. Don't you know anything about the Catholic Church?" Kid said with some embarrassment.

"Yeah, confession. I'd like to do one of those ... sir Father, but I'm not even a Catholic ... so it probably wouldn't really ... what ... take ... or would it?"

Father's mastery of keeping a straight face was certainly being put to the test here, and now he also had a new title. "It certainly would 'take' if you are genuinely sorry for what you have done."

David nodded. This was serious stuff. "Would you perform a confession for me, sir Father? There are an awful lot of things ... inside of me ... difficult to live with ..."

"Yes David. We'll work something out, OK?"

David beamed.

"Where is your husband, Kid?"

"On a reporting trip ... be home tomorrow night. But I'm sure he already knows that something has gone pear shaped ... he feels these things you know Father. And David, you mustn't say sir Father, just Father, OK?" Now she started to fidget in her bed, the painkillers were wearing off and the pain of her crushed ribs became unbearable. David held her hand while Father fetched a nurse.

"May I kiss you now, Kid?" he asked hopefully.

"On my forehead, not on the lips, I told you before. But thanks for coming and for being concerned." He bent over and kissed the top of her head just as Father and the nurse entered the room.

"Please, would you leave the patient now. I'll give her a pain killer and something to make her sleep," nurse said to Father.

"Sure. Come David, Kid needs to get some rest. Sleep well, Kid," he said. The two men left the room and made their way noiselessly along the empty corridor.

Father and David were about to enter the car park when Father said, "Would you like to come to my house, David? We could sit in my study and then you might like to tell me about the events of your past that have been causing you so much pain. Would you like that?"

David stopped in his tracks. "Yes, please Father."

"I go and brew a pot of coffee," Father suggested once they were inside his home. "Please go through to my study and make yourself comfortable."

David looked around the room which was cluttered with books and loose papers, letters and magazines but he made nothing of it. He stood facing a wall of books but rather than read the spines of any of them, he tried to gather his thoughts while his mind was awash with memories he was unable to control. He concentrated on getting all his anxieties into words and comprehensible sentences. He needed to express how sorry he was, how ashamed and how guilty. Father will then communicate my deep felt regret to his God and ask him to forgive me and let me get a fresh start, he concluded in his mind.

"Do sit down, anywhere you like." Father's voice pulled him out of his thoughts.

"I'd rather stand," he said, "I'm better able to concentrate in a standing position, if it's OK with you."

Father nodded. "Before you start David, I want you to know that nothing of what you tell me will ever go beyond these four walls."

"Thank you Father." Then a pause. "It was during the war ... that's when my life started to become a nightmare. You see, that's where I committed the worst crimes anybody can think of. I killed people ... often with my bare hands ... people who were only half my size and not even trained in the same skills I was. No one explained to me why these little people were my enemies ... what they had done to me or to my country. They were communists, we were told, and that was bad - bad enough to die for. How was I to understand? I am a karate fighter, Father, and the military made me into a killer. I started learning karate when I was very young but I never meant to hurt anyone."

There he stopped abruptly as if remembering to straighten out a misunderstanding. "Father, Kid is not my sister, Phillip is my brother. Kid and I just look alike ... for no reason at all."

If Father noticed that David's sentences were rather jumbled, he did not let on, instead he smiled and said, "I knew that. Kid just loves to think that she has a brother."

"You see, Father, we are not allowed by law - I mean martial arts law - to use our skills in a ... umm ... worldly way, you know as a weapon for destruction. Karate is an art, that's what it is. But when the officers gave orders you had to ... to obey. Horrible pictures come back to me in my dreams still now ... can't get rid of them. I feel so guilty ...

I've brought misery to families. I might have killed a son, a brother, a husband or a father ... I didn't know. We were all turned into robots ... we executed orders ... never stopped to think ... no time to feel sorry, no time to grieve."

It became more and more obvious to Father that David was now speaking through a voice that came from a different time and place. David stood straight and motionless. The perfect karate stance at all times, Father mused.

"I can see David, that you are carrying the guilt of our whole nation on your shoulders. But even for a powerfully built man like you, this is bound to be too heavy a burden. War, as we all know, is the most abominable evil humanity has ever invented. You were a victim, David, the same as the soldiers and civilians who were our enemies."

David seemed to turn this over in his mind, then he said unexpectedly, "The President of the United States ... he organized the whole debacle, right? Maybe he did confession too ... and felt sorry once he realized ... the extent of the damage he had done ..."

Father lowered his head. Rather too late then Mr. President, to feel sorry, he thought with some irony. Aloud he said, "Yes, maybe he did."

"Do you think your God can forgive me for what I've done?"

"I'm sure of it, David. God knows that you are truly sorry ... and God is not just my God, you know, he is everybody's God."

"Thanks Father, and please thank ... God from me. That means that I can now start ... like from scratch, right? I already had to start from scratch once ... when I came back from the war. I was sort of dead then ... I didn't know where I was ... didn't even recognize my parents ... but I came alive again ... at least to a degree. I don't really understand what happened. I was a complete imbecile at first ... could do nothing right - nothing except karate. I never forgot any of it but ... I sure got myself into trouble because of it. That's why I spent so much time in jail. But I'm done fighting in the streets ... I'm an instructor now ... got a real good job. You see, Father, I had nothing else to fall back on when I was released."

Father needed every shred of concentration to follow David's incoherent life story but he had already decided that David was not an imbecile and that he certainly had his heart in the right place.

"But Kid tells me that you are renovating the house you are living in. She said you were the master builder ... that's something, isn't it?" Kid had also told him that Robert made all the plans and that David was often unable to read or interpret them.

"Yeah, I'm very lucky ... I love working on his house ... Robert is a great guy." David finally sat down. The first healing signs started to manifest themselves in unmistakable ways. He felt light, and he felt somehow new. It was as

266

if a newly created life force was cruising through his body offering him a fresh start. "Thanks Father," he said, "I feel good inside ... somehow."

Father knew the moment the soothing effects of confession were setting in. This confession might have been rather free-style but it is working. It's the results that count, he thought with considerable satisfaction.

XVIII

While Kid was in a medically induced sleep in her hospital bed and David revealed the crimes of his past to Father, Phillip's mind was in turmoil. It was now after midnight and he was restlessly tossing and turning in his hotel bed in Nashville. Phillip was well aware that something was wrong, his telepathic senses had never deceived him. He had tried to call Kid three times during the course of the evening and had gotten no answer. She could of course, be working a late shift at Alfredo's, or she might have been invited for dinner at Anita and Bob's house. Or I might also just be deceiving myself, Phillip thought a little helplessly. His schedule had been rather sketchy when he left home in the morning which had made it impossible for him to tell Kid where he would spend the night, so now Kid could not contact him and put his mind at ease. He felt in his bones that something had gone very wrong, but he could not get back home because of some damned conference the following morning.

The 'damned conference' finished at eleven o'clock, Phillip refused the invitation to stay for lunch, got into his car and made his way home driving above speed limited all the way.

When he reached his home there was no sign of Kid. He tried Alfredo and got no information, then he tried Father and got the full story. He rushed to St. Mary's hospital and reached the reception desk, distressed and breathless. "I need to see my wife ... the name is Kid McCabe." He didn't notice the curious looks he got first from the nurse and later from the doctor, all he knew was that his darling Kid had been viciously attacked and was probably in pain and he had not been around to comfort her.

The curious looks from doctors and nurses all originated from the same thought, 'who is this guy who thinks of himself as Kid's husband? We've all seen Kid's husband yesterday - the huge, blond, good looking guy.' No one was prepared for the scene which followed Phillip's entry into Kid's room. She would have jumped out of bed with joy if it had not been for the pain of her crushed ribs. Phillip put his arms around her, made soothing noises and soon the two were in an intimate embrace which went on and on. To everyone around, it looked like David had lost his husband status in one fell swoop.

Phillip was informed that Kid had to spend one more night in hospital. He was devastated and inconsolable as he returned home alone that night. He entered his house and found that it had lost all its warmth and all its charm since Kid was not with him. A little absently he opened the refrigerator and looked at all the food which he had no intention of eating, then came a knock on the front door. If it's someone who thinks I need looking after, he said to himself, I'll scream.

"I'm coming," he said with some annoyance, then he went to open the door and found himself looking at a man he had never seen before. He was black and rather shabbily dressed, he wore two jackets one on top of the other even though it was not cold enough for that. The zipper of the outer one had obviously packed up and the two sides were held together by a couple of safety pins. A hood was loosely thrown over his head of fuzzy black hair, he wore loafers and no socks. The man was slightly stooped and held in his hand what Phillip instantly recognized as Kid's red and white backpack.

"Does Mrs McCabe live here? Need to talk to her," the man said without looking at Phillip.

"She lives here, yes, but you can't talk to her right now. She is in hospital," Phillip said truthfully and at these words the man lifted his head for the first time and gave Phillip a rather unsavory look. Then he pointed to the backpack in his hand and said, "Do you know this?"

"Looks very much like my wife's, yes. Where did you find it?"

"Found it at the scene of the ... accident yesterday." The man seemed a little unsteady on his feet. Maybe a little drunk, Phillip thought.

"So you've come to give it back ...?"

"Yeah mate ... but it'll cost you ... I mean, I found it and I brought it all the way here."

"Sure," Phillip said. It did not take much to see the situation for what it was: a feeble and rather transparent scam, an opportunity for this possibly homeless man to make some money - money he was likely to turn into alcohol or drugs as soon as he left this place. "Why don't' you step inside so I can close the door ... a bit cool out there," Phillip said in a flat voice.

The man did not answer but followed Phillip's invitation to enter the house. He walked slowly, swaying a little and Phillip could see a piece of plastic sticking out of one shoe. Plastic bags as a replacement for socks, Phillip concluded. "Come through to the kitchen. Do you want a cup of coffee?"

"I have a beer," the man said rather grumpily as he sat down on the bar stool Phillip had pulled out for him. In the enclosed space of the kitchen the smell of the man's dirty clothes and unwashed body became rather overpowering, Phillip's politeness started to fray at the edges and he had

271

to make an effort not to show his distaste as he handed the beer bottle over. The guy started to unscrew the bottle top, his hands - in fact his whole body - were visibly shaking. As Phillip shot a quick glance at the guy's face and saw the deadness in his eyes and the dilated pupils, there was no longer any doubt in his mind that the man was under the influence of drugs. Maybe a cup of coffee would have been more sensible under the circumstances, he told himself belatedly.

"How much do you want for the backpack then?" Phillip asked.

"Fifty bucks."

Phillip turned his head and gave him a quizzical look over his shoulder, "A bit steep, isn't it? Have you checked what's inside?"

"Just books ... that's all. So are you going to give me the money or what?"

Phillip puzzled over the inconsistency in the guy's words. If there were only books in the bag, how did he know it belonged to Mrs McCabe? Maybe this guy was one of Kid's attackers and was now trying to cash in on the backpack as well.

"I'll give you twenty-five," he said.

"No way. Fifty or you won't get the bag."

"Please yourself, I don't really need my wife's backpack, and anyway ... if there are only some books in it ..."

"How about forty …"

"Thirty."

"Thirty-five."

"OK, I give you thirty-five dollars. Happy?"

For the first time the guy showed something akin to a smile on his face. It was not an ugly face, Phillip decided, but it was dirty and the beard was straggly, his nose was running and he kept wiping it with the back of his hand. Phillip was slightly disgusted but at the same time he felt sorry for the man. Just for a minute he wondered what had happened in this guy's life … what had propelled him to the bottom of society. At that point in his thoughts, Phillip heard the man's voice from the breakfast counter, "Is Kid badly hurt? Will she be OK?"

So he knows Kid, it went through Phillip's mind, he has just used her first name. But looking at the his unwelcome visitor, Phillip doubted that this guy would physically attack and rob Kid, then decide to come to her house and return the backpack … in exchange for fifty bucks. And now he asks me if Kid is OK – it just doesn't follow. Phillip said none of this but answered the question honestly, "She will be alright, but she is in some pain, got a few crushed ribs and lots of bruises. Do you know my wife?"

"No, don't know her."

I bet you don't, you're a bad liar. How then do you know her first name … and you just used it in a rather familiar way, or didn't you notice? Phillip thought with some irony but didn't bother to say it.

"I have another beer," the man said unexpectedly. Phillip understood then that this guy had forsaken all manners and niceties of our society. Life for him meant to survive one day at the time. If there was a chance to get another bottle of beer, he would not hesitate to ask for it - the opportunity might not arise again. You never knew what the next day might bring ... and the next ... and the next. It was at precisely that point that Phillip connected with Kid's compassion for the homeless and the downtrodden. It could well be that this poor guy knew Kid from one of the shelters organized by the Catholic Church where she helped feed and look after the people in need. It was possible. "What's your name?" Phillip asked without warning.

"Oliver ... Oliver is my name. Yours?"

"I'm Phillip."

Oliver got up now holding his second bottle of beer still in his hand, unopened. Then he slowly proceeded to stuff it into an inside pocket of one of his coats. He carefully folded the three ten-dollar bills and the five-dollar bill Phillip had given him, started to fumble with his clothes, stuck each bill in a separate pocket, coats, pants, pockets front and back. This task took some time to complete and was seemingly of utmost importance. And all during this time Oliver took no notice of Phillip who watched this unusual show with fascination. When Oliver felt that his treasure was well hidden and all things were in the right places, he turned around and made his way to the front door without saying another word. Phillip followed, he was nonplussed. Oliver stopped at the door, then probably remembered where he was. He turned to look at Phillip, "Thanks mate," he said and to Phillip's surprise he finished with, "Hope Kid will be OK ... and home again soon." Then he let himself out and walked away, slowly, unsteadily, his hood up, his head bent.

Phillip was stunned. He stood in the hallway and stared emptily at the front door shaking his head in disbelief.

The following day was Saturday. Phillip had been told he could pick up his wife at around eleven. He had made the bed and was in the process of washing the coffee cup and his last night's wine glass, when he heard a car turn into his driveway. It was Kid's car, driven by David.

"It got left in the parking lot," David explained, "so I drove it back here." With this he handed the keys to Phillip and turned to go.

"Hey, hang on, come on in ... and how do you think you are going to get back home?"

"I'll walk."

"Right, that will only take you a couple of hours. Come and have a cup of coffee."

It was over coffee that David embarked on what he thought would be a harmless conversation only he had bad-

275

ly miscalculated. "As soon as Kid is well again I'm going to start training her in karate," he said truthfully.

"Say what? You will do no such thing ... too rough, too dangerous, she'll get hurt ... I won't hear of it."

"What's the matter with you? Kid asked me to teach her ... she wants to learn. Anyway, there is more than just brutal fighting involved in karate. You don't know what you're talking about."

"Yeah, but there *is* brutal fighting involved. Didn't you give us ample proof of it? I said she will not take up karate and that's final."

"But if she wants to ... you can't make her decisions ... that's not right."

"Are you calling me a control freak? Well, don't insist. Kid and I talk about issues and decisions in our lives like two grown-ups. She will see that it's impracticable ..."

"So you *are* controlling her ... making her see stuff your way."

"Just shut up, will you?" At that moment he noticed David clenching and unclenching his fists, his size and his stance were more intimidating than a minute ago, his features hardened and his eyes took on a menacing expression. Phillip registered instant panic. "OK I'm sorry I ... over-reacted. For god's sake ... you frightened the living shit out of me when I was just a little lad ... you're doing it again now." His flimsy barrier of self-control was breaking down completely now. "I bet you'd flatten me just the same now even though I've done some growing-up since."

"I could, yes ... but I'm not going to." And then, for reasons unknown to Phillip, David's eyes filled with tears.

What's this? The deadly fighter in tears? Phillip was mystified. But before he got a chance to air his puzzlement, he heard his brother's choked voice.

"I'll never hurt you ... I never would have done at mom's home either." There he took a break, wiped his face with his sleeve, then continued with some urgency, "Don't you understand ... I took up karate so I could protect you ... not hurt you." It sounded like a message from the heart. "You were so little ... so helpless ... and mom had put me in charge of you. All my mates laughed at me because I spent every spare minute with you. I used to get you in that little push chair and strapped you in ... then I ran all around the neighborhood with you. I learned to do everything for you - all except feed you of course - but I always watched mom. I changed your nappies, stuck you in the bath, put you to bed, picked you up every time you cried. Don't you remember anything at all? I thought I was the one who suffered from memory loss."

How could I possibly remember having my nappies changed, Phillip didn't know whether to laugh or to cry. David just kept getting things so wrong - things to do with time mainly. "I'm sorry David, but I don't remember. I was only very little, don't forget," was the best he could do.

"Yeah sure, you were that little when mom brought you back from hospital ... I could just about hold you in my two hands. Must have been winter ... you were wearing a little coat with a hood over your head and tiny little gloves," he said dreamily.

"David, if I was just a few days old it *would* have been winter, I was born on November eleven."

"Uh-huh," David nodded as if to say 'you remember that one alright'.

So David started to learn karate in order to protect me, his baby brother. He obviously had a talent in that field, the talent got shamelessly exploited by the military, and after David got back from the war, more dead than alive, he was this country's top karate guy – the guy who won every tournament in sight. And no one ever thought of telling me about it, Phillip recapped. What a watershed. "I'll be picking Kid up from the hospital shortly. Let's both go, shall we? And thanks for being there for Kid while I was away." In a spontaneous gesture, Phillip put his arms around his brother's shoulder. David looked puzzled.

XIX

David called Kid at home and summoned her to the dojo for her first karate class after her lunch-time shift at Alfredo's. With time David had become more familiar with the use of the telephone but he could not memorize any numbers. It had been Kid's idea to compile a list of the numbers he was likely to use on a daily basis and David now carried in his pocket a card containing these numbers all written in big bold letters. They were: his own, the dojo, Robert's office, Kid and Phillip's and Alfredo's. David had decided on the time when Kid's ribs were sufficiently healed, he did not take the doctor's verdict into consideration. Only *he* knew when she would be ready since he alone made all the decisions on how much and what type of physical effort was going to be put into her initial karate lessons.

But Kid proved to be a difficult student right from the start.

279

"The doctor said more than a week ago that I was fine," she insisted.

"Too soon for karate training ... I'll start you on a one-to-one basis."

"I want to be in a class."

"Later." David had given her a karate outfit with a white belt and was now showing her how to bow as she stepped onto the mats.

"When do I get another color belt? Nobody has a white one."

"When you pass your grade ... now, here is how you stand, inhale and find your centre of gravity," and he demonstrated. "And if you keep up this argumentative attitude ... you can find yourself another teacher."

This last statement finally found its mark. Kid knew it was time to accept David's authority. "I'll shut up, Sensei," she said solemnly.

"How come you know that term?"

"I'm not just a pretty face ... I read it somewhere."

A smile appeared on David's face. "Good, let's start then."

Kid and Phillip had discussed the issue of her karate training, although not exactly like two grown-ups as Phillip had expounded on the morning of Kid's return from hospital. Kid was not prepared to deviate from her conviction that had she known how to defend herself, she would not have ended up battered and bruised in hospital. "And I don't want this to happen ever again," she concluded stubbornly.

"And if you had known some self-defense, you would have easily wiped out three guys all by yourself, right. Come on Kid, get real."

Phillip had been against the idea of Kid taking up karate when he first heard about it and he was not about to change his mind. Kid would have to see the issue his way - the only sensible way there was. He emphasized that karate was too rough and totally unsuitable for her. He was prepared to be as unyielding as she was. Deep inside however, there were other reasons for his opposition to Kid's being tutored in karate by his brother - reasons as yet only vaguely formulated in his mind and based mainly on his own overheated imagination. Kid would be spending a lot of time with David in that dojo, just the two of them, and Phillip didn't like it. The fact that he and Kid now knew for sure that David could not father children still did not mean that he could not have sex, did it? Phillip's rational thinking mechanisms had temporarily departed from his mind, he was vaguely aware of it but paid no attention to an inner voice that told him he was not only unkind but also wrong to suspect his wife of unfaithfulness.

Then an event at David's dojo took place and Phillip saw an opening to find out more about karate classes and about his brother's teaching methods ... including possible seducing opportunities.

Kid told him that Robert had plans for the karate school where he and David taught. It was Robert's belief, she said, that karate - and martial arts in general - should be made better known to young people of all walks of life, and that Mr Blythe's school should be in the forefront by offering the public an insight into the art of karate and the possibility of easy access to membership at his school.

"So Robert is organizing a special recruiting fête to be held at the dojo," Kid was full of enthusiasm when she got to this point in her story. "He wants it to be a real little fête, you know, attractive for children ... the dojo all decorated with balloons and colorful ribbons ... coffee and soft drinks, cookies, sandwiches and all. He'll print flyers advertising the date, place and nature of the event and we students are going to distribute them around town. David will teach a couple of master-classes and ... there is going to be a photo of him in one of his flying positions ... I've already seen it ... very beautiful. Robert put me in charge of handing out en-rolment forms and pamphlets." She had insisted that Phillip and all his friends come along even if it was just for the entertainment. "And to see David in action," she had added rather importantly.

David's master-classes however, proved to be more than just entertainment – they were a true experience for most people present. Phillip watched his brother in his role as karate expert and he saw a completely new person. He saw a man who was in total command of himself and of every one of his movements. Phillip was overwhelmed by David's mastery of the art of karate and as he looked around at the people in the hall he could tell that his brother's supremacy escaped no one. The aura of power which surrounded him affected everyone, children and adults alike, and David's natural good looks and his charisma certainly made him the undisputed star of the event.

Later that day, Phillip inadvertently learned more about his brother during a brief conversation with David's landlord and friend, Robert.

"You know Phillip," Robert said, "David's mind and even his physical body undergo some sort of transformation when he slides into his karate-skin, as it were. He becomes who he is, rather than who he needs to be seen to be. In everyday life he makes an effort to learn and become a regular guy, but in the dojo he makes no effort at all. That's where he naturally is ... himself."

Interesting, Phillip thought, and a good way of putting it too.

It was David's second master-class that provoked Jim's remark, "I never thought him capable of anything so ... what ... masterful." And he finished rather tactlessly with, "I bet he has women falling over themselves trying to get into his pants."

Phillip had planned a show-down with his brother and

now seemed the right time for it. He walked to the table where Kid was handing out enrolment forms. "Kid, could you please get David for me? I'd like to talk to him."

Kid opened her eyes wide and looked at her husband in complete puzzlement, "But Phillip, he is in there ... in the shower room with a dozen naked men ... I'm not going in there to get him ... no way."

"No ... of course not. I quite understand," Phillip said trying to keep a straight face.

When some time later, Phillip found himself face to face with his brother, his earlier resolution to inquire into the possibility of David using his teaching time to seduce his wife suddenly seemed out of place. Phillip felt foolish and wished he had never asked for this meeting. In a lame effort to give the whole thing an air of casualness he downgraded his provocation to, "Those master-classes you taught ... they were quite extraordinary. Bob and Anita's son Michael is going to be one of your students. He can't wait to start his first lesson ... and one of my friends has also enrolled ... although he did have second thoughts. He said something happened to him while watching your second master-class."

"Who? Do I know the guy?"

"Yes, you do. It's Mario."

The expression on David's face showed concentration and seriousness. "Mario," he repeated, "he would have to be ... well tuned in to ... to the essence of karate. He'll be alright."

Phillip understood not a word of what David had just said, but he was not about to query it. Maybe this is what Robert meant by 'David gets transformed when he is on the dojo mats', he thought.

XX

The argument over Kid's taking up karate classes with David was the first issue in the McCabe's married life - the first since Kid's original discovery of David - that had not been satisfactorily settled. Kid and Phillip were both aware of it and both did everything possible to try and convince themselves that it was not so. The result was that an uncomfortable atmosphere of uncertainty - and in Phillip's case of fear - prevailed in their home. It manifested itself in their everyday life: over dinner, while doing housework and even in bed.

Kid suffered terribly. This was exactly what she had sworn to avoid in her marriage. Phillip had always understood and respected all her wishes, her interests and her needs, why did he balk at this issue? Kid told herself that she could well have wanted to play tennis or join a yoga group, and she was sure her husband would have made no fuss at all, but the issue of martial arts he just could not handle. There are times of quiet during my karate class. There is sitting still and breathing correctly ... not so different from yoga, she reasoned with herself. David is the master instructor, he wouldn't make me do stuff which could hurt me, and he is a stickler for safety on the mats to boot ... he never has any accidents in a class. The debate inside her went on and on. There was just one point – and it was the decisive one - that eluded her troubled thoughts, namely Phillip's lack of trust in her faithfulness and his self-created suspicion of David's intention to use training time to seduce her.

As Kid's training with David went ahead against his wish, Phillip gave the outward appearance of being annoyed and upset since he did not want to let on that his soul was in fact tormented by fear and jealousy. The strained atmosphere between him and his wife hurt him as deeply as it hurt Kid. What hurt him even more however, was the knowledge that he had started to mistrust Kid. And what if my mistrust should be misplaced? This would be tantamount to doing her an injustice and Kid does not deserve that. Then why, his rational mind asked, why do I persist in my suspicion that David is trying to seduce her? I have as yet not a shred of evidence to uphold such a suspicion. It's all just a figment of my imagination. But rationality and reasoning never quite managed to take the upper hand in his mind and since he meant to be seen as a reasonable man and an understanding husband he knew he could not continue to nag her about these lessons. Where was the solution to this dilemma?

There were however, times when Phillip found peace and relaxation and when his bad conscience was not given an opportunity to bother him, and these were the times spent playing music either at home, in his music studio or on stage. Music always had the magic power to encompass all his senses and make him forget the world around him and all that happened in it. Even the knowledge of David's presence in the audience during a performance on Friday or Saturday night could not dent his deep felt enjoyment of music-making.

David had no inkling of the fact that he was the cause of a domestic drama that was taking place at his brother's home. Phillip had assured him that he and his wife knew how to discuss all issues in their lives like the two intelligent adults they were. David had considered this to be the green light from his brother and had consequently started to instruct Kid in the art of karate. She had been rather a handful at the beginning but had become quite docile now. David felt safe in the assumption that Kid and Phillip were in agreement over this issue, since as a rule, he believed what people said. He was not one to conjure up suspicions; he took people and their words at face value.

During this time, David often reflected on those two incidents when he had wanted to kiss Kid, but he now understood her admonishing words. He was allowed to kiss her cheek or the top of her hair but not her lips, and it was OK to give her a hug and hold her in his arms for a little bit. He liked that ... he loved her ... she was his sister.

It had been a very long time since David had felt genuinely close to a woman – close enough to want to kiss her. His sex-life had been severely interfered with during his time in the war, and ever since then he had been carrying the burden of his sexual inadequacy around with him. He had made the painful discovery of his sexual handicap shortly after his escape from the clinic in St. Louis while still recuperating from his temporary death and battling to keep his head above water in everyday life. The doctors in the hospital had simply told him that as a consequence of having been exposed to some deadly weapons he was now sterile - could never have any children of his own. The fact that he was going to be unable to lead a healthy sex-life he had to find out the hard way. All these years later David still shuddered at the mere thought of the hurtful and embarrassing situations he experienced at the start of his life as a civilian. From then on he avoided women ... they scared him. No one ever understood why.

Why was it then, he now reflected, that women always wanted *me* - wanted me to sleep with them and told me I was sexy even though *I* never made any attempt at flirting ... never tried to seduce a woman?

The only person David had ever been able to confide in about this problem was a doctor in jail in California. The doctor had stitched up his arm after he had settled a fight between two guys wielding vicious looking knives and a vet – a mate of his. A nice guy, the doctor, David remembered, he had no trouble understanding my problem. He said there was nothing really wrong with me, I just needed to be confident and I should not be afraid.

Still, David never had much luck with girlfriends even though later he overcame his affliction - at least to some extent. He stayed away from women as much as possible and tried not to have anything to do with them and as a consequence, he never really learned how to talk to girls and how to treat them nicely and correctly.

But with Kid it's different, David knew that for sure. She likes me with all my shortcomings, she is honest and straightforward. David's thoughts now turned to Kid's work at the shelters where she helped the homeless people. I meant to help them too, he reflected sadly, only I went about it the wrong way ... got myself arrested and put behind bars. One thing however, during all his bad years David had never become homeless. He was physically fit and he knew he could work for a living. He worked at any job that was available, he always had a roof over his head and he never walked around looking bedraggled.

However, there had been times when his frustration got the better of him, and those were the times when he went on the rampage, got into conflict with the law and was sent to jail. But all this was behind him now. He would never fight in the streets again, he was leading the life of a decent citizen, he had family and friends and Father had assured him that his God had forgiven him for all his past crimes.

Phillip sat in front of the television set, but rather than watch the program he stared right through the screen at images in his own mind. When did I turn into the jealous guy I am now, he asked himself for the hundredth time. He had always thought of himself as a 'SNAG' - a sensitive new age guy - rational, logical and sensible, yet now he found himself suffering from some self-created disease. I must be going mad.

But doubting his own sanity did nothing to diminish his fear of losing Kid - and of losing her to his own brother. Many a time he had decided to talk to Kid about the type of friendship she had with David, and to query her about the time before and after her classes alone with him in the dojo and about her feelings for him. But every time his courage had deserted him at the last moment. He knew he was responsible for the tension between them. He wished he could turn the clock back to the time when he and Kid loved each other unconditionally – the time when he did not hide any secret thoughts from her.

Kid was still at Alfredo's working a one-off evening shift and would be back in half an hour or so. Phillip promised himself that he would take his whole life in his hands and tell her about his problem when she got home. Then he heard a knock on the back door. Not Kid, too early, he thought, and why the back door, anyway? Phillip went through the laundry, opened the back door and found himself face to face with David who stood towering over him and holding two big books in his hands. The expression on his face showed concern.

David was the last person Phillip wanted to see right then. Still he motioned him to come in ... what else could he do. "What have you got here?" he asked, indicating the books.

"Kid gave them to me ... they're about Japan. They are from the library she told me, and they need to go back tomorrow ... so I'm bringing them here. Where is Kid?"

Phillip felt a strong urge to scream at his brother for sounding so damn innocent, instead he said, "She is at work ... will be home soon."

"How is she?"

"What do you mean? Or do you know something I don't?"

"No need to yell at me ... I only thought I'd ask. She wasn't right somehow, this afternoon in class ..." He never got to finish his sentence. Phillip was about to fly in his face.

"What are you saying? How 'not right'? Come on, out with it."

"She didn't concentrate," David said truthfully. "She couldn't sit still at the start and again at the end of class. I had to reprimand her twice for not paying attention. You know ... one student's inattention can put others at risk ... cause accidents."

Phillip was listening in silence. He had a very good idea of the reasons for Kid's 'inattention' in class. Kid must be suffering much more than she let on, and of course, it had to be her brother who noticed it rather than her husband.

David continued. "She looked unhappy ... had tears in her eyes ... I saw them."

"What did she tell you? And what did you do?"

"I did nothing at all. I also had another class directly after hers ... no time to talk. I was hoping to hear from you ..."

David had put Phillip in a spot without knowing he had. David, Phillip realized with some relief, had obviously no idea of what was going on between Kid and himself. Kid had not talked about their domestic affairs. Suddenly it struck him that he could well be completely wrong about his brother's feelings and intentions. And before he knew it, he asked, "You like Kid, don't you? I mean, you are concerned because she looked unhappy, right?"

"Yeah, I like her ... we get on well. I trust her ... something I haven't done in a long time." He answered truthfully not realizing that his honesty and his innocence infuriated his brother and stretched his patience almost to the limit.

Anyone would have caught the unsubtle innuendo in my question, Phillip thought, anyone except my dumb brother who has the mental capacity of a ten-year old. It was then that it dawned on Phillip: it is precisely this absurd innocence and childlike honesty which protects my brother from ever getting into the kind of muddle I find myself in right now. Slowly his thoughts began to circle back to the trust David had mentioned - the trust he had in Kid. Surely, years in prison would have to be the most efficient recipe for avoiding to trust anybody. Was that what David meant when he said he had not trusted anyone in a long time? Phillip was momentarily lost for an answer, but right then Kid's car could be heard to turn into the driveway, then her voice rang out.

"I'm back." She walked in through the laundry and saw Phillip and David standing at the breakfast counter. Kid chose to ignore the looks of confusion on their faces and gave Phillip her customary hug and kiss. "What an evening," she exclaimed and shook her head. "Alfredo must have had everybody with even the remotest link to the 'Motherland' in his restaurant. I never heard one word of English all night." Only now did she turn and look up to David, "Hi brother," she said and gave him a little hug too. Phillip watched rather more closely than politeness allowed as Kid put her arms around David's waist and leaned against his body, the top of her head reaching no higher than mid-chest. David folded her in his big strong arms for just a second then Kid stepped back; she had more news to impart. "I served Mario's parents and a couple of aunts and uncles I think, and also Father. I must have run miles between kitchen and dining room tonight."

"Relax now, Kid. Sit down I make some coffee," Phillip suggested but there was a hollow ring to his words. He had not seen Kid so carefree for some time and he wondered if her display of lightheartedness had something to do with David's presence.

"I brought the books, Kid. You said they were due back ... soon. Are you OK?"

"Of course I am. Oh, you mean because of this afternoon in class?" Now she turned to Phillip and explained, "I didn't do very well ... scatterbrain that I am, so I was told off." She refrained from mentioning her tears or what caused them. It was hard enough to keep up a cheerfulness she did not fully subscribe to just now.

Phillip nodded. David looked at her wide-eyed and with a question mark on his face. Kid affected not to notice, but she knew she could not keep up this charade for very much longer. She didn't have to since David soon got up and turned to go, "I start a six in the morning ... better go now."

Phillip waited until he heard David's car drive away then he asked, almost casually over his shoulder, "Tell me what really happened this afternoon in your class."

"As I said, I had to be told off by the teacher. That's it."

"What did David say?"

"He just said 'Kid you're not concentrating'. Why? Did he tell you anything else?"

"Should he have?"

"I don't like it when you answer with a question of your own. What do you want to hear?"

Phillip sat on the sofa, he was very quiet and looked down at the carpet when he said, "Is there anything going on between you and David?"

"No nothing," she said defiantly.

"I'm sorry Kid, that was a stupid question. It's just that David said you were crying, and he seemed real upset. *Were* you crying, Kid?" While asking this question, Phillip miraculously felt a warm feeling of love and tenderness towards his wife. It was right then that the truth of his unfounded suspicions finally hit home. He knew he had been unfair; he felt ashamed and guilty. All he said was, "I'm real sorry Kid," but did not give a proper explanation for his apology.

Kid did not understand but decided to answer truthfully

nevertheless, "Well, just a few little tears," she said, "I was kind of embarrassed after having made a fool of myself, that's all."

It was unfortunate that at this crucial moment Kid failed to truly communicate with her husband. Weeks of tension and uncertainty had hardened her senses and her goodwill even though her love for Phillip had not been impaired. She didn't know therefore, that with her pragmatic - if truthful - answer, she did not acknowledge Phillip's honest apology.

Phillip nodded but he no longer needed to take comfort from the knowledge that Kid was not lying to him. His decision to trust her was made, his optimism and his love for her were back in place now. "That's alright Kid, come let's go to bed, you had a long and busy day." He put his arm around her shoulders and guided her upstairs.

The night of David's unexpected visit and Phillip's insight into the injustice he was doing to Kid, finished in peaceful harmony in the bedroom of the McCabes. All seemed to be well again, all suspicions of unfaithfulness discarded. But not long after, it was Kid who slipped up, and she slipped up big-time.

XXI

It was a Friday in late October, the days were getting shorter and the temperature had been falling steadily, but still the trees along the streets and avenues were ablaze with colors. Phillip and the musicians were rehearsing in the music studio late in the afternoon while Kid did some work in Father's parish. She was scheduled to join the band in the evening to hear their performance.

Kid had caught a rather nasty cold the day before but did not make much of it as was her usual way. Colds came and went, she knew, this one was no different. Unfortunately, this one proved to be a little more stubborn. By the time Kid finished work at the soup kitchen, she was coughing almost uninterruptedly, her eyes were watering, breathing became labored and painful and she had just about completely lost her voice.

Jennifer, the lady in charge, suggested that it would be

wise to refrain from driving. "Maybe your husband could come and pick you up?" she suggested.

"Good idea," Kid spluttered. She wrote down the number on a piece of paper and held it out to Jennifer. "Please will you ... call him?"

Jennifer nodded and went to the phone. She dialed the number and Kid could hear her asking for Mr McCabe. If she was a little apprehensive as she watched Jennifer explain why and where he should come to pick her up, she made sure not to show any sign of it.

"He'll be here in a tick," Jennifer called cheerfully. What she did not know was that she had spoken to the wrong Mr McCabe. Kid had given her the number of her brother, not her husband.

David was only halfway out of the shower when he heard the phone ringing. It rang and rang, Robert was obviously not around to pick it up. David remembered to tie a towel around his waist before he made his way downstairs.

"David speaking," he said.

"Mr McCabe?" he heard an unfamiliar lady's voice.

"Yes ma'am."

"Mr McCabe, my name is Jennifer. I'm calling you on behalf of your wife. She has a real bad cold, can hardly talk. Please can you come and pick her up? I don't think she should drive right now."

What is this? My wife? I don't have a wife. Is this Kid

playing some kind of trick on me? A dozen questions went through David's head. Had Jennifer not been so quick and insistent, David might have had time to give voice to his confusion and in the process give Kid's little scheme away. As it happened however, his slower than average thinking and talking mechanisms saved Kid some embarrassment.

"I tell you exactly where we are." Jennifer continued and gave the address and detailed directions how to get there. She even told him the best place to park his car. "Take a warm blanket with you," she added before ringing off.

David ran upstairs, put on some warm clothes, took a rug from his bed and flew out the door. He knew Kid would explain all to him once he had her in his car. The most important thing was to get her home safely.

A short time later David walked through the door of the shelter with big bold strides and immediately saw Kid sitting at the end of a long table. Her head was lying on her folded arms, she did not notice him as he approached. "What happened Kid?" he asked, "and stop coughing, you can't talk like this."

Jennifer was now standing next to Kid. She laid a hand on her shoulder then looked up at the tall, blond, good looking man she took to be Kid's husband. "Take her home and stick her into a hot bath," she advised wisely.

"Yes, ma'am. Thanks for calling. Come on Kid," and since Kid did not move he scooped her up in his arms, making it look as though she weighed no more than a child of about ten. Jennifer draped the blanket around Kid's small body and sent them on their way.

"Where is Phillip?" were David's first words once he had her settled and wrapped up warmly in his car. "Why did you tell the lady I was your husband? What's going on?"

"Too many questions ... just drive me to your place ... please," Kid managed to say between fits of coughing.

David did as he was told and as he drove, he threw a sideways glance at Kid who sat in the passenger's seat, a miserable little heap, coughing and shivering. Yet rather than feeling distraught or apprehensive, David felt absurdly flattered for being the one she had asked for help. He was going to be in charge of her wellbeing that night and he was determined to do everything she needed and help her get better. He knew he could do it.

"Don't move," David told her on arrival at his house, "I'll come and get you out." He wrapped the blanket around her, lifted her carefully out of her seat and carried her inside. She lay motionless in David's arms when Robert caught a first glimpse of them. He was not immediately sure what was inside the bundle David was carrying. "Kid," David said in answer to Robert's quizzical look, "she is sick – needs a hot bath." Then he went upstairs taking the steps two at the time. Above his head, Robert could hear David's footsteps as he made his way to the bathroom at the end of the hallway, then he heard the sound of water filling the bath tub.

"The bath is just about ready, Kid." David announced, "get in ... quick as you can." Just before he stepped back out into the hall, he noticed Kid fumbling ineffectively with the zipper of her jacket. She pulled the shoelace into a knot then started to kick at her shoes in a vain effort to get them off with the shoelace still tied, and all the while her whole body was shaking, David could not be sure whether because of the cough or because she was cold.

It hit David right then: Kid needs my help – and she needs it now. Without another thought he stepped back into the bathroom, then closed the door to keep the steam inside. Kid sat on the little stool and let him peel off her clothes. She was like a rag-doll ... she seemed to have no will of her own. She docilely lifted her arms so David could pull her sweater over her head. She let him take off her shoes, socks and jeans.

When David got to that point, his mind started to play tricks on him. Suddenly Kid turned into one of the little Vietnamese children who were fleeing their burning village. The children had lost most of their clothes, some were completely naked, all of them were crying and screaming in sheer terror. The blazing fire was right behind them. It was like a slow re-enactment of a dream. David's head began to spin, tears filled his eyes and blurred his vision. He quickly got up from his crouching position and left the bathroom without another word. Once in the hallway, he leaned with his back against the wall beside the bathroom door and tried to bring his erratic breathing under control.

An anguished Robert was awaiting him at the bottom of the stairs. "What's happening to you? You look like you've just seen a ghost."

"I have." And to Robert's surprise, David told with at least a measure of accuracy what he had just experienced. This was not the first time that Robert had been witness to one of David's recurring flashbacks but it was certainly the first time David was able or willing to elaborate.

"What's the story about Kid? Why did you bring her here rather than take her to her home?"

"She didn't say. But she asked me for help, so it's my job to ... to care for her. I have to brew some tea now."

About ten minutes later David made his way upstairs again carrying a mug of steaming hot tea. At Robert's insistence he had sweetened it with honey. "May I come in Kid?" he called outside the bathroom door. He heard a muffled voice saying something unintelligible, so he ventured in.

Kid sat immersed in the bubble bath right up to her neck and as she now turned her head she gave David a little smile. "I'm better now. What's in the mug?"

"Tea ... and you must drink it hot ... and there is some

Aspirin, too." He sat on his heels beside the tub and handed her the mug. "Hold it still ... don't spill it," he cautioned. "Let me help." He supported Kid's head with his left hand and with his right he carefully fed her the hot tea by the spoonfuls. "You must get out before the water cools down. I wait outside."

Kid lifted one hand out of the soap bubbles and placed it against David's cheek for a few seconds, then let it slip back into the water. A minute later, outside in the hallway, David could still feel the touch of her hand against his face. The warm soapy water was running down into the collar of his sweater. He made no attempt to wipe his face dry.

"You may come in now David," Kid's voice woke him from his reverie.

On entering he found Kid fully dressed. In a spontaneous gesture he put his arm around her shoulder and guided her to his room which was two doors down the hall. "Are you feeling better, Kid?" He asked.

"A little weak but lots better, yes."

Once inside his room he lifted Kid up and placed her gently on his bed, then covered her with his quilt and sat down on the edge of the bed. "You need some rest."

Then something happened to Kid, something she could not and did not even try to understand right then. And it was something she would later have trouble explaining to her husband. "Come David, lay down next to me," she said lifting up the quilt for him to slide under.

David's heart almost missed a beat. He kicked off his shoes and stretched out beside Kid, gently putting his arms around her. Then he lay very still and enjoyed her nearness. Kid did not move and David assumed that she had gone to sleep. Suddenly Kid turned her head and looked into David's eyes. It was an unmistakable invitation – an invitation to be kissed. If David was puzzled he did not take the time for analysis. He bent his head and very slowly, very gently touched her lips with his. It was not a passionate embrace, it was just a sweet kiss. Unfortunately, David had not closed the door and as Robert passed on his way to his own room, he could not help but see David and his sister-in-law entwined on David's bed immersed in a kiss. I only hope they know what they are doing, he thought a little distractedly, then proceeded to mind his own business.

Kid's emotional aberration didn't last very long, she soon found that she was out of breath and as she was forced to turn her head aside her rational thinking came back. What am I doing, she asked herself with horror, how could I? Now she tried to push David away from her, but she might as well have attempted to push a brick wall out of place. David held on tenaciously, he was having the time of his life and he was in no mood to give up quite so easily.

"Please David," he heard, "we mustn't ... it's not right ... I'm sorry ... my fault."

"No no Kid, this is nice ..." he said in his slow and

gentle way, "don't push me away."

Kid was horrified at the situation she herself had created. How was she going to get David to understand the dire consequences this was bound to have. "I have to go home, David. Please will you drive me ... let me go now ... get up."

In complete bewilderment David let her go and got out of bed. He was of course, fully dressed, he had never dreamed of an opportunity to be intimate with his sister. But Kid asked me to kiss her, he told himself, I'm certain of it. She wanted me to be near her and hold her in my arms. Why is she so upset now? Why did she say 'my fault'? David could not detect any fault at all. "I don't understand Kid, you liked me to kiss you, didn't you?"

Kid was gripped by a fit of coughing, she sat miserably on the edge of the bed dangling her legs. She was in tears. When she recovered her voice again, the only thing she could say was, "Phillip will probably never forgive me ... I've ruined our marriage ... but it's not your fault David, so don't worry ... I'll deal with it as best I can. Please take me home."

Robert had deliberately been eavesdropping on the disjointed conversation between Kid and David. He seized the moment when they were at the bottom of the stairs to fill some of the gaps in the story he had heard so far. "How are you feeling Kid?" he asked harmlessly. "Come and sit down, let's have some coffee or maybe more tea in your case."

"Thanks Robert," Kid said. She didn't have the energy to oppose his invitation.

"Why did you ask David to take you here rather than home? Will you tell us, Kid?"

"It's because ... because Phillip and the boys were rehearsing at home in the afternoon for a performance. That's where they are now ... quite a big concert I think. If I had gone home ... sick like ... Phillip would have felt responsible for me. He would have foregone the concert and stayed at home and cared for me. But I don't want him to miss a performance ... playing music means so much to him ... you have to understand."

"So what are you going to tell him when he gets home tonight?"

Kid sat very still but her inside was all in a turmoil. She took a few more moments to regain control of herself, then she said, "You know Robert, don't you."

Robert concurred with a nod then threw a quick glance in David's direction and to his surprise he saw a dreamlike contentedness in his friend's eyes. Oh my God, he thought, I hope this is not what I think it is. From far away he heard Kids voice, "I'm going to tell Phillip ... everything. I have to. I lapsed, didn't I? But I meant no harm ... just made a mistake. Do you think Phillip will understand and forgive?

Would you if you were in his shoes?"

Robert could not hide a little smile at the way Kid had put the question to him. "I believe that ... yes, I would Kid ... but I'm not Phillip ..."

"Thanks anyway, Robert," she said.

David took her home soon after the talk with Robert. The house was dark when they arrived and Phillip's car was not in the driveway. "Thanks David," Kid said and turned to face him. "Thanks for looking after me. You do understand, don't you, that we should not have kissed. I'll tell Phillip the whole truth ... I hope he will forgive me ... and you."

David must have understood since he leaned over and gently brushed the top of her head with his lips, then he went and opened the door on her side to let her out. Kid had to wonder for a minute where he had learned such gallantries. Just before he pulled away from the curb, he called through the window, "I'll drive your car back here tomorrow."

XXII

Phillip stayed for only one drink after their concert on that Friday night. He was just a mite worried about Kid's absence in the audience during their performance. She might have had to work late, he tried as an excuse, but an inner voice told him that Kid would not have wanted to miss this special night. So what happened?

When he returned home he found that Kid's car was not in the garage, there was however, a light on in the bedroom and Phillip was struck by some unfamiliar vibrations that prevailed all through the house.

He found Kid sitting in bed, a box of tissues, a glass of water and a packet of Aspirin on the bedside table. She either sniffed or sobbed, Phillip couldn't be sure which. She blew her nose then looked at him with tear-filled eyes. But before he could ask any questions she threw herself into a full-blown confession of her sin. She had rehearsed what to say over and over, yet now that her husband stood in front of her, she found that she was completely departing from her script right from the start.

"I'm sorry, Phillip ... I know you'll be angry with me ... it was all my fault ... I don't know what got into me ... are you going to throw me out? You could, you know ... but I'm real sorry, deep inside, I mean it ..." at this point she had to come up for air and just as well because Phillip had had quite enough of her babble by then. But even though he was annoyed at her incoherence he was more concerned about the state of her health. Fear now began to undermine his annoyance and it was imperative, he knew, that he discipline his curiosity as well as his annoyance and address her health issue first.

"Kid, you look and sound like you have caught a rather nasty cold. I'll go and make you a hot drink. Do you need anything else?"

Kid shook her head and sniffed.

"We'll talk when I come back and ... I'd appreciate if you could revert to English. So far I have not understood one word of what you mean to tell me."

Kid nodded dutifully.

As Phillip turned and walked out of the room he left her with his image and with the sound of his voice still hanging in the air even after the door had closed behind him.

Kid knew she would have to go through the whole thing

again. Phillip's departure only served to give her more time to conjure up his reaction to her abominable sin. Phillip would be angry, of that she was sure. But what would he do with his anger? Would he kick her out? Or would he himself walk out and never come back? There was only one thing she could really be sure of: Phillip would not be violent towards her; he was not that sort of man. All that and more she had had plenty of time to turn over in her mind while waiting for her husband, yet now that he was down in the kitchen and could walk back into the room any minute, Kid was suddenly seized by yet another possible outcome: Phillip might turn his anger away from her and aim it at David. He might see David as the seducer, the ultimate villain and the one who made the advances. And what then? Phillip could blame her for insisting on making David a member of the family again, for taking him here and for offering him assistance. Kid realized it all with horrifying clarity. Phillip might regret having given in to my family feelings and say that if David had not appeared in our lives nothing like this would ever have happened. And the worst thing was that he might well be right in saying that. Kid's distressing thoughts were interrupted by Phillip who entered the room carrying two cups, a tea pot and a sugar bowl on a tray. He placed the tray carefully on the table on Kid's side of the bed, "Sugar?" he asked, as if this was of utmost importance right then.

An unnatural silence now took hold of the room, and as the minutes ticked away, Kid became more and more uncomfortable. Phillip sat on the edge of the bed, he was looking down at her but said nothing. Might as well jump in at the deep end, she thought, "Phillip, I kissed David, that's what I have to confess. I kissed him a few hours ago in his house, in his room."

Phillip sat motionless and Kid saw all the color drain from his face, his eyes went dead, his hands started to shake and he barely managed to put his cup down before spilling the hot tea. "Why Kid? Why did you kiss him?"

Kid made an almost superhuman effort not to show her tears and embarked on an account of her evening including as much detail as she could remember. "I didn't want to up-set your musical evening, that's why I asked David to take me back to his place," she put in rather lamely even though it was the truth. "And after I came out of the bath he put me on his bed because I needed to rest and then ... then ... it wasn't him, he didn't try to seduce me ... he did nothing, nothing at all ... fully dressed both of us ... it was all my fault." Kid didn't know that her desperate effort to defend David was useless as well as unnecessary as Phillip had not said another word since his initial question. In her confusion she rambled on, "David ... you see, he wanted to kiss me before but I told him 'no' so he didn't. He only meant to show that he likes me as a sister, that's all. He never touched me ... I mean indecently ... even when we kissed on his bed. He doesn't ... umm ... he is not like that ..."

"Kid why are you harping on about David's innocence? I'd rather like to hear your side of the story. Did you like his kiss? How did you feel? What did it mean to you? That sort of thing. Can you?"

Kid was lost for words. This was not a situation she was familiar with. Finally her tears started to flow, her nose was running, she started to cough and all the while she wanted no more than to die on the spot.

"Come on Kid, you can do better than that," she heard Phillip's voice, it sounded flat and unfeeling.

Right, she thought, I never wanted to be weak ... now is the time to show that I can go on against all odds. She blew her nose, wiped her face and took a deep breath concentrating her strength on the spot David had taught her to call 'hara' - her centre of gravity. Then she said, "I wanted to show David how grateful I was for his help tonight. Why I did so by asking him to kiss me, I don't know. After a little while, I knew it was a mistake. I turned away and said I was sorry and I shouldn't have and you would never forgive me and ..."

"... and David had no idea what you were talking about, right?"

"No he didn't, how do you know?"

"Never mind that now ... go on."

"I'm really very sorry, Phillip, very very sorry, from the bottom of my heart. It really was my fault, not David's ... please don't blame him and don't be mad at him."

"There you go again, Kid. I have made no mention as yet of wanting to blame my brother."

Kid was momentarily puzzled but didn't know what to make of her puzzlement. "Please can you forgive me Phillip? It meant nothing more to me than a 'thank you'. I'm not at all in love with David, not one little bit ... I'm in love with you only ... always ... forever. Please believe me. I just made a mistake, that's all. Father says that all humans make mistakes and that his God always forgives if one is honestly sorry and that we ordinary guys should learn how to forgive because this is very important and he says that by accepting other people's apologies we make the world a better place and that ..."

"Yes yes, I get your drift Kid, no need to go on."

"That means that I'm forgiven, doesn't it?"

In a gesture of resignation, Phillip shook his head, lifted his hand to his face and covered his eyes. "I'm disappointed Kid, and I'm hurt rather than angry. Do you remember our discussion at the very start of our life together when I told you about my 'unsavory reputation'? Kid, I kept my promise, and not only that, I haven't found it difficult in the least to change my ways. So can you understand why I feel ... the way I feel right now."

Kid understood well enough, but it was what followed that threw her completely off balance. What she heard next was the one reaction she had completely missed in her rehearsals.

"I'm not blaming David and I'm not mad at him for what happened but I'm determined to talk to him about it."

From there on Phillip's words turned into a monologue – into something like a confession. It seemed like he no longer spoke to Kid when he continued, "I know I was slow in re-acquainting myself with my brother, and even slower in understanding and accepting that he was not responsible for what happened to mom, but then ... I started to warm towards him once he became a part of our little family. Oh sure, we had the occasional brotherly shouting match and he did frighten the living daylights out of me on one or two occasions. And there was a time at the beginning of your karate classes with him, when I feared that he might try to seduce you. The two of you do spend quite a lot of time together in that dojo, after all. But I got over all that. I was ashamed of doubting your faithfulness as well as of suspecting him. You see Kid, I really like my brother now. I know that his heart is in the right place and that's what counts. I can handle his lack of social skills and his memory gaps." At this point he turned to look at Kid and said, "All your defense strategies Kid ... they were not really necessary. I've long stopped fearing that David would try to seduce you. To do this, he would have to be devious, calculating and cunning. David is none of those. His almost childlike belief in people's goodness ... it has its advantages."

Kid had been mesmerized by Phillip's words. Why did I get Phillip so wrong, she asked herself? I completely underestimated his kindness and goodwill, how could I be so insensitive? The realization made her feel ashamed.

"I'm really sorry, Phillip, I should have known how you felt towards your brother ... I was very insensitive. You see, ever since I started training with David ... and doing so against your wish ... the tension between us has filled me with unease and unhappiness. It was all very difficult for me. I wasn't sure if your anger was directed at me or at David ... or at both of us."

Phillip shook his head. "No Kid, it wasn't like that at all. The tension between us was my own doing. As I just said, thinking of you and David alone in that dojo ... I turned into a jealous husband. I never knew I could be. I was afraid of losing you, I guess. Then, one night, I realized that I had done you an injustice and gaining this insight made everything right again for me. I should have enlightened you right then but I didn't. So, I need to apologize for suspecting you of wrongdoing, long before you ..."

"... before I actually did something wrong. What's going to happen now that I have?"

In answer Phillip bent over his wife and put his arms

around her as best he could. "Maybe we should concentrate on getting you better, Kid ... first things first."

Kid was moved by Phillip's words and by his embrace but still, this was not enough, she needed absolute certainty that she was forgiven. "You know, Phillip," she started, her voice serene and calm now, "I always knew, from the moment we met, that our relationship was ... sacred, made in heaven ... different from all other relationships in the whole world. I still think of it like that. The mistake I made ... it's done nothing to make even the smallest dent in the love I have for you." She stopped just long enough to cough and blow her nose, then she continued. "Do you still love me ... same as before? Tell me, will this incident overshadow our marriage from now on ... and never go away again?"

"My own thoughts have been following along very much the same lines, Kid." Phillip said slowly, "I don't want a shadow hanging over our marriage but ... the image of you in David's arms ... the two of you kissing ... when it flashes through my mind ... it hurts Kid, it really does."

There was nothing Kid could say, so she simply nodded.

"I do love you Kid. Remember Father in his wisdom said that we were bonded together by our love and that love would help us get through difficult phases in our lives? I truly hope that he is right."

Life flowed easier and more harmoniously after Kid

and Phillip had made their respective confessions. Their minds and their souls were more at peace ... their smiles had once again returned to their faces.

Phillip, true to his word, arranged a time and place for a talk with his brother. Something told him that an in-depth talk would offer him a solid basis from which to start working towards a better understanding of what had taken place between David and Kid.

Phillip suggested that they meet in a bar in town rather than in either of their homes believing that neutral ground would provide a more favorable atmosphere for the conversation he had in mind. He carefully rehearsed his opening sentences and the subsequent questions. He was going to ask them one at the time. He decided to make them so they would not sound like accusations; he did not want to frighten or confuse his brother. Phillip's mind was all set as he approached the bar. He saw David as soon as he entered, you could not miss him in any crowd. His brother always stood a head taller than everyone else. He wore an off-white polo neck sweater, his hair hung in a wild tangle around his head. There was a serious expression on his face but it bore no signs of apprehension. David did not know why he had been summoned.

Phillip made his way through the crowd looking and feeling quite confident. Nothing could go wrong now.

David's face broke into a warm smile the minute he

saw his brother. "I only just got here, I ordered a beer for you too." And without a moment's hesitation he embarked on an account of the reasons for his present high spirits. "Starting from tomorrow, I'm teaching a few classes at the martial arts department of the university. Can you imagine? Me inside a university?"

So much for all my preparations for a serious man-to-man talk, Phillip thought, a complete exercise in futility. How could I forget such a trivial issue as my brother's unpredictability? He said, "Sounds great. They must have gotten wind of he fact that there is a master instructor in town, eh?" The beers arrived right on time and the two brothers toasted David's good fortune. A minute later David was in full flight again.

"The Black Belt at university ... the head of the department ... he gave me one look and asked 'where have you been hiding since your sensational tournament tour around the country?' Pretty scary that ..."

"What did you tell him?"

David shook his head, "Nothing ... just shrugged. I never thought anyone would remember that."

"Just shows how memorable an event it was," Phillip smiled. "Let's go grab a seat, shall we?" The bar offered a number of niches and corner tables which guaranteed at least a modicum of privacy. Phillip was still determined to get to his subject. The brothers were just about to pick up their glasses when there was a commotion right behind David. A lady carrying a tray on which stood three or four full glasses tripped and lost her balance. David's left arm shot out backwards in a flash to stop her from falling. With his right hand he snatched the tray and lifted it high above everybody's head, stabilizing it to prevent most of the drinks from spilling. The lady clutched David's arm as if it were a life-belt. Now she was on her feet again and began looking for her drinks. The entire intermezzo lasted only a few seconds but it earned David a big round of applause from everyone who had witnessed it.

"How the hell did you see her? She was right behind you," somebody asked the obvious question. Phillip thought he might as well supply an appropriate explanation.

"My brother has exceptional peripheral vision, no accidents ever happen when he is around. I have a feeling he sees around corners just as easily." More laughter.

David was pleased with his brother's answer. Although seeing around corners, he thought, was probably going it a bit.

A little later, as the brothers sat opposite each other at a small corner table, Phillip asked, "Do you know David, why I wanted to talk to you tonight?" and since David did not reply, he answered his own question. "It's about you and Kid ... this is really important to me. Tell me what happened that night ... tell me how it was, can you?"

320

David sat with his hands locked together prayer fashion, his forearms lying on the table. He was talking to the triangle of table top in front of him when he started, "Kid asked me for help ... I did what I could ... I saw it as my duty to ... to get her better. I fed her the hot tea by the spoonfuls ... she was in the bath, bubbles up to her neck. It was after the bath when ... I screwed up, didn't I? I did wrong to kiss her. Kid was weak ... kind of not herself when she asked me. Yes, I kissed her ... I did. Just a kiss. Kid and I are best friends. She loves *you* Phillip ... you only, no one else."

Phillip watched his brother carefully. He could almost feel how hard David had to concentrate to get this story out accurately and understandably. David continued doggedly. "When I was in hospital ... long time ago ... do you know ... the doctors told me the war had made me sterile. That's all they told me, but it wasn't all ... my whole life was stuffed. Once I was out in the streets and on my own ... that's when I found out. I was a real mess." He stopped to gather his thoughts still looking down at the table. "Women scared me then ... jail was a good place to get away from being exposed ... I never understood ... why women kept pursuing me ... I mean, I never showed an obvious interest."

Phillip could not stifle a little smile. He shook his head when he said, "I know why David ... it's because of your stunning looks ... your blue eyes and ..."

"Oh, shut up, will you?" David lifted his head and made

eye contact with his brother. He didn't know what to make of Phillip's explanation.

"I knew you were not going to like it, but it's true, believe me."

David thought about it for a minute, then continued where he left off, "Even now ... I don't know how to handle women ... I usually avoid them. Kid and I ... we are friends. I'm fond of her. You guys, you and Kid ... you have been real good to me. Please Phillip, I don't want to lose you again because I screwed up that night. I'm real sorry."

After David's last plea, Phillip started to feel tears burning behind his eyes. He tried to blink them back but David saw them anyway. Phillip had never been good at hiding his tears. David reached across the table and put his large hand on his brother's wrist. "I'm sorry if I caused you pain, Phillip."

Phillip nodded, tried to smile and changed the subject. "How is my little wife doing as a martial arts student? Is she still in the same class? And is she concentrating now?"

"Umm ... I wish you wouldn't ask a dozen question in one go. Remember that's what got me into trouble with your mate Jim? OK, she is not a very good student ... got the concentration span of a ten-year old and ... oh yes, she is not in that class any longer."

"Private tuition again?"

"Not quite. I'm teaching her together with a young lad, a new student who joined only a few weeks ago."

Little did either of the brothers know at that time that the tuition of this new student was going to develop into a major drama for his master instructor.

XXIII

The new student's name was Thomas Clark. He was thirteen years old, he was small for his age and rather fragile looking, but what distinguished him from most students of his age was his radiant smile and a visible interest in everything around him.

Thomas was seen standing by the side of the dojo watching first a children's class immediately followed by the training of a group of intermediate students. Thomas had read about the phenomenon of the master putting himself in a karate mind-frame, 'a state of absolute composure - a state of mind which excludes all mundane and non-karate related issues' the book stated. That must be the mind-frame this master is in right now, Thomas thought. I can feel a sort of aura surrounding him. Without knowing it, Thomas was already close to worshipping the man he saw as his future karate instructor and he felt as if he was about to ask for a private audience with the Great Master.

"Can I help you?" he heard a voice beside him. It belonged to one of the students who had also been watching the class.

"I'd like to speak to the instructor, but I can wait ... I'm in no hurry."

"This is his last class," the student said, "he will talk to you after that."

David had seen the young boy the moment he entered the dojo, but had only registered him on the periphery of his consciousness. David never missed anything. At the conclusion of his last class, still wearing his white karate outfit, David approached Thomas.

Thomas looked up at David, he had to bend his head way back as if looking up at a skyscraper. "My name is Thomas," he said bravely even though David's size intimidated him greatly. "Sir, I've come to ask if you would accept me as one of your students, please sir. I've never been able to learn karate, but I know quite a lot about martial arts. I've read every book available on the subject. Please sir, will you let me be your student? No other school in town has agreed to enroll me."

David had been listening carefully and he could feel the intensity in the boy's words. Now he lowered himself into a crouching position as he asked, "Why is karate so important to you? And please call me David."

"It's important to me because ... it's not just like sport, I mean competitive sport where one wins and the other loses, is it sir ... David? It's an art ... it's to do with concentration and breathing and that. That's what I've read. That's what I'd like to learn."

David nodded in agreement. "You said other schools didn't enroll you, why?"

"Oh ... just because I'm ... not very big and strong. I've got something wrong with my blood, but I'm really OK ... most of the time. I can pay the tuition fees; I've got some money of my own. My parents ... they think karate is too rough, they just don't understand."

David liked the reasons Thomas had given for wanting to learn karate, they pretty much coincided with his own ideas and beliefs of the art of karate. He didn't make any detailed inquiries about the illness the lad had mentioned, instead David relied on his knowledge and on his conviction that meditation and controlled breathing would be beneficiary to Thomas. His parents, it seemed, were either wrongly informed or not informed at all.

"Yes, I will take you on as my student. I'll start you on a private course ... then we'll see."

Thomas was so happy, he wanted to hug this huge man who was going to be his teacher - the man who would re-

326

veal to him all the secrets of karate. But Thomas also wanted to be tough and not show any tears, so he simply held out his hand to shake that of his future instructor, then they arranged day and time for his first lesson.

"I can get here on my bike after school," Thomas said. "Mom and dad are both at work all day and can't drive me here."

David nodded, then remembered to ask, "Would you please write down your home address and phone number for me before you leave? And don't worry about fees just yet." With this the deal was sealed; both student and master were happy, each in his own way.

It was a couple of weeks later when David unexpectedly asked Kid to wait for him after class. "I'm teaching this new student, Thomas," he said, "I'd like to train you and him together. He is only thirteen, a beginner but real promising ..."

"... unlike me, you mean. Am I even too useless to remain in the class I'm in?"

"Something like that, yes," David said in all seriousness.

"You know David, you couldn't tell a lie ... not even to stop me from feeling like an absolute idiot."

This produced a warm smile on David's face. He placed his hands on her shoulders and looked down at her, "You're alright Kid, you just need to stop a million thoughts going through your mind twenty-four hours a day. Oh yes and ... would you pick Thomas up at his home and take him back after class? Here is his address."

And that was how Kid and Thomas started training together, talking together before and after class in Kid's car and becoming friends. Everybody was happy with the way things were if only it hadn't been for the fact that Thomas wanted to pay for his own fees. This issue weighed heavy on David's mind. He would gladly have charged Thomas no fees at all. But can I do it, he asked himself, or will this go against the rules of the school? I must discuss it with Kid, she is good at stuff like that.

Kid's answer, when he consulted her on that subject, confirmed his fears and doubts. "You can't just teach him in your working time and at the school without enrolling him, I mean without telling anyone. There is paperwork to be completed and that," Kid told him competently.

"So, what do I do? Thomas said he was going to pay with his own money ... that doesn't sound right. Maybe his parents can't afford the fees. Maybe they are a big family. Seems like both mom and dad work all day."

"Umm, yes possible ... I have an idea," Kid beamed at the mere thought of being able to solve a difficult problem. "You have to enroll Thomas, do all the right things for the school, but then ... and you don't say that to anyone ... *you* pay the money into the account rather than Thomas. Have you got enough? If not I can pay half of it. How's that?"

"Sounds good. So Thomas thinks it's for free, right?"

"Yes ... that's the general idea." Kid was quite confident in the success of her scheme.

The training sessions continued twice weekly, the money was paid by David first, then with some help from Kid. All was well.

But Kid's clever idea unfortunately, did not work for a very long time, since neither David's teaching nor Kid's payment scheme met with the approval of Mr Clark, Thomas' dad.

Mr Clark found out quite inadvertently one evening when he watched Maria empty the washing machine. Maria was the live-in cook, maid, cleaner and erstwhile nanny. She was loved by everyone, she was irreplaceable, she was part of the family. "What's this white jacket, Maria? The one you just took out?" Mr Clark inquired.

Maria, unlike mom and dad, was in the know of Thomas' secret martial arts training. Now she was cornered and knew she could not tell Mr Clark a lie, so she said, "Sir, it belongs to Thomas. It's ... a sort of uniform he wears for his training."

"What training?"

"I'm sorry sir. Thomas should have told you ... it's karate training."

Mr Clark was close to screaming his anger and frustration at Maria but thought better of it. He took a deep breath before he said, "I'll have this out with my son ... thanks for telling me, Maria."

The Clark family home was one of the most beautiful places and in one of the most expensive and high-class suburbs of Knoxville. The large downstairs living and dining rooms were decorated with antique furniture, paintings of great beauty and great value - all of them originals - hung on the walls, the floors were covered with soft Persian carpets of delicate colors and intricate patterns, a wide curved staircase led up to a number of bedrooms, all with en-suite bathrooms. There were wide verandas, a games room, a den which was Thomas' domain at all times. The house was surrounded by beautifully manicured lawns and gardens. There was also a large swimming pool with adjacent spa pool. The Clarks had indeed everything money could buy.

Mr Clark took a few bold strides past the kitchen and came to a halt at the bottom of the stairs, "Thomas, come down here at once," he called in a peremptory tone of voice.

Thomas was lying on his bed, he was listening to his favorite music through his headphones while reading the latest issue of a magazine called 'Martial Arts Today'. He was blissfully unaware of his father's summons. The first thing Thomas knew of the drama he had created was when his dad burst into his room without knocking, an expression of anger and outrage on his face.

"Turn that music off, I need to talk to you."

Thomas needed no more than those words to fully understand the nature of his father's exasperation. *He has found out about my training somehow, there is going to be big trouble*, he thought. He obediently removed his headphones, switched the music off and sat up bracing himself for the approaching storm.

"How long has this karate training been going on? You knew very well that your mother and I did not give you permission to join a martial arts school. We have been through this many times. I find it hard to believe that you simply went behind our backs. Please explain." And that was an order.

"If you had only tried to understand when I explained about martial arts, its essence and its beauty, this would not have happened, dad. I wanted nothing more passionately than to study the art of karate. You knew that, yet you stubbornly denied me the privilege of doing what was closest to my heart ..."

"Oh, cut it out Thomas. You know as well as mom and I that karate is totally unsuitable for you."

"Look dad, I'm sick of being seen as and treated like I was some sort of freak. Ever since I've been diagnosed with this blasted leukemia I'm being singled out as the poor little boy who is dying ... the poor boy who can't do anything other boys do. I know my ... my life expectancy is ... nowhere, so can't you at least let me make the best of the time I have left?" When he got to this point, Thomas was close to tears but they were not tears of self-pity, they reflected genuine anger and frustration.

The father closed his eyes momentarily, his son's words seemed to have hit an exposed nerve. "What school did you join, Thomas? And who is your teacher?"

"It's in Market Street, right in the centre of town ... there is only a small sign saying that it is owned by a Mr G. Blythe. But they have *the* top karate master there and he teaches me ... kind of privately at the moment ... with just one other student. The teacher's name is David McCabe."

"And who, may I ask, is paying your tuition fees?"

"He is not charging me anything." A flat statement, but the truth as far as Thomas knew.

"Right, and are you telling me that it is the appropriate thing for a responsible adult to do to go behind the back of a student's parents? You don't think that the teacher should have made sure to get parental consent before taking you on as his student? Or didn't you tell him ... about your health condition ... ?"

"I did ... sort of."

"OK, here is what I'm going to do. I'll talk to my lawyer ... we'll find this precious master of yours ... I'll sue him ... I'll take him to court ... I will not let him get away with this." And as an afterthought he added, "On top of all that, it looks like he is cheating the school management out of their tuition fees." With these final words Mr Clark left the room, stormed downstairs and started pacing up and down the length of the entrance hall. When he had convinced himself that the teacher, and not his son, was the culprit, he went to the phone and dialed his lawyer's private number.

David was training a group of four aspiring Black Belts - one of the highlights of his job. The two detectives - a man and a woman - entered the dojo ten minutes before the end of the training session and found that they were inadvertently treated to a master-class worth televising. They consulted with each other in whispers before deciding to watch the class and give second priority to their orders of taking Mr McCabe back to the station to answer a few questions. The two detectives were simply mesmerized by the spectacle that played out in front of them. A number of students sat on the side of the dojo mats observing the course and seemingly following it with every fiber of their being; there was complete silence in the hall. At the end of the class, the four students stood solid and straight facing the tall blond man - the one who wore a black belt. They bowed, then following the master's example they knelt down and sat in silence for as long as the master deemed necessary.

Once teacher and students had bowed themselves off the dojo mats, one of the spectators approached the detectives. "Can I help you?" he asked politely.

"We are from the police," the female officer said. "We're here to talk to Mr McCabe."

The student looked at them, stunned and wide-eyed. "I get him for you ... he is the master you just saw, ma'am." .

A little while later David walked up to the two detectives, he moved in harmonious and elastic strides, his face showed neither curiosity nor apprehension. He was completely unfazed when he said, "You want to talk to me?"

"Warrant officers Foster and Kershaw," the officers introduced themselves, showing their identifications. "We need to ask you a few questions. It's about one of your students, Thomas Clark." No change of expression on David's face, so the officer continued, "His father is suing you for training Thomas without seeking his permission. The boy is thirteen, therefore still a minor. What do you have to say?"

"What do you want me to say? Yes, I am Thomas' teacher ... he is an excellent student. What now?"

"Will you come to the station with us? We need to talk about this some more."

"Like this? Or do I get a chance to shower and change?"

"Does everyone here know that you are training Thomas?" Warrant officer Foster asked.

"Not the people I've just taught ... they are not from this school."

"Better if you don't talk about this right now, OK? We wait here while you have your shower."

What the detectives didn't know, was that among the students who had watched the class was Mario, the soon-to-be lawyer, and with his acute lawyer's senses he had over-heard just enough of the conversation to be put on alert. He said nothing in the shower room not wanting to compro-mise David, but he made a mental note to inform Phillip of this development as soon as possible.

David was made to wait for his interview in a small room near the entrance of the police station and a young uniformed police officer was quick to use these few min-utes to ask, "You are a karate fighter, we're told ... do you cut bricks in half with your bare hands?"

David had heard this silly question so many times be-fore, he felt like telling the cop to just shut up, but thought better of it. "No, I don't," he said. "I could of course, but what would be the point?"

Just then David was called into one of the interview rooms. It contained a square table with four chairs, a tape recorder and not much else. David was now in his street clothes as he sat down opposite the two detectives. He leaned back in his seat, his hands folded in his lap, both feet flat on the ground, his face a mask of stoicism.

It was the male detective, officer Foster, who started the interview. "How long have you been training Thomas?"

"A few weeks ... couple of months maybe."

"We understand that he came looking for you. He

wanted you to be his teacher. Is that correct?"

David nodded, then remembered that it was all going to be on tape, so he said, "Yes."

"Didn't it occur to you then, or later, that a lad of thirteen needed his father's consent to enroll at a martial arts school?"

"No, it didn't. Thomas made it very clear that karate training was ... was of great importance to him. He gave me all the best reasons for wanting to learn ... he is a very dedicated student. He knew quite a lot about martial arts ... all out of books." David spoke in a flat tone of voice; he sat perfectly still, didn't fidget with his hands, never crossed and uncrossed his legs, never moved a muscle. Both officers noticed his calm demeanor and started to admire the complete control David had over his body. It looks like he has control over his mind as well as his body, it crossed their minds.

"Did Thomas mention anything about the state of his health?"

"Briefly ... yes. He said something was wrong with his blood ... but that he was quite OK, really."

"And that still didn't make you think that karate could possibly be the wrong kind of sport for him?"

"No ... quite the opposite. The study of karate ... can and will be of great benefit to him ... to his health and ... also to his mind. I know it's important that I get everything right with his training." He came to a halt, took a deep breath then continued, "Karate is not a sport ... it's an art and a philosophy. The class you watched today gave you a perfect example of that."

"Was this a special class?"

"Yeah, I'm preparing these four men for their Black Belt grading test."

"I see. Do you think they'll pass?"

"I know they'll pass ... it's my duty to make sure of it."

Uncertain looks passed between the two officers, neither was sure how to interpret this last assertion. They had been told that Thomas thought of Mr McCabe as the greatest karate master in the whole country, and they had naturally assumed this to be an expression of juvenile over-enthusiasm and teacher-worship. Now however, they began to wonder if there could indeed be some truth in Thomas' statement. But the officers knew not to show any signs of their doubts and of their growing insight into this man's personality. They continued their questioning.

"So you firmly believe that you have done nothing wrong. In fact you are convinced that Thomas will benefit from your training. And you stick with this?"

"Yes. One thing Thomas said was that ... that his parent's didn't understand anything about martial arts ... and about karate in particular. He also said he would pay the school fees ... he said he had money of his own."

"And what did that tell you, Mr McCabe?"

David had no trouble finding answers. At least the cops know to ask one question at the time, he thought. "That maybe Thomas' parents could not afford the extra fees for the karate school... could be that they are a big family ... his mom has to work full time, Thomas told me."

As the two officers listened to David's interpretation of Thomas' words, they both had to make a conscious effort not to smile. How could he have gotten things so terribly wrong? Mr and Mrs Clark were extraordinarily wealthy people and Thomas was their only child. But by the same token, the officers were touched by David's innocence, his concern and his truthfulness. "And *did* Thomas pay his tuition fees?"

"Umm ... no, but you had better talk to Kid about that."

"Who is Kid?"

"Her name is Kid McCabe ... I've been training her and Thomas together ... they make a good team. Kid is also my sister ... sister-in-law." And for the first time since the start of the interview, a smile appeared on David's face and a sparkle could be seen in his eyes. Warrant officer Kershaw, the lady officer, who had been fascinated by David's stunning looks from the moment she saw him in his role as instructor, almost melted now as she saw his smile. His deep voice brought her back to the interview room.

"Why don't I talk to Mr Clark?" she heard. "It's just a misunderstanding ... can easily be sorted if I could just speak to him."

"Mr Clark does not think so." It was a rather lame answer but the best the police officer could do at the time. The interview was terminated and the tape recorder turned off. Then a knock on the door. A uniformed cop stuck his head through the partly opened door and handed a pile of documents to her colleague. David waited patiently while the officers scanned the pages, conferred with each other in a whisper then sat down again.

"Did you ever consider that karate could be too tough for Thomas ... even dangerous maybe?"

"Karate is not dangerous when practiced on the dojo mats. I also know how to go easy on a student ... with the physical part."

Detective Kershaw now looked up from the documents she had been reading; they were David's criminal record. "But then, you spent more than five years in jail, didn't you, for killing a man in a street fight ... using karate."

So that's what they're reading, David thought, should have known they would dig up stuff to use against me. "Yes. I paid for having killed that man ... but for all the other people I killed ... in the jungle of Vietnam ... I was decorated instead."

An uncomfortable silence hung over the room after this

last statement which David had made without any sign of pent-up anger. What sort of answer could anyone give to such obvious and incontestable injustice? And why was this man not resentful of a system that had treated him so unfairly? "We'll need to talk to your sister-in-law. That's all for the moment, Mr McCabe."

David bounced up from his chair in his usual manner and stood towering over the two officers making them look like garden gnomes. He said nothing, asked nothing. It's best to let the cops think that they are in charge, he thought remembering similar situations in his past. He ducked through the doorway and walked into a big open entrance hall.

There was some commotion at the front desk; someone gesticulated trying to explain something; someone shouted an order; a black toddler cried helplessly in the confusion then started to run. The little boy saw David further down the hall and ran in a direct line towards him, grabbed his leg and held on desperately. Without undue agitation and without a word, David reached down to the toddler with one hand, the little boy grabbed the extended arm and held on as if for dear life. David lifted him up effortlessly and sat him comfortably on his hip, then he put his other arm around the little boy in an effort to make him feel safe. The boy started to calm down as he dug his little hands into David's long thick hair. David let him do as he liked. Now the toddler burrowed his tear-streamed face and his runny nose in David's shoulder and a minute later a contented giggling sound could be heard. A whole brigade of police personnel stood and watched the incident as though it was some form of entertainment.

David walked up to the baby's mother who was still trying to explain her situation. She was a tall, slim, dark skinned lady. David placed her son gently into her arms.

"Thanks brother," the lady said with a smile.

David simply nodded, "Take care now."

At that point finally, one of the officers came out of his stupor and asked the silliest but most obvious question, "Do you know each other?"

"No," was the extent of the answer which came from both the mother and David.

"Then why ... why did your son run ... to this man ... if he doesn't know him?"

Another stupid question, the lady thought, typical cop. "My little baby needed some comfort in this confusion," she said. "Children know where to find that ... they are clever that way." She said it with maybe just a tinge of condescension.

David ruffled the baby's woolly black hair and smiled at the cleverness of the lady's answer. On his way out he saw a lot of heads shaking in obvious disbelief.

That afternoon, a few phone calls related to David's

crime of teaching Thomas, were made around town ... some were successful, others were not. One was made by Thomas to Kid's home, he did not reach her there. Another call was made by Mrs Clark from her office to her son at their home, she did not reach him either since Thomas was staying at the house of a school friend. The revelation of her son's karate training and her husband's boundless anger had come to Mrs Clark at entirely the wrong time. Over the previous few weeks she had found her son in almost permanent good humor and high spirits. She had been pleased to see him more relaxed when she came home at night, she had found him more confident and generally happier than usual. But since his father had aired his wrath and started procedures to sue Thomas' teacher, her son had lapsed into a despondency that worried Mrs Clark greatly.

A third call was made by Mario to Phillip at work. Mario knew this was risky since Phillip's workplace was in a big office where a dozen telephones rang simultaneously and almost constantly and Phillip had very little time for private conversations. Still, Mario's information was important enough for him to take that risk. "Phillip," Mario said, "there is something you need to know, I shall be brief." Then he lined out in a few well chosen sentences what he had heard in the dojo earlier that afternoon.

"Does that mean David is going to jail?" was Phillip's first question. He was in a state of instant panic.

"I shouldn't think so ... not really. I mean, the guy *can* take this to court but ..." he left the sentence unfinished then added, "David will probably need a lawyer. I can get one for him."

"Good idea and thanks, Mario. Does Kid know?"

Mario was only guessing when he said, "She might by now. I'm sure the police will want to talk to her. But don't worry ... she'll know how to handle the cops."

"I'm sure she will ... in her very own and totally unorthodox way. Got to go, thanks Mario, I'll call you tonight."

Phillip had only marginally managed to sound cheerful and unperturbed. The truth was that he was terrified. If any remnants of ambivalence over David's little stint with Kid had still been lingering in Phillip's mind, they were now replaced by genuine concern for his brother's future. I'll not see David go to jail again, he swore to himself. I'll do absolutely anything ... anything to help him win a court case if there should be one.

The detectives made some phone calls too. They found out a few things about Mrs Kid McCabe. They knew where she lived, where she worked and what shift she was doing on that particular day. Now they were on their way to Alfredo's restaurant.

Kid was working in the shop that afternoon. She stood behind the counter when the two investigating officers entered. They were the same officers who had spoken to David earlier on and they took one look at Kid and shook their heads in unison.

"This is ridiculous. She's got to be the guy's sister ... not sister-in-law, "detective Foster whispered to his partner. Now he addressed Kid.

"Mrs McCabe?" Both officers showed their badges and identified themselves then came straight to the point. "We understand that you are taking karate classes together with Thomas Clark."

"Yes, I am."

"We need to ask you a few questions."

Kid nodded but showed neither surprise nor concern even though she had no idea what was going on. Instinct told her that it was better to humor police officers rather than to confront them.

"Are you aware that Thomas is suffering from a serious ... affliction, and are you also aware that his parents were against his taking up karate?"

"To the first question: yes, only he never said it was serious. All he said was ... something to do with his blood but that he was really OK. To the second question: no, I didn't. I have never spoken to his parents."

"I see. We'd like you to come to the station with us. We have a few more questions."

"I need to ask my employer, my shift is not finished." Kid said, then walked into the family room. The short conversation the officers overheard took place entirely in Italian to their utter amazement.

At the police station, Kid was ushered into the same room where David had been questioned earlier ... now they started to buttonhole her.

"Mrs McCabe, Thomas' father is suing his teacher for training his son without having obtained his parents' consent. Did you know that Thomas is: a) a minor and b) suffering from leukemia?"

"What's Thomas suffering from?"

"Leukemia, it's cancer of the blood and is ... terminal. So, do you understand now why his father is against letting his son train in karate?"

"I didn't know about his illness, but now that I do, I think Mr Clark's decision is completely the wrong one to make. You see, karate is an art, and that's how Sensei teaches it ... it will help Thomas, it will make him feel better and stronger in body and mind." It was quite inadvertent that Kid and David had expressed their convictions in almost identical terms.

The detectives did not miss it and immediately concluded that brother and sister – in-law – could well have coordinated their replies. Detective Kershaw asked, "When did you last speak to your ... teacher? What did you call him?"

"Sensei, that's the Japanese word for teacher and master. David is our Sensei, we all call him that in the dojo. I

345

saw him last ... two days ago, during class ... but we didn't kind of speak. When David is in his karate mind-frame he doesn't talk to us ... like in general conversation."

"I see," detective Kershaw said, even though she did not see at all. "Tell us how Thomas' tuition fees were paid."

"Well, Thomas said he would pay ... he said he had money of his own but David felt bad about that. You see, we figured that his parents were not financially in a position to pay extra school fees ... maybe a big family ... many children ... college fees and that, so I came up with this idea." Kid explained her 'big idea' and concluded with, "so the school does not get cheated, and Thomas is happy thinking that his tuition is for free. It works both ways." She looked proudly at her two interlocutors. "Also, I pick him up and drive him back after class so he doesn't have to ride his bike. You see, his mom can't drive him. She has to work all day."

The two officers shot each other understanding glances, then, "Do you pick him up at his home?"

"No, he waits for me at a corner, only three minutes from his home - a spot where it's easy to pull up and drive off again so I don't have to go into the cul-de-sac." It was only then that Kid noticed the puzzled looks of the two cops facing her. "Yeah, I know ..." she said out of the blue, "I know you think that David is my brother, but he isn't my very real brother ... he is my husband's brother ... make of our facial resemblance what you will." This finally provoked two smiles. "What is Mr Clark intending to do?"

"He says he will sue David ... take him to court if need be."

"I don't understand. What about he and David talk together and smooth out all these misunderstandings? David is doing the best he can for Thomas ... surely that is what his parents want, too."

And for the second or third time, it became clear to the detectives that Kid and David talked, thought and reasoned on exactly the same wavelength. There was no need for them to conspire or rehearse their answers.

"Can you talk to the man?" Kid asked. "Suggest a time and place for them to discuss the issue?"

"We'll see what we can do." This was slightly more encouraging than the answer given to David ... but still far from promising.

A conference took place in Kid and Phillip's lounge room that evening. Kid went to the kitchen to prepare a few plates of finger food to hand around. Phillip got the drinks ready while the four men in the lounge were making small talk. Kid was proud to be hostess at such an important gathering and she wanted to make sure not to miss even one word. Present were Mario, Robert, Mr McDonald, a gentleman Kid did not know, David and of course Phillip. Mr McDonald was a friend of Mario's, he was also of the 'lawyering trade', and Kid guessed that he was an authority on criminal matters. He lined out all the facts in a lawyerly fashion. He stressed David's mistake of starting Thomas' training without seeking the consent of his parents, then he added the fact that Thomas was still a minor. He emphasized the seriousness of omitting to consider Thomas' health condition, and only then did the lawyer talk about Thomas and his family. He mentioned that Mr Clark was the owner of a chain of department stores and that Mrs Clark had her own career in the fashion trade. Mr McDonald had already done a lot of research in the few hours since Mario had approached him.

"Excuse me, sir," Kid could curb her confusion no longer, "are you saying that the Clark family are filthy rich? Sorry, I mean very wealthy ... big mansion, swimming pool, mom and dad a career each? Then why would Thomas suggest he'd pay the tuition fees out of his pocket money? Makes no sense ... none at all." Kid was of course taking the words out of David's mouth. The other four men in the room however, had trouble hiding a smile at the way she misconstrued the situation with such genuine outrage.

It was Mario who knew how to appease Kid, he had expected just that reaction from her. "You are on the wrong track here, Kid. Thomas wanted to pay ... not because there was no money in the family, but because he knew that his father was dead set against him taking up karate training, and the reason dad opposed karate was ..."

"I know ... it's because Thomas is not altogether a healthy young lad, right?"

Everybody nodded silently as Kid pronounced the obvious in vintage Kid fashion. But no one had counted on David's opinion - an opinion which would up-end the whole issue once again.

"But I didn't make a mistake ... it's his dad who made it. I know that my teaching will help Thomas. I'm just as concerned about the lad's health as his father is. He shouldn't be accusing me of wrongdoing ... maybe better if he came and watched some of our classes, then he would understand what his son's training is all about."

Mr McDonald realized that David was taking an approach based strictly on common sense, instinct and goodwill. Maybe David is indeed the supreme master instructor Mario has portrayed, the lawyer thought. When he spoke again, Mr McDonald made sure he spoke in David's language.

"I understand that you have set your mind and your heart on using your art to help Thomas, and I personally believe that you have some power to do just that. We have another karate expert her," and he inclined his head towards Robert. "Would you second that statement, Mr Conner?"

"Yes, I would. I am convinced that David's approach to karate and his teaching can be of considerable benefit to Thomas."

"Good. But there is the legal side to this issue, David, and that is what Mr Clark's accusation is based on. Do you understand that? He is very angry at not having been consulted. He is the father, he is a rich man, he owns big department stores and is used to having people around him do as he says. You have offended him ... he is taking revenge."

All through the lawyer's speech, Phillip and Kid sat side by side on the sofa. Phillip had his arm loosely draped around Kid's shoulder, she was trembling almost imperceptibly.

"If Mr Clark decides to take this to court, there is going to be a trial by jury," the lawyer's explanation was directed at David. "The jury will consist of twelve citizens – men and women of all walks of life - and they will decide if you are guilty or not. Some of the jurors might be mothers or fathers of thirteen year old sons and they will empathize with Mr Clark. Other jurors could be convinced of the healing powers karate could have on Thomas and would feel that you are doing the right thing. You see, there is no way to second-guess the verdict of a jury. We would call character witnesses: your brother, your sister-in-law, Mario and Robert. Mario has also pointed out Mr Goldberg who has a very high opinion of you. Many of your students and some of their parents will want to stand by you. They will tell the court that you are a decent, law-abiding citizen and that you had Thomas' welfare at heart when you made your decision to take him on as a student." He paused for a second then added, "Mr Clark would call witnesses too. He has a high standing in society and we don't know who his witnesses would be. Do you understand all that David?"

"Yes sir. But ... Mr Clark's lawyer will also use my criminal record against me, right? The police guys had already dug up the whole lot."

"Yes, there is that, too," Mr McDonald nodded seemingly deep in thought. "But I'm still hoping that this whole issue can be settled in a conversation between you and Mr Clark. Are you prepared to talk to Thomas' parents David, and explain your side of the story?"

"I would like that, sir."

Time for Kid to hand around more nibbles, Phillip fetched a few more bottles of beer; the official part of the evening's discussion had come to an end. Phillip was worried about what could happen to his brother, Kid was confident that David would triumph in a court case, Mario was ambivalent and Robert admired David's firm belief in the healing powers of martial arts. That left the lawyer's feelings ... he was determined to win this case if it should go to court.

Mr Clark was sitting in one of the soft leather seats in his luxurious lounge room behind an open newspaper. But rather than read the print which stared at him, he was deep in thought. He was a very troubled man.

It's our son's diagnosis, he reflected sadly, that has changed my whole life. My relationship with my wife has deteriorated because of it, we have practically ceased to communicate. I don't even know how my wife is coping with the devastating knowledge of our son's predicament. We have never been able to share our sorrow and our pain. To the outside world we both pretend to be OK - we give the impression that we are coping - but I know it's only a façade. Mr Clark was deeply saddened.

And as if this was not enough, just a few days ago, Mr Clark had found out that his son had started to train in martial arts, the one hobby he and his wife had most vehemently objected to. Mr Clark remembered that some time ago, Thomas came home with a flyer announcing a recruiting fête at a martial arts school. The flyer showed a photo of a karate instructor in white garb and black belt in some impossible position, seemingly flying through mid-air. Thomas had asked to go and watch the master-classes advertised on the flyer and he and his wife had given their permission. We meant to appear reasonable and open-minded, he remembered sadly, maybe it was a mistake to let him go. Thomas was thirteen years old and Mr Clark knew he had to give him the freedom to choose how he wanted to spend his Saturday afternoons. Father and son had come precariously close to a full-blown argument over the issue of Thomas joining this school: the father could not understand his son's fascination with martial arts and the son was not prepared to accept his father's reasons for not allowing it - a hopeless deadlock.

And now Thomas had simply gone behind his father's back and started training with this fancy master of his. Mr Clark had been beside himself with anger. At first it had felt as if his son had thumbed his nose at his own father, had ridiculed him and cheated him. But almost as soon as his anger had taken hold of him, Mr Clark had shifted it away from Thomas and put the blame squarely on the shoulders of his teacher. The man is an adult and should have acted in a responsible way, instead he used cunning and deviousness, and in an underhanded way forced himself between father and son, Mr Clark repeated in his mind. It was the perfect justification for his present initiative to sue. Mr Clark had decided not to let this guy get away with it ... he wanted revenge.

But his decision to take the teacher to court started to backfire very soon. Thomas' health deteriorated, he lost his recently acquired energy and his new joie de vivre. He lapsed into a depression so deep it caused his parents grave concern. He gave no explanation, he refused to talk, he spent most of his time locked in his room in a kind of inertia. He seemed to be giving up on life, on his future ... on himself.

It was this behavior combined with his wife's insistence that Thomas had been noticeably healthier for some weeks and her conviction that the clandestine training may have been the real reason for his relative wellbeing that led Mr Clark finally to concede to holding a talk with the karate instructor. It had taken some negotiation to make Mr Clark change his mind but when he did, he decided against his lawyer's advice to meet on neutral ground in the impersonal surroundings of a lawyer's office. Instead he chose to conduct the meeting at home. Now, Mr Clark, his wife and his son were all awaiting the arrival of the karate instructor David McCabe.

Just before Mr Clark folded his paper in preparation to receive his 'guest', he briefly pictured the sort of person this karate master would be. Probably all muscle and powerful physique, he thought, the fast-talker who has all the reasons for the vital necessity of karate in my son's life well rehearsed and ready for all the world to hear. Mr Clark could just imagine the guy, probably with a crew cut, sweeping through the door, taking over the whole room by his mere presence, displaying little samples here and there of his supremacy in this God-given sport. The thought did not anger Mr Clark, rather it made him smile and shake his head at the futility of it all. Just then he heard a car pull up in the driveway and a minute later there was a knock on the front door.

"Dad, mom this is David McCabe," Thomas said politely when he showed David into the room then, "David, my mom, my dad."

Mr Clark looked David up and down trying not to stare. So this is the monster-karate-guy I pictured in my mind only a few minutes ago. He sure is a giant, he stands tall and straight, maybe that's how karate masters stand, Mr. Clark thought with some amusement, but I must not judge simply on appearances, that wouldn't be right either. He was somewhat reassured when he realized that at least there was no arrogance in the man's facial expression.

"Thanks for agreeing to talk to me," David said slowly in his deep baritone voice. He had made an effort to look his best. He wore a freshly ironed white shirt, tailor made black pants, his long wavy hair brushed and neatly combed. David looked very respectable indeed. At Mrs Clark's invitation they all sat down, although David would have preferred to stand. A standing position always made him feel more confident in a difficult situation.

David knew exactly what this meeting had to achieve and there was no doubt in his mind that he would leave this house after having obtained Mr and Mrs Clark's permission to continue with Thomas' training. David had an extra sense for these things. Now he waited for Mr Clark to speak.

David remembered Mr McDonald's instructions not to press his point straight away but to listen carefully, then answer all the questions that were put to him truthfully.

Mr Clark started in a flat but rational tone of voice. "You do understand Mr McCabe, that you were not legally entitled to start training our son. At the age of thirteen he is still a minor and hence needs our permission to become a member of a martial arts school."

"I do understand that now, sir."

"You also know the reason why we are against our son's karate training, don't you?"

"Yes, I know your reason but ... with all due respect ... I cannot agree with it ... sir."

Now it was his wife's turn to state her opinion. She delivered it in a businesslike and unemotional tone of voice, it sounded rehearsed. "Before you continue Mr McCabe, surely you can understand that this sport of yours is too strenuous and too rough for Thomas. Do I have to spell it all out ... the precarious state of his health, the constant threat of dramatic and unmanageable symptoms? It's not real hard to see why my husband and I cannot possibly allow him to continue with this most unsuitable hobby. You can see that Mr McCabe, can't you?"

David knew instinctively that now was the moment to state his argument in support of her son's training. He didn't trust himself to look at either of Thomas' parents. He sat on the edge of the soft seat, his feet firmly planted on the floor, his hands palm down on either side of his thighs, like a wild animal ready to jump. He looked straight ahead at his own thoughts and convictions.

"Ma'am, karate is neither a sport nor a hobby ... it's a philosophy ... a way of life. It is not just the tough fighting that you see sometimes on television ... karate includes self-control, concentration, controlled breathing and ... meditation. I know that karate ... practiced the proper way ... will be of great benefit to Thomas ... to his mind, his body." David was delivering his convictions in a measured way. It was clear to him by then that Mr and Mrs Clark did not have any concrete knowledge of the essence of martial arts. They saw it as a rough fighting sport with a high risk factor and therefore unsuitable for their son. Period.

Not exactly the fast-talker I imagined, it went through Mr Clark's mind, and he is also not making much headway in his task of convincing us of the value of his art.

"Ma'am," David continued doggedly, "maybe you might like to watch one of my classes. It could help you ... I think ... to get a clearer picture ... of karate in its purest form. I do a lot of meditation with my students ... at the beginning and at the end of every class ... even with the youngest ones ... six year olds ..." It was after this last statement that David thought he saw a shadow cross Mrs Clark's face. What was it? Suddenly the hard and suspicious look he had seen in her eyes mellowed and her defiance was replaced by an expression of deep sorrow and pain. This lady is suffering a great deal, David now realized, why didn't I understand that first up? What a tragedy for a mother to know that her thirteen year old son lives with a life threatening illness. David suddenly saw the real Mrs Clark and he was ashamed for having inflicted additional sadness upon her. Now he quickly got up from his seat and walked around the little table to where Mrs Clark was sitting. She looked at him uncomprehendingly and there were tears glistening in her eyes. Her husband could not help but marvel at how nimble this huge man was. He seemed to move with the soundless tension - with the control and precision of a cat.

David lowered himself onto one knee in front of Mrs Clark and said simply, "I'm sorry ma'am, real sorry for having caused you ... more pain. But I know I can help Thomas ... to deal with his life. I know I can, ma'am. But I realize ... that I can only do it with your permission."

While David apologized and offered his help to her son, Mrs Clark was looking unwaveringly into David's deep blue eyes, trying hard not to show her tears. Then she nodded, and with this one gesture, she unmistakably gave her consent.

"Thank you ma'am," David said as he lightly touched her clasped hands which lay in her lap. Then he pulled himself up to his full height, turned around and walked to the other side of the lounge room. He sensed that Mrs Clark broke down in tears after his last words, and he also knew that her husband was now holding her in his arms giving her the love and comfort she needed. He stood unobtrusively in the darker part of the room for some time, then he heard Mr Clark's voice,.

"May I get you a drink, Mr McCabe?"

David turned to face Mr Clark in answer to his question and to his surprise he saw Thomas and his mother holding each other in a tight embrace. It was Thomas who was comforting his mom not the other way around. David closed his eyes for a second, he did not want to give an unguarded display of his own emotions, not right then.

A little later, they all found themselves sitting down in silence, each holding a drink. To an outsider it could well have looked like a companionable silence, but it wasn't. The silence was enforced and awkward. Mr Clark's mind kept going back to this most unforeseeable outcome of their discussion. He had watched in wondrous amazement as his wife had bared her soul to this man who was a complete stranger to her. She had done so without saying a word. It apparently all happened through vibrations or some other mysterious connection. Why did she let this stranger see right into her heart, he wondered, when she has not been able to do the same for me, her husband? How is it that this man and my wife communicated on such a deep level - if only very briefly? It could not have been based simply on the guy's good looks, he thought, this would be totally uncharacteristic of my wife. Mr Clark found no answer to this puzzle. He re-experienced this short intermezzo maybe half a dozen times before he realized that rather than feel pangs of jealousy, he was actually grateful to this master instructor for having in some miraculous way broken through the shell his wife had built around herself in an effort at self-preservation. David had opened new channels along which he, the loving husband, could now pursue his efforts to get his marriage back on track.

Thomas' thoughts went along similar lines, but to him, the little episode between his mom and the master had felt more like watching a magic show. All things fell into place without any indication as to why they did.

Finally, Mr Clark broke the silence, "I feel that my decision to press charges against you was somewhat hasty. I have decided to discontinue the process."

David was close to tears with relief. He lowered his head for just a second trying to hide his loss of control. "Thank you sir, ma'am ... I promise to put everything I've got into Thomas' training ... you are welcome to ... come and watch us any time you like. I'll continue to go easy on the physical part. I've been training Thomas with just one other student ... I'd like to keep it like that."

"There is one more question, Mr McCabe. Thomas tells me that you've charged no tuition fees. Wouldn't that be cheating the school?"

"It would sir, but the fees *were* paid ... by me and my sister-in-law. We didn't tell Thomas ... we didn't understand the ... circumstances."

For reasons David could not understand, both Mr and Mrs Clark smiled. "We'll give you that money back," Mrs Clark said, "and we'll pay the school fees from now on."

"Thank you, ma'am," was all David could say.

While the outcome of David's all important talk with Mr and Mrs Clark was still hanging in the balance, quite a crowd of friends had gathered at Robert's mansion. They were all waiting with a mixture of trepidation and uncertainty to hear whether David was to go on trial, and their feelings barely improved even after Kid had made it quite clear that Thomas' parents would see the light, as she put it. They would understand the healing powers of David's teaching and they would not proceed with the charges against him. "I have personally seen improvement in Thomas' health already ... I mean, I'm the one who is training alongside of him ... and he is a top student ... he can sit in meditation ten times as long as I ...and ..."

"... but that's not much of a reference, is it Kid?" one cheeky student piped up from the back of the room and unfortunately, his remark was greeted with laughter.

"Thank you," Kid said. She was totally unfazed. "We are going to celebrate and Mario will call the lawyer and tell him the good news. Why all the sad faces? There is nothing wrong with a bit of optimism, is there?"

Right then David's car could be heard turning into the

driveway and minutes later he walked in through the back-door. Kid took one look at him and knew. She ran up to him, her arms open for a hug. But David was one step ahead of her, he swept her off her feet and lifted her high enough for their faces to be on a par. He held her like this while Kid gave him a kiss on his cheek. Once her feet touched the floor again she said, "You'll keep training Thomas and me together, right? I can learn how to sit still in meditation ... they all laughed at me ... let's celebrate now."

XXIV

David's life as a free citizen was playing out like a dream. Small hiccups like the threat of going on trial over the issue of Thomas' teaching were of little consequence. You dealt with them, then you concentrated on what came next. After years of monotonous and useless prison routine, every one of David's days now promised new challenges, more surprises. Kid had advised to live one day at the time and to worry about the next one when it came. David interpreted this to mean that you approached each day as if it were your last.

At the beginning he had been shy in public and insecure when making decisions. He had felt inadequate and ill-equipped to re-integrate into society - into the life of an ordinary guy. He had been slow to pick up confidence in his abilities and in his resources, yet now he worked a busy schedule at two martial arts schools with the additional bonus of having Mr and Mrs Clark visit the dojo regularly so they could watch Thomas in class. Weekends and mornings he worked as 'master builder' renovating Robert's house which was by now turning into a stately mansion. Three upstairs bedrooms were ready and furnished, one more to go. An invitation to the Clark's house for dinner one night had given David the idea of making the attic into a small movie theatre, similar to what Thomas had in his den.

At around that time, David developed a serious interest in cooking. He soon realized however, that in order to really make headway in this hobby, he needed to be able to read cooking books since they contained all the secrets of his newest fascination. David's reading skills had improved some since the start of his new life but he knew that they were still far from sufficient for the task at hand. So now, even though he was shy and embarrassed about his inadequacy, he saw no alternative but to learn how to ask for help.

In prison asking for help had not been a problem, after all everyone who was inside was a felon and everyone had his shortcomings. Owning up to them amongst his prison mates had not been a big deal. But out in the real world – in the world of the free people – he found that it was not quite so easy to admit to a lack of reading and writing skills. Everyone took those for granted. For a long time David debated in his mind over a course of action, then one day his eagerness to learn about cooking took the upper hand and his mind was made up.

I'll ask Phillip and Kid, he decided, at least there I won't be laughed at. What David did not know was that his brother was manifestly delighted at David's honesty and at his genuine interest in learning.

"You know David," Phillip said while he helped him work through the general lay-out of the recipes in Kid's curry book, "you got yourself a completely new lease of life now, right? A job that you like and are good at, the house renovation at Robert's, new interests - a busy and challenging life." He took a break there before he continued in a somewhat different key. "You have no idea how terrified I was that time when we didn't know if you would have to stand trial. Kid, in her usual carefree and optimistic manner, helped smooth things over ... made it easier for me to deal with my fear."

David looked at his brother in amazement, as if to say 'why are you bringing this issue up again?' For reasons Phillip did not bother to analyze, he understood his brother's reaction. David had certainly been afraid at the time, but once the issue was resolved satisfactorily, he simply dismissed it from his mind and turned his attention to new days filled with new events. That's how David saw life and that's how he lived it.

Then came David's rather unrelated remark, "Kid

had one of those as well, didn't she? I mean new leases of life. She told me once about how her house burnt to the ground."

Phillip was by now so well tuned in to David's disjointed conversations that he found no difficulty in going on with this thought. "And so did I ... I mean meeting Kid and starting a life with her. Yeah, I know, I screwed up a couple of times but ... we found a way to sort things out again. My life with her is simply magic ... I know how lucky I am ... I wouldn't want to be without her ... I couldn't."

David smiled. "You two are a top couple, eh? Can you help me some more with this cook book reading? I want to get some from the library ... probably never find my way around in there, though."

"Take Kid along. She goes there almost every week."

Robert and David sat at their large kitchen table, the latest plans for the attic spread out in front of them. "I'll be going away for a week or two," Robert announced unexpectedly. "Need to see my family ... seems like mom had a bad turn ... heart trouble. They live in a small town north of Nashville ... place called Clarksville." Then he turned back to business. "You know the ropes around here, you can start on the attic in my absence."

"Yep. I'll look after this place ... and after the school ... you can trust me."

Robert smiled and nodded. "I know David, thanks. And

by the way, I might bring back another house sharer, we've got plenty of room here after all. Dad has made some reference to a lad - son of a friend of his – who is going to start his studies here shortly. The father of the young guy will pay rent no questions asked."

Ten days later, Robert came back accompanied by a young man. He was about twenty, he was of below-medium height and rather too thin, David thought. He had curly brown hair cut short almost like a crew cut and he wore very small round eyeglasses. The eyes behind those glasses were alert and intelligent and David didn't miss the kindness and gentleness in their expression.

Robert introduced him to David. "This is James. He is going to be sharing the house with us." Then, "James, this David."

James looked up at David in amazement for a while, then remembered his manners and said, "Nice to meet you David."

James had lived with his parents in Clarksville all his life and now he had come to Knoxville to start his medical studies. He was filled with enthusiasm and determination to fulfill his lifelong dream of emulating Albert Schweitzer. Ever since James was a little boy he had told his parents - and everyone else who wanted to hear it - that he was going to be a doctor and specialize in tropical diseases ...that he would then go out and work in Third World countries of Africa and Central or South America where, equipped with the knowledge of modern western medicine he would care for and heal the poor and the underprivileged. He was prepared to accept substandard living conditions, be it in the jungle of the Amazon or in the Sahara Desert, it was all part of his vocation. Now the time had come for him to take the first steps towards achieving this aim.

Robert's head and shoulders were still stuck inside the boot of his car as he was retrieving James' luggage when he called out, "David, will you show James up ... you know which room. I'll brew a pot of coffee - as a welcome gesture."

David picked up James' two big cases making it look as if they were empty, then led the way inside and up the small staircase which led from the laundry to the upper level. The bedroom Robert had indicated was as yet sparsely furnished, it had a bed, wardrobe, a chest of drawers and not much else.

"This is your room ... there will be a carpet and curtains too," David said a little apologetically. "We are working on it. Do you have sheets and pillow cases and that?"

"Some, yes," James said, feeling rather more intimidated by David now that he was standing inside a room designed for regular-size people. He has probably long ago stopped noticing that he intimidates his fellow human beings, it went absurdly through James' mind, since he has lived all his life being a giant. David's deep baritone voice roused him from his thoughts.

"I'll help you make the bed. Let me show you around first." They left James' room and made their way along the corridor. "Here is the bathroom ... there is another one downstairs next to the laundry. The big curved stairways in the front cannot be used for another few weeks ... they are still under construction and not safe to walk on." He pointed out Robert's and his own bedroom. "The fourth one is as yet no more than a junk room and a working area," David said. James followed David like in a dream. It was all so new and unfamiliar; this was the very first time he had left his family home.

"Do you think you'll like it here?" Robert asked casually while the three sat at the large table in the kitchen – it still had to double as a dining room - having their promised cup of coffee. "Your mom seemed a little worried about letting you go."

"Oh, mom just doesn't understand that I have grown up now. You see, I'm the oldest of four children and the first one to leave home. Mom can be awfully sentimental ... she started even before I left. She was already worrying about my absence at the dinner table every night, can you imagine? She'll soon get used to it ... she just has to."

369

Robert felt like smiling, David took what he heard at face value.

It was now twenty-four hours later, the three men were having their dinner when the phone rang. "Probably mom," James said with a mixture of hope and embarrassment.

The phone still stood on its temporary cardboard box in the hallway. Robert left the table and went to answer it. "It's for you James," he called a minute later and added in a whisper, "Your mom."

"Hi mom ... yes fine. Don't sound so concerned, I'm not five years old any more you know. I can stand on my own feet - well, in a way. Thanks for paying my rent though."

Robert and David had unintentionally overheard that part of the conversation from the kitchen but now they made a conscious effort to eavesdrop. "Yes I have ..." they heard James' voice, "his name is David ... he is absolutely huge ... oh about six foot ten or eleven at least and real fit ... not sure, maybe a football player ... No no, totally inoffensive, nice guy ... yes, right next to mine. Uh-huh ... just stop worrying, will you?" Then a longer pause while he listened. "Oh good ... how much? Thanks dad. Yeah, in a week's time. Of course I know ... you too dad. Give my love to everyone. Thanks for calling ... bye."

The two eavesdroppers in the kitchen looked at each other and smiled in mutual understanding. Clearly, mom had a tendency to mother James, but the one-sided conversation they had just overheard left no doubt in their minds that James was part of a loving and caring family.

As James sat down at the kitchen table again he said, "Dad put money into my account so I can buy a car. He is real good that way. The money for rent will come out of that account too." Now he shot an uncertain glance at Robert then at David. "My parents spoil me ... I know it, but I'm trying not to take them for granted. I'll get a part-time job soon ... I hope. Will you come with me to find a suitable car, Robert? I don't know much about cars."

"You'll be better off with David. He'll get you what you need."

David concurred with a nod. "We can go tomorrow morning ... after breakfast. I'll be back by ... about eight ... start work at ... two in the afternoon." He turned to Robert with a look that seemed to say 'that's right, isn't it?'

If James was a little puzzled by this arrangement, he preferred not to mention it right then. "Good, I only want a small vehicle ... doesn't matter how old. Thanks David." Then curiosity got the better of him. "Are you a professional football player? I was only guessing when I told mom."

"No ... I'm a martial arts instructor."

"Oh, same as Robert? Dad told me about that."

"Yes, the same as Robert ... at the same school."

Robert shook his head in disagreement. No way 'same

371

as Robert' he thought, more like 'about ten grades up from Robert', but he kept his thoughts to himself. He rather enjoyed listening to this little dinner conversation.

"So you teach afternoons only? Or evenings ... for grown-ups after work, I suppose. Then why do you come back at eight in the morning?"

"Umm ... yeah, I teach children's classes in the afternoon and some classes in the evening."

"But that still doesn't explain your eight-in-morning-return." Maybe I'm overstepping somewhat, James thought and looked at his new friend a little uneasily.

Robert too, felt rather uneasy right then. He had this sinking feeling that David was going to give up and storm out of the house ... anything could happen. But he was wrong.

"You do ask a lot of questions, James," David said in a mild voice. "I don't mind answering so long as you ask them one at the time."

"Sorry, I tend to get carried away a little ... it's all so new and interesting ..."

He sounds just like Kid, it went through David's head and the thought made him laugh.

"... didn't mean to be funny ..." James said.

"... didn't mean to laugh. OK, I spend some time every morning in the dojo ... at the karate school I mean ... on my own."

"Working out? Training and that? But you are also the builder here, aren't you? Robert told me ... he is doing all the designs, isn't he? Maybe I can help some ... you know small jobs ... I can learn if you just show me ..."

"You are doing it again, James," David said seriously. "Let's concentrate first on getting a nice cheap little car for you. Then you can help me with some of the jobs here. But won't you be too busy with your studies?"

"Well yes, I will be busy. I know there is an awful lot of stuff to learn before I'm a doctor but ... I still like to learn how to work with my hands too," James said. "I'm also going to specialize because I want to work in poor countries where people need the First World's sophisticated medical technologies," he added importantly.

"You mean in small villages in the jungle and that?" This conversation was turning very serious indeed.

"Probably yes. Have you ever been to such places?"

"Umm ... yes, I have ... but I wasn't there to help the poor people ... it was different for me."

"Is this difficult for you to talk about? I didn't mean to pry ... honestly?"

"I know you didn't, James. I spent some time in Vietnam ... long time ago now ... but I didn't choose to go there."

James instantly understood even though David had hardly given anything away. James knew about America's war in Vietnam which took place when he was only a little boy. He had read books and seen movies, he was made aware of the miseries and the hardships which had been inflicted on the people of Vietnam as well as on the American soldiers. He looked up into David's eyes now and his expression left it no doubt that he meant to say a collective 'sorry' on behalf of his country to David and all the people who had been made to suffer.

David nodded. "There is stuff ... that still haunts me sometimes ... comes back in pictures in my dreams. But I'm learning to look to the future ... trying to make something of my life."

"You *are* making something of you life. It's this house you are re-building, the atmosphere here ... it's wonderful."

"Thanks James."

Robert sat unobtrusively at the other end of the dining table, his presence apparently forgotten. But he had listened carefully and observed the progress of this in-depth conversation between two men who had known each other for no more than twenty-four hours. To his utter amazement these two people who had seemingly nothing in common - different background, different generation, different interests, different outlook on life - had just established the framework for a sincere and meaningful friendship. The realization filled Robert with an inner contentedness. This new friendship, he mused, will surely make for a smooth and harmonious life in our home. He leaned back and relished the warmth this feeling provided.

It was one of the rare times when Phillip went to David's martial arts school. He considered the place to be David's turf and he respected his brother's authority in the domain of martial arts. On this day however, Phillip had to pick up his wife after her karate class. He had just locked his car and started to walk towards the entrance when he heard a voice behind him.

"It's not often we see you here, Phillip," Robert said, "what's the special occasion?"

"The special occasion is that my wife's car packed up yesterday, or to put it in her vernacular 'it has run out of motor', and like a miracle the whole thing didn't blow up while she was driving it."

The mere fact of having to repeat Kid's near tragedy brought Phillip close to tears. "Anyway, I'm here to pick her up," he added trying to hide his momentary display of emotions.

"She'll be another ten minutes or so. By the way, we are planning to hold a house-warming party ... Saturday, next but one. I'd like it to be a big event ... with lots of people, students, their parents, old Mr Blythe, Thomas and his parents. You wouldn't, by any chance, be willing to supply some musical entertainment ...?"

Phillip had to laugh at the way Robert sneaked the

question in. "I would love to but it's not for me to decide, I'm just one of the band-members, but I'll talk to Bob. He might agree ... he is good that way. I'm looking forward to seeing your mansion in its full splendor and beauty. I only saw it twice: once when it was more of a ruin than a house and the second time was just after David had done some wiring or something underneath, I believe ..."

Robert didn't let Phillip finish the sentence, "... don't remind me of that day. It was the most scary part of the whole enterprise." And in answer to Phillip's unasked question, he continued, "OK, here is what happened: big parts of the plumbing needed to be replaced and this had to be done under the house. Now just imagine, David props up the whole place on six or eight jacks - very much like the ones you use to jack up a car - he places one guy at each of those, 'make sure it doesn't slip sideways' he calls out, then goes on his belly and slithers under the house to do the repairs. I mean ... any of those contraptions fails and David is crushed to death by the weight of the whole damn house. I don't think I was the only one whose heart skipped a few beats while waiting for David to come out from under the house that day."

Phillip simply shook his head. "He has no concept of fear, does he. Maybe he has already experienced the most horrifying and frightening stuff ... at an earlier point in his life. Whatever happens now ... it cannot possibly be worse. Maybe his perception of fear as been killed altogether."

"I know what you are referring to. David and I have talked about his past ... in a way. It predictably got us into a bit of a verbal muddle, though. Oh, before I forget, the party will take place in the day time since a lot of our guests will be children ... David is a champion with his little students. We'll probably have lunch outside. David has built outdoor cooking facilities and - wait for it - David is going to do absolutely *all* the cooking for everyone. There will be dozens of people. He is already studying his cooking books ... he buys them now, you know, and he reads them from cover to cover."

Phillip felt a mixture of amazement and admiration and - yes, love for his brother.

"Have to run and get changed," Robert called then added with a smile, "Sensei doesn't like to be kept waiting."

Phillip went down to the basement then walked along the corridor towards the dojo. There was silence. He stopped after turning the last corner and now he could see David and his two students, Kid and Thomas. They stood straight and erect facing their master. David gave some sort of command which Phillip did not understand, then they all went into a kneeling position, hands placed on thighs, spine straight, chin slightly tucked in, and they maintained this position until David again made a sound to indicate the end of the meditation. Phillip watched as his brother jumped into a standing position in one single leap. Kid and Thomas tried to imitate him. They both failed, so they just stood up like ordinary human beings. While marveling at David's authority and agility, Phillip had not noticed Mr and Mrs Clark standing right beside him and watching the same ritual in stunned silence.

"You must be Kid's husband," Mr Clark said hoping not to startle Phillip. "We are Thomas' parents - got here too late and missed the lesson." He hesitated for a second then said, "Your brother ... he is quite extraordinary ... I find it fascinating to watch him in his dojo. His teaching seems to help Thomas ... in mysterious ways."

Mrs Clark took over from there. "Our son is more confident, positive, optimistic - hard to describe - but I feel that he is happier since ... you know ... since he started with these classes. There is also a degree of hero-worship involved," she said with a little smile, "and that would lift anybody's spirits, but I understand that Thomas is not the only one of David's students in the 'worshipping category'." She added cryptically.

Phillip smiled, the best he could do to hide his lack of knowledge of his brother's charm and of his charismatic potential vis-à-vis his students. "I think you know more about my brother - the Sensei - than I do." And for some inexplicable reason he continued, "My brother and I ... we were separated for many years. The alienation which resulted was mostly my doing I'm afraid."

"I'm not sure that David sees it this way, Mr McCabe, but I'm simply going by a hunch here. David has not told us much about his life and his past, but judging by the few things he did say ... he certainly seems to be very fond of you."

Phillip nodded then started haltingly, "David and I ... even though we are brothers, our lives played out quite differently. While mine was easy and carefree most of the time, his was marred by drama and tragedy of such enormity ... I can still only guess at." Phillip felt that he had Mr and Mrs Clark's undivided attention and he knew he had to do his best now to make some sense of his introductory statement. "David was sent to fight in the jungle of Vietnam and after his return he had no choice but to continue fighting in the concrete jungle of the city streets in his home country. My late father used to say that the military had reduced David to a senseless killing machine. It's only now, since David got out ... out of prison, I mean ... that I've come to realize that his soul has survived along with his body, and against all odds his heart has remained in the right place. I really have to thank my wife for having forced me into this realization. Kid has inadvertently established a playing-field for me to re-connect with David."

"What did your wife do to create this situation? Would you mind telling us?"

"Umm ...she ... I'm sorry my thoughts are a bit muddled at the moment. I've never actually talked about this to anyone. You see, I didn't tell Kid for some time, even after we were married, that I had a brother, and when I did, she instantly wanted to meet him. I was against it ... it was difficult for me. David was in the St. Louis State penitentiary serving a sentence for manslaughter. Eventually I got over my stubbornness and my antagonism and then Kid and I agreed to take him home to Knoxville after his release. Now I'm real glad we did."

Phillip just had time to see Mr and Mrs Clark nod when he heard Kid's cheerful voice.

"Hi darling, thanks for picking me up." Then she turned to Mrs Clark and threw in casually, "My car is undergoing surgery as we speak, so ..."

"No surgery Kid, I have ordered a brand new car for you. I can't handle any more drama."

"But my little Ford is fixable, I like it."

"Kid, you were lucky your little Ford didn't blow up with you inside. It's going to be scrapped, full stop. Thomas, where does your vote go - scrap the Ford or fix it?"

"Scrap. Mom, dad?" They both agreed with Thomas.

"My darling wife, your are out-voted. I love you ... I've already bought you a brand new Honda. We are approaching a new episode in our life." He took Kid in his arms, she responded in true Kid fashion by snuggling against him. Kid loved her husband. He was now as always, the centre of her life.

On their drive back, Mr and Mrs Clark sat silently side by side recapping what they had just heard and forgetting that Thomas had not been privy to this first little glimpse into David's past.

"Why are you both so gloomy?" Thomas asked from the back seat. "And why didn't you come to watch our class today? It was an interesting one. Sensei showed us a few super kicks. We are not to do them straight away though ... too difficult, but he performed a whole series for us to watch ... he is superb, mom."

It seems like I didn't exaggerate on the hero-worship then, mom thought with some amusement. Now she turned in her seat. "Sorry Thomas, we were late today ... just couldn't make it, but we'll come and watch again, you know it, as often as we can."

"Yeah, I know." He took a deep breath before he asked, "Mom, what did you and Phillip talk about? You stopped when Kid and I arrived. It was about Sensei wasn't it? Phillip said some horrible things about his brother, right? I don't think he likes him. What did he say? I'd like to know."

It was time for dad to get involved in the conversation. He spoke straight ahead as he drove. "Of course we will tell you Thomas; we'll tell you exactly what Phillip told us. What made you pronounce such a harsh judgment on Phillip, though? You know that judging people is not only unkind but can also be dangerous. And I can tell you right

381

now that you are wrong. We'll talk when we get home."

The conversation which took place in the dining room of the Clark's home directly after their return did not go as well as it should have. Thomas had set his mind on disliking Phillip or at least his attitude toward David, and his parents resented their son's opinionated ideas about Phillip. They tried to remain reasonable, the way adults should be, but failed to get through to Thomas.

"Phillip told us that throughout his life David had encountered hardships while his own life had been smooth and easy, and that he and his brother had been separated for a long time. Phillip blames himself for this."

"See? That's just what I mean," Thomas said rather petulantly. "If David's life was hard, his brother should have helped him. Instead he sent him away. Not much brotherly love there, right? What sort of hardships, anyway?"

Dad's patience started to fray at the edges by then. Mom noticed it and took the initiative. "David was sent away to fight in the war in Vietnam. We have to understand that the separation between the brothers happened after he came back ... Phillip was not very specific. I believe however, that Phillip is much younger than David which means that Phillip would have been too young to fully understand what happened in his brother's life."

"Maybe? But David came home again, unharmed and well ... many soldiers died there. So why did Phillip send his brother away then instead of ...?"

"From what Phillip said, I don't think David was 'well' when he came back. War experiences sometimes do terrible things to soldiers' minds and to their souls. Look Thomas, we have all noticed that David is a rather slow talker and thinker, no need to deny that and these could well be remnants of war trauma. I believe that this was implied in Phillip's words ... somehow. And Phillip finished by saying that his brother's soul had survived and was still intact. Thomas, Phillip loves his brother. Your father and I could both feel it. You are doing him wrong by condemning him the way you do."

Thomas' look of defiance did not change but he refrained from protesting.

His father continued almost immediately, "Phillip and Kid brought David here after his release from prison. He served a sentence for manslaughter in St. Louis."

"What? Are you saying that David murdered someone? It's not true. Sensei wouldn't do that and he couldn't have spent years in prison. I know what prisons are like, I've seen it on television and in movies. Prisoners fight and kill each other ... they are vicious and horrible. Sensei is not that sort of person. I don't want to hear." Thomas put his hands against his ears to stop hearing more slander against his master - his hero.

Mr Clark took a deep breath in an effort to control

his mounting irritation, then he started in a steady voice. "Manslaughter is not the same as murder, Thomas. It means to kill somebody unintentionally ... by accident. Phillip did not tell us the exact circumstances. We all know that David is a professional fighter and we have to assume that he used his fighting skills to survive the war. It follows therefore, that he would know how to survive a prison sentence. Don't you agree?"

Thomas agreed but did not get himself to say so. "How long is a sentence for what David did?"

"Phillip didn't say but I believe it is around four or five years, probably depends on the prisoner's behavior and such ..."

The mere thought of his beloved teacher incarcerated in a dark, damp cell without a window, given bad or no food, having to suffer the cold and most likely being mistreated by the guards brought tears to Thomas' eyes. He quickly got up and ran out of the room to hide his loss of control. Both parents watched him, trying to empathize with the sorrow and the pain their son was experiencing.

It was Maria who saved the situation. She followed Thomas and gently knocked on the door of his room and without waiting for a reply she opened it and went to Thomas who was lying across his bed sobbing uncontrollably. Maria had been an important person in Thomas' life ever since he was a baby, and in critical situations like this, she spoke to him in her native Spanish, a language Thomas understood and spoke fluently. "Don't despair my darling," she said in her soothing voice as she put her arms around his small body, "your teacher is a free man now, he is a good man and he will never go back to prison. You need to be confident and trusting and you have to believe in the goodness of his heart. Can you do that?"

It took a little while for the sobbing to cease and for his voice to return. "Yes Maria, I can ... I love my Sensei ... almost as much as I love mom and dad."

Hand in hand, Thomas and Maria re-entered the dining room. Thomas went to his mother and put his arms around her, "I'm sorry mom, I was stubborn. The thought that Phillip didn't love his brother really hurt. I was not angry, just scared." Now he looked at his father and said, "I kind of like Phillip ... he and Kid ... they really love each other ... that's so nice to see."

The reconciliation was complete then. "You will both come to Robert and David's house-warming party, won't you? Please make sure you're not busy on that Saturday."

"It's a promise," mom and dad said in concert.

XXV

Robert's house-warming party was a huge success and images of it were to remain in the minds of many of the invited guests for a long time to come. It was a good thing that none of the guests was endowed with the gift of seeing into the future so no-one was able to predict the tragedy and the disaster which were soon to follow that enjoyable Saturday.

The newly renovated mansion was in top shape on that day and David lent the event a special quality by putting on a culinary splash of unparalleled proportions. David had put himself in his party-cooking-frame-of-mind on Thursday night and had given all his Friday lessons to his two assistants, Robert and Jason. David planned everything - he planned all the dishes to be cooked and the sequence in which they were to be served. He wanted only one helper and that was James.

James wrote down the list of dishes as dictated by David, he gave a hand when more than David's two were required, he stirred sauces, checked the oven, turned meats over on the grill and acted on strict orders from the chef - and he loved every minute of it.

David had chicken in one marinade, beef in another; he had fashioned small sausage rolls and quiches to be served as finger food for starters, a variety of kebabs, some with seafood, some with chicken interspersed with onions and tomatoes and other vegetables. He made salads and prepared fruit baskets.

"James, please make sure the colors are right," David had said indicating the fruit selection, "this is important, it makes the dishes look appetizing." James knew that David was unable to distinguish colors, so this job gave him extra responsibility.

David baked bread and buns, and he now excelled in his newly discovered art of baking cakes. For the housewarming he made a carrot cake and a chocolate cake. Both those confections he produced by faithfully following the instructions in the book - he had never made either of these cakes before.

Since it was a warm Saturday in September, it was decided to hold the party outside. All the guests, approximately forty of them, admired the house inside and out while Bob and the band played in the big downstairs room. At one point the children miraculously produced a football and a minute later they all gathered around David pleading with him to give them a game.

"David is a first class football player you know," one boy informed Kid.

"Is he just? I always thought of him as a karate expert." Those guests who were near enough to hear it smiled. Most of them were parents of David's students and they knew that David was a champion with the children.

At that moment Kid's mind inadvertently wandered back to the curious occurrence at the police station directly after David's questioning. The police officers had told her about the incident with the black toddler, hoping to get an explanation. At the time, she had simply smiled and said that her brother had a special understanding with children. But now, watching the children clambering all over David with their request for a football game, it seemed like the right time to tell Phillip what she knew. "David had never seen that little boy or his mother," Kid explained, "yet the child ran to him for comfort, apparently without a minute's hesitation and the mother understood, she asked no questions of David. That's what the police lady told me. Now look at the children here. Phillip, what is it about David that attracts children like that?"

"Magic Kid. He radiates a type of magic that children understand. He communicates with them, he speaks their language even when he doesn't speak."

A voice behind Phillip unexpectedly expanded on his explanation.. "It's like he is the father of all the little ones here. Some sort of compensation ... it may well be." Father Pasquale had overheard Kid and Phillip's words. "I'm sorry to butt in on your conversation," he said with a smile.

"So you know about David's past, Father." Phillip was puzzled. He had no idea that there was any connection between his brother and Father.

"I know some, but you have to understand that I cannot divulge the circumstances under which I acquired that knowledge."

"You are not suggesting that David did conf..."

"Yes I am. True it was a rather free-style confession, but I believe that improvisations are justified so long as they bring help and supply comfort. David and I have stayed in touch since that day. Actually, I received his invitation to this house-warming party only this morning, rather short notice, you might say, but I was certainly not going to miss it."

Typical David, was Kid's immediate reaction, but she was truly fond of her brother, so she said instead, "Did you also know that David had taught himself to become an expert chef?"

"I had an idea ... yes. He is positively excelling today. I'd better go and talk to him ... and eat some of the delicacies he has prepared."

When Father had disappeared in the crowd, Phillip turned to Kid, a sheepish grin on his face, "Did you know about David's confession, Kid?"

"Sort of ... it was around the time when I was in hospital." Then she said without preamble, "Darling, you *do* love your brother now, don't you."

Phillip did not answer Kid's question, instead he shrugged and shook his head in a gesture which could mean anything from 'yes, it's true that I love him now' to 'I'm glad you insisted on meeting him' or 'miracles do happen'.

There was to be one small hiccup however, before the party was over. It happened late in the afternoon when some people were already preparing to leave. Thomas started to feel unwell; he knew the symptoms, he had experienced them many times since his diagnoses eight years ago. He approached his mom and dad as unobtrusively as possible, he never liked to make a big issue of his ill health. His parents took in the situation instantly. Mrs Clark had made sure of the location of the phone as soon as she entered the house and had informed Robert of her reasons. Now she ran and made the call to the special care unit at St. Mary's hospital. Thomas and his father started to make their way to the car when David caught Thomas' eye. He flew across the room, and effortlessly picked Thomas up and carried him in his arms. James instantly supplied expert medical help to settle Thomas comfortably in the back seat - he was, after all, the medic in this place.

David and Robert had both been given Thomas' medical history and a quasi first-aid course once Thomas' tuition had become legal. They were told that the symptoms could be sudden and unpredictable. Thomas wore a special bracelet with his name, direct dialing number to the hospital and blood group inscribed. So far however, no emergencies had occurred while Thomas was in the dojo. On two occasions, the school had received a call saying that Thomas could not attend that week's lesson but would be back the following week. Both times Thomas was back in class for the next lesson, no questions were asked, no explanations necessary.

David was devastated at Thomas' departure from the party. He went upstairs and found refuge in his room and locked himself in. Kid pleaded with him outside his door, she tried to reason with him to open up but failed.

Finally it was Father who was successful in gaining entrance to David's room. He and David spent twenty minutes together, no sounds and no words could be heard. When they came downstairs, David was back in control of his emotions thanks to Father's unparalleled gift of inspiring confidence and giving love.

Robert answered Mr Clark's call about thirty minutes later. Thomas was in good hands and in a stable condition, he would be back in class as soon as possible.

XXVI

Two weeks after the house-warming party, the house next door to Robert's burnt to the ground. Some said it was arson, some said it was an accident. At the time the house was inhabited by a group of young people who rented it from the owner and ran it as a sort of communal living set-up. They were not interested in looking after the house or the garden around it, the place was therefore rather ramshackle and run-down. The number of members of the group changed frequently, sometimes eight or more people lived in the house, sometimes only three or four, sometimes they included children and even small babies. There were times when sounds of music - sounds of peace and harmony - drifted across to Robert's house, at other times screaming and shouting and vicious fighting could be heard. Robert and his two mates had an agreement amongst them: they would never get involved and they would never call the police, no matter what they heard or even what they thought they heard. On a few occasions, one of the neighbors had come over to ask if Robert could help out with some milk or bread, a light globe or some washing powder. Robert's team always helped and never asked personal questions.

On the evening of the fire, James was in his room studying. His and David's rooms were side by side and faced away from the neighboring house. Robert was downstairs in the living room watching television. David was at the dojo and was expected back at ten o'clock. James had covered David's dinner with aluminum foil and put it in the oven ready to be re-heated when David came home.

The first thing Robert noticed was the smell of burnt rubber, or was it melting plastic? He couldn't be sure. He quickly checked his own kitchen, then he heard crackling and hissing sounds of flames. A minute later the air was filled with the roaring sound of the fire which was consuming the house next door. "James," he yelled up the stairs, "fire next door."

James charged down the steps, and together they went outside and moved their cars away from that side of the house. David arrived back at exactly that moment. He too, parked his car some fifty yards away from his usual place in the driveway. By that time the fire had already engulfed the biggest part of the house. The tenants, five of them, were outside. Two women were in flimsy nightshirts, they were gesticulating wildly and screaming at the top of their lungs.

Robert and David heard it simultaneously. "Is someone still in there?" Robert asked rather helplessly, "is that what these guys are yelling about?"

David did not approach the screaming group. He stood stock still, listened carefully then declared, "Two people ... I can hear a woman and a baby. Let's go get them out before it's too late."

The two men communicated with gestures for a couple of seconds as the noise made no allowance for verbal communication. James watched as they breathed in deeply and took control of their bodies and their minds in preparation for the dangerous task at hand. That's just what I saw them do in that dojo of theirs, it went through James' mind in a flash, a sort of preparatory stance in readiness for an attack. When he got to this point, he realized that the building had already swallowed both his mates. James braced himself for the worst, he knew he had to stand by and supply first aid when necessary.

David and Robert followed the sound of the woman's voice. It took them to the upper level and into the first bedroom on the left. A woman lay sprawled on the floor, part of the ceiling had caved in, the flames were precariously close to her body and she was pinned down by one of the beams that had fallen across both her legs. She screamed and screamed. "The baby, the baby ... over there ... get her out ... please get her out."

In the corner of the room lay the little cot on its side, the baby still wrapped in some blankets, the flames only inches away.

"Grab the baby, Robert," David said in a calm voice, "call James and have him meet you on the stairs. Hand the baby over to him, then come back and together we get the woman out." Then he turned around and started to talk to the lady. "We'll get you out, don't be afraid. The baby is safe," he promised.

Now he started to shift bedclothes, carpets and burning furniture out of the way as best he could and when Robert re-entered the room he yelled over the roar of the fire, "I'll lift the goddamned beam ... you pull the lady out from under ... gently."

The room was by now filled with thick, black smoke, the heat of the fire was almost unbearable and the beam David had to lift looked like it could easily weigh a ton or two. Robert was beyond questioning David's strength or his stamina, he just mechanically followed instructions. David wrapped some cloth around the lady's face to reduce smoke inhalation, both men were now coughing desperately but nothing could stop David from making this almost super-human effort of lifting the beam which was crushing the woman's legs. Robert moved her slowly, carefully, he had to assume that both her legs were broken. David dropped the beam, turned around and scooped her up. She had stopped screaming now and her limp body hung like a rag doll in his arms. He ran down the steps behind Robert who did all he could to clear a path down the smoke-filled stairway which by then was cluttered with fallen debris. The fire engine and the ambulance had already arrived when the two men with the unconscious woman emerged from the burning building. Somebody took the lady out of David's arms, of that he was sure, but afterwards everything became a blur of flames and heat and smoke.

The baby James had taken out of Robert's arms half way up the stairs had burns on her arms and feet, she was coughing and crying but she was alive. The condition of the baby's mother however, was far more serious. Her legs had indeed been crushed and they were covered with burns. Her nightdress was singed in places and had melted against the skin of her arms and shoulders. While mother and child were being carefully placed in the ambulance, the firemen were working with coordinated precision, slowly succeeding in bringing the fire under control and finally extinguishing it. Robert lay half conscious on the pavement gasping and forcing some fresh air into his lungs. His right forearm, wrist and hand were covered in blood. David stood over him, blood pouring down his soot covered face from a wound on his forehead. This didn't deter him from picking up Robert and carrying him away from the heat and the smoke. David's hair was plastered to his face with sweat and blood, he was coughing and breathing with difficulty, his jeans and his shirt were shredded all the way down one side, his thigh was streaked with burns. There was a searing patch on his ribcage which raged with pain but he couldn't take time to see the medics. First of all Robert needed his help, he was suffering badly from smoke inhalation.

James watched as David carried Robert past the now burning oak tree. "Over here," he called in a voice that carried, "we need stretchers for these two men ... smoke inhalation ... burns all over their bodies."

The ambulance staff recognized authority in the voice they heard and came running with two stretchers. Robert was barely conscious as he was carried to the ambulance, David was determined to walk. "I'm OK," he gasped, then used the back of his hand to wipe the blood from his forehead and out of his eyes thus making an even worse mess of his face.

The first thing David recognized when he re-gained consciousness, was a smell. Dishwashing liquid, it crossed his mind, window cleaner maybe. Next he felt an oxygen mask sitting on his mouth and nose. He cautiously started to open his eyes, just a slit, and found he was alone in a white cubicle. That's when it happened.

In a flash he found himself back in the clinic where

he woke up right after he had come back from the war - years ago. He saw nurses and doctors all dressed in white. They all said they meant well, they gave me drugs and stuck needles into me, said they were going to help me. David's thoughts were not following any rational pattern, he was confused and he was scared. He shook his head vigorously, he was in tears and unable to stop this unguarded display of fear; his mind was racing. Not again ... I'm not going back to those times ... the times when I was no more than ... than a vegetable. He followed his immediate urge and pulled the mask off his face, tore the intravenous needle out of his arm, roughly pulled off his hospital gown and threw it on the bed then started to run towards the door. Where was Robert? Was he OK ... and the woman and her baby?

Two nurses had heard him but had not understood his words. They came in quickly and held him by his arms and shoulders. They tried to place the oxygen mask back over his nose and mouth and slip the discarded gown over his naked body. David defended himself energetically even in his weakened state, and he was shoving the nurses out of his way just as Phillip and Kid were shown into his room. Kid needed just one second to take charge of the situation. She placed herself squarely in front of David and took hold of his big powerful shoulders with her small hands.

"Now you just stop pushing the nurses around, hear me? They are trying to help you. Here, let me put your nightshirt back on ... patients are not allowed to run around naked." Then Kid took the mask out of the nurse's hand and continued, "I'm going to stick this thingamy back on your face ... you leave it there or you will suffocate." Following this rather wayward improvisation, Kid placed the mask rather indelicately back over David nose and mouth and pronounced, "now ... breathe!"

"... and this is an order," Phillip heard next to his ear. He had been watching Kid's ministrations with suppressed amusement. Now he realized that the words had been said by a doctor who stood right next to him. Both men soon found it difficult to suppress their amusement as they continued watching the patient and his new nurse.

David immediately stopped fighting and did as Kid ordered. The big strong man was suddenly as docile as a lamb. He let Kid lay him back down on the bed and cover him up with the white sheet. Kid seemed oblivious to the fact that there were professional and competent hospital staff in the room. She looked down on her brother and gently brushed some of the tangled hair out of his face. "All will be well. Phillip and I will check on Robert and on the lady with the baby. Just get some rest." With this she placed a very little kiss on David's cheek and smiled. David closed his eyes and relaxed.

"His wife?" the doctor asked Phillip.

"No, *my* wife," Phillip said without rancor. He had long

ago stopped puzzling over Kid's expert way of handling David, of getting him to submit to her orders and even be afraid of her threats. Phillip simply put this down to their chemistry, and at this particular moment he was seriously concerned about his brother's wellbeing.

David was back on the dojo in his role as Sensei two weeks later. He still had a number of stitches in his head and bandages on his legs and his torso but he had obtained green light from James to resume his teachings albeit with a caution not to exert himself more than necessary.

Robert was forced to spend some time at home. His hand got seriously burnt and was, for a time, useless to him since as an architect he needed it to draft plans. He was at home therefore, and watched when the bulldozers arrived next door and demolished the remaining parts of the burnt-out house and cleared the whole block. It left an ugly gap amongst the stately houses on Jefferson Street, and an unpleasant smell lingered over the area for some time to come.

In Robert's mansion, James had put himself in charge of all matters medical: he tended the wounds of his mates, changed bandages, checked every scratch and even the smallest burn carefully to avoid any possible onset of infection. He ordered rest when necessary, he forbade Robert to use his right hand for any household chores. James did all those himself. Robert watched James with an inward smile, while David acted on James' instructions naturally and obediently. As far as David was concerned, James was the medical expert in their team, the fact that he was still only in his first year of medical school notwithstanding.

David's stitches were removed and all his wounds had healed nicely when nature, in a vicious and seemingly undeserved way, turned against him once more. Disaster came from a different quarter this time, and it hit David a blow so devastating he found it almost impossible to parry.

XXVII

David was on the mats, he was warming up, concentrating and getting his body and his mind in the right frame for the final series of lessons of the day. He heard the phone ring but did not interrupt his meditation, Robert would get it.

It was a very short conversation. Robert replaced the receiver and stood motionless for a second. Then he took a deep breath and re-entered the dojo. He bowed as he stepped down onto the mats and in a very low voice said, "Sorry to interrupt Sensei. This is important."

David gave Robert a questioning look but did not speak.

"That was Mr Clark on the phone. Thomas had a bad turn ... he is in hospital. Could you go ... right now ... sounded urgent."

David's features turned hard, he leapt to his feet and

started to make for the shower room, "OK, I get changed …"

"Go as you are, David ... fast as you can. Mr Clark said he'd be waiting for you at the main entrance. I'll take this class. Jason will be here in an hour, we'll take the following ones together." David nodded thanks, turned and ran down the hall.

He parked his car in the visitors' lot behind the hospital, jumped out and slammed the door shut. He ran towards the main entrance, weaving through parked cars at top speed, his long yellow hair flying in the wind. He met Mr Clark at the entrance as Robert had said. "Thanks for coming David," Mr Clark said in a somber tone of voice. The two men were by then on first names; David now addressed Thomas' father as Clive and his wife as Caroline. "Follow me," Clive said and lead the way.

Neither of the two men noticed the curious looks they got from hospital staff as they made their way along the corridors to Thomas' room. David's white outfit conformed almost perfectly to that of nurses and doctors, the only difference was that David's white outfit had a contrasting black belt which was tied around his middle ... plus the fact that David was barefoot. Clive carefully opened a door on the left; it opened first into a little anteroom where Caroline was waiting. David saw a sad and hopeless look in her eyes and before he found his voice and could put any of his ques-

403

tions into words she put her arms around him in a spontaneous gesture. David reciprocated briefly, shyly. A curtain was drawn back and all three could now approach Thomas' bed. He looked small and frail, his eyes were closed, he did not move and did not respond immediately to David's 'Hi Thomas'. It was only when David took his little hand in his that Thomas opened his eyes and tried a little smile. David ignored all the medical paraphernalia which stood and hung all around the bed - they were all gadgets he did not understand anyway. He only looked at the brave and smiling face of his darling student and friend.

"Please Sensei," Thomas' voice came in a whisper, " ... will you ... meditate with me?"

David shot a quick questioning look at Caroline. She nodded her head and he understood. He went down on one knee at the side of the bed while Caroline fluffed up the pillows to make Thomas more comfortable. Now David started to talk to Thomas, slowly but with authority.

"Breathe in Thomas ... into your centre ... remember 'hara'? Now let the air out ... and think of nothing but your breathing." David reached out and gently massaged Thomas' shoulders. "Good. Again ... breathe in ... and ... out." David took Thomas' hand in his, closed his eyes and started to breathe rhythmically ... in and out ... and soon Thomas followed his master's example.

Clive and Caroline watched the procedure with a sense

of wonderment. They felt the tranquility that pervaded the room. They saw Thomas' features relax and take on an expression of serenity, his breathing became even and regular. Clive and Caroline were now also in the grip of this newly created peacefulness.

David knew when it happened - he knew it instantly, instinctively. He felt it when the pulse of life went out of the little hand he was holding in his; he knew when the boy took his last breath, he knew when Thomas was no longer with him. David opened his eyes and got to his feet, then turned to look at Clive and Caroline. It took another few seconds then they too, understood.

The last thing David remembered was Caroline leaning over Thomas and kissing his head then, in floods of tears, she threw herself into her husband's arms. David found himself staring at the lifeless figure of Thomas, and suddenly all hell broke loose inside his head and his mind: everybody was now dying around him, women and children, soldiers, his own mates, everybody was screaming, bodies were lying all around him, burnt and mutilated, women with babies on their backs running for their lives. Now he too, started to scream - or did he? David took one step back, gave his head a vigorous shake and realized that he had probably not screamed since nobody was looking at him, but he knew he had to leave this place - just disappear quietly and be alone.

Since he was barefoot, nobody heard his footsteps as he left the room and sped down the corridor. He ran down the stairs and out through the side entrance into the street. He found his car, got behind the wheel and closed the door. David gripped the steering wheel with both hands, leaned forward, laid his head on his arms and wept and wept. After a while he turned the ignition on and drove off just letting the car take him where it wanted to go. Eventually he found himself at the river bank; he took the blanket from the back seat, wrapped it around himself and went to sit cross-legged under a big tree.

Just sitting very still will bring me some peace of mind, he assured himself. It was very quiet; the noise from the distant highway was no more than an continuous hum. David sat and watched the mass of black water go by in a monotonous and steady flow. Now he turned his head and looked upstream. There he fixed his eyes on one little spot of water and followed it as it inexorably made its way downstream past him and then further and further away until he could no longer be sure which spot it was. Then he turned his head and looked upstream again. He focused on another spot and repeated his little exercise imagining how his very own little bit of water would make its way through town then further downstream for miles and miles until in the end it would join the ocean.

Maybe I should just follow them ... just go ... no matter

where. Who'd care anyway. All these people who say they are my friends ... none of them know that I am responsible for the death of so many harmless, innocent little jungle-people. Why is it that good people like Thomas and my mates from the army ... they all had to die ... and I am still alive?

Mustn't think like that, David ordered himself, I'll only get to ... to where I'm no longer able to stop my tears. They made me take some medication ... against being depressed or something ... never again. When David got to this point, he knew he had to will himself to control his breathing, to slow down and relax. He started to empty his mind and to rid himself of his erratic thoughts. Eventually they all disappeared ...and then there was nothing any more ... nothing to fear, nothing to cry over.

David didn't know how long he had sat in his self-created void but now he opened his eyes again, and in his mind he re-played all the months since he started teaching Thomas and subsequently became friends with his parents. Caroline thanked me for dedicating so much time and patience to her son, David remembered her words very clearly. She said Thomas was happier, more confident since he started training with me. One Sunday afternoon I spent with Thomas and his parents at their beautiful home and on that same day, I taught Thomas to swim in his pool. Thomas was a little miracle.

"I loved you Thomas," David said out loud. "I hope you are in a peaceful place now - in a place where there is no more pain. I'll ask Father to pray for you." What David re-experienced was like a movie - a live-movie - one wherein he himself played an important role. He kept listening to the gentle splashing and gurgling sounds of the water near the river's edge until he started to feel its soothing effect on his tortured soul.

Robert returned home later than usual that night. He had been roaming around town aimlessly, hoping against all odds, to find David. When he finally did get home, he called almost before he entered the house, "James, is David back?"

"No, why?" James called from the kitchen. He took one look at Robert and knew something was out of kilter. "What happened?"

"It's Thomas. I had a call from his father. Thomas had been taken to hospital. I sent David there immediately. Later we got another call ... Thomas died."

James momentarily closed his eyes, then he took a deep breath, "Do we know if David made it in time to see Thomas ... before ...?"

" Probably yes, but then ... David sort of evaporated ... disappeared soundlessly, nobody saw, nobody knew. He didn't come back to the school, he didn't come back home ..." Robert was frantic.

"We need to call Phillip and Kid. Maybe that's where he went."

Kid picked up the receiver and said, "This is Kid speaking." Phillip stood right next to her, they had just finished washing the dinner dishes. "Hi Robert. No, he isn't. Why? ... What is it?" Then a longer pause while Kid listened. "Oh, how sad ... that would have hit him a real blow ... what? ... of course I am. He is hurt ... and grieving ... understandably so ... Yes ... we'll let you know if ..." then she replaced the receiver and shook her head.

"It was Robert," she said unnecessarily ... as if Phillip had not gathered as much by following her side of the conversation. "He wanted to know whether David was with us." Then she relayed the sad news she had just heard from Robert. "I really don't understand why Robert is in such a tizzy over David's temporary absence. Of course he would need to be by himself ... he is probably crying, so he doesn't want people around, right?"

"Quite likely. But you know that David is prone to have some sort of flashbacks. Seems like any odd thing or situation can trigger something in his mind." And then as an afterthought he added, "The parents must be worried - I think I'd like to talk to them."

"Talk to them about what? They know nothing about David's past, about possible flashbacks and that. David would never have told them because he thinks that it would lose him their friendship."

"But they do know some, Kid. *I* told them."

"I don't believe it ... Phillip you went behind David's back. That's not right."

"Don't fly at me like this. You don't know the circumstances ... and Thomas' parents were not shocked at what I told them either."

"What were they then ... the circumstances?"

Phillip truthfully repeated the conversation he had with Mr and Mrs Clark while waiting to pick her up at the dojo and he concluded with, "And I'm positive that Thomas wanted to know what had been said and that his parents obliged."

"You betrayed your brother. All he wants now is to become an ordinary guy. He doesn't want anyone to know about his bad past. He will never offend again ... you know that as well as I do."

"I don't see that I did anything you could call betrayal. I disagree with you there, Kid. What I told them would merely have supplied answers to questions they had asked themselves but didn't think they could ask David personally."

"Are you implying that David's shortcomings are *that* obvious?"

"Some of them are ... yes. But Kid, their friendship has not been affected or damaged by what I told them. Maybe the opposite is true - maybe it has been strengthened by what they now know. That's why I want to talk to them."

An expression of defiance still lingered on Kid's face. Phillip knew what was going on in her mind. "Look Kid, I understand that being loyal and truthful is crucial in your life, and I appreciate that. I wasn't being underhanded when I talked to Thomas' parents and I promise that I will own up to my brother."

"Good," was all Kid said. In her heart, she knew that Phillip had a valid point, and he had also indicated that he respected her side of the argument. She knew she had over-reacted but wasn't quite ready to admit it.

Phillip read her thoughts. He tenderly put his arm around her shoulder, "Come darling, let's go to bed. I don't believe that David is in any danger, do you?"

"No, I don't. He just needs to be alone for a while. Sorry about flying in your face darling."

The phone rang a second time. "You take this one, Phillip," Kid said over her shoulder. She was already half-way up the stairs.

The call was from Mario who repeated the news Phillip had already heard. "Do you know where David is now?" Mario asked. "He apparently just sort of slipped out of the hospital. You know he can move like a wild cat on silent paws."

"Yes I know. He might just need some time alone,

411

Mario. We'll let you know if he should turn up here, OK?" That was the extent of their conversation.

That night, Phillip lay awake for some time. It wasn't worry that kept him awake, it was just the sort of night when he liked to let his thoughts roam back over his life - his life with Kid. His memory touched on that very first evening in the hotel in Australia and he recalled his theatrical and mildly absurd behavior of that night and the thought still stirred a feeling of embarrassment deep inside. The fact that he couldn't have known then what was to come seemed like rather a cheap excuse at this point. Yet the following morning at breakfast I could suddenly see into the future, he recalled with some amusement. I know I made a fool of myself by charging after Kid's truck, but I was following an impulse. Even now Phillip remembered clearly hearing this little voice that was telling him not to let Kid slip away from him.

Kid was sleeping peacefully, her head resting against his shoulder. Phillip listened to her regular breathing. He loved her – he would love her all his life. Their relationship had indeed strengthened and deepened as Father said it would.

"Phillip, wake up ..." Kid said urgently, "can you hear what I hear?"

"... can hear nothing, Kid," Phillip said sleepily.

By that time Kid had already slipped on her bathrobe and was holding Phillip's up for him to put on. "Quick, I heard the door go ... a burglar I suppose. Come on, lets get him." Slowly, carefully they descended the steps hand in hand. Neither of them had a clear idea however, of how to 'get' a burglar if there should indeed be one.

David had let himself in with the key Phillip had given him before he moved in with Robert. 'Consider this to be your home,' Phillip had said, 'anytime you want to come here ... you're welcome'. David knew the hour was late but his brother had never specified time of the day or occasion, he had simply said 'you'll be welcome'. David had entered the house quietly by the back door, turned on the little light in the laundry then walked slowly into the kitchen. His heart was filled with grief and sorrow and he was a little unsteady on his legs. At this difficult time he felt the need to be with Phillip and Kid - they were his family, he loved them both. Like in a dream he pulled out one of the stools at the breakfast counter and sat down a little uncomfortably. He propped up his elbows and buried his face in the palms of his hands.

This was how Kid saw him as she and Phillip tip-toed down the stairs. She took one look at the sitting giant and knew. Something is very wrong ... David is sitting ... David never sits ... David always stands ... on both feet, never even leans against something. This can only mean that we have a real crisis on our hands. "David?" she said almost in a whisper. "David, darling," then she approached him and gently, awkwardly put her arms around him.

David didn't quite know how to respond even though he meant to.

"I'm glad you came here, David," Phillip said as he sat down next to his brother.

David nodded. "I just needed to come home. When things are difficult ... this place here ... it gives me the feeling of ... home."

Silence for some time.

"David, Robert and James called earlier on, they were worried, wondering where you were. I promised to call back ..."

"Oh come on, they'll see me soon enough ... when I get back. Why should they worry?"

Phillip decided to ignore this and continued undeterred. "Actually, Mario called too. For pretty much the same reason."

"Why all the fuss ... nobody needs to worry about me."

Kid and Phillip shot each other quizzical looks, then Phillip made one more attempt, "What about Mr and Mrs Clark? Surely they would like to know that you're OK."

"Why the hell would they be thinking about me? They've just lost their only son ..."

Phillip had had enough. "Look David, all these people

are your friends, right? Why are you so dismissive?"

David looked up now, bewilderment written all over his face. "What do you mean?"

He just doesn't get it, Phillip thought. Alright, I'll spell it out for you. "What I mean is, you don't seem to know how to accept people's honest friendship. You sound like your mind is going back to your past, to the times of fights and arrests, the times of handcuffs and jail, the days when people used you and laughed at you. Forget it David, now is different. You are a decent citizen and an honest guy and people respect you. Remember the party? All those students and parents and everybody ... they see you as their friend. They honestly care David, they have your wellbeing at heart, and the littlest ones practically worship you ... I've seen it. David, all these people are true friends, they all love you ... I've been there, I felt it. Where is your confidence? What are you doing to yourself?"

It was after these last words from his brother that David broke down. He lowered his head, buried his face in the crook of his arm and started to cry ... and he cried bitterly for a long time. Kid and Phillip looked on helplessly but did nothing to try and comfort him. They could not grasp the full extent of David's sorrow, so they simply let him cry himself out.

When the sobbing ceased, he said somewhat shyly, "May I stay here with you tonight?"

"Of course David, you have your room – always." Kid offered.

"No, I mean ... I'd like to stay with you guys ... not on my own ..."

This time it was Phillip's answer which came instantly as if rehearsed, "Sure, I understand David. Let's all go upstairs." And with these words he pushed his stool back, took his brother by the arm and led him out of the kitchen. Kid had to marvel at her husband's display of competence. Phillip's turn, she thought a little uncomprehendingly, to put into practice a scenario of full-blown ménage à trois.

David was wearing his white karate outfit, his Black Belt around his waist and he was barefoot. Phillip was in his dark blue toweling bathrobe which reached down to mid-calf, he was barefoot too. As Kid watched them slowly make their way upstairs, she felt as though she was watching a soppy family-reunion movie.

"I quickly call Robert and Mario, OK?" she said. And without waiting for a reply, she picked up the receiver and dialed. The call to Mario lasted for about one minute, the one to Robert and James a little longer. Mr Clark had apparently inquired about David's whereabouts, and James thought that he sounded real worried.

"Please James, can you call him? Tell him that David is with us tonight. David is ... not in the best of shapes. But Phillip and I are looking after him ... in standard McCabe family tradition. Don't worry about anything, OK?" Then she went upstairs knowing that she would be sharing her bed with Phillip and David. An interesting if a little scary prospect, she thought but didn't pursue it any further.

Kid saw David's karate outfit laying in a heap on the carpet in the corner of the room, he was just getting into bed on the far side and Phillip was covering him up with the quilted bedcover. Without a word, Phillip helped Kid out of her robe, hung it up on the inside of the bathroom door then shed his own robe. As naturally as if it were an everyday occurrence, Kid climbed into the unoccupied space of her and her husband's matrimonial bed. Phillip followed and settled down beside her. Kid now found herself sandwiched between two naked men - one her husband, the other her brother. It was quite involuntary that some mischievous thoughts crossed her mind then. What if ... during the night while I'm asleep ... I should turn over and cuddle up to the wrong man? Her own explanation to justify such a situation was instant: not responsible for what one does in one's sleep. Then another 'what if'. What if David gets into one of his nightmares? I would be the one to cop it ... and cop it big time. She felt her mischief vanishing and fear flooded in to fill its place. From the corner of her eye, she saw David curled-up and seemingly asleep.

She turned toward Phillip and rested her head on his chest. "Now we are real family, aren't we," she said maybe just a tad uncertainly.

"Yes, it's nice ... and thanks for ... for..." the answer came unexpectedly and sleepily from the other side of the bed, then David wriggled around a little and buried his head back in his pillow. Kid waited for a few minutes and when she was quite sure that David was fast asleep she whispered very close to Phillip's ear, "Darling, David is touching my hand."

Phillip chuckled.

"This is no chuckling matter, Phillip," Kid said urgently.

"No, of course not, he just needs some re-assurance of our nearness. David had a difficult day, don't forget."

"OK then."

David slept like a baby for the rest of that night. His mind and his soul were filled with family feelings; he felt safe close to his brother and sister-in-law and there was no room in his heart for the ugly pictures of his nightmare.

He woke up early since his inner clock was tuned to his usual pre-dawn meditation, and as he started to stir, Kid woke up, too. She reached out sleepily and landed her hand smack in the middle of David's face. She let it slide down and come to rest on the soft hair on his chest. That feels nice, she thought a little cheekily, "Are you going to your dojo, David? What time is it?"

"It is ... umm ... I don't know, the clock is on Phillips'

side."

"It's ten to six," Phillip said. "Can you have a pre-meditative cup of coffee?"

"Yes, thanks." With that David got out of bed, rubbed his eyes and walked unsteadily across to the bathroom. He was completely naked.

Is this how things are done in this house now? Kid asked herself briefly. OK then ... I just follow suit. "I go and brew a pot of coffee," she said while getting out of bed - she wasn't wearing anything either. Then she turned to Phillip, "You have to get up, darling. These are the new rules of the house, you see."

Phillip did as he was told, then embraced Kid. "I make the coffee, Kid. You go back to the family bed for another ten minutes, eh?"

XXVIII

It was a few weeks after Thomas' funeral. David had been able to make some sense of a life without his darling student, thanks to the healing effects of a night spent with his brother and Kid and also thanks to Father's patience and to his loving words.

One day around lunch time, David was studying his newest book. It dealt with herbs and explained how, where and when to grow them. In the last section there were some recipes using the herbs that were grown in the first and second part of the book. Reading was still a highly demanding enterprise for David and required every bit of his concentration. This was the reason why James' news that the block next door was now for sale, and his following discussion with Robert on that subject, went unheard and unnoticed by David. He was not one for multi-tasking.

"The block is quite a bit bigger than ours," Robert

said. "Hope somebody is not going to construct some architectural monstrosity on it or an ugly food outlet of some description. It would kind of damage the whole image of Jefferson Street, don't you think?"

James nodded. "I just had a good look around the area. It reaches right down to that little creek bed ... kind of pretty down there ..."

Then the phone rang.

"Yes, Mr Blythe," James heard. "At seven thirty? I'm sure we can make it ..." James decided that he was not interested in that conversation and turned his attention to David.

"Are you going to cook us some of these?"

"Umm ... I'm thinking of growing herbs. I'll make a herb garden - a real rock garden - at the back near the laundry door where the plants will be sheltered from the wind ... get plenty of sun, then I will ..."

"David, listen up," Robert interrupted. "Do you have classes later this afternoon?" And before David's thinking mechanisms had time to switch from herbs to karate, Robert continued, "Anyway, Mr Blythe wants to see us ... you, me, Jason, secretaries and all ... at seven thirty, OK?"

"Why?"

"Big news apparently, but he didn't specify."

The next minute, David was back with his herb studies as though nothing had been said.

"I'm glad you are all here," said Mr Blythe, "I have news for you ... good and less good. I start with the latter. I have decided to close the school." He paused momentarily, then said in the same tone of voice, "Now don't look at me as if this were the end of the world. I'm getting older and my wife, as you know, is not in good health. It has been suggested to us that she would benefit from warmer and milder climate so we intend to move to California. I always hoped that my son would take over the school but he has, unfortunately, never shown any interest in martial arts. He also lives California, in San Francisco, so we might have some sort of a family reunion. My son is married now and has a baby daughter. He has a business and a life he enjoys. That's it. Now, the closure is not going to happen tomorrow or the day after. I just thought it was the decent thing to do to inform you all of my intentions."

Nobody made any comment.

"Now ... here comes the good news. The school has received a donation - and a very generous one at that - in the form of a check. It is from Mr and Mrs Clark. Attached to the check was a note which says that the donation was made in recognition of the benefit karate training had been to their son during the last months of his life and that they hoped the money could be used to help other students too. The note finishes with a personal thanks to their son's Sensei for his dedication and for the wisdom he had taught Thomas."

At that point Mr Blythe looked up, then continued, "You have done our school proud, David," he said and got up to shake David's hand.

David looked bewildered but remained in control. He simply nodded.

Exactly two weeks after the conference in Mr Blythe's office, the subject of the land for sale next door to Robert's house came up for discussion once more, this time by David. His approach indicated clearly that he thought he was the first to have noticed the 'For Sale' sign. He, James and Robert were sitting comfortably in their vast lounge room having a pre-dinner drink.

"The place next door ... it's for sale," David announced solemnly, "and I'm going to buy it and build a dojo on it ... a real proper dojo. Robert please, you design it for me, in true Japanese style: sliding doors with rice paper, straw mats, showers and changing rooms, the lot."

"Have you hit the jack-pot David?" James blurted.

"The what?"

"Sorry. Do you have the money for all this, I meant."

"No, but I can get a loan from the bank ... everybody takes out a loan when they buy property or build a house, right? You just pay it back bit by bit." These were his final words on the matter, then in one of his by now familiar leaps of thought he said, "I go and start dinner." His two friends were left sitting in their soft seats as though glued to them.

They shook their heads in stunned silence, and if there was a collective feeling of a bad omen looming in some corner of their minds, they did not show it.

That night, David got very little sleep. The idea of buying land and constructing a dojo that would be all his own had come to him like a dream of the distant past, suddenly surfacing again in the present. David was determined not to let that dream disappear again ... ever. He decided to ask Kid to come with him to the bank, just in case he should get stuck filling out forms. But there was one little problem with that: he and Kid had not been on very good terms for a few days even though apologies had been made after their shouting match.

It happened a few days ago. Kid was early for her class and sat waiting on one of the benches in the little square at the back of the building. A young man sat down next to her and tried to engage her in conversation. Kid was not in the mood. She was reading a book and had no time for making conversation. The man did not give up immediately, instead he made a renewed attempt at talking to her. Kid in a rather brash and petulant way shut the book, shoved it in her backpack and started to walk toward the back entrance of the building without saying a word. The young man followed and when he held the door open for her, he made the almost fatal mistake of placing one hand on Kid's shoulder.

That did it.

Kid turned around briskly and in the following few seconds gave a text-book performance of a defense against an imaginary attacker. She soon had the man pinned against the wall, the palm of one hand in his face and pushing upwards, her elbow ready for a vicious blow to the ribcage. Then she saw two people walk towards her; she let go of the man and turned to walk inside the building and to the dojo. The two people also happened to be David's students and it was unfortunate for Kid that they went straight to their teacher and told him what they had witnessed.

David approached Kid after class. He was livid and he gave her a proper teacher-student dressing down. "Kid, you are not to use the skills I teach you in public. As your teacher I'm responsible for your actions. Why don't you listen to what I tell you? You completely overreacted. Karate isn't just a game, OK?" Then David pointed out that talking to someone in a public place was not a crime and that she had attacked a probably harmless guy. "It is a lot worse to punish someone for a crime he has *not* committed than to let a real culprit go free," he told her in no uncertain terms.

Little did he know that he was not the first person to be confronted with this critical issue. David was of course, unfamiliar with the judicial decree of 'presumed innocent until proven guilty'.

Kid had been subdued and a little intimidated by his harsh words. They had both apologized, but they had spoken little since then and David wondered now if it was OK to ask Kid for help with his bank loan.

He needn't have worried, Kid never did sulk or bear a grudge for any length of time.

On the following morning, Robert and James watched with considerable misgivings as David got ready to leave. He was wearing his best shirt and trousers, meticulously polished shoes and his hair, now shoulder length, was nicely washed and brushed.

The two men left behind at the kitchen table after David's departure shared another cup of coffee, in silence.

"David looked real respectable, didn't he?" James was the first to speak. "But then ... he is good-looking no matter what he wears. His chances of being eligible for a loan ... they are slim, aren't they Robert? He has no assets or anything to inspire a bank with confidence of his trustworthiness."

"His chances are not only slim, they are non-existent. Lack of assets is only one argument against him, James. Remember, David has a criminal record a mile long. They'll dig it up for sure and ... no money lender is going to overlook that."

"But what about his good behavior since he...."

"It's no good James, he just has to accept that he will not be granted a loan by any institution. But there are other things he can do with his life ..."

"....in this 'Land of Opportunities'," James added cryptically.

"You can say that again." They left it at that.

It was a difficult day for David. His visits to various banks all proved to be dismal failures for exactly the reasons Robert had lined out to James. His criminal record would mysteriously appear on the banker's desk after the first ten minutes of the interview. The initially friendly talk would instantly mutate to a refusal, uttered in suitably embarrassed tones of voice. He would hear words like 'regretful' and 'we are afraid that under the circumstances ...' or 'your record tells us ...'.

Kid stuck by her brother through every one of his failures. She commiserated, encouraged, moderated depending on David's mood. But the moment she caught the first signs of possible loss of temper on David's part, she decided it was time to refer to drastic measures of her own: she threatened him. She threatened to physically subdue him if he did not calm down and see reason. Her tactics worked like a charm. "No Kid, please ... no fight ... let's remain friends," he pleaded.

"OK, friends again," she sounded conciliatory, "and I won't ask you to give me the precise reasons for the loan you're after, you tell me when you are ready. Now, you have to go to work ... you need all your concentration there.

Think about the money issue later, OK?"

"Thanks ... I love you Kid."

"No you don't."

"In my own way I do."

Whatever his own way is, she thought, I love him too, just a very little bit ... that's OK.

When David came home that evening, all Robert and James could see was an expression of impassiveness. But it was more than just a display of senseless bravado, there were signs of determination and studied calm. David's behavior demonstrated just how much control he was capable of.

David went straight into the kitchen and busied himself with the preparations for dinner. He had by then assumed full responsibility for all the cooking in the house, Robert's erstwhile distribution of chores notwithstanding. James had a dozen questions ready to shoot and only with great difficulty did he manage not to be needlessly provocative. He continued vacuuming the carpets in the lounge and Robert proceeded with sorting out the washing. Disclosures of David's success or failure had to wait until dinner time.

David did not give much away that evening, except that the bankers he had spoken to today had not been co-operative, but that he was far from giving up on his idea of building a dojo on the block next door.

That night was much more restful for David than the

previous one. He was even more determined to have his dojo. Nothing could stop him now, certainly not an insignificant little accessory like money – or the lack thereof. David had made a decision. Tomorrow, he would go and talk to Mr Goldberg. That was it. Mr Goldberg said he wanted to help if he could, now was the time. David remembered that on his card were the words finance-something-or-other, that meant he was something to do with money. With this reassuring thought, David let himself drift into a peaceful sleep.

David never thought of making an appointment with Mr Goldberg. He had the address on the calling card and that's where he went the following morning after his regular pre-dawn routine and mediation in the dojo. He wore his light blue shirt, the one Kid insisted reflected the color of his eyes, his tailor-made grey slacks and black shoes. He put on his black suit jacket which was made of a velvety material. Where the colors of his clothes were concerned, he still relied almost exclusively on Kid's advice ... it had never deceived him.

At the reception desk, David simply asked to speak to Mr Goldberg. He stood tall and straight facing the receptionist with a smile. David did not know that the lady broke the rules when she let him see the boss without the required appointment, and she herself was not quite sure if she did it because she was intimidated by David's size and by his statuesque stance or because she was charmed by his good looks.

Mr Goldberg was positively delighted to receive David in his palatial corner office on the top floor of the building. There was a big beautifully polished mahogany desk to the left and four soft seats and a small table to the right. Two potted trees in the corner gave the room a comfortable atmosphere. "Good to see you, Mr McCabe," Mr Goldberg offered. "Please sit down. What brings you here?"

David would have much preferred to stand for this important encounter, but Kid had long ago told him that it was not polite to stand in a room especially when one was six foot five. 'You intimidate people', she had admonished. So he sat. He had not rehearsed his sentences. He knew it was no good since he would not be able to remember them at the right moment anyway.

"Sir," he started, "I'm here to ask for your help." He took a deep breath as a measure of controlling his agitation then continued. "I wonder if you could give me a loan." Robert had worked out the approximate costs of the dojo then added the price of the land, and it was a hefty six digit amount that David now stated to Mr Goldberg.

Mr Goldberg listened and didn't blink an eye. "I see," he said, "what are your plans?"

"I want to buy the piece of land right next to where I'm living - the one where the house burnt down - and I want to

430

build a gym or rather a dojo on it. Our martial arts school will soon be closed, you see, and there are many students who want to continue practicing and studying ..."

"Now that you say that, I remember having seen a flyer around town - long time ago - it had your photo on it, right? I didn't recognize you straight away," Mr Goldberg flashed a little smile at David, "You were shown in a rather unusual ... a rather sophisticated position."

"Yes sir, I was. I'm a karate instructor. The school where I teach organized a recruiting fête on that day and I taught two master classes." And right then in another sudden change of course and seemingly unrelated, David asked, "How is your little girl, Mr Goldberg?"

The banker only just managed to stop himself from shaking his head in disbelief. "She is fine - her name is Sarah, by the way. She remembers the day when she fell into the river and she has asked after the 'man with the long yellow hair' on more than one occasion."

David gave one of his most charming smiles and nodded, but said nothing.

"Now back to your project, Mr McCabe. I'm only too happy to help. Of course I'll let you have the money you need."

"Thank you sir ... you're very kind. Please will you work out my pay-back schedule? I intend to build the dojo myself and then I'll be teaching full-time ... I will be able to pay your money back ... all of it."

Unexpectedly, Mr Goldberg got up from his seat, took a few steps then came back and sat down again. "Mr McCabe, I don't want you to pay the money back. It's not a loan ... the money is yours, it's a gift. I know that money can never really pay for what you did for my family but I see this as my opportunity to thank you for saving the life of my daughter."

David was speechless.

"It's OK, don't say anything. How would you like the money? A check? or shall I transfer it to your bank account?"

It was after the business part had been settled that David suddenly felt pangs of guilt for not having told Mr Goldberg the truth of his past. Is not telling lying, he wondered? After all it's because of my past that no one wanted to give me a loan ... I must tell him. "Sir," he now started haltingly, "umm ... I've been to other banks ... they refused me because of my record. I feel I have to tell you." He shot a quick glance at the banker who sat opposite. Mr Goldberg was unfazed.

"In the years since Vietnam ... I've spent time in jail ... more than once. But I'm no criminal, sir. It's just that I was wild and strong ... and my mind was sick ..."

"It's OK Mr McCabe. What happened in your past will not make me change my mind. I am aware of the damage our involvement in Vietnam has done to our people. My own brother ... he was drafted, too. He came back minus one leg and ... he wasn't ever the same person again. He couldn't re-integrate into our society ... he is dead now."

"How did he die, sir?"

"He shot himself ... left a wife and two little boys behind." And after a pause, "Oh, they got plenty of compensation from the government. My brother was an officer of some rank ... still, it didn't bring the family their father and husband back." The question implied in the look he gave David was unmistakable. And David answered it simply by saying, "No sir, nothing ... but I came back in one piece and physically fit ... and also I was not an officer, just a soldier."

The phone started ringing, business took it's course. "Please stay in touch. I'm looking forward to seeing your martial arts school up and running."

That evening when David got home after his last class, he was in high spirits and his heart was filled with happiness. He could hardly wait to tell his mates his good news.

He almost didn't have to, it was apparently written all over his face. "Success David?" James asked before he was properly inside the house.

"Yep. Got the money. Now I can start ..."

"Tell us all," Robert called as he came bouncing down the stairs. "Can I start with the design of the dojo?"

David very carefully took Mr Goldberg's card out of his pocket and held it out to Robert, almost like an offering might be made at a shrine. "This is the man who gave me the money," he said truthfully.

Robert quickly picked up on the improbability of this statement, but assumed that it had merely been David's unfortunate choice of the word 'gave'. The guy who 'gave' me the money David said, Robert recapped. Nobody 'gives' money, you lend it or you borrow it depending which side of the deal you are on. He said, "So, this then is the person who gave you a loan, right? What terms ... interest ... come on, tell us, don't keep up the suspense."

"No no, it's not like that. He *gave* me the money ... as a gift ... don't need to pay it back. Remember the little girl I fished out of the river? Well, Mr Goldberg is her father ... he is kind of saying thanks."

"This sounds like straight out of a fairytale," James exclaimed. "I'm so happy for you David ... this is fantastic, let's celebrate."

XXIX

By the time Mr Blythe closed his school, David's dojo was practically completed. All it needed were a few finishing touches from the master.

Robert had designed the dojo along the lines of a Japanese house with sliding doors although not fitted with the traditional rice paper, but with soft off-white frosted glass panels. The front door opened onto a small entrance area with a wooden floor - the place where everyone had to take off their shoes. All other parts of the dojo were entirely done in tatami mats - the straw mats which are used in Japanese houses as floor coverings. On these mats everyone only ever walked barefoot. The actual dojo was a couple of steps lower than the rest of the place. Two large windows faced east, David and Robert had agreed on the importance of letting in as much of the morning light as possible. Robert had designed bathrooms and showers to be separated from the dojo by another sliding door. The whole building was done in light colored timber and the roof featured exposed beams in keeping with traditional Japanese houses. The attention to detail gave the dojo a tranquil and serene atmosphere.

David had a lot of willing workers who helped with the construction of the new dojo. They were all students who enjoyed working, not for money, but simply for the benefit of camaraderie and personal satisfaction. An inauguration ceremony was organized and David prepared a 'universal course' - a course where everybody would participate regardless of age or grade. It was to be a highlight in David's teaching career. On that day, David had an unusual gathering of students on his new dojo mats: advanced students and beginners, children no more than six years old side by side with Black Belts. David put all of them through an hour-long session which was designed to instruct and challenge everyone present. It was a masterpiece in-so-far as karate classes went, and was to be remembered by many for a long time to come.

Conflicting thoughts about using karate as a sole means of making money however, surfaced in David's mind shortly after inauguration day. David had always wanted to practice karate as an art form not as a mundane means to make a living. But what could he do other than run this dojo as a regular martial arts school? He was a karate fighter - nothing else. He had no trade and no skills to fall back on. He was aware of his inadequacy in everyday living skills and he still had to rely on some help and guidance from family and friends in that field. David spent sleepless nights turning this issue over in his mind. He knew he needed to make an income by some other means than karate,. only then could he train his students without having to charge them tuition fees. That's what he wanted to do with his life. In this particular matter David did not ask for assistance - not from Robert and not from Phillip and Kid - he was simply too shy to approach anyone.

Surprisingly and quite inadvertently, the answer to his dilemma came from his brother during one of their regular dinners. Kid was the first to sense David's unease and she thought she knew its origin. "I know what's troubling you, David," she said seemingly out of the blue, "I can read your mind. It's to do with using your karate teaching to earn an income, that's what it is."

David nodded. He felt absurdly relieved that this issue had come up without him having to ask for help.

Being his student had given Kid a clear insight into David's passionate desire to treat karate as an art and not as a money-making enterprise. She also knew that directly after his release, he had accepted the job as karate instructor only because he had had no alternative; he had no other training and no trade. But he is clever with his hands and with tools, she now thought, and he is strong and hard-working and reliable ... there must be something he can do.

"But you are clever in many ways David ... there is stuff you can do. Let me think. You can renovate houses, build a dojo and ...".

"Yeah sure, but I often can't read or interpret the plans, right?"

Without warning, Phillip now spoke up, "Remember the backyard we had when we were little? You did a lot of work there and turned it into a beautiful garden ... fruit trees, flower beds, strawberries. You're good with plants and landscaping and all that. Why not try to turn *that* talent into a money-making enterprise - a business of some kind?"

When Phillip got to that point, David was shaking with helpless laughter.

"Would you care to share the joke, David?"

"Yeah, I'll try. In that backyard ... I also built a sandpit for you ... nice big one ... and Poppa bought you plastic shovels and stuff."

Kid's turn to giggle.

"You were still very little ... just old enough to stand on your own feet ... and you played in that sand for hours building God-knows what and all the while you sang all the baby songs mom had taught you. I never thought of that for years but now ... I can see it all like a movie in my head."

Kid was jumping up and down with delight by then,

"My darling husband singing baby songs in the sandpit ... what a scream."

Phillip took some time to decide whether to laugh along with Kid or to be embarrassed. But as it turned out, he was not given much time for inner debate. His initial suggestion had triggered off something in David which now seemed to be unstoppable.

"That's it," he said. "If I plan carefully and use all the land I have sensibly, I should be able to produce fruit and vegetables, grapes, strawberries, heaps of stuff ... I can sell to shops or at week-end markets. I can also establish a nursery ... trees and shrubs in pots. Maybe I can advertise to landscape other people's gardens ...." David's mind was made up. "Great idea, Phillip," he said, and right there in his brother's living room he saw his future clearly lined out for him.

"Brilliant ... and I can give a hand. I'm real good at digging the soil, you know," Kid added, she thought, help-fully.

David's dream enterprise soon started to take shape. He purchased garden tools, wheelbarrows, water hoses and fittings, soil-mixture, fertilizer. He set up a potting shed and a greenhouse; everything was possible when you had a seemingly inexhaustible bank account. He selected the best spot for his fruit orchard, he planted saplings of apple trees, pears, plums, peaches and apricots. He built three lines of trellises for grape vines. He marked out the vegetable garden and dug the earth into deep furrows and filled them with good soil and manure. He wanted the best for his plants – he was a serious and conscientious gardener.

He continued living in Robert's house - it had by now become his home. David spent the first hours of each day in his dojo then taught classes in late afternoon and evening. In between he worked tirelessly on his land. Robert and James watched him with a mixture of amazement and admiration from their vantage point next door.

There was one issue in his newly found life however, that David diligently pushed into the background, hoping it would eventually just go away: it was the actual running of his dojo as a martial arts school. Almost all the students from Mr Blythe's school had followed him to his new place in Jefferson Street. He taught a series of classes every day, he had his assistant teachers when he needed them – in short, the teaching side of his school ran smoothly and to everybody's satisfaction. It was the organizational side which was somewhat haphazard. David lacked the sophistication and the savoir-faire needed to run the school as a business.

Even though Kid had no head for business either, it was nevertheless she, who one day came up with an ingenious scheme to put David's mind at ease. She now worked regularly in David's garden, once or twice a week, strictly under his supervision. The boss, as she now called David, usually allowed her a short break after the first two hours, and it was during one of those precious breaks while Kid and David were sitting on Robert's veranda having a cup of coffee, that Kid addressed the issue of the school management. "David, I have a very clever idea on how to solve your school managing problem. Do you want to hear?"

"Sure Kid."

"OK. It's plainly obvious that all your students mean to pay for their lessons, right? I've heard them ask how much it was and how to pay it on more than one occasion. You see, people don't know - or have forgotten - that one can get something for free," she said rather pompously.

"So, what you do is: you tell them that you *don't* charge any fees but - and here comes the but - if anybody *wanted* to give you something anyway they were free to do so, and that it didn't matter how much or how little. And you tell them that the money will be used exclusively for the upkeep of the dojo. Good so far?"

"Yep."

"Now, at the entrance of your dojo you place a box with a lid and a slit cut into it. Those who want can then stick some money in there ... but nobody would be made to feel that they had to and no one can see what's in it. You could always use that money to build up a depot of second-hand outfits and distribute them to students who are not so well off. What do you think?"

David sat in silence for a long while, then he reached out and took Kid's hand in his holding it as a lover - or a loving brother - might. "You are wonderful Kid, thanks." Then he got up and pulled Kid to her feet. "Just a little kiss. You know I love you ... I mean, as a brother ... just as a brother." He clasped her in his big arms and gave her a kiss on her forehead. "I'd never want to upset your relationship with Phillip. I'm happy knowing that my little brother is married to the woman he loves. Let me love you just a very little bit, too."

Kid looked at him wide-eyed. She had never heard him say so many consecutive, correct and coherent sentences.

"Time to go back to work. We have to finish preparing the soil where I'm going to plant the onions and the garlic," David said in one of his usual mind leaps. "The Chinese say you have to plant them on a full moon. I read it in my gardening book."

Kid couldn't be sure she had heard correctly but then, her husband had told her more than once that his brother was a mixed bag of improbabilities and surprises.

XXX

It all started as a secondhand story. Mario was the one who heard it and it caused him considerable anguish. It was not just the fact that the story he heard was completely implausible and utterly improbable which disturbed him, more than anything, he puzzled over the reason why someone found it necessary to concoct such a bag of lies. Mario told first Phillip and Kid, then Robert who related it to James at home. It later spread amongst the other students as rumors are wont to do.

This was how it all came about. The martial arts department of the university had approached David once again after he had officially resigned from his job and started teaching in his own school. Could he take a class for just a month while one of the instructors was away on business, the head of the department had asked him. It was a class of relative beginners, young ladies, some of them teenagers.

David was known to teach all classes, big or small, men or women, advanced or beginners, children or adults. This particular group however, was to become a problem class. David came home after the first lesson saying, "They are an impossible lot ... can't shut up ... can't concentrate. I don't like it ... this could lead to accidents ..."

A week or two later, Mario was sitting in the university canteen having his lunch alone, an open law book on the table next to his plate. This was when he overheard a group of girls at a nearby table chatting and giggling. The first words that caught his attention went something like, "Did you see the look on his face when Jessica took off her top, indicating the exact spot where it was supposed to be hurting?" Some rather childish giggling followed. Mario didn't know who they were talking about, but he had a feeling that these girls were up to some mischief. He kept staring at the open page in his book without however, reading it. Mario was engaged in some deliberate eavesdropping.

"Yeah ... and then you went and improvised some thigh injury ... as high up as possible. Anything goes in karate training, right? You might as well have taken it off altogether then." More laughter followed.

Another girl continued. "He believed every word we said, right? I mean, by rights he isn't allowed to come into the girls' changing room at all."

Mario kept listening but did not dare look in the direction of the speakers.

"Still, we didn't get any ... results, did we? I mean, he is just gorgeous looking, and so damn sexy but he showed no reaction ... no visible reaction, if you know what I mean." This last comment was greeted with peals of laughter. "All through class he never acknowledges anything any of us says. He is like a robot ... he is good at his job but ... no fun at all."

"Not only 'no fun', but he can be quite rude and arrogant. Did you notice how he just sort of dismissed us all after class ... too high and mighty to take us out for a drink, the master instructor," the young lady added in a voice charged with sarcasm.

When the girls got to that point, Mario knew that the object of their interest was his own teacher and friend, David. What did they want from him? What results were they talking about? Why did they trick him into entering the changing room ... what was going on? Mario was deeply troubled by this inadvertently acquired knowledge. But there was one more comment, and it was that which disturbed Mario more than all the other nonsense he had heard so far.

"If he keeps treating us like shit ... we can get him, you know, legally ... for entering the girls' shower room ... touching us where he shouldn't. He has no witnesses ... it won't do him any good to say we asked him to come in to inspect our injuries ..."

"... especially since there are not going to be any signs of injuries at all."

445

Now Mario got the whole picture of their scheme; he was angry and outraged. He shut his book with a bang, scooted back his chair and walked away, his lunch only half eaten. What has David done to deserve this? Mario decided there and then to tell Phillip exactly what he had just over-heard, and he would do so the minute he got home. These girls were playing a cruel and disgusting game. A game? This could well turn into something much more serious than just a game - given enough time, Mario reflected sadly.

What Mario meant by 'getting home that night', was in fact Phillip and Kid's home. He was living in their spare room – temporarily - until he found somewhere else. It was a sad story and Mario had spent many nights crying in his room at the end or the hallway in his friends' house. Mario had finally, after many long and agonizing years, found the courage to tell his parents about his homosexuality and their reaction had been devastating. Not even his worst fears had prepared him for the shock his revelation gave both his Mama and his Papa. His parents were of Italian descent, a second generation American by now and they were stout Catholics. Their only son being gay was simply unacceptable. His Papa had kicked Mario out of his house and out of the family. He didn't know what to do or where to go, and in his misery he had turned to Phillip and Kid, his best friends. They had listened to him, made no comment, showed neither shock nor disgust. Instead they reassured him of their continued friendship and offered him accommodation in their home.

"That's what friends are all about, Mario." Kid had said straight from the heart. "You are welcome here for as long as you need, Phillip and I love you."

So tonight he would have to tell his friend and landlord that he had news of a plot against his brother - a scheme that had the potential for dramatic consequences.

Mario let himself in through the back door and found Kid and Phillip in the kitchen engaged in a combined effort of preparing dinner.

"What is it Mario?" Kid said as soon as she saw him enter through the laundry door, "you look as if you had been put through a washing machine."

"I feel as if I had, Kid. There is stuff I have to tell you both." And before he even took off his jacket he started to give a verbatim account of what he had overheard at lunch in the canteen. Mario had an accurate and reliable memory for words.

"I don't get it," Kid said when he stopped to take a breath, "... and don't look at me as if to say 'oh, but you are so pure and innocent and your mind is so utterly uncorrupted, of course you don't get it'. It is important for me to understand all this since it concerns my very own brother."

"Excuse me Kid, *my* very own brother." Phillip managed to put in.

"Oh stop squabbling over the ownership of a brother you two," Mario admonished, "Phillip, you need to tell me what this is all about, I have a feeling that you know. I was struck by two things, both of which might provide a clue for you. One, 'David is no fun' and two, 'he treats us like shit'. Phillip?"

Phillip looked down at his feet considering his answer. "Let's sit down. I'll uncork that bottle of wine ... "

Kid fetched three of their best crystal glasses, stood them on a tray together with the bottle and the corkscrew then carried it to the lounge room.

"Yes I do know, but I don't really want to say. I feel I should talk to my brother and set this straight with him face to face ... not behind his back."

"Oh come on Phillip, don't be melodramatic. These girls are planning to get David into legal trouble and I won't let it happen. But you need to enlighten me on a few issues here, OK?"

"This is the lawyer in you speaking, I assume. OK here is what I know. Things happened to David in Vietnam. I was about thirteen years old when he came back and didn't understand what trauma and post traumatic symptoms meant. Now I do to some extent." Here Phillip started to recite, "Tendency to periodic depressions, memory gaps, lack of self-confidence, and in David's case ... a stuffed-up sex life."

"But Phillip, you can't be sure of that, can you? We mentioned it, remember? But our discussion was rather inconclusive since we had no real idea if David was affected by this ... sex-thing ..."

"I remember Kid, but I feel that I know the truth now. You see, in the time since our discussion I've become quite close to my brother, so I'm putting two and two together. I don't have evidence to substantiate my theory - you just have to take my word for it. David found out about his sexual handicap the hard way after he escaped from the clinic. No-one had told him ... probably because no-one knew about it. He was on the run from the police, from the law and from jail. He knew that a lot of things were wrong with him ... then suddenly and unexpectedly he found that his sex-life had gone down the drain as well. I'm sure that the crimes he committed and all the fights ... it was all the result of this unbearable frustration. David is no criminal, there is no evil in him, he doesn't know what vengeance means ... he just didn't know how to handle being a free citizen in his homeland after what he had experienced in that dreadful war."

Phillip glanced at his two listeners, there was a look of resignation in his eyes. "I know I sound hopelessly sentimental here but let me finish anyway. I can just see the whole scenario: David is a good-looking guy, tall, fit and sexy, very attractive to women ... so they fall for him wherever he goes. During these first and difficult months after leaving the clinic and having to cope on his own David experienced failures in ... satisfying women, consequently he made every effort to avoid these situations ... to avoid women altogether. This explains the girls' words of disappointment and of anger: 'He is no fun', and 'he treats us like shit'. That's what they said, right?."

Mario nodded, he was deep in thought. "Yeah, makes sense. Do you think he is still ... I mean it could well have been ... temporary only."

"I don't know that for certain. But going by a hunch, I would say that if place and circumstances were good, he'd probably be OK. He might just need to get over some sort of fear of women in general ... maybe that's why he gives the impression of being arrogant. So what do we do next, Mario?"

"One, I go and talk to Robert and others I can think of, then we all keep our ears and eyes open so we won't miss anything of what these students are scheming. At the first sign of them trying to go public with their lies, I'll step in as an witness."

Kid had been listening to the conversation between Mario and Phillip with mounting unease, she could not help remembering what happened during one of the band's performances only a couple of weeks ago.

The concert took place on the campus and was organized by university students. It was quite a big venue with a stage across the whole front of the room. A bar was at the back and two extended counters on either side of it. The whole area was set with rustic looking tables the same height as the bar and everybody sat on bar-stools. The whole place, except the stage, was in comfortable semi-darkness - a pleasant atmosphere altogether.

Kid had been working at Alfredo's that night and had not been able to get away on time, so she missed the first two or three songs. She found the room crowded, warm and smoky when she entered but had no trouble locating David, he was a difficult person to miss in any crowd. He looked smart in his beige cotton shirt with buttoned pockets and shoulder flaps. The musicians looked smart too, they all wore black slacks and black shirts ... all except Jim. He wore a white shirt. Probably because of his black skin, Kid reasoned, white shows up nicer indeed.

David vacated his seat and motioned for Kid to sit down. "I get you a drink, Kid," he said, "what would you like?"

"Glass of red wine, please." My darling brother can be so gallant, she thought proudly. Then she felt Robert's eyes on her and when she turned around, the look on his face reflected her own thoughts of a second ago.

It was during the second part of the concert that David

blew his image of the gallant guy. Kid excused herself and went to the bathroom, and as soon as the seat beside David was empty, he heard a lady's voice very close to his ear, " ... enjoying the concert?"

The next minute he felt cigarette smoke being blown directly into his face. He got up, shook his head and turned away. He didn't say a word.

"What's the matter?"

"Don't like smoke in my face," David said after his customary thirty second silence between hearing a question and giving his answer. Anyone not familiar with this delay always started to repeat the question before David was ready with his answer. Some people found this irritating.

"Oh, I'm sorry. Mind if I sit down here?"

Silence for a couple of minutes. "It's somebody's seat," he said without looking at the person he spoke to.

"Whose? Wife, girlfriend?"

"No. Umm ... aren't you here to listen to the music?" David said making it quite clear that he was in no mood for making conversation.

"Yes, I sure am ... they are good, too. By the way, I'm Pat." She waited and just as she opened her mouth to repeat her statement she heard, "I'm David." But David was still not looking at her, his attention was focused on the musicians and on the song they were playing.

"Are you a student here, David? Don't think I've seen you around. What do you do?"

For the first time, David looked at the lady called Pat and if there had been more light in the room, she might have seen an expression which spelled out 'just leave me alone, will you'. "I'm not a student," he said. Pat was watching him very closely, he could feel it and he knew very well what she wanted ... he had experienced it a hundred times before. Why can't she go get herself another guy, he thought with considerable annoyance, all she wants is a screw. Why bother me? Just then Kid came back to the table,

"You sit down here Kid," he said, getting up from his stool. "You know I can stand for the rest of the night."

Kid smiled then noticed the young lady who sat beside David. "Friend of yours, David?" she asked.

"Nope."

Not so gallant after all, Kid thought. "I'm Kid," she said cheerfully.

"Am I occupying your seat?"

"Never mind, I don't own it." The conversation was temporarily interrupted by applause all around, then Kid continued, "... top concert, isn't it. David's brother is one of the musicians ... the one who plays the acoustic guitar." What else can I say to stop the situation from deteriorating, she asked herself now close to panic. If David would at least acknowledge the woman's presence, instead he puts his hand almost possessively on my shoulder. Kid turned around and gave David a pleading look; he did not understand. He only asked if she wanted another drink.

"A coke please."

"How about a drink for me, David?" Pat asked rather cheekily.

David either didn't hear her or didn't want to hear. He simply walked away and tried to disappear in the crowd.

Kid was close to despair, she looked at James and Robert who sat at the other end of the table but got no help from them so she just hoped this whole uncomfortable situation would simply go away. Finally in a fit of piqued, Pat got up and turned to walk the other way. The last thing Kid heard was a muttered '...arrogant bastard', then Pat was gone.

This must be how David's students felt, Kid thought, the ones Mario heard complaining about their instructor's arrogant behavior.

As promised, Mario went to see Robert the following day. Robert listened attentively and never interrupted Mario's account of what he had overheard in the canteen. The fact was that this story did not come to Robert as very much of a shock. He clearly remembered David's own comment on this particular class after his very first lesson.

"It all falls into place," he said, "these students have very little interest in karate and a lot of interest in their instructor. David does not recognize the signs of flirtation or possible intent of seduction." There he paused to take a breath. When he continued it was as if his voice had changed to a minor key. "David does have a difficulty when it comes to talking to women. Maybe he is shy ... I don't know. I've watched him a couple of times after class when he was approached by women, mostly single mothers who come to collect their children. He gives the appearance of being rude ... almost arrogant." Right then, Robert too, remembered the incident at the concert.

"Are you implying that these mothers had romantic - maybe sexual - interests on their minds?" Mario broke into his thoughts.

"Absolutely. Look, whether David likes it or not, he is terribly attractive to women, his problem is that he doesn't know how to handle them."

At this point Mario had to reveal Phillip's theory to which Robert simply said, "Right. I believe Phillip is spot on. I'll go and watch David's next class with these girls... might try to take Jason and others with me ... you for that matter."

"I'll be there. Phillip promised to talk to his brother on the subject of how he treats women," he added with an uncertain shrug of his shoulders.

Robert's suggested strategy worked the treat. It worked for everyone except for David's students. In an effort to save David from being further used and abused, Robert had managed to speak to the head of the university's sports department, Mr Grey. He listened carefully as Robert gave him a full account of all the facts, including his personal fears and apprehensions concerning the devious ways the students had chosen to try to seduce his friend. So, the following week, and without David's knowledge, four men watched his class from a vantage point outside the dojo. Two of the clandestine observers, Robert and Jason, were Black Belt holders like David and with their expert knowledge of karate, were able to keep a close eye on David's teaching as well as on the students' performance as the course progressed. They soon got the picture of David's initial concern and of his continuing irritation with this particular group of students. They giggled during the starting meditation, there was constant chatter amongst the students once the lesson had started, instructions were only partly followed and David had to stop and repeat certain movements. On more than one occasion he asked for more concentration and less talk. "This must be hell for David," Robert sighed.

It was around then that things really started to go wrong.

"How do I do this David," one of the students interrupted, "I can't do this position right. Come here and show me again." An unmistakable invitation to be close to the instructor and to be touched by him.

"Now I see what you mean," Mr Grey whispered, "... wonder if they dare go any further."

They did.

"I'm hurt ... my rib cage ... right here ... hey David I

need help." The spot the girl indicated where help was apparently required was about one inch below her breast.

"Dammit, she's not hurt at all," muttered Mr Grey. He had had enough. He ostentatiously walked into the dojo area and sat down on one of the benches without saying a word. The other three men followed silently and sat down beside him and together they watched the continuation of the class right to its conclusion. David could be seen to apply every bit of self-control to keep his calm; there were no more incidents but the chatter and the giggling continued. After he had bowed himself out David made sure that none of the students remained on the mats unsupervised then walked over to his visitors. He did not know why they were there. Robert introduced David to Mr Grey.

"Nice to meet you, Mr McCabe, not one of your easiest classes to teach, I understand."

"No sir ... and I'm absolutely sure ... that there has been no injury. I never have accidents in my classes. Robert and Jason ... they can vouch for that." Both men nodded.

"I believe you. I'll catch the students when they come out of their changing room. By the way, were you asked to attend to some sort of injury before ... in their changing room?"

"Yes sir, but there was nothing wrong with any of them. I think they were playing games with me. I don't understand ..."

Mario rolled his eyes, Robert and Jason shook their heads. Mr Grey looked at David and said, "I'll sort it, Mr McCabe. I know you are a top instructor, so don't worry about anything."

David went to have his shower. As far as he was concerned, Mr Grey was in charge and the problem class was taken care of. Not long after that day David was informed that the university instructor had returned unexpectedly early and would take the class again. David was nevertheless paid for the full month he had signed up for and was thanked for helping out.

One day shortly after the termination of David's ill-fated karate course at the university, Phillip decided to go and see his brother at his home. He had several reasons for his visit. One, he wanted to confirm that his hunch concerning women had been correct; two, he wanted to hear it directly from his brother and three, he wanted to see David's property. Phillip hadn't visited his brother in his new surroundings for some time, he had either been too busy at work or else had spent time in his music studio with his friends practicing and rehearsing. Weekends he loved to spend with Kid going for a drive, a picnic or simply staying home enjoying her company.

Kid had kept him informed on David's work and on his business progress. She knew every last detail since she worked with David in his garden on a regular basis and she called him a slave-driver. Phillip understood the joke behind this, it made him smile.

On this particular night Kid was working a late shift at Alfredo's and Mario was studying with some friends and Phillip didn't feel like spending the entire evening on his own so he decided to go and see his brother.

David was coming up from the bottom of the garden pushing a wheelbarrow full of compost. He beamed when he saw his brother walk leisurely across the lawn towards him. "I'm taking this soil to the back of the dojo ... want to plant some shrubs and flower bulbs ... make it look real pretty next year. Have you been inside my dojo at all?" He asked, then gently slid the door back to reveal the small entrance and behind it the area of the tatami mats. David kept his dojo spotless, he made sure that there was always a vase with fresh flowers on the small bamboo table by the entrance - the only piece of furniture as dictated by Japanese tradition. David loved his dojo - his inner sanctum - as Phillip thought of it.

David's dream property had by now turned into a beautifully landscaped area. The lawn adjoining the road with the two large shady oak trees and now a variety of flowering shrubs gave the impression more of a park than a man-made garden. The small Japanese house that was his dojo, was not immediately visible from the entrance, you had to walk down a winding path to get to it. All vehicles had to stay out front where David had provided some parking spaces. The dojo was surrounded by leafy bushes and now there were the beginnings of a flower garden on the side facing Robert's house. David had removed the fence between his and Robert's property to extend the park-like area right across to Robert's mansion. The vegetable patch and the fruit trees were down at the bottom of the property. Phillip could just see the grape vines and a part of the tool shed.

Phillip sensed an atmosphere of peace and tranquility the moment he stepped onto his brother's property, he found that he relaxed easily and felt at peace with himself. This is like a retreat, where people go to meditate and find their inner peace, he said to himself, I'll make this pilgrimage more often. He was glad that his long-lost brother had finally found a place where he felt happy and where he could spread his talents, both landscaping and karate. The whole atmosphere set Phillip's mind wondering whether there existed in fact some sort of supernatural justice - a justice which now allowed David to enjoy some good times in his life. He had missed out on all of that long enough.

"Have you finished your teaching for today, David?"

"Umm ... no, one more session later ..."

"You know that class you taught at university ..." Phillip said casually.

"Yeah, I know all about that now ... the little devils."

"David, when you said that your whole life got fucked in the war ...did you mean like your ... sex life, too?"

"Yes, the lot. It was difficult ... I got hurt ... and embarrassed, many times ... during my bad times ..."

"It *was* difficult? Is it in the past?"

"Mostly ... yes." David said but continued as if this was just a minor issue, "Come, let's walk down here, I show you the vegetables and the fruit orchard."

They walked side by side in silence for a while then Phillip said without warning, "You know, I often think how easy and carefree my life has been, while you've been made to endure so much hardship. And then you told me that you looked after me when I was little ... and later I kind of dismissed you from my mind - from my life. It makes me feel guilty now."

"No need to get all sentimental about it," David said in a rare attempt at casualness. "I loved you when you were a tiny baby ... and I still do now."

Silence between the brothers for a few steps.

"That nightmare David, do you still have it?"

"Yes, it never goes away. James takes care of things when it happens ... he is wonderful. He is a doctor you know."

Phillip knew full well that James was far from being a doctor, but David did not see it this way. His mind works a

461

bit like Kid's, Phillip reflected with some amusement, she sees Mario as a lawyer just because he is a law student. Aloud he said, "Kid told me about your rock garden, where the herbs are. Did she help you build that?"

"No no, I did that long before I bought this joint. Why do you ask?"

"Umm ... the way she described its construction, I was sure she personally picked up rocks the size of a house and placed them in strategic spots."

David threw his head back and roared with laughter. "No, she didn't, you know I wouldn't let her. She helps me with the vegetables, pulls out weeds and spreads the mulch. She's asked me to help her build a rockery in her - your garden. I like it when she comes and works with me ..." he finished a little dreamily.

"I'm sure she likes it too ... she calls you a slave-driver, though."

"What does that mean?"

"It's an expression referring to the old times of slavery in the south, when white farmers owned black people ... like they owned sheep and cattle. Some white masters overworked their slaves, they drove them too hard." Phillip could sense an uncomfortable tension coming from his brother, so he quickly added, "Kid used the expression jokingly, of course."

But his explanation of Kid's true meaning came too

late. David's mind had already leapt way back to wartime and the jungle. He saw the long column of little brown men in ragged clothes, some without shoes. They walked in single file, carried no weapons, their hands folded and placed on their heads. Behind them were a few equally little men, the same features same color only these men were carrying machine guns and they were shouting and prodding the others roughly with their weapons. David knew that they were all brothers. What were they doing to each other? Why was it that some were armed and powerful and some were victimized and defenseless? Suddenly he felt a hand on his upper arm. He whirled around and shook the hand off. At that moment the poor bedraggled soldiers vanished as quickly and as noiselessly as they had appeared. David felt a stinging pain in his head, he buried his face in his hands for a second then he was back in his garden, only a few steps away from his beloved dojo. He turned to face Phillip, who was leaning against a tree, a pain filled look still on his face.

"What happened?" David asked, "did I hurt you?"

Phillip shook his head. "Probably no more than a bruise." David had delivered a vicious blow to the forearm of his imaginary attacker. "But it's nothing, really," Phillip added. Then why did David now put both arms around his brother, press him against his chest and start sobbing? "I'm OK David, honestly. Try and tell me what happened before it all fades away again, can you?"

"Horrible stuff ... in the war ... prisoners. They were shoved around like cattle ..."

Just these few words sufficed for Phillip to realize with utter horror that his own explanation of the expression 'slave-driver' had triggered David's flashback. It had lasted less than a minute but Phillip knew with terrifying clarity it's potential to do damage. But how was I to know, a voice inside Phillip lamented.

When David had his emotions back under control, the brothers sat down on the grass without saying a word. "Show me your arm."

Phillip rolled back the sleeve of his sweater and bared his right arm. On the underside of his forearm a patch of discoloration had already started to show.

"I'm sorry Phillip. I didn't know what I was doing ... just felt that I had to defend myself. Kid will want to know where this came from. Please tell her that I didn't mean to ... to hurt you."

"Sure, and I'll also tell her not to use that silly word again. Do you experience these ... flashbacks frequently?"

"Used to ... all the time. Got me into trouble when I lashed out at people without knowing it ... did some quite serious damage, too. But since I've been here - I mean since St. Louis - it's been really good ... only very few."

"Maybe because you feel safer now and because you

are more at ease with yourself and with life in general," Phillip ventured, then in a surge of courage, he said, "There is something I meant to ask you a long time ago, may I?" But instead of waiting for David's answer he plunged right in, "Remember when Kid threatened to throw you out of our house? You reacted and sounded as though you were afraid of her ... what went on?"

"I *was* afraid, believe me. If Kid attacked me ... she'd have me flat on my back in seconds. I couldn't defend myself ... couldn't do anything at all. And that night was not the only time she threatened me. I think she knows her threats frighten me ..."

Phillip listened to this absurd but fascinating story in amazement, then he surprised himself by asking, "Is it OK to talk about Thomas?"

David nodded but did not answer.

"You are still friendly with his parents, aren't you? Did they ever talk to you about your past? I mean, did either of them ask you any questions?"

"I have a feeling that they know ..." David said, not answering his brother's question. "Maybe my failings ... my flaws and memory gaps are all too visible, too noticeable, and they give me away before I even know it." There he stopped, as if realizing suddenly that he was still talking to his brother. "Why?"

"I should have told you some time ago, David. I once

465

talked to Mr and Mrs Clark about you, about us being brothers, about our lives. I don't really know how it happened, I
just found them easy to talk to, and I know they have a high
opinion of you ... and they respect you." Now I've started, Phillip thought, I better tell all, then I brace myself for
whatever reaction I'll cop.

"Kid was real angry with me when I told her. She
feels that I went behind your back ... kind of betrayed you.
But that was not my intention, I promise. I just knew that
Thomas' parents wanted to know more about you. I have
seemingly answered their questions before they even asked
them. I promised Kid I would tell you and apologize to
you." At this point he stopped. They were still sitting side
by side under the tree.

David didn't face his brother when he said, "I told
Mr Goldberg too, when I asked him for help ... thought he
needed to know a little about me ... it was a very big gift
after all. Clive and Caroline, Thomas' parents ... I wanted
to tell them that I'd done time and that ... but then suddenly
I had this feeling that it wasn't really necessary. They knew
anyway ... and knowing about my bad times did no harm to
our friendship ..."

That means he is not going to be angry, Phillip thought
with considerable relief. From far away he heard David's
voice, "I just remember something ... Kid told me while we
were working in the garden. She said the Jews believe that

… umm … if you save the life of one Jewish child, you save an entire world. It's in their bible … whatever they call it."

"Interesting," Phillip said. He found he had no trouble following David's mind leaps. "Of course you did just that - I mean, save the life of one Jewish child. I seem to have heard or read that once … somebody prominent said it in connection with what happened to the Jews in World War II, and I think they call their holy book the Torah. What made you think about this right now, Dave?"

"Don't ask … that's just how screwed up my thinking is."

Phillip chuckled. "What time is your class, David?"

"Nine, I think. James will come and get me when it's time."

"Let's make our way back. Do you change at the dojo or at home?"

Before David could answer, they heard the sound of three very short, piercing whistle blows.

"That's James … it's our sign." This was just one more feature of this amazing friendship between David and James.

That evening had one more surprise in store for Phillip. He found out the minute Kid came home. She was no hero at hiding important news.

"It's written all over my face, isn't it darling," she said. "OK, you tell me your evening's adventures first … then

467

me."

Phillip didn't argue. He related faithfully what he and David had discussed leaving nothing unsaid and Kid was mighty proud to hear that her scheme to scare David worked to such perfection. It never occurred to her to inquire into the reasons why.

"Now ... your turn Kid."

"Right. It happened at the end of my shift," Kid started. "I was getting ready to leave when I noticed Giovanna and Mrs Visconti talking kind of agitatedly in the family room. Mario's Mama was very upset, she was in tears ... I saw them. Of course I instantly guessed the reason for her anxiety: It had to be Mario. Giovanna asked if I had time for a cup of coffee. So I sat down at their table. I was a bit nervous - understandably so, I suppose. I needed to make sure not to blurt out stuff ... as I usually do in a tricky situation."

Phillip was still fashioning his sandwich but listened carefully to Kid's story and kept a very straight face.

"When I saw how distraught Mario's Mama was I decided to come straight to the point. 'Mrs Visconti' I said - and of course all of it was done in Italian - 'I know why you are upset. It's because of Mario. You are terribly worried about him now that you and your husband have kicked him out of your house ' She looked at me then, sort of puzzled and very sad - very sad indeed - so I felt I had to set her mind at ease. 'Don't worry now' I said in a very gentle tone of voice, 'Mario is in good hands. He is living in our house, in the spare room, and Phillip and I are looking after him.' Nothing wrong with that, is there?"

"No, nothing at all," Phillip said and encouraged her to go on. There wasn't anything really wrong with what Kid said, it was her way of relating it that was perhaps a little unorthodox.

"Mama Visconti then spoke for the first time. You know, Phillip, *she* never meant to throw her son out ... she just wasn't able to reason with her husband. Why, I wonder, can't men be wise and understanding like we women can ... a shame really."

Phillip looked up from his sandwich raising an eyebrow in the process, but Kid was completely oblivious of his reaction.

"You see Phillip, I had spoken with Father about this issue so I had all of Papa Visconti's arguments at my fingertips. 'Its because of Mario's sexual orientation ... it's seen as a sin, isn't it?' I said, 'that's why your husband is so angry with Mario. But you know ma'am, what I don't understand is, Father tells me that God made all the people and that he loves us all. So that includes Mario and men like him. Maybe God should have thought more carefully before making gay men and then call them sinners. Mario is a decent and kind person and a very good friend to me and my husband', and I added truthfully, 'he loves you and his Papa. He told us'."

"You said that to Mrs Visconti, a believing and practicing Catholic? That God should have done some thinking?"

"Shouldn't I have? It's true though, isn't it?"

"Yes Kid, it's true enough - maybe a little lack of subtlety, that's all."

"Hmm. Mama and Giovanna both looked at me but said nothing. I took it that they meant for me to continue. 'Please ma'am', I said, 'will you open your heart to your son and love him again, and please ask your husband to do the same? Father told me that forgiving is real big in the Catholic faith'. That was alright to say, wasn't it Phillip?"

Phillip took a deep breath before he answered. He couldn't really fault Kid's good intentions or her dogmatism.

"Diplomacy is a fickle thing, isn't it Kid? Not everybody's cup of tea," was the best he could do. "Now you are facing the task of telling Mario."

"No, you tell Mario."

"No way, you questioned the wisdom of his God ... you tell him." Phillip was adamant, but when he saw the despair in Kid's face he got up from his bar stool and put his arms around her. "If you need my help, I'll be there for you darling."

XXXI

David received a phone call late on Saturday night. It was a long distance call, his first one ever. Robert answered and heard a smooth man's voice, it sounded educated, even sophisticated.

"My name is Chuck Talbot. I would like to speak to David McCabe. I hope I have the right number."

"You have. I get him, just a minute."

"David, it's for you," Robert said as he re-entered the lounge room. "A man called Chuck Talbot ... mean anything to you?"

"Yes, thanks." Came an unusually flat reply from David.

"Hi Chuck, this is David speaking."

"Glad I got you ... had a hell of a difficult time to locate you. How are you doing David?"

"Fine. Where are you calling from?"

"I'm in Chicago, my home town if you remember. It's about Tony."

"What's about Tony?"

"OK. He and I got out about the same time ... we stayed in touch. His family is in Chicago too. Dave, Tony is very sick ... it doesn't look like he is going to make it. He is now at his parents' home, he's been asking for you. He needs to see you ... before he goes."

Silence.

"Are you there David?"

"Yeah, I'm listening."

"Look, can you get here ... I mean as soon as possible? You have to fly ... do you have the money?"

"Yes I do."

"Good. Book the next possible flight then let me know the flight number and the exact arrival time. I'll meet you at the airport. Here is my number, write it down." He stopped and chuckled, "how are your figures, Dave?"

"Cut it out mate," David said in as benign a voice as he could muster then he called over his shoulder, "James!" Just that. Into the mouth piece of the phone he said, "What's the number then?" David now carefully repeated the number he was given, one digit after another, and James wrote them down on the pad provided for just such emergencies.

"David, Tony's parents and all the family would really

472

appreciate it if you could get here. I can't talk too long right now ... be good to see you and hear what you've been up to. You haven't been back in, have you?"

"No mate ... never again. You?"

"Nope. I'm good and straight now. See you soon."

"Sure, take care."

James was puzzled by the staccato conversation of which he had just heard one side. David put the receiver down and kept his hand on it as if he were waiting for the answers to all the questions he had not asked. He seemed not to notice James who stood beside him, silently like the devoted personal secretary awaiting further instructions. When David came out of his reverie he gently put his hand on James' shoulder. "I'll make us all a hot drink," he said.

"David where is this number I wrote down? And who is Chuck? You've never mentioned him to any of us. Sounded like something urgent, was there?"

David shook his head and smiled in a resigned sort of way. "Chicago. I need to get there as fast as possible," he said trying to answer some of James' questions. "A mate of mine is very sick ... apparently wants to see me before ..."

"What's wrong with your friend," asked James the doctor, this time.

"Chuck didn't say ... just that Tony was very sick. Can you help me with flight arrangements and that, James?"

"Sure. We have to call the airport at this time of night

473

... see what we can get. Leave it with me." And with these words of reassurance James picked up the directory and got down to work..

"Who is your educated friend Chuck?" Robert asked a little later when David entered the lounge room carrying a tray with three mugs of hot chocolate.

"He's an old mate of mine ... haven't heard from him in a very long time."

"Good friend?"

"Yes, we were close then ... always looked out for each other. Chuck and I shared a cell in prison for ... don't know how long. He is a clever guy ... read every book in the prison library."

"Why was he in jail?"

These were the first words James heard as he came into the room with the results of his inquiry. He stopped abruptly in his tracks and listened to the conversation which was in progress.

"He was a businessman ... made a heap of money, but ... he told me he started to make money illegally somehow ... umm ..."

"Embezzlement, maybe fraud of some kind, I suppose. How long did he get?"

"Don't know exactly ... much less than I got. Tony, the guy who is sick ... he was with us in jail ... a Vietnam vet. He is Italian ... we were good friends the three of us. Tony should never have gone to jail, he couldn't handle it. He was kind of soft and gentle, a very little guy ... I rescued him a number of times ... fighting gangs always target the weakest ones."

Chuck's call for help had seemingly triggered something inside David – something that made for one of the rare occasions when David reminisced. Robert and James knew better than to interrupt.

"Tony wanted to be an engineer, build bridges and that ... but the war fucked up his life ... like most of us. He lost all his hope ... never found the energy again to go to university ... got into drugs and dealing ..." Suddenly David remembered where he was, "Sorry, got carried away for a bit there," he said rather pointlessly.

James had managed to book a seat on a flight leaving the following morning; it would get to Chicago by lunch time. David informed Chuck as promised then started to pack. He was going to purchase his ticket at the airport before his departure; he now had a checkbook and a sound bank balance, he started to feel like the 'regular guy' he always wanted to be. During his absence, the business part of his life would be taken care of by Robert and James: Robert in the karate department and James in the fruit and vegetables.

"I need to tell Kid and Phillip. Too late to call now?"

"You might get them out of bed but I don't think it will matter greatly," Robert said casually.

Kid answered the phone. "No, I was not in bed ... still watching television. Phillip is away on a reporting thing ... back tomorrow night."

"Kid, I'm off to Chicago tomorrow ... don't know for how long. I'm going to see a mate of mine."

"You're going by plane?" That's what interested Kid first and foremost. "Will you keep the airline menu card for me?"

"Yes Kid."

"Oh and they'll give you a small, packed-up, moist and perfumed towel. Keep that for me too, please."

"Yes Kid."

"Will you tell me all about your trip when you get back? I've never been to Chicago."

"Yes Kid."

By that time, both Robert and James were in stitches and wondering what Kid could possibly be saying to have provoked three consecutive 'yes Kids' from David.

True to his word, Chuck stood waiting in the arrival hall at O'Hare airport in Chicago. He smiled as he approached David, "Can't miss you in any crowd, you will always stick out a head above everyone else. Your hair looks good shoulder length like that."

"Thanks, you look good too. Back in business?"

'No mate, I've changed. I'm done with the sales business. I'm studying now, art and literature. Remember our classes back then?"

"Yeah ... improved my reading since. I got a job as a karate instructor straight away after my release. I learned how to be a chef, too ... now I'm growing fruit and vegetables ... making money so I can teach my students for free ... was real lucky with money ..."

He still talks in his characteristically disjointed way, Chuck thought. Kind of suits him though, adds a gentle and lovable tinge to this giant. "I'd like you to tell me more about your new life ... later."

It was during the long drive to the suburb where Tony's family lived that Chuck started to air his personal feelings concerning their mutual friend. "Tony was in hospital for a while," he started matter-of-factly, "but they let him go home ... not because his health is improving ... in fact I suspect the opposite."

"How long has he been sick? Do you know anything?"

"Not much. Cancer I'm told ... to do with coming into contact with some horrible weapons during the war, I believe." He took a deep breath then said tentatively, "Try not to show shock on your face in front of the family when you see Tony. You are tough Dave ... I know you can do it."

David was deeply disturbed. He didn't quite know how to take Chuck's advice since he didn't know what to expect, so he just nodded.

Chuck stopped the car a block away from Tony's house and turned the engine off. "OK David, listen. Ever since Tony got real sick, he has been asking for you ... sometimes he is only half conscious. He's been painting a picture of you as his hero - his savior - he never explained why. Do you know?"

"Yes."

"And that's all you're prepared to tell me?" One look at David told him that his guess had been correct and that it was useless to push for more detail. "OK, when you enter that house over there, you will be surrounded by a big family. They are Italian and emotional as hell. They will all be in tears most of the time ... can you handle it?"

"I'll try."

"Trying is not good enough, David. You have to do this right. They all count on you to put their son's soul at peace ... or whatever Catholics do. These guys are waiting for you to perform some sort of a miracle. Are you up to this?"

"Yes."

"Good. Let's go in and face the music."

David and Chuck entered the house by the front door and found a crowd of people waiting for them. It's like some weird reception committee, it struck David. They all had to look up at him, their faces showed a mixture of anxiety and expectancy, Mama, Papa, grandmothers, sisters, brothers, aunts, uncles and cousins. David felt like a giant amongst a family of dwarfs, no one was taller than about five foot three. He greeted them with a collective 'hi' then introduced himself.

"I got here as fast as I could after receiving Chuck's call," he said slowly in his deep baritone. Some of the people around him were openly weeping, others showed traces of tears which had been shed before his arrival and were now being bravely suppressed. A lady David assumed to be Tony's Mama led him along a corridor and into Tony's room.

Tony was not in bed as David had expected, he was dressed and on a sofa with a blanket thrown casually over him; he sat facing a television set and had a couple of newspapers and a book on a small table within his reach. But Tony was neither reading nor watching television. His head lay on a cushion, his eyes were closed, he did not immediately react to David's arrival. Mama ushered him in, then retreated noiselessly back into the hallway.

"Hi Tony," David said gently and as he saw a fluttering of Tony's eyelids he prompted with more cheerfulness than he felt, "Come on mate, open your eyes, it's me, David."

David remembered Tony as being a small guy but now he saw a very tiny person lying on the couch. His friend looked grey and gaunt, there was almost nothing left of him. David felt that he might not have recognized him had the circumstances been different. That's what Chuck's warning was about, he realized with a jolt. But Tony is still the same guy... inside ... in his heart ... it's only his material body that's undergone a change, David assured himself. He crouched down beside the sofa so his and Tony's faces were more or less level. "Talk to me, Tony," he said.

Tony spoke with difficulty. "David ... I want to thank you ... for ... all you did for me ... and for saving my life ... in jail ... that day in the shower block." He halted to take a couple of breaths. "I had some good times ... since I came out ... spent most of it with my family. Thanks ... thanks again David." He stopped and closed his eyes for a second and as David looked down on his friend he could feel Tony's pain as if it was his own. Then Tony made an effort to continue. He seemed to be determined to say all the things that needed to be said ... and he needed to say them now, while there was still time. David took Tony's hand in his and waited in silence until Tony was ready to continue.

"David ... tell my parents ... tell them later ... as much as you can remember ... of that time. Will you do that?"

"Yes. Will it help them... do they want to know?"

"Yes. Now tell me about your life ... since you got out ... I just want to listen to you ... talking is too much of an effort ..."

Without further ado, David started to recount the main events that had taken place in his life as a free citizen. He spoke slowly, carefully, but no matter how hard he tried to remain coherent, he could not stop his thoughts and memories from jumping back and forth in time and place. He told about his piece of land, his dojo, his gardening business, then he mixed in sentimental thoughts of his loving friendship with his brother and sister-in-law. He mentioned Robert and the house he had renovated, his special friendship with James, his endeavors to become a chef, the little girl he had rescued from the river and how her father had become his benefactor. At that point, David was sure he saw a weak little smile appear on Tony's face. He waited.

"I'm happy for you ... you're doing great." Tony said then he seemed to fall into an instant sleep. David gave his hand a squeeze and to his surprise felt a very small squeeze back from Tony's fingers. David got to his feet, touched Tony's head very gently then walked out of the room. "Ma'am," he said to Tony's mother, "please, would you go and sit with your son now."

Chuck took David to stay at his apartment that night and promised Tony's family that they would return the next day. He had a keen sense of how David was feeling after speaking to Tony and he was sure that David needed some time and distance to get things straight in his mind. Also Chuck wanted to give David some information on what was really going on. "You do realize, David," he told him on the way home, "that Tony did not just fall asleep as you told his parents. He is in a coma ... it's a little like a sleep, only people often don't wake up again."

David sat very still and listened attentively to Chuck's words.

"I spoke to the medic ... he is, I believe, a cousin of Tony's. He told me about the coma. He also said that Tony had suffered a lot over the last few months and that it had been almost unbearable for the family to stand by helplessly and watch as he deteriorated. He just kind of faded away. The medic said it was one of the worst ways to go - for the patient as well as for family and friends."

"How long does a coma last?"

"I don't think anybody knows but when the body is weak and when there is no more resistance ..." he let his unfinished sentence trail off.

David and Chuck spent an evening together, neither was in the mood for a night on the town, so David cooked dinner for both of them. "I told you that I am teaching myself to be a chef," he said with a little chuckle.

"So you are a chef, a karate master, a fruit and vegetable growing expert and a house renovator ... anything else I need to know?"

The two friends spent a pleasant evening talking and reminiscing. David learned that Chuck and Tony had been released almost at the same time, only a couple of months after he had left. Since then the two friends had stayed in loose contact.

"Tony was in rehab for a while and he also went to counseling," Chuck said. "I'm sure it helped him. He did well for himself ... went back to school, so to speak. He was again serious about wanting to be an engineer." Chuck had lots of worthwhile information to impart and he was an excellent talker.

"Tony asked me to tell his parents about ... about what happened while we were mates ... in jail," David said uncertainly. "I know I'm not a good talker ... I'm afraid I might make a mess of this ..."

Chuck had to laugh at David's misgivings. "You sure are the worst talker David, but Tony's family won't even notice that. They want to know just why Tony had been asking for you and they might well feel that it is thanks to whatever had been said between the two of you, that Tony found some sort of peace. Aren't you going to tell me?"

David breathed in deeply then let the air out of his lungs very slowly. "Not now ... I don't feel I can tell it twice."

David was sitting in the large dining room in Tony's house and was once again surrounded by many tearful members of the family. An atmosphere of sadness and pain seemed to engulf the whole house. It was the day following his arrival and he had not spoken to Tony again.

A little later David was shown to Tony's room. Tony was now lying in bed, he was still in a coma. David looked down at his friend for a long time, he didn't understand the meaning of 'coma', so he decided that Tony was asleep and that he was at peace now.

When David came back into to living room he was offered food and drink as was the custom in an Italian family. It was lucky that Chuck knew about that; he had advised David not to eat anything at all before their arrival so that he would be able to eat with a healthy appetite. "Refusing their hospitality would be a great insult," Chuck, in his wisdom, had told him.

The crucial question came from Tony's Mama as David had expected. "Please, David what was it that Tony needed to say to you? He has been asking for you repeatedly, so ..."

David gathered his thoughts before he started. "It happened while Tony and I were mates ... in jail." No immediate shock registered on the faces of the family members at the word 'jail', so David thought it was safe to continue. He pushed his chair back from the table and crossed his legs. He would have preferred to stand but he had learned some time ago that his size intimidated the people around him.

"I'm a Vietnam veteran too ... and it was always my job to look after the other vets ... when times got rough. Umm ... there is a lot of fighting in prison ... and fighting is the only thing I can do."

"And you should see this guy fight ..." Chuck addressed the room at large in an attempt to brighten up the atmosphere some. He didn't need to finish his sentence as his meaning seemed to be quite clear to everyone present.

David took no notice of Chuck's words. "I'm not clever like Tony ... or like Chuck ... but we helped each other in any way we could. There was one day ..." here David turned to look at Chuck, "...and this was some time before you were there, Chuck. Inmates often attack in gangs ... they went for Tony in ... sorry ma'am, it was real bad ... I'm not sure I should tell right here."

"Please, continue ... you don't need to spare us."

David nodded and took a deep breath. "Those guys would find the time and place where one is most vulnerable ... so they chose the shower room. Somebody had smashed the light and was about to use a piece of broken glass ... as a weapon. I wasn't in the shower when it started ... you see, nobody would start a fight when ... when I was around ... I kind of terrorized the whole place at that time. But the guys didn't know that I was on my way to the shower right then. There were three of them and they ... they would have killed Tony ... I know they would ... big, square guys ... all of them bigger than Tony. It was a horrible fight ... turned into a proper blood bath ... and all of us wearing no clothes, of course. Tony's arm got cut but not very deep ... left a scar though." David saw Tony's parents nod. So they've seen that scar. "Yesterday Tony thanked me for saving his life that day ... that's what he said."

Chuck had a distinct feeling that this story was going to be greeted with more tears, so he quickly put in, "How did it end?"

"Umm ... the three guys were taken to hospital, I remember that. I took the broken glass from them and threw it away. Then I ... just knocked them out." And turning towards the family he explained, "When I get into a fight ... it's like I'm back in the war ... I act without thinking ... kind of automatic ... don't often know exactly what I'm doing. That's what got me into jail in the first place."

After these words from David, there was complete silence in the room. Chuck was sure everybody felt that an injustice had been done to David, but no one knew how to put thoughts into words.

"What happened to *you* after that battle, David?"

"Solitary confinement ... can't remember how long though."

A young boy, about ten years of age, now walked up to David. He looked down at his feet and seemed to be concentrating before he said, "Uncle Tony says you were a karate fighter."

"I'm still a karate fighter now," David said, "but I only fight on the dojo mats. I have a school ... lots of students ... but no more street fights."

"I want to learn karate but my mom says it's too violent, too dangerous. Is that true?"

486

"No, it's not dangerous and it's not violent ... it's an art ... it's beautiful. Maybe I could talk to your mom ... explain about martial arts."

"Yes please sir."

"I'm not sir, I'm David." This quick reply put fleeting smiles on a few faces.

All during this talk, David noticed people quietly moving back and forth along the hallway between the dining room and Tony's room. David, thanks to his extraordinary field of vision, saw the expressions of pain and sorrow on their faces without having to turn his head and look directly at anybody. Then he saw a woman who he took to be Tony's grandmother or great-grandmother; she looked older than anybody David had ever seen. She was very small and spoke Italian only. She came out of Tony's room and walked along the hallway slowly and a little unsteadily then suddenly she started to falter. David was on his feet in a flash and caught her in his arms just seconds before she collapsed on the floor. He lay the tiny lady on the couch and everyone gathered around them. The medic was now in charge and David received many hugs and thanks. It was at times like these that David wished with all his heart that he was more like the same size as everybody around him. It would have made receiving all these heart-felt hugs so much easier.

David and Chuck left Tony and his family late that afternoon. David had been with Tony one more time and on that last occasion he had firmly decided that his friend had found his ultimate peace and that he would not wake up again to more pain and agony. It's best like this, he convinced himself, his soul is at rest now and in a safe place.

During their drive to the airport David and Chuck spoke little. It was only while standing in line at the airline counter that Chuck said almost to himself, "Surprising that your horrible story didn't shock people more than it did. They really needed to know the connection between you and Tony, I guess." And when David did not reply, he continued in a different vein. "So you're going back to a good life now, eh? Have you ever thought about getting married?"

"No." David's answer came quicker than any Chuck had heard so far. The two men looked at each other for a minute, Chuck with incomprehension, David trying to formulate an explanation of his hasty monosyllabic answer. "No one wants me for a husband ... and I wouldn't make a good one, either. I'm happy the way I am ... I like my life as it is ... I have friends and I love Kid, my sister-in-law, and my little brother."

Chuck thought it wise not to dwell on the subject of David's love for his sister-in-law, so he just pretended that he understood the circumstances.

"What about you, Chuck?"

"I'm thinking about it all the time ... haven't found

the right lady yet, but ... who knows. Anyway, let's keep in touch, OK?"

The two men gave each other an approximation of a hug then David boarded the plane.

While sitting comfortably in his window seat, an orange juice on the small foldable table in front of him, David's mind replayed all the sounds and images of the past two days. He felt the hugs and the kisses on his cheek, he saw the sad and tear-streaked faces and the collapsed great-grandmother. But again and again, his thoughts would circle back to Tony - Tony who had been no more than a very small, grey and shrunken body, eaten up from the inside by the deadly disease.

David knew now that he was going to be next in line. He had been exposed to the same devilish weapons ... it was going to get him just as it did Tony. But I'm not going to put my family and friends through the agonizing process of seeing my body decay, he promised himself right there on the plane which took him back to his dojo, his home and his small family. He promised himself that he would not end up in a hospital bed surrounded by sad and mournful faces - by people trying to hide the shock and disgust at watching him shrivel up and die.

David was not afraid of dying.

He had witnessed death many times before - the death of friends and mates, of enemy soldiers, women and children. He had been there when all movements came to a stop, he had seen breathing cease, eyes loose their shine, souls leave their bodies, pain and suffering and torment finally end. In those moments he used to convince himself that the soul would go to a place where there was peace, harmony and light, and since he now expected to die any day – any time - this self-created certainty helped dispel the fear of his own death.

But right now he was a member of a community, he had family and friends, people he loved and respected, and the last thing he would do in this life would be to make sure that they all remembered him as the guy who was their friend, their brother, the chef, the gardener and vegetable grower, the house builder and the karate master The last image I want them all to keep of me should be of the fit and healthy six foot five guy I am now. David made this pledge to himself on the plane back from Chicago. It sat deep inside his heart; it was the most important promise he had ever made. He would not tell anybody about his intentions, it was to remain his secret, and at the right time he would know exactly what to do.

It was past two in the morning when his plane landed in Nashville. He had to take another plane from there to Knoxville and it would almost be morning by the time he reached home. That suits me, he thought contentedly, I'll go to my dojo until the sun rises as I always do. The atmosphere of peace and quiet inside his sacred place would help him find the perfect balance of body and mind. He could then reach that state of weightlessness in which he would empty his mind and be free. In his heart, David once again thanked his Sensei in Okinawa, who so many years ago had introduced him to the secrets and miracles of meditation.

XXXII

It was Phillip's idea to celebrate David's birthday that year.

"Great," Kid exclaimed spontaneously, "only problem is, David does not have a birthday. I've buttonholed him more than once on this."

"You might well have, darling, but the answer to David's day of birth lies exclusively with me - his very own brother."

"... and my status of sister counts for nothing at all, right? So when is it then?"

"My big brother was born on August eight, that's in a couple of weeks' time, and being his sister does count, Kid. Don't look so disappointed, you know my brother loves you." Phillip said it lovingly and without sarcasm.

David's birthday celebration consisted of a special dinner at his brother's house. Kid and Phillip combined forces to prepare a lavish three-course meal, complete with entrée and dessert. They invited friends: Mario, Robert, James, Jason, David's other assistant, Bob and Anita and their son Michael. All the guests were gathered and sipping on a pre-dinner drink - all except the birthday boy himself. He had called earlier and apologized in advance for an inevitable delay due to an extra class he had promised to teach.

"You do know David," Kid had said on the phone, "that it's *your* birthday we are celebrating ... yes of course ... what's that? ... Shut up ... we'll all be waiting for you."

"What was the 'shut up' for Kid?" Phillip inquired with a cheeky smile on his face. "He wouldn't be making advances, would he just?"

"He did ... in his very own clumsy way. But I'm not telling."

So, the party proceeded with a few more pre-dinner drinks. It didn't matter that David was absent; this was something David would not have participated in anyway.

An odd conversation took place however, in Phillips lounge room while everyone was waiting for David.

Robert and Jason had inadvertently gotten into a discussion on technicalities of karate and Kid noticed it when she handed a platter with little goodies around. "You are talking shop here ... stuff that no one but you two can understand," she reminded them.

493

"Sorry Kid ... sorry everybody ... not very polite," Jason apologized, then addressed the room at large, "we were talking about David's meditative powers just then," and looking at Phillip, he said, "David is quite incredible, you know. He is capable of relaxing every muscle in his body at will, I believe, and he can go real deep in meditation. He knows how to empty his mind - somehow - of all thoughts and images and of everything that happens around him. I always think that he goes someplace where he is totally on his own. Maybe not for long stretches at the time, but I'm sure he does get to the point where he reaches some sort of otherworldliness ... for lack of a better word. He knows how to get rid of all the monkey business that goes on in our brains."

"But he is like that right through his training, isn't he? Sort of makes him untouchable and invulnerable. How did he learn that, I wonder." Robert said. It was a statement not a question.

"Monkey skills." Kid volunteered competently.

"How do you know about those, Kid?" Jason asked in astonishment. "We sometimes used that expression in the Air Force, among flyers."

"I know because I've just recently read about this phenomenon. It was described as ... umm ... 'unteachable and esoteric skills'. Is that what your Air Force jargon means?"

"Pretty accurate definition ... yes." Jason said displaying a smile. "I never thought of using the expression in any field other than in flying, but it's spot on in this context. David does seem to be guided by some forces that none of us can access."

"Are you still a flyer, Jason?"

"Yes, I'm a pilot. I fly commercial aircraft now, sometimes private Lear Jets, when I get lucky."

James had been listening attentively. Meditation was not a field he was well versed in - not yet – but since it was an aspect of the human brain - or the mind - he instantly took a great interest in this topic. One thing however, he did know and this was the moment to say it.

"David also has a very high threshold when it comes to the perception of pain. I'm thinking of the night when he came out of the burning building. He insisted on walking to the ambulance even though he was practically unable to breathe. Would this be in any way connected with what you have just told us?" He addressed his question to Jason.

"Difficult to say, but ... yes, I think there could be a connection. He might get to a point beyond registering physical pain. I had never really thought of it this way."

"Does that mean he does not *feel* pain?" Kid inquired. "Or does he conquer it somehow? I mean, does he have the power to kind of overcome or channel pain?"

"I believe it's a combination of all that," James said. "I'm not sure if one has to be born with this type of resilience, or if one can acquire it. To tell you the truth, I have no idea of what a human being can and does acquire when exposed to the atrocities David was exposed to during his time in Vietnam. One thing however, I have a distinct feeling that he would never choose to undergo medical treatment if he should get ... sick, you know what I mean."

"You might well be right there, James," Phillip said pensively, recalling David's escape from the clinic directly after his return from Vietnam, where he had apparently been 'filled with drugs'.

Kid's turn for one of her mind leaps. "Do you know," she said out of the blue, "about those tribes in far off Pacific Islands, where some people meditate their whole metabolism down to an almost standstill? You see, they know when they are approaching the end of their lives. Then they climb up the mountains into a cave and sit in meditation and kind of ... die themselves. Do you think that's true?"

Everybody appeared to be inward looking for a while, then Phillip said, "I believe it's true, I have read about this, too. It's awesome though, to think that ..." he left his unfinished thought hanging in the air.

"And do you think that David ... could he, maybe ...?" Kid asked tentatively.

Jason answered almost immediately, "I'm tempted to believe that, yes. Rather a morbid subject for us to discuss tonight, though?"

"No, not at all," Kid's reply was instant, "I mean, nobody expects to live forever. When our time is up, well … It's just that we ordinary guys don't have that inbuilt sense of the time of our … what … demise, right?" Kid of course, had no inkling that night as to the amount of truth that lay hidden in her statement, and neither did anyone else, which was why no one thought her story worth remembering when David arrived a few minutes later. But James made a mental note to do some research on this phenomenon. This was a line of thought his doctor's mind had so far not pursued in any detail, but since it concerned his very special friend David, he now put it on the top of his list of further studies.

Kid greeted David with a big hug, one of those where she jumped high enough to be able to put her arms around his neck rather than only around his waist. It was important that David was the central figure that evening. "Happy birthday darling brother," she breathed into his ear, then in her normal voice, "When did you last have a party for your birthday, David?"

"I never had one."

"Not so brother," Phillip said, putting on a mock air of wisdom. "I personally remember your birthday party just before or after you got your Black Belt." And then an afterthought, "I was about eight years old at the time … but I do remember that one. Mom and Poppa were real proud of you."

David listened and shook his head in amazement. He knew a whole lot about that time in his life but all of it was to do with his little brother ... none of it with himself. Now he heard a voice from afar.

"How big an age gap is there between you two?" Jason asked.

"Ten and a half years," Phillip supplied, thankfully before David had a chance to admit that he was not sure.

It was as though in a dream that David now said, "We always had a party for *your* birthday ... a cake with candles ... toys, balloons, paper hats ...lots of children, aunts, uncles, cousins the lot. I don't know why I can remember some things and not others." David did not notice the smiles on everybody's faces.

And he did not see the tears welling up in Phillip's eyes, either. Is it David's innocence, Phillip asked himself helplessly, his undisguised love for his baby brother that stirs my emotions like this? In an effort to hide his near loss of control, he turned to the kitchen and called over his shoulder as casually as he knew how, "Anyone for a refill before we start dinner?"

As far as David was concerned, this was his first birthday dinner in his life and he enjoyed it thoroughly. He felt happy and safe in the company of his friends and family and he savored the warmth that pervaded the whole house.

It was a wonderfully happy evening for all of them, and the thought forming in David's mind, that it would also be his last birthday ever to be celebrated, was no more than speculation created in his subconscious.

XXXIII

During the weeks following his birthday - which as David now knew, was in the middle of summer - he dedicated a lot of time to his trees and his vegetables. He checked his plants carefully for possible diseases, for caterpillars, grasshoppers or aphids. David felt closely connected with all the plants in his garden, he respected them, spoke to them encouragingly and was happy when he was able to harvest cabbages, cauliflowers, lettuces and tomatoes. But David never took nature for granted. He and Kid had often marveled at the miracle of plants and their growth.

"Just think," Kid had said only recently, "how does that small seed you put in the ground suddenly know how to make two little leaves, then a stem, more leaves, a flower and ... pronto, a cucumber."

David knew it was his job to provide the best conditions for his plants and love them all through their growing cycle, but he was also aware that there was a higher Authority out there - and a real powerful one at that - that was ultimately responsible for the growth and the health of every plant in his garden.

Then quite suddenly, intuitively ... David knew. He caught the first signals effortlessly and calmly. 'Watch' he heard an inner voice, 'but don't worry ... not yet ... you still have some way to go'.

It was a day in late October, there were still some vegetables in the garden, the trees were giving a last show of color and beauty before shedding their leaves in preparation for winter. David was not scared even though he knew what was coming his way. He looked at his trees and shrubs and they seemed to say 'we will soon go to sleep for a few months, and then we'll wake up again. You might not see us dressed in our new leaves next spring but we will remember the loving care you gave us during these last years'. This thought made David smile. If that's how they feel about me, he mused, then my friends will surely feel the same way. And with this reassuring thought, David approached the last phase of his life.

His first decision was to make quite sure that he left his gardens, the orchard and his dojo in top shape. He continued to deliver his vegetables to Alfredo's restaurant and to the two shops that had bought his garden produce from him ever since he started his business. He also took a box of fruit and vegetables regularly to Mr Goldberg's residence and one to Clive and Caroline Clark. David saw no need to say any special good-byes, he did not want to alarm his friends unnecessarily. Nobody needed to know or even suspect that anything was going to change ... in the near future.

There was one thing however, that was close to his heart: he wanted to make love to Kid, just once, before he died. It was crucial to David to show Kid his gratitude for her help and assistance, for her kindness and her un-wavering friendship. He had loved Kid for a long time; he loved her as a sister and she had reciprocated his love in her own sisterly way, David was sure of it. Making love to her would not be an act of deceit, he reasoned with himself, it would not be seducing her and trying to take her away from her husband. Kid and Phillip are such a loving couple, he thought, nothing could destroy the bond which ties them so tightly together. Kid would understand, she would feel the same way as he did about making love. Kid's earlier repri-mand that kisses and intimacies were strictly for husbands and wives were not the sort of words David remembered at this point in his life. He was convinced that loving Kid was not a sin but an act of thankfulness and respect. He just knew that Phillip would see it like that too.

David made no concrete plans for the execution of this last wish, he simply relied on god-send, providence, force majeure and other expedients to be there for him at the right time and in the right place. In the meantime he led a busy life.

Some time ago he had also undertaken the task of landscaping Robert's garden. His idea was to join the two properties to form one big park-like area. He dug flowerbeds along the front of Robert's house, he had already built a brick barbeque at the back between his dojo and Robert's back entrance and was now adding a pergola to the side of the dojo to allow the creeper he had planted there in spring to climb and eventually cover the whole area, thus creating a leafy roof to sit and relax under.

"I won't be around to see it," he told the plant while he was working right next to it, "but I know you will do a wonderful job and it will look beautiful."

Once a week, David had dinner with his brother and sister-in-law, sometimes at their house, other times at his. These evenings remained highlights in his life. Having found his beloved brother again after all the bad years and having finally made friends with him was a dream come true. All through his bad times - times he spent roaming the country and times he spent in jail - he had never forgotten the good times of his early life with his baby brother. During the course of these last magic years since his release he had told Phillip repeatedly, in his awkward disjointed way, how important their friendship was to him and how much he appreciated it and how thankful he was.

Sometimes when Phillip felt that David was too sentimental he would simply shrug at his brother's assertions of love and affection but deep inside his heart, Phillip cherished his love for his big brother more than he liked to admit.

As winter slowly set in, David started to experience the occasional bout of pain. He felt stings inside his chest which he took to be reminders of what he was facing. But he had long ago learned to ignore pain and to channel his strength where he needed it most. He knew how to control his breathing and how to concentrate his whole being into his center. That's what he did during the long hours he spent alone in his dojo.

David had revealed nothing of his decision to anyone. However, on two separate occasions he had inadvertently given a little of his secret away. One such occasion was when Chuck called a few days after David's return to say that Tony had 'died in his sleep'. That's how Chuck put it, knowing that these would be the words David could understand.

James had stood next to the phone when David received the sad news and as his doctor's curiosity got the better of him, he blurted almost before he knew it, "Tell me about your friend David, the one you went to see in Chicago, please."

"He got sick after stuff happened to him in Vietnam,"

David said truthfully. "When I saw him, he was almost dead ... the disease was destroying him ... reducing him to nothing ... I hardly recognized him then. Tony fell into a deep sleep and ... never woke up again."

"Probably in a coma ..." James ventured.

"That's the word they used ... but it looked like a peaceful sleep to me. It was real hard for his family to have to watch ... they suffered maybe more than Tony himself did."

That had been the extent of their conversation that night. David could not have known that James read more into the few incoherent sentences than the words suggested.

The other time when David said more than he knew he was saying, was the day when he helped Father fix the roof of one of the shelters. A storm had brought down a tree, it had crashed into the roof and done considerable damage. When the job was completed, David and Father sat together having a cup of coffee in Father's study.

"Kid told me you spent a few days in Chicago some time ago," Father said conversationally.

"I did, Father. I went to see an old mate of mine ... he died soon after I came back."

"What happened to him?"

"Umm ... he was a war veteran like me. He and I ... we were mates years ago in prison. He got sick because he ... and all of us ... had come into contact with some of the horrible chemicals that were used in the war. That's what my friend Chuck told me."

Father instantly registered David's implication. David knows, he thought, that the same thing is bound to happen to him one day. Father made sure however, not to show any trace of the deduction he had just made. He kept listening.

"When I got there the whole family were gathered ... big Italian family ... generations of them ... all in the one room. You know Father, it must have been terrible for them all to watch Tony ... slowly waste away. I've seen them ... they all suffered. Maybe it was worse than to just receive the telegram saying that he had died for his country."

Father nodded. He was putting two and two together. David's thoughts manifested themselves as clearly as if they had actually been pronounced.

Ironically there were now two people in the know of David's secret: Father and James. David had underestimated James' doctor's instinct as well as Father's wisdom. Both men knew now that David expected to meet the same fate as his friend Tony and that he did not want his family and friends to suffer the way he had seen Tony's family suffer.

Father was deeply troubled by the thought of David's future. If David should get sick, how is he going to handle the situation, the pain and the slow deterioration of his physical body, Father puzzled? Suicide? Is that what David has in mind? The mere thought terrified him.

James was in a slightly better position to figure out David's way of solving the issue. He now reflected on the conversation that had taken place on David's birthday. The two karate experts had both agreed that David had unusual meditative powers, James remembered, skills that were inherent - skills that could neither be taught nor learned. And there was Kid's rather wayward story about people who could, through sheer will power, reduce their metabolisms and bring them to a complete standstill. Sounds like hibernation in frogs, James reflected. He knew about these things, they were all in some way connected with his study of human anatomy and psychology. James was almost sure that David would use these magic powers in some form ... at some stage.

Father and James were of course unaware that they shared knowledge of such importance. Both kept that knowledge to themselves. Neither mentioned it to anyone, not even to Robert or to Kid and Phillip.

Kid still worked with David in his garden regularly, she had also taken it upon herself to handle the business side of David's enterprise. Not that Kid was very good with figures and accounts, but for one thing, she was more confident and for another, she could always rely on her husband to untangle her mistakes. But what Kid really enjoyed was working on the land, with her hands in the soil. This brought back some vague and remote memories of the home and the garden she had once owned in far-off Australia. She had land-scaped, worked the soil and planted her vegetables there ... it was all a lifetime away now.

On this particular day Kid and David were working in the vegetable patch. It was time to tidy up and clear the area of all the remaining weeds then cover it with the left-over mulch and leave it for the winter months. When David decided that it was time for a break, he handed Kid a blanket and told her to spread it under the big oak tree while he went about brewing coffee. He had now set up a coffee maker, cups, sugar and milk in his tool shed. Soon, brother and sister sat in companionable peace on their blanket each nursing a cup of steaming hot coffee in their hands. Kid loved those moments of rest. David casually laid his arm around her shoulder and pulled her to him, "I like this spot," he said, "I can see almost all my fruit trees from here."

"Take that arm away or I'll spill my coffee," Kid said in mock anger.

"Put the cup down then, because I'm not going to let you go," he said trying to sound menacing.

Kid put her cup down on the grass and tried to wriggle out of David's grip. "Just you watch ... I'll show you how to get out of a tight spot. Don't forget that I'm a karate student ..."

David laughed. "Show me how well you learned your lessons then."

The play-wrestling between the two unlikely opponents continued with Kid trying every one of the tricks she had learned, momentarily forgetting that she was using them against the very person who had taught them to her in the first place. Her endeavors got her nowhere. David tried to make his defense look real but in truth it was delicate and gentle. Suddenly Kid found herself in an inescapable and all-embracing grip, pressed against David's chest. It felt warm and safe and intimate. Kid gave up her struggle then and enjoyed the touch of David's body against hers.

As they were lying on their picnic rug, Kid put her arms around David and they held each other; he was her brother and her best friend, she loved him like a sister ... or maybe at this moment like a lover. And that's where it happened. Kid and David made love for the first and only time under the big tree at the far end of David's property.

Brother and sister stayed there for some time afterwards, without speaking, without either explaining or apologizing. It had been just the way David knew it would be. There had been no haste, no lust and no greed - simply true and genuine love between brother and sister, or rather between brother-in-law and sister-in-law.

The thought that she might have been unfaithful to Phillip did cross Kid's mind fleetingly, but it was barely a proper thought, more like a wisp on the periphery of her mind. Kid was not having an affair with David, he had not seduced her, he was her brother and they loved each other as brother and sister. Making love, she reasoned, was our ultimate expression of genuine friendship ... and that's what it was. Phillip knows that we love each other – he has said so more than once.

A little later she and David resumed their work in the vegetable patch, neither of them deemed it necessary to discuss what had taken place during their break, neither felt embarrassment and neither felt guilt. They kept their feelings and memories of their togetherness contentedly sealed inside their hearts.

The day came when David decided to close the dojo for a month or so. He wanted to install a proper heating system in both the dojo and the shower rooms. The other, more personal reason for the closure, David did not reveal to anyone. He did indeed install a heating system but when that job was done, he was glad he had closed the dojo and there were no classes now. He needed to spend more time in there on his own, most of it in meditation. David knew that his time was short; he found it increasingly more challenging to ignore his pain. He went through periods of dizziness and nausea, but the difficult times came and went, he was still strong, nobody noticed that he had lost some weight.

Winter had set in quite suddenly and Kid spent a lot of her time helping Father in the shelters. The cold weather brought more hardship to the homeless in town, more people needed to be fed and kept warm. Father was thankful for every pair of hands that could help with these tasks. Kid would usually work her mid-day shift at Alfredo's and then go straight to one of Father's soup kitchens and put in another few hours hard work. She and Phillip had discussed the issue and Phillip had assured her that he understood. 'I'll never stop you from helping the poor and the destitute, darling,' he had said, 'I know how important this is to you.' Phillip had even made himself available on a few Saturdays to give a hand in feeding the homeless people.

Kid knew she was going to tell Phillip about herself and David, she meant to tell him and she was going to tell him. She did not feel that she had committed a sin. This was not like years ago when kissing David had turned into disaster. She and Phillip had come a long way since then. Knowing that David loved her no longer disturbed Phillip, he had even said so without hard feelings and without sarcasm. It was therefore, not Kid's guilt or shame which caused the delay in her confession, rather it was sheer exhaustion at the end of her days during this busy time that was responsible for her postponement. She and Phillip always managed to relax over dinner with a bottle of wine, and with these blissful moments at the end of her days Kid simply forgot to tell Phillip about having loved David. Then, suddenly, it was too late.

The phone rang at a quarter to six in the morning when Kid and Phillip were still fast asleep. Phillip answered it since the phone was on his side of the bed. "Yes?" he said sleepily.

"Phillip, please come quick ... you and Kid ... don't ask any questions, not right now ... just get here as fast as you can ... thanks." James did not wait for a reply but put the receiver down immediately.

Phillip was speechless and looked rather absurdly at the phone with the now disconnected line.

"What is it Phillip? You look strange."

"I feel strange. James wants us to come over ASAP."

"How much?"

"As Soon As Possible. Come on, let's go."

The previous evening David had prepared Lasagna. He had set the dining table nicely for four people: Robert, his girlfriend Jean, James and himself. Jean had been spending more and more time at the house lately and was in the process of becoming a part of the little family. David put a bottle of red wine near Robert's place, he was the one to uncork it and pour the wine. David didn't drink any alcohol at all.

Robert and Jean had planned to go out after dinner; James had an important exam looming and disappeared right after dinner to his newly created study which took up one part of the attic space. David didn't mind tidying up and washing the dishes, he liked to do house work. When all was done he sat down to watch some television but soon got restless. His recurring pain caused him considerable discomfort now.

Almost unconsciously he got to his feet, stretched and tried to get comfortable then he started to make his way to his room. He took his karate gear out of the wardrobe and went up to the attic. There he stuck his head around the study door. "Good night James," he said, then went downstairs, opened the backdoor and walked across the garden to his dojo. James didn't think that there was anything out of the ordinary in the 'good night' he had heard and neither he nor Robert and Jean knew that David was not in his room that night.

He spent the night in his dojo - his inner sanctum - where he could empty his mind and find his ultimate peace.

James woke up before dawn, very unusual for him especially since he had studied late the night before. He didn't feel too good when he opened his eyes, there seemed to be a lump stuck in either his stomach or in his throat and an unfamiliar pain had lodged itself inside his chest. He walked unsteadily down the stairs to the kitchen to get a glass of water.

Later he could never be sure just what made him do it, but he suddenly put the glass down on the sink and ran out through the backdoor. He could see the little bluish light right outside David's dojo door and it showed him the way in the dark. He slid back the outer door. Since he had not bothered to put on any shoes he could make his way straight to the dojo by sliding back the second door. In the pale light of the fading moon, James could distinguish the shape of David in the center of the dojo mats. He was curled up lying on his side. As James got closer he started to try and reconstruct what had taken place: David had been in his meditating position, on his knees and sitting back on his heels. He had fallen forward and then sideways. His hair was spread out on the straw mats, his eyes were open, he lay motionless. James quickly put his face against David's, he felt no breath; he put his hand to the side of David's throat and to his wrist and felt no pulse.

James sat looking down at his lifeless friend and like in a dream, Kid's story of the tribe in the Pacific Island came back to him. But Kid couldn't have known, none of the people present at the party could have known, it went through his mind. It was no more than idle chat. James was sure that he had been the only one to see some truth in it, some time later, when David told him about his friend Tony. Still, I didn't see it coming, James reflected sadly. Lasagna last night, convivial talk around the dinner table, 'good night' through the crack of the door to my study ... no, I didn't see it coming, and that's exactly the way David wanted it.

James knelt down and held David's head in his hands

and with tears streaming down his face, he kissed David's head very gently. "I love you David," he whispered, "you are my hero ... thanks for having been my friend."

Phillip's car turned into the driveway approximately twenty minutes later. James stood waiting on the front veranda; he had not woken Robert and Jean. By the curious looks on Phillip and Kid's faces, James could tell that neither of them knew or even suspected what was coming their way. He led them to the dojo without a word of explanation and as he slid back the first door he simply said, "I won't come inside with you."

XXXIV

David's lifeless body, dressed in his white karate outfit and Black Belt, was now stretched out on the dojo mats. Kid and Phillip were sitting cross-legged on opposite sides of him. Kid was cradling David's head in her lap, Phillip was holding his brother's hand in one of his and with his other hand he was holding Kid's thus forming a circuit to allow their love to flow freely between them.

Phillip was at pains to blink back his tears but he was determined to follow Kid's lead ... crying had to wait until later.

The hand Phillip was holding still felt a little warm; he sat very still and looked down at his dead brother, and right then he heard an inner voice that said 'you still look just as fit and strong as the brother I have learned to love. Your hair is thick and beautiful, your features as handsome as always, your skin smooth.'

I've always liked you in your karate outfit David, Phillip continued his silent monologue, it lends you strength and it gives you that charisma ... we all felt it when you appeared on the mats the day of the recruiting fête – the day you taught your master classes. I did love you David, you knew it, didn't you. Kid taught me how to love you again after all the bad years when I tried to forget you and, sad to say, quite often succeeded. You're a great guy ... you're gentle and caring and loving ... and you're certainly the greatest karate master ever; that's how I feel about you, David. Phillip was sure he could see a smile on David's face. Could this mean that his brother had found his inner peace in the moment of his death?

Kid read Phillip's thoughts and said dreamily, "He looks just the same as always, doesn't he Phillip? Do you remember when he told us about his friend in Chicago ... the man who died slowly, painfully? Better like this. In my mind and my heart, I shall always keep the image of David, my six foot five brother with the beautiful blue eyes and the long blond hair, the chef, the gardener, the Sensei. Do you feel that way, Phillip?"

"Yes Kid, these were my exact thoughts, too. Now there are just the two of us ... the last McCabes."

"Our love will help us be strong ... we can do it darling."

They both fell silent after that and sat motionless in the

center of David's beloved dojo until the sun was right up in the sky.

A new day had begun – life had to go on.

EPILOGUE

The cause of David's death was officially put down as heart failure.

Phillip and Kid, hoping to follow David's unspoken wish, decided that David's ashes should be buried right next to his dojo, on the side where he had planted a number of flower bulbs. They would all start to grow in a few months and the entire area would be a beautiful show of colors.

Phillip wanted to hold a wake on the day the urn was lowered into the ground; this should be an opportunity for all David's friends and for everybody who knew him to come and say their last good-byes.

"Please remember," he said as the people started to arrive, "David would not like a crowd with sad and tearful faces here now. That's not the sort of guy my brother was. He wants us all to have a good time, and I'm sure he would be happy to be remembered as the Sensei, the friend, the brother. Please will you all help Kid and I to make this the sort of gathering David would have liked."

Many people were there on that day, students, children and their parents, instructors from other schools where David had taught. Mr and Mrs Goldberg and their daughter Sarah, Clive and Caroline Clark, Alfredo and Giovanna, Mario and, to Kid's and Phillip's delight, his parents, James' parents and two of his sisters, and some neighbors, too. Bob, Anita and their son Michael who had worshipped David as his instructor, Joshua and his new wife, and unexpectedly even Jim turned up.

"I, too, would like to say my good-byes to your brother, if I may." Jim said seemingly in all seriousness. "But ... tell me Phillip, this brother of yours ... he didn't just cave in like that. He was fit and tough and powerful ... sudden heart attack? .. do you believe it?"

Phillip had no answer other than, "Well, his heart did stop in the end, right?"

Father Pasquale said a few wonderful words about David, about the honest and trustworthy person he had been, the man everyone had respected and loved and about the goodness which resided in David's heart.

It was towards the end of the event that an unfamiliar face appeared in the crowd. It belonged to a man in his forties, well dressed and confident in his appearance. He looked around, located Phillip and addressed him in a manner which indicated that he knew him. "Hi, I'm Chuck Talbot. You are David's brother, aren't you?"

"I am." Phillip was mystified. "I don't think we have met."

"No, not really ... but I have seen you and your wife once ... and I remember. Your brother and I ... we were mates some time ago. I'd like to say my last good-bye to him ... if that's OK."

Phillip nodded. He could not remember ever having seen this man Chuck before. "Come and get a drink, Chuck, over at the big house ... when you are ready," he said.

Kid was talking to Mario and his parents and had not seen he newcomer. Mario had introduced Kid because his Mama had asked him to.

"Ma'am, I'm so glad to know that you and your husband are reconciled with your son," Kid blurted in true Kid fashion, then she walked right up to Mrs Visconti and spontaneously put both arms around her.

"Thanks Mrs McCabe, you are very kind."

Meanwhile Phillip and Chuck got talking. "Where was it you saw me and Kid? And how well did you know my brother?"

"David and I ... we were mates in prison, in St. Louis. I only caught a glimpse of you the day you came visiting. I was the lucky one who got to be David's cell mate." There was a look of embarrassment on Chuck's face for just a moment, then he continued. "I was in for ... fraud, but I've certainly learned my lesson. I'm studying now ... literature and art. I certainly wouldn't have survived my prison term without David's protection." Chuck stopped to take a breath, then added, "David was so excited when you and your wife first visited - excited and just a tad scared, I have to add."

When Kid approached she simply said, "I'm Kid. Are you David's friend from Chicago?"

"I am ... though why you should know that, I can't imagine."

"Just a hunch ... please continue, I didn't mean to interrupt." Phillip gave Kid a puzzled look but said nothing, he never questioned Kid's hunches.

"So, David and I shared a cell. David needed help in literacy, I needed protection. Guys help each other out in whatever way they can. Prison is a tough place."

Kid just had to interrupt once more when curiosity got the better of her. "How did you know ... about the death of my brother?"

"I too, have hunches, Mrs McCabe, or maybe it's just that special understanding which exists between prison mates."

"Uh-huh," was the best Kid could do.

"One night I called to summon David to Chicago ... it wasn't all that long ago. A mutual friend of ours was dying ... his name was Tony." Chuck recounted everything that happened during those few days David spent in Chicago and he finished with, "Dave was a great guy. He might have been made to *take* lives out there in the jungles of Vietnam... but he certainly *saved* lives in jail ... I know that for sure. David was the greatest fighter. He fought guys who were armed with knives, guards with loaded guns. He knew no fear ... he was unbelievable. Lots of guys, when they're that good ... their personalities get jaded ... they become arrogant, but not David, he knew no arrogance." Chuck quickly lowered his head, but too late, Kid saw the tears in his eyes.

"Can you go on?"

"I'll try. David was real excited knowing that his brother and sister-in-law were coming to see him again after that first unexpected visit. But he was also embarrassed and insecure and God-knows what else. We shared a very small place, he and I ... kind of sat on top of one another, so we got to know each other well ... we confided in each other ... we were real close.

"I knew that David had suffered during the war, but I don't believe that his trauma handicaps altered his character ... never made him mean or devious." Chuck took a deep breath then added, "I loved your brother ... I did. David would never have wanted his friends to watch him die slowly ... like Tony. I'm not sure why I'm saying this."

"Thanks Chuck, for your kind words," Kid said, then gave him a little hug before moving away. She didn't want to make a show of her own emotions right there.

"The last time I saw David," Chuck addressed Phillip now, "in Chicago, I casually asked him if he ever considered getting married. You are smiling Phillip, why?"

"It's just that ... David was not very good with women ... shy and awkward. What did he say?"

"He said 'no' and that no one would want him for a husband and also ... he said that he loved Kid ... just like that."

"I know he loved Kid ... in fact they loved each other ... but they didn't have an affair, it was not that sort of love."

After this conversation, Phillip joined Kid who was talking to Father. Phillip just caught the last words of Father's sentence, "... you see Kid, I put two and two together, but that still didn't provide a complete answer." Then he saw Phillip and repeated, "I was just telling Kid that David was quite sure he was going to get sick ... the same as his friend Tony and that he was determined not to put his friends and family through what he had witnessed in Chicago. He felt that Tony's family had suffered terribly having to stand by and watch helplessly as their son deteriorated and died. But that is all I know."

A few days later, James appeared unexpectedly at Phillip and Kid's doorstep. "Sorry Kid, to barge in on you like this," he said, "I just wanted to see you and Phillip before I leave on my first mission."

"It's wonderful to see you James," Kid exclaimed with genuine pleasure. "Where are you going? Some jungle country, undoubtedly. Can you stay for dinner? Phillip will be home shortly. I'm doing one of my curries tonight?" She and James gave each other a big, long hug.

"Darling," Kid greeted her husband with a kiss then turned to business almost immediately, "It's curry tonight, please you're in charge of the rice ... you're the all-time expert. I've asked James to stay."

James waited until after dinner and when they had shifted to the lounge room for coffee he asked the question he'd been burning to ask, "Is it OK to talk about David?"

"Sure James," Phillip said, "what is it?"

"It's about the circumstances of his death." James said bravely. "Do you know ... did anyone tell you?"

"Tell us what, James?"

"David's death ... seen as heart failure. I'm not sure how to say this ... please bear with me. Kid, on David's birthday you came up with this weird and wonderful story about some tribes in remote Pacific Islands. I'm not saying that David knew about this but ... we all heard about the depth of David's meditation, remember? Maybe he *was* in some way able to control the forces of life and death. David didn't want to expose his friends and family to the ordeal he had witnessed in Chicago - to the slow and painful death of his friend Tony. David might somehow have been responsible for ... for the way he died. I mean ... it's possible. David was an incredible person ... he was my hero ... I loved him ... I did." James broke down in tears after that.

"David loved you too, James. Please, you have to be brave ... we all have to." Phillip said.

Later that night as Kid and Phillip were comfortably reclining in bed Phillip said almost casually, "Did it strike you Kid, that we have now heard three versions of David's death wish - two at the gathering at Robert's and one tonight? The same words ... the same thoughts ... first from Chuck, then from Father and now from James? Oh, and by the way, Jim came out with another interesting half-thought. David was too strong and too fit to just collapse and die of heart failure, Jim said. He sounded as if he suspected some sort of foul play; he certainly does not believe in the heart attack theory. Isn't that very much what James said earlier on?"

"They all said, all except Jim that is, that David didn't want us and his friends to watch him deteriorate and die slowly. But how, I wonder, did not wanting this to happen influence the way he had a heart attack? Any truth in that story of mine on David's birthday, you think?"

"Hard to say, but ... who knows. David was an extraordinary guy. I believe the bit about him not wanting us to see him die slowly, though. He wanted us to remember him the way we all knew him. You know Kid, David has seen death ... I think many times ... and he knew that deep inside, one keeps last images of people. He wanted that last image he left for us to be a good one."

They were silent after that, each following their own train of thought.

"What else did Chuck say to you after I had gone? Anything important?"

"Nothing mind-boggling, only that David said he loved you. But then, I knew that anyway. I said that you and David didn't have an affair."

What is he getting at, Kid wondered. What's this special inflection in his voice all of a sudden? Then she heard Phillip's voice again as if from a distance.

"I didn't tell him that you and David made love. I know it was only once but I still didn't say."

"You knew all the while? And you said nothing?" Kid felt shame and embarrassment, she didn't dare look at Phillip.

"I'm saying it now, Kid, and yes, I knew on the very day. How? That odd telepathy between us still works you know."

"I should have told you ... I meant to, I really did, but then ... I didn't. I'm sorry, Phillip."

"Are you sorry for not telling me or for making love to David?"

"For not telling you. I didn't think loving him was a sin, it was more like a token of our friendship ... something like that."

"It's OK Kid, I'm not angry and I'm not jealous. You know, when I looked at David's face that morning in the dojo, I saw a smile there and I thought to myself that David had died happy because he had been able to show you how much he appreciated your friendship, your kindness and your sisterly love. It was his way of saying thanks."

Kid felt tears running down her cheeks; she had no will to stop them. "I love you Phillip," she said, "I love you and I respect you and I appreciate your generosity and your wisdom and ..."

"Enough ... I can't handle so many compliments all at once," Phillip said laughingly, then out of the blue, "You know what's the best thing I ever did in my life?"

"No, come on, say it. The suspense is terrible. What was it?"

"Running after that truck outside the hotel in Fremantle ... or rather ... catching up with it."

ISBN 142518491-X